T0270115

Acclaim for

OATHBOUND

"In this nautical fantasy, McCombs keeps the stakes high, maintaining a melodramatic dynamic between the protagonists that emphasizes their youth . . . alongside the threat of mutiny."

— PUBLISHERS WEEKLY

"This story has all the beloved elements of a classic pirate tale, including ferocious sea monsters, captivating merfolk, legendary treasure troves, and haunting black ships."

— CITY BOOK REVIEW

"Victoria McCombs's young adult novel *Oathbound* is filled with danger, romance, and a good dose of piracy. Arn's ship, *The Royal Rose,* is a good backdrop for laughter and heartache alike . . . A story that's sure to awaken readers' thirsts for adventure."

— FOREWORD REVIEWS MAGAZINE

"Full of magic and romance, *Oathbound* is a swashbuckling adventure that will leave you breathless!"

— CASEY L. BOND, author of *House of Eclipses*

"A binding contract, a deadly illness, a mysterious treasure, and a deadly mission aboard *The Royal Rose, Oathbound* is hauntingly enchanted. A perfect read for the sea-lover in us all!"

— DANIELLE HARRINGTON, award-winning author of the Hollis Timewire Series

"*Oathbound* is a swashbuckling tale that's just as vivaciously full of life as it is full of dark peril. McCombs spins a tale that satisfies as a pirate's tale while diving into the deep waters of love, loss and the gradients in between. Come for the adventure and stay for a toothy story that will linger with you long after you finish the last chapter."

— AUTUMN KRAUSE, author of *A Dress for the Wicked*

OATHBOUND

Books by Victoria McCombs

The Storyteller's Series
The Storyteller's Daughter
Woods of Silver and Light
The Winter Charlatan
Heir of Roses

The Royal Rose Chronicles
Oathbound

OATHBOUND

The Royal Rose Chronicles
Book One

VICTORIA MᶜCOMBS

To August,
Mommy finally wrote you a pirate story.

1

EMME

The creaky door of the Banished Gentlemen tavern swung wide as a young man with a cutlass strapped to his side sauntered in with his fists raised in triumph. He hadn't bothered to lace the front strings of his shirt, showing the curls of his tattoo underneath. Golden waves for the ocean he loved so dearly.

He practically sang as he declared loudly enough for the room to hear, "He's dead! Finally."

From my seat in the back, I cursed. Further news of death was not welcome here. This week had brought enough of that.

Whosoever death this was, Arn danced in the face of it. He paused to shake a few hands and tip his head in greeting. To a few he even bowed. *Bowed.* As if he'd waltzed into a fancy establishment among fine nobles instead of a seaside tavern with the smell of fish and saltwater filling the stale morning air.

Pirates. Always so dramatic.

As if he could read my thoughts, Arn threw his head back and bellowed, "It's a great day, indeed." His voice reached the dusty rafters above and settled over the tavern like a promise—a vow that today would be the start of something wonderful.

To reinforce his point, he raised an imaginary tankard, then scanned the heads of our few customers.

With a strained smile I raised my hand in greeting.

Arn sighted me.

He bounded across the floor and pulled out the seat opposite from mine. "Emme, did you hear? He's dead." Though less than a meter away, his slurred voice paid no regard to volume as he spread out his arms and grinned.

"There you are. My closest friend and the fairest maiden in all the land. The wise, the majestic Emme. Truly, there is no one like you across all the seas."

From behind the bar, Bart and I exchanged glances.

Had I not confessed yesterday how I longed for my friend's ship to come into port? And now the Fates, who had been cruel this week, sent him the very next morning. Drunk.

In the rare times Arn chose to get soused, trouble always followed—and when trouble came after him, it often brought difficulty to me. "Arn, I'm not helping you hide the body this time. That turned into a huge mess."

He wagged his head. "I'd always hide the body for you." When my brow raised, he laughed. "No need, I didn't kill him this time. The old pirate is dead of his own accord." Arn crossed his fingers and twirled them in the air as a promise. He removed his pistol belt and laid it on the table, then leaned forward and whispered, "It's old Barnacles."

"Bernabe De?"

Arn hushed me and motioned to lower my voice but nodded. He had some nerve to hush me after his grand entrance. They could probably hear him from the docks.

Wild glee frolicked in Arn's eyes. "You know what this means, don't you?"

He'd never looked so disappointed in me as when I shook my head. He leaned forward even more. "The treasure?" He slapped the table, and my plate clattered. "This is it, Emme. This money will get you out of here."

When my eagerness didn't follow, Arn slumped against his chair, crossed his arms, and looked at me. "What?"

Over our four years of friendship, Arn had rambled about so many treasures that I'd lost count. For all his talk, he'd never acquired a decent loot—most of his wealth came from plundering small merchant vessels, then bringing the silk or spices back to this cloudy seaside town to trade. I expected this trip to end no differently than his others. "Remember a few years ago when you went after Winfred Varlow's hoard and you got so lost that you couldn't find your way out of those seas for weeks? Or the next year when you sought the perfumes from the ship that went down on the cliffs, and you wrecked your own vessel? Or four months ago when you chased the ruby ship and got struck by the poisonous sea creature? You and your whole crew almost died."

His grin widened with each recount, and he leaned back and folded his hands behind his head. "Where's your sense of adventure? All a part of the pirate life. Besides, I have a better feeling about this one. My plan is failsafe."

"Almost died, Arn."

Before I could challenge Arn further, a voice as deep as the ocean rumbled over us, and Bart lumbered up to the table, floorboards creaking under his weight. He had wide shoulders made more intimidating by the grand size of his arms but eyes so kind that it was impossible to fear him. Those eyes locked on me, and I silently begged him. *Please don't say anything. I'm not ready.*

He nodded, ever so slightly, and I loved him for it. Bart was the closest thing I had to a father since mine died, and he'd given me a home here at the tavern along with a job. There weren't many things I loved about this town with the smell of fish stained into the air and the questionable folks coming in off the seas—even the king of Julinbor seemed to have forgotten about us here—but Bart made it bearable.

He dried his large hands on a rag. "Arn, haven't seen you in a few months. Recovered from that poison yet?"

I smirked, but Arn ignored me. "Quite recovered, thank you."

Bart peered closer. "What's this? You've got nine . . . ten hairs on that little chin of yours. Why, ten's nothing to laugh at."

I suppressed a snort.

Arn huffed. His honey-colored hair on his head grew in thick little waves, and he had handsome almond-shaped blue eyes and a strong, square jaw, but at almost twenty-two, Arn's skin was as smooth as the sails on his ship, and he feared he'd never grow a proper beard. "It's a sign that I can be trusted. Honest men don't hide their faces behind beards." He stroked his skin. "People trust me because of this face."

Bart nodded knowingly, but the humor in his eyes lingered. "And what's these plans I hear about? Still trying to take my Emme out to sea? I'm surprised you haven't kidnapped her by now."

"She might kill me if I tried that." His wary eyes found mine, and I bared my teeth. Then I grinned, and he grinned back before glancing over his shoulder to the other tables where the fishermen weren't giving us any attention. His low voice dripped in anticipation and adventure as he told us, "It's Bernabe De's treasure, but don't go telling nobody. And yes, I'm hoping Emme joins my crew for this one. She'd make a fine pirate if she got over her peculiar distaste for the water."

Many seafarers who sailed through trusted Bart with their stories, so if there was anything to know about the treasure, he'd hear it first. From our seaside town at the southern tip of Julinbor, we saw many pirates stumble through our doors with tales of the beautiful mermaids of the north or fabled items claiming to hold powerful magic within them, and they shared such tales with us as their blood turned to alcohol. We'd make a game of guessing who told the truth and who didn't.

At this story, Bart's mouth tipped open before he snapped it shut. "I won't say a word, but that bit of gossip has already graced my ears. In fact, I heard it's guarded by his ghost."

When my eyes widened, Arn chuckled. "Ghost. As if. Say, could you get me some grog?" Bart was never one to deny a man his grog, no matter the hour, so he turned for the bar.

"Water," I called after Bart. "He doesn't need grog, he needs water. Really Arn, you're swaying."

For a man who usually avoided the bottle, he chose the worst week to show up drunk. I couldn't tell him like this. At least the rum prohibited him from sensing that I hid anything, and my ugly secret could remain hidden until I found the courage to share it with him. I might need rum of my own to accomplish such a thing.

Bart returned and set a glass of water in front of Arn, who refrained from complaining. He raised the glass to me. "My lady." Then he gulped.

A nod of approval came from Bart. "There's a good lad. Word of advice? Watch your step going after this dead pirate's treasure. It's a far cry from the easy robbing of merchant ships."

Arn spat out the water. "Easy? Easy? I'll have you know, it takes years of experience to pull off robbing merchant vessels."

"Just be careful, lad."

As Bart left, I threw a rag to Arn and pointed to the table he'd just spat all over. He diligently wiped as I looked after Bart. With a voice as low as the bottom of the sea I asked, "Do you think there's a ghost? Why, you'd never get the treasure then."

Arn set the rag down with a sly smile. "Don't let this influence your decision, but here's the thing . . . there's a ghost."

I stood up. "No. *No.* I'm not going," I said. "Do you know what you're getting yourself into?"

He looked happy that I asked and pulled his chair over next to mine, grabbing my hand to tug me back into my seat. I tore my hand from his grasp as he spoke. "We all know that old Barnacles scored quite the loot after taking down that merchant vessel in the Borrinswail Strait. Then he found those caves and scored big on gems."

I nodded as I recalled. Arn thought this man had more wealth than any other pirate alive. "He was obsessed with his wealth—never spent a penny of those loots."

Arn snapped his fingers. "That's right. Well, he became consumed with the idea that people were coming to take it from him." I raised my brow, and a devilish gleam entered Arn's blue eyes. "He may have been right. But it drove him mad. So, he went to the Island of Iilak and vowed to protect it forever. That wish was granted. He gave up his mortality to become a ghost so he could guard his treasure until the end of time. Quite the dramatic fellow, really. Sent his whole crew home on meager rowboats and wrecked his beautiful ship. Now his treasure sits on an island with hardly anything to protect it."

"Besides a ghost, you mean."

He waved his hand, almost knocking over his glass. "Yes. Besides that. So, what do you say? Will you come to the Island of Iilak with me?"

An unease stirred within me at the familiarity of that name. I'd heard it this week, though not from Arn's lips. It took a moment to place where, and once I did, I sucked in my breath. "What is the island called?"

"Iilak."

That was undeniably the same place. In our extensive search for what could keep me alive beyond eighteen, that island had come up. It was rumored to hold something that could cure any illness, though the island itself was hardly more than rumors. Bart and I cast the idea aside as an impossible mission, for I had no ship to get me there and no account that what I sought existed besides rum-stained scribbles in the back of a book.

But no other answer came.

Perhaps the Fates weren't as cruel as I thought them to be. And perhaps I needn't tell Arn my troublesome news after all. The Elmber Nut could make all my problems vanish if I got to it in time. Six months, maybe a year. That's all I had.

The hope of that rare nut and the safety it offered me was worth joining with pirates—just this once.

I rested my head in my hands as for the first time I debated venturing out with Arn on one of his far-fetched quests; however, he'd need to prepare for this trip with more diligence than usual before I felt comfortable about the decision. He'd often been like this—giddy with glee and ready to chase after a ghost on a distant island that was near impossible to reach.

But it wasn't often that he took my hand and begged me.

"Please, come with me. You keep me sane, and I need your practicality on board. And I happen to know that you need the money. The amount of silver we can get from pawning his treasures will allow you to buy back your childhood home in the valleys."

Arn knew me too well. When my father died, I couldn't afford to keep my childhood home running, though the memories of that place stayed with me like an anchor that tethered me to those hills. Those days in the sun, far from the smell of the ocean, tending our flock, few worries on our mind—those were happy times. After the events of this week, I'd given up ever getting back there.

Arn leaned closer. "You can buy back your sheep."

A smile threatened to crack my cheeks, breaking my reserves.

"*Baaaaa.*" Arn's mimic drew a laugh from me. The bliss sounded foreign upon my lips, as the news of this week provided little opportunity for laughter, but Arn's smile was so big that it was difficult to resist.

This was usually when I said no. I'd allow Arn to tell me about his mission, get excited with him, offer some practical advice, then remind him that I preferred the land. But things were different now. I sighed. "Have you made plans?"

His head rose and eyes perked up. "I've mapped out the route we'll take. My exact plans are on the *Royal Rose*. Come aboard my ship to inspect them and decide for yourself." He gestured out the door to the pier.

The idea of going to his boat on the moving water was enough to make me scrunch my nose, but he grabbed my hands. "Please, Emme. I know how skilled you are with the blade, and your knowledge of the sea is unsurpassed. I need you."

I sighed again. I did know an unfortunate amount about the sea, thanks to my mother.

"I will look at these plans," I said. Arn's jaw dropped, and he bounced in his seat. "But you need to wash out your mouth before breathing that close to me ever again." I pulled my hands from his and pushed his face away. Delight radiated through his expression, and I tried to smile back.

"You mean it?" His eyes searched mine, and I nodded.

"Yes."

Arn knocked over the chair as he hopped up and shouted, "She said yes!" That earned loud cheers from the fishermen who knew me well. Arn bowed again on his way back out the tavern, tripping several times while I followed behind.

As I passed Bart, I whispered, "It's on the Island of Iilak."

It only took a few moments for his brown eyes to widen. "The Elmber Nut."

I nodded. "It may be my only chance to survive past the winter."

The sadness remained in his eyes, but no argument came.

No reminder that this nut might not exist. No reminder that the seas were a dangerous place. He did duck his head and whisper into my ear, "Listen, there's something about this island you need to know. The rumor of the ghost? I've heard it's a lie set up by the old pirate to lure the sailors who sought his treasure to the island where he can kill them. A ghost is one thing, but you might sail to a very dangerous and very much alive man."

All thoughts of my own troubles vanished, and my knees quivered beneath me as unwelcome thoughts of Arn slaughtered on the island came to mind.

This time, he might be in over his head.

"I've got to warn him."

Bart shook his head, glancing to Arn, who stumbled through the doorway. "I doubt he'd listen to you in the state he's in or remember it when the alcohol is drained from his blood. Besides, you know how rumors are—never know who's telling you the truth. But it's something to be wary of. You keep a mind on it and tell Arn when he's sobered up." He twisted his hands together and looked toward the docks.

My feet were as heavy as lead and my legs reluctant to move toward the wild, unpredictable ocean. Questions swam through my mind, but only one stumbled out.

"Do I have a choice in going?"

Bart's expression softened as he looked at me. "I would bear this burden for you if I could, but if you hope to be healed from this disease in your blood, it must be you who goes. You'd be dead before I returned to our port." His giant hand stroked my cheek. "And I fear Arn may be your only chance to get there, little one. But I worry for what awaits you on that island."

2

ARN

By Valian's Crown, she actually came with me. I thought she'd laugh in my face and tell me to leave. But instead Emme followed to load the *Royal Rose* from the wharf. I treaded lightly and kept my mouth shut against saying anything to make her turn back to the safety of the old tavern. I'd only convinced her to board my vessel a few times, and only once did I take her for a jaunt around the port. But never on a voyage.

It must have been my devilish good looks that finally swayed her. I knew one day she wouldn't be able to resist.

Her face pinched as the deck swayed beneath us. Her dislike was ironic, considering who her mother was. The daughters of pirates were usually anchored to the sea, but not Emme.

"You'll get used to the movement," I promised, but it did nothing to remove the unease from her eyes.

She looked older than when I saw her last. When I'd met Emme, she was a girl of fifteen, made from nothing but blood and bone. But that was years ago. This lass before me was a woman with meat on her arms and a face more filled out, so her cheeks dimpled when she smiled. She kept her long, dark hair braided through a scarlet ribbon embroidered with an octopus at the end—a token from her father, as she'd once confessed to me. An octopus ribbon for his daughter who had squirmed as much as an octopus as a baby. She never forgot to wear it, and I tried to be at Kaffer Port each year on the anniversary of his death because of how hard that day was for her. Sometimes she didn't see me at the tavern, but I always stopped by to ask Bart how she fared.

Emme would be displeased to know how often I asked after her.

The sun climbed higher over the ocean, and I squinted into the harsh light. The water was beginning to help, but my head still felt thick. A fierce headache would soon be upon me. The copper rim of my flask met my lips to prolong the avoidance of the sting of sobriety, reminding me why I so often avoided getting soused. I stumbled on the quiet deck where only my first mate, Ontario, picked through old knots. The other few men were either still resting or off to find something to entertain themselves for the morning and stretch their sea legs. We had a long journey ahead of us, and our time on land would be limited.

Ontario walked with a steady certainty that a drunk man should not possess, and I narrowed my eyes. I'd almost fallen off the slipway, but my first mate pulled on the riggings and moved the wash bucket with ease. He had a better head for rum than I did, or he hadn't drunk as much as I'd thought.

We'd landed at Kaffer Port last night but waited to disembark until morning came and Emme would be awake. We'd gotten news of old Barnacles' death two days ago and sailed straight here, so we'd had little time to celebrate. I'd been waiting for this day.

This trip was crucial for more reasons than I cared to admit to Emme. She'd never consider going with me if she knew the whole truth, so from here on out I must be diligent in keeping the rum out so the secret stayed in.

Ontario waved a hand to us, his skin the same olive tone as the young woman beside me. Sleeves the color of frothing waves were rolled carelessly at his elbows, allowing the purple scar traced down his forearm to be seen. He covered his other arm with tattoos, but that scar he liked to show off. He'd concocted many wild stories of how he got it to tell the women on land. Emme knew the real tale, which was far less grand than he liked. "Morning, Emme." He leaned heavily on his northern accent, the only sign he showed of rum in his belly. "I can't believe you came. I thought you'd send him back to the ship with a few choice words." He made a drinking motion.

She laughed, but both her hands stayed tight on the taffrail, and her knuckles were white. Her eyes continuously glanced back to the land. As Ontario came closer, she hid her discomfort behind a smile. "I heard you were in on the drinking antics."

He shrugged. "What can I say? Even a reputable fellow like myself enjoys the occasional drink."

"So what will you spend your money on, if you get this treasure?" Emme asked him. "Drinks?"

His brown eyes widened slightly and flickered to me. With as much stealth as I could muster, I shook my head. *Keep your mouth shut, mate.*

He recovered quickly and coughed. "Haven't given much thought to it yet."

I grimaced. Not a good enough answer. Anyone else might be content, but this was Emme. Her head tilted to the side. "You haven't thought about it? I would have guessed you pirates dreamed of little else."

From under his thick eyelashes, he glanced to me again. I'd asked him to keep quiet about this certain topic without anticipating her asking such questions. I stepped in. "My men think about more than just money, you know. We are one of the only crews that have books for studying on board. These are educated men." I pretended to be offended.

Ontario pasted a grin to his face and nodded. "Love me some arithmetic."

From the corner of her eyes, Emme watched me. I shrugged. She swiveled her head to scan the boat, as if answers might lie there. The *Royal Rose* had been cleaned since she last came on board, a fact that I took particular pride in. No other pirates could boast a ship as clean as mine. The golden railing leading from the main deck up to the helm shone in the sunlight, as did the caps on the tips of the wheel and the knob from the cabin below. The square window was polished, letting us see into the room where the bookshelves and narrow table stood, free of dust and droplets of rum. Across the deck, the two main masts stood tall with sails as white as the clouds and ropes meticulously examined for fraying.

It was a decent ship. Frame built with fine mahogany wood, planked with polished cedar. Small enough to fly across the waves.

The man I'd taken it from was no doubt still missing it.

Emme's keen eye took in all these details, until at last she crossed her arms. "Where are these grand plans?"

Relief flooded my chest, and I resisted exhaling as if I'd been holding my breath, which I had. "Right this way."

As she passed him, Ontario darted me a glance, but I moved on.

The plans hid in a box under my bed. It'd taken me two long days to write them out, but years to plan this in my mind. From what I'd heard, I had guessed it'd be years before Bernabe De kicked the bucket and never envisioned he'd plant the treasure on an island first. It was almost too easy.

Emme kept close as I opened the hatch and led her down into the cabins. Her sweet smell of wildflowers and vanilla hit my nose, two scents not usually encountered on my ship. For a moment, guilt pricked me, but I shoved it away. I was doing this for her too. This wasn't selfish.

She'd forgive me for this.

The cabins where the crew slept were nothing more than two small rooms with twenty bunks lining the walls, eight on one side, eight on the other, and four against the back wall. My cabin was adjacent to theirs, with one bunk and a table and a few drawers. The doors to the crew's rooms were open, and Emme stopped in the first doorway.

"It looks cleaner since last time, if that's possible."

I tried to shut the door, but she stepped in the way. "Where are all the things?"

"Like you said." I twirled my fingers. "Clean."

She tapped her foot. "No, when they are clean, the bags get placed on their beds. There's only . . . six beds with bags. What's the other room look like?" She twisted and pushed open the other door before I could stop her.

"And six occupied beds in here. The rest are filled with supplies, not belongings. You only have twelve men on crew with you?"

Blimey. I didn't feel drunk anymore. My mind sobered up quickly as it scrambled to respond. "Thirteen, actually. A few of the lads have found honest work in Julinbor, but we manage without them. There's more room for storage, though," I added.

She spun on her heels. All discomfort of being on a boat disappeared as accusation filled her eyes. "Arn Mangelo, where is your crew?"

She was too smart for me. It was what attracted me to her. Usually I was smart, too, but right now I couldn't remember much more than my own name. She waited for a reply, and my mind clambered for something decent to give her. With an airy voice I said, "Money is tight currently, so we are managing with a smaller crew. Turns out we don't need as many men as I thought to make this ship float."

I smiled and leaned against the doorframe as her gaze

swept over the cabin again before it fixed on me. In an action I hadn't predicted, she turned away from the empty cabin without further question. "Show me your plans."

Her voice sounded more serious now, as if she understood better how much I needed this. I gestured toward my cabin and followed her inside, where her bright yellow dress was the only color in the room. Everything else was a washed-out hue of red or gray or gold—the colors of the captain from whom I acquired this vessel. The opposite from the saturated blues that the king of Julinbor sailed under. That part pleased me.

I had little love for the king I used to work for.

She viewed the land outside the small porthole while I fetched the plans from inside a cherrywood box with metal brackets holding it together. A fake gem sat on the latch, but I kept it clean, so it shone like a real one. I flipped it upward and opened the box. My crisp papers sat inside. Emme kept a hand on the wall for as long as she could while she took a few shaky steps toward the table where I laid out the plans.

"This is the map of the path we must take." I slid the curled parchment, where I'd drawn out the islands we'd have to stop at on our journey for supplies, toward her.

She lifted it and studied the map while twisting the end of her braid in her fingers. The sunlight from behind her glittered off her hair, and my breath caught in my throat. I wasn't used to such beauty being on board. Again I was struck by how much she'd changed over the past few months; gone was the girl who stared at the ground as she talked and stumbled over her words. I wiped my awed expression from my face before she looked up. "Are you certain this is the path to the island? I've heard rumors of the Island of Iilak, and I thought no one knew the way."

I stepped in to look over her shoulder. She shifted slightly away. The smell of wildflowers filled my nose again. "It's a tricky path, but it's not impossible. See these islands here? They move. So the exact path will have to be adjusted to account for those. And this island here"—I pointed to a large mass of land in the middle—"sometimes appears and sometimes doesn't. No one knows why. The waters are dangerous here and . . . here, and the Never-Ending Land can be tricky, but I've heard of a channel through . . . here. It's small and hard to find, but I spoke to a man who crossed it once. That's the only way to get to the island. Not many know about this little channel; it's a well-kept secret. Ontario is the only one of my crew to know."

She was quiet as she studied it. "And why do we have to stop here?" She pointed to an island shaped like a hand. "It'll be quicker to avoid the island and all the unpleasantries of that place."

I agreed that I wouldn't stop there unless necessary, but we didn't have a choice this time. "A weapon lies there, one riddled with magical properties that can best a ghost. It's not the only magical token we can use—this map indicates where a few others are located—but this one is the most practical and closest to our route." My fingers drummed against the paper.

"That one's closer." She pointed to a scratched-out mark.

I frowned. "Aye, but I don't care for the man who owns it. Hence, it's scratched out. But the woman who possesses this one"—I pointed her attention back to the circled dot—"is a reasonable trading woman."

"And what will you trade?" Emme asked, but I knew that question was coming. I reached under my bunk and pulled out a different box. This one was long and thin with silver embellishments on the tips. When I opened it, she gasped.

"Your old naval outfit?"

I looked at her face instead of the blue jacket, gold buttons, and high collar of my former self. I'd worn this outfit when I was sixteen and enlisted in the king's navy. I wore it up until the day that I cast it aside for the pirate life. Emme didn't know the full story behind that, but she knew how my lip twisted at the mention of my time on the king's ship.

The first time she'd met me, I was in the king's navy. I doubt she would have spoken to me had I appeared as a pirate. I'd seen the way rapscallions vied for her attention and how she rolled her eyes at them, but when I walked into the Banished Gentlemen as a younger lad with my crisp suit and polite manners, she allowed me to befriend her. Never more than friends, but I didn't take the relationship lightly.

Even when I disowned the king's navy and swore a pirate's oath, she allowed the friendship to continue with hardly a question about it.

I closed the box. "It's worth nothing to some people but a lot to others. This trading woman happens to desire something like this. It's a valuable thing to masquerade as one of the king's men."

Her eyes studied mine for a while, but I shielded my emotions from her.

She glanced to the plans. "Do you truly think you can get that treasure?"

I gently placed the box back under the bed. "Aye. I know I can. And I know the money will be enough to buy you back that home and the sheep." She smiled, but it pained me to think of her so far away from the water where I could see her. She turned to look out the porthole again, where we could see the side of the Banished Gentlemen sitting near the pier.

I stepped behind her. "I won't let you get hurt," I promised.

She snorted. "I can protect myself. That's not what I'm worried about." I waited, but she didn't say more.

"If we don't get the treasure," I said, "I will rob a merchant's ship and give it all to you, even the crew's portions."

She turned around and took a step back when she saw how close we were. I tried not to be bothered by it, but I subtly smelled myself. The sharp smell coming from my jacket was nothing like wildflowers.

"You really need this, don't you?"

I raised my hands before letting them fall to my sides. "I do."

She cursed lightly as she returned to the table and leaned over the maps. She surely didn't understand how desperately I needed this, how my life was on the line if I didn't get it, but I'd told her enough. Over the years of me asking her to join my crew, this was as close as she'd ever gotten to saying yes. My breath hung in my throat while I waited. Emme sucked in her cheeks, then answered through a puff of air. "Okay, fine. I'll do it. I'll go with you."

My heart leapt inside me, and I resisted the urge to pick her up and spin her around. That'd be a sure way to get her to change her mind. Instead I leaned over the table to hide the foolish grin on my face that threatened to give away too much of my enthusiasm.

When I raised my head, her lips were bent into a deep frown, and her eyes pointed to the land outside the porthole. Her voice vibrated with uncertainty. "Where's the first stop?"

Maybe she'd change her mind now. I closed my eyes as I answered. "Arwa Isles."

I peeked through my lashes. Her face remained unchanged. Perhaps she didn't know. "We need one more companion before setting off. From what I hear, he's educated about the seas, a strong fighter, a skilled sailor . . . and you get along nicely."

Her face turned white. She knew now. "Emric."

"Yes. I think we need your brother."

She cursed again, more vividly this time, but didn't argue. Emme's relationship with her brother was unusual. There was much love between them, but many differences. Due to their unique ways of life, they hadn't seen each other in ages. Emme had grown up in that time. But while Emme knew a lot about the ocean, Emric lived on it. His expertise would be valuable. And I knew how much Emme missed her older brother.

More than that, from what Emme told me in the past, Emric needed the money too. It wouldn't take much to convince him to join us.

Emme put the papers back in the box with surprising calmness. "I better pack my bags."

"Bring something other than dresses," I told her, then flushed as she jerked her head up and glared at me. "It's not practical for a pirate ship. You could snare the skirt on the riggings."

Her lips pulled tight. "I'm not a pirate. I'll wear what I please."

I waited until she'd climbed the ladder to follow behind, standing on the deck with Ontario as she descended the slipway. She took a deep breath as soon as she hit the pier.

"Did you tell her?" Ontario asked.

My head shook. "No."

He gave me a sad look, but I turned away. "Don't ever look at me like that, Ontario. She needs this too. That money will save us both."

3

EMME

The small waves met the sandy shore and lapped against the planks of the pier, each sound warning me. *Beware of the bitter waters. Beware of the seas where your mother drowned. Beware of the pirate life.*

I'd diligently heeded their warnings my whole life. I'd not taken up my mother's legacy or set sail with Arn. I'd kept to the safety of the land and the certainty of hard ground beneath my feet. I'd not answered the call to the water.

But the luxury of land was no longer mine to claim, and the certainty I'd always clung to began to slip through my fingers. Now, because life was cruel, the nut that could save me grew on an island almost impossible to reach, forcing me onto a ship and across treacherous waters in a desperate search.

So, to the water I go.

And, if there was a twinge of excitement that stirred within me as I looked over Arn's plans, or a moment of anticipation at the thought of setting sail, I chose to ignore it, for that thinking could only bring devastation. The high seas could only bring ruin.

Beware.

I wasn't a pirate. I wasn't my mother.

My mother had been one of the fiercest pirates to sail the

high seas, either feared or loved by all who knew her. She left me and Emric in our father's care while she made her fortune, hardly returning to her small family on the sheep farm.

Until one day, she didn't return at all.

None could say for certain which sea held my mother's body now, but my father grew further troubled with each passing day, and he never recovered from that stress. Eventually he died, sending my older brother and me to Kaffer Port to work alongside the man who grew up with Mother. Our days tending sheep under the hot sun were replaced by foggy air and salt in all the food. Emric remained by my side for two years, but his heart longed for adventures bigger than the tavern, so I let him leave with the next sailor who came through. He wrote several times a year, but I'd only seen him twice since.

Emric was like Mother—he always had been. Wild and ambitious. His free spirit couldn't be contained, just like the mass of brown curls on his head.

Remembering how Arn had praised him made my stomach turn. Of course he would think Emric was a more valuable shipmate than me; I was probably little more than a token to convince Emric to sail with us.

I loved Emric, but he loved the sea, and I didn't.

The smell reminded me of Mother and of sorrow, and the salt burned my eyes. The sea was a place where people went to get lost, not where people made an honest life. I'd lost enough people to the sea. I refused to lose myself.

Arn might be the only one who could convince me to get on a boat. But I saw how much he needed it, and I needed this too. More, in fact. I had more to lose than he did.

I started packing.

It didn't take long to gather my things. My room above the tavern wasn't much more than a few blankets on a straw bed and a trunk for my meager belongings. All my letters from Emric were inside, as well as the few I'd exchanged with Arn.

I had one pair of shoes and three linen dresses in addition to the one I had on now. I wrapped them up in my blanket and tied the edges together.

That was it. My entire life packed up in a faded wool blanket.

My hand caught on the splintered doorframe. It wasn't too late to stay here. I'd be safe, I'd be happy, and I'd be on dry land.

But I'd be dead within a year.

When I thought of it like that, it was easy to forget the moving ocean and the high waves in storms and the endless smell of fish filling my lungs and the sunburnt skin and tiring work on deck.

One year.

Or the chance at having a lifetime.

My foot pulled the door closed behind me, and I didn't look back. Bart waited downstairs with a sack in hand and somber look on his face. "Provisions for the trip," he said as he set it down with a thud on the table. The tavern was empty now that all the fishermen had gone out to sea. Soon I'd be out with them, but while they returned in the evening, I wouldn't see another port for a long time.

His arms wrapped around me like a wall of safety, and I pressed my hands against his sturdy back. "I love you," I whispered. When I pulled away, tears glittered in his dark eyes.

"I love you too." He cleared his throat. "Be safe. The ocean is a dangerous place. The storms, the pirates, the sea creatures, the unpredictability of King Valian . . ." His voice trailed off, and he touched my cheek. "It's a treacherous world on the high seas. And who knows what stirs on that island."

My hand clutched his. "I'll be careful. And I don't believe in the Sea King Valian."

His face told me he did, but he stepped back. "If you change your mind, you're welcome to come back home."

He got that sad look in his eyes again. If this was our last time seeing each other, I didn't want that to be the last look he got of me, so I pulled back my shoulders and threw on a smile. "Thank you, Bart. For everything."

With his dark skin and large body compared to my small frame and olive complexion, most assumed Bart adopted me as his daughter when I was a child. We didn't correct them. In a way, he had adopted me, and it hurt to leave him almost as much as it hurt to leave my deceased father buried under the old willow tree back home. The same dull ache pulled at my heartstrings. Bart's wide frame filled the doorway as he waved one last time before I crossed the causeway and onto the pier, where small pebbles filled the cracks in the old planks and dead fish gathered at the edge of the frothing water. The *Royal Rose* swayed in its berth, as small waves lapped against its hull.

Again, the water called out to me. *Danger, danger, danger. The water holds infinite dangers. Your mother was lost in its waves.*

My breath tripped and I stumbled. I glanced behind me to where Bart still waited, watching me leave. Seagulls squawked, mocking my conflicted heart. The bags grew heavy in my arms, and I willed my feet to continue. I'd given my answer; I wouldn't go back on my word now. Not when Arn was counting on me. Not when I needed this to survive to nineteen.

Arn stood at the helm of the ship, gazing at the other ships bobbing in the crystal water. As I lurched near, he swung himself over the side of his boat and landed on the pier with a slight stumble. Still drunk. As he straightened, he shook his head, and I laughed. "You need to sleep."

He gave me a lopsided grin. "All in good time. Two bags?"

I tossed one of the bags to him, which he narrowly caught. "Food from Bart."

His face lit up as he peered into the sack. "Jolly good, I knew I liked that fellow. Fresh rolls?" He dug into the bag. "Bless him." He took a bite, then spoke with his mouth full.

"Ontario just went to grab some more provisions, but we plan to leave at midday."

Midday. Very soon I would set sail with a band of pirates in search of a treasure. *If my mother could see me now.* She'd been sailing for years at my age, and already had a healthy list of enemies.

Emric wasn't going to believe his eyes when he saw me on a pirate ship. I felt as if I was observing someone else's feet go up the rickety gangway and onto the deck where the ground swayed, the saltwater splashed, and a suspicious smell of rum tainted the air. Arn opened the hatch to the ladder below deck and gave me an apologetic look. "I would offer you the deckhouse, but it'll rock more violently. You can have my room." He waved a hand. "I see you ignored my advice to don some pants. You may regret that one."

I knew I wouldn't. This dress kept me separate from my mother. The moment I put on pants, there'd be little distinction between me and the woman who chose sailing the seas over her family. This dress reminded me of the colors of home and of who I was.

"I'm not a pirate," I reminded Arn.

The corners of his lips rose. "We'll see."

After getting set up in Arn's room, which consisted of little more than dropping my bag under the cot and checking to see if any crawly creatures roamed under the mattress, I rejoined Arn above deck. It might sway more here once we set sail, but the open air was comforting.

Arn made a bed for himself in the on-deck cabin by laying some fleece blankets down under the table. Several built-in shelves were stacked with thick books, all their colors faded by the years of sunlight coming through the four portholes.

"Why do you not sleep with the other crew?" I asked. "You certainly have enough empty bunks for it."

He gestured to the room. "Because I'm a captain. I have the privilege of privacy. Besides, my men need to bathe more often before I'll lie next to them." He took his dark blue jacket off and laid it over the table. His leather gloves were worn through the fingertips and looked to be scorched, but his belt buckle still shone. He'd cut off his blond ponytail since I saw him last, and the ribbon that once held it was now tied to his wrist. It was easy for me to forget how handsome he looked when he stopped creasing his brow in worry.

I moved to join him at the table's side. "How bad have things been?"

It took him a few moments to respond, but when he did it was through a strained smile. "It's not too bad."

"Arn?"

A sigh. "All right. Remember last year around first snowfall when I told you things were pretty bad?" I nodded. It was the first time Arn had showed signs that pirate life wasn't as grand as he'd claimed. After turning from the king's navy, he was eager to prove he knew what he was doing and hesitant to show weakness. His pride meant a lot to him.

"But remember how I came back two months later after scoring silk from a merchant vessel and everything was fine again? It's like that. Things are tricky right now, but they'll turn around." He pushed the worry from his face until only his calm blue eyes, narrow nose, and his reassuring smile remained.

My mouth opened just to snap shut. Questions on my end could lead to questions from his, and I wasn't telling him the whole truth either.

"Now, let's see about getting you a weapon, ey? I've got a fine cutlass here and a dagger if you'd like." He crossed to the wall where a chest sat with crimson engravings. It creaked as he opened it to show the few weapons inside. "Isn't much, I'm afraid, and the pistol is a little rusty. Are you still a solid shot?"

The weight of the pistol once felt natural to me, but now it felt unbalanced. Still, if faced against a foe, my hands would remember what to do. "I could hit a chest shot perhaps, though I'm not keen on the idea."

"Chest shot is fine. Here, this belt will fit you." His fingers grazed my sides as he brought out a brown leather belt and wrapped it twice around my waist, tying it in the front. To the belt he attached a small dagger on my left side and a cutlass on the right. Then he stepped back to take a good look.

"Look like a pirate to me. I've got extra pants right over here if you want."

"Don't even think about it." The weapons brought me back to that little sheep farm inland where Mother would let us shoot against bales of hay and spar with us in the mornings as curious little sheep watched. Even when she was gone, my father would keep up our training so Emric and I could impress her when she came home.

Emric always impressed her more.

The door opened, and Ontario paused in the doorway, his eyes sliding over me. "You look great," he said. His eyes lingered before they turned to Arn. "Captain. We are ready to sail."

Something frolicked in my chest, a feeling I couldn't describe. Many times I'd heard Ontario tell Arn it was time to set sail as he came to fetch him from the Banished Gentlemen, but this time I was on the ship with them. This time when they set sail, I'd be sailing too.

This was it. After this, I couldn't change my mind. If we didn't get the Elmber Nut, I'd be dead before we ever returned to Kaffer Port. The strings in my heart pulled so tight that I had to use all my strength to anchor my feet to the boat and remind myself this was where I needed to be if I hoped to live. My mind knew that, but my fluttering heart still didn't.

Was this feeling in my bones from anticipation, or was it my gut warning me to flee back to land? Was my mind excited by the water, or trying to save me from it?

Arn grinned as he announced, "To the Island of Iilak we go."

4

ARN

"Anchors and sails, boys!"

On deck, everyone moved in seamless fashion to prepare to set sail. One of the crew members untied the ship from the wharf and threw the ropes on deck where others swarmed to wind them up. The furled sails were let loose, then pulled taut and tied in place. Emme grabbed the portside railing and clenched her jaw as she cast a longing look back at the Banished Gentlemen. I offered her a smile, but she hardly noticed. She looked moments away from hurling or jumping from the ship.

The *Royal Rose* glided forward as the oars below began to move. We veered slightly right, and I glanced over the starboard side. "Where's Ursula? Her oar isn't moving."

Ontario sheepishly rubbed his hands together. "Sorry, Captain. She informed me this morning that she won't be rejoining the crew. Seems she was offered honest work a few months ago, and she's decided to take it."

Blast. We were stretched too thin as it was. I tried to control the disappointment on my face so the crew wouldn't pick up on my troubles.

"I suppose it's too late to kill her new boss and bring her back to the seas?"

Ontario's grimace deepened. "That might make her company most unpleasant, don't you think?"

"I suppose. Frankly I couldn't care less what sort of mood she's in, as long as she's rowing." I ran my hands through my hair and groaned. "I didn't even know she was offered work."

"Well, Captain," Ontario said very matter-of-factly. "Is that not what you intend when you teach your crew how to read and write?" He cleared his throat. "Perhaps it's time to stop those lessons before another finds a new job."

The idea had occurred to me more than once. But I sighed. "No. I want to give them opportunities. It's just a terrible time for them to be finding them. We have no quartermaster. We have no decent cook. We have no second. No carpenter. No doctor. If other pirates could see us, they would laugh." A mist from the sea came up and splashed my face, as if the very waters were chuckling at our misfortune.

"Our crew is still young," Ontario reminded me. "Give it time. Many pirates prefer to sail with more experienced crews, but soon enough we will be a force to be feared. Men's teeth will quake at our names."

We'd been pirates for three years now. I ought to be grateful we had a nice ship, but if we didn't have the crew to manage it, then it might as well be at the bottom of the ocean. "We must first survive that long."

Ontario gave me another pitiful look. "I'll go take over her spot below. But Captain, consider halting the crew's lessons so they don't get new jobs. Or at least teach them a few wrong things—that'll do the trick. I could teach them, if you'd like. I'm guaranteed to do it poorly."

I waved him off with a chortle that soured as soon as his back turned. I had twelve sailors with me on my crew. One less mouth to feed and portion of plunder to offer, but also one less sailor to help us navigate through the rough voyage ahead.

Thank the stars for Emme and her brother who would

follow. Their mother's diligent sea lessons and ruthless weapon training when they were younger would be invaluable to us during the grueling months ahead.

If anything, their lineage might deter others from attacking.

The son and daughter of Arabella the Ruthless.

The woman who could shoot a bottle at seventy meters and whose sense of hearing let her track through the night. The one who ruled the high seas before she died five years ago, leaving a slew of pirates behind regretful that they hadn't been the ones to spill her blood.

Even as a fresh recruit in the king's navy, I had known who she was. I should fly her flag below mine to elicit fear in all who crossed us.

That might come off as taking advantage of Emme's presence and lead her to doubt that I desired her company regardless of who her mother was. She could be the daughter of two corn farmers, and I'd still want her at my side.

My own flag cracked in the howling wind—a black tarp with a golden rose dripping golden blood. The blood had been Emme's idea. She thought the flower made me look weak.

Right now Emme was leaning her head over the side of the ship with her eyelids pressed shut. I slid to her side and placed a hand on her back, where her muscles startled at my touch. "By stars, Arn. This is worse than I remember."

"You haven't vomited yet, so I'd say we are off to a swell start." I tried to be optimistic, but the shore was still near, and she already looked green. As the days went by, she would only grow more miserable. Without thinking, I said, "You don't have to do this. Stay here, and I'll bring the treasure back to you."

Warmth filled her eyes, but she shook her head. "No, I have to go. Your cook, Bishop, promised to make me a concoction that should ease my stomach." Saltwater splashed up the side of the boat and spat mist over Emme. Pure disgust crossed her face. "I'm going to smell like fish."

She would, and I would miss her usual smell of wildflowers.

She turned away from the water. "I think I'll go rest for a while."

My face twisted apologetically. "It's best you don't, love. Stay above deck and keep your eye on the horizon. It'll be the fastest way to get over this seasickness."

A shaky breath escaped her lips. "But it doesn't reek as bad down there, and I can't be as sick if I'm not awake." Before I could attempt further argument, her hand squeezed my elbow, and she moved away from the railing.

Timmons, one of the men on crew, passed by. His eyes roamed over Emme, and he placed a hand on her shoulder. "Looking a little sick. First days at sea will do tha' to you. Have ye tried a cotton ball?" His face got close as he inspected her skin.

"Cotton ball?" She reached back to stabilize herself on the railing once more.

Timmons stepped back. "You don't know that trick? Where's Bo, he always has cotton balls. Bo!" Timmons's eyes wandered over the ship until Bo's head popped out from the cabin. "Gimme a cotton ball."

Asking no questions, Bo pulled one from his pocket. Timmons held it between his fingers and thumb. "Thank ye kindly, you odd man. Here you are m'lady. Put it in your ear."

She glanced between us. "Will that help with seasickness?"

"'Bout as well as whatever Bishop could give ye," Timmons swore. I, who hadn't found that particular trick to work well during my early days, merely shrugged.

Percival, with his bright red jacket unbuttoned over his unlaced shirt, came out of the on-deck cabin a moment later. "Give her a green apple. That'll fix her."

"Henrik told me that trick this morning; it didn't work," Emme informed him.

Percival stroked his chin for a moment, then threw back his head to holler up toward the crow's nest where little Lewie perched at watch. "You know any good tricks for seasickness?"

He leaned over the perch so far that I worried he might fall. "You tried cotton balls?"

Percival groaned and waved an arm at him, and he went back to watch. Emme gave a faint smile. "Thank you all so much for trying, but I'll be fine." Her words got cut off by her stomach lurching. She placed a hand over her belly and hurried to the ladder.

Guilt coiled around my heart, but I didn't let it show. Perhaps I should have let her remain on dry land where she felt safe instead of selfishly wanting her near me. A few moments after she descended the ladder, Ontario came up.

"We've caught a good breeze; should carry us a fair distance." He fixed the fallen hair from his long ponytail and straightened his wrinkled jacket. His dark eyes shifted to the hatch across the deck. "How's Emme?"

I shook my head in reply and climbed to the helm to take the wheel from Henrik. He nodded and trotted down the stairs.

Ontario kept an eye on him until he was out of earshot. "Should we tell her?"

My chest tightened, but my mind tried to soothe it. She'd hate me if she knew. "Once we get that treasure and pay the dues, the rest will go to her and her brother. They needn't know what we needed the money for."

Ontario and I watched the men working below. "They might like to know the danger that follows us."

He made a fair point, but it was one I already knew. Work had been scarce recently, and we had to resort to less than honorable methods of keeping afloat.

Now we needed this treasure. Robbing merchant ships wouldn't be enough. If we didn't get the money, I would lose my ship, and without the *Royal Rose* I was nothing but a man who'd left a comfortable life in the king's navy and dared to believe he could be a pirate.

Ontario fiddled with the twine around his wrist. "Have ye considered, Captain, leaving this all behind? Finding honest work inland, perhaps as a bookkeeper, and being free of this nightmare that holds us?"

The twitch in his eye and detail of the question told me that he had thought of it, but I couldn't claim the same thoughts. "Nay. There's nothing else for me. No life. No family. This ship is all I've got."

If I dwelt on that fact, it would put a weight on my heart so great that I might never be free of it, so instead I cast the sorrow aside. All was not lost yet.

"But surely your father would welcome ye back to the business?"

"He'd take one look at these pirate tattoos upon my arms and never love me again. Nay, Ontario. I have no other options but this."

My first mate fell quiet beside me, but I cared little for his pity. My hand clasped his shoulder. "We will make it through this, my friend. I promise you that. And Emme never needs to know the danger we are in."

Ontario nodded. "Tell me, is her brain the only reason we invited her along with us? The lass doesn't mean anything to you?"

I snapped my head to look at him. "I don't like using her like this. She's a dear friend."

He waved his hand in a circle. "Aye, I know that. But what I'm asking is if she's more."

Ah. An answer came to my tongue, wanting to say that we were sweet on each other, but she'd given me no indication of that being true. In fact, she seemed rather ignorant to the advances I'd made—standing close to her and listening intently when she talked. If a lass couldn't tell that I liked her from that, then I didn't know how else to say it. "Nay, mate. She's merely a friend."

I hadn't failed to notice how Ontario had looked over Emme when he saw her with the pirate's cutlass and dagger strapped to her waist. Similarly, I hadn't failed to notice as she blushed when he complimented her. Or how she stepped back every time I got too close.

Blast, I should have said we were sweet on each other.

His face brightened in a way that made me frown. I distracted myself with checking the compass. "Three days until we should reach Arwa Isles. If you want to take some rest, you should get it now."

He bobbed his head, but his eyes were glazed over already, lost to his own thoughts. Before heading below deck, he ducked into the cabin and came back out with some bread. I could guess who he was taking it to.

Still your jealous heart. She's not yours. Focus on getting the treasure and staying alive.

5
EMME

"I like Emme." A voice stopped me in the hallway before entering the captain's cabin. A man spoke from inside one of the bunk rooms, though I didn't know all the crew well enough to identify based solely on voice.

"From what the captain says, she possesses a great knowledge of the sea and of the creatures who roam within. She knows as much as a pirate who's been sailin' for fifteen years, that's what he said."

I grinned. I'd just turned away from the thin door when a second man spoke.

"I don't trust her."

I recognized this voice as Svid, one of the twins. His comment gave me pause. "She's the daughter of Arabella the Ruthless. I heard her mother once killed her entire crew because she suspected them of plotting mutiny."

That wasn't true. Mother had spared nine lives. But she also killed twenty-three while they slept, then took over another ship to rebuild her lost crew.

I removed the cotton ball from my ear and leaned forward. The door to their room was barely ajar, so I took care not to get too close to be seen through the crack. "Well, I like her," another said.

"But don't you think she's distracting to the captain?" Svid asked. "Do you see how he looks at her as if he's found a priceless pearl inside an oyster?"

Heat flooded my cheeks. I had noticed that.

One of them snickered. "Were you not distracted by Ursula? Nearly fell from the riggings into the ocean for that one. Perhaps it was your blubbering that drove her from the crew." The other man had a good laugh at that.

"I think it was your foul mouth, Brother. Or your horrid odor," Svid combated, labeling his twin, Sims, for me. "Besides, I'm not captain. I'm allowed to be distracted. But Arn has been off lately. Something ain't right."

My feet inched nearer to the door to catch the conversation as their volume dipped.

"I asked Captain what the matter was, repeatedly, but he said he'd hang me from the crow's nest if I bothered him about it again," Svid claimed. My eyes widened, but his brother chuckled.

"I'd like to see that." A thud followed. "Ey, watch it. I'm just joking. I asked Captain what was going on, too, but my punishment was language lessons. I can almost write my name though."

I hadn't been wrong in thinking Arn hid something. Now my determination to know what it was only grew. I inched even closer to the door.

"I don't know, men," Svid said. A silence followed that concerned me, so I backed away. The floorboards creaked under my weight, and my breath froze in my throat while my heart pounded in my chest. Svid's next words found me as they drifted through the crack, as light as the wind. "Perhaps it's time for a new captain."

A latch at the end of the hallway opened, and I flew away from the door. Bishop emerged from the kitchens with a wooden cup in hand. "There you are," he said too loudly. I grimaced. "I brought you that drink I was telling you 'bout."

I hurried to take the cup as fast I could. "Thank you very much, Bishop," I whispered. "You're a lifesaver. I'll drink it in my cabin." I fumbled with the handle and slid through the doorway. "Thank you." I shut the door as quickly as I could.

The cluttered thoughts in my mind prevented me from gagging upon the foul taste of the gray liquid in the cup. If I didn't notice a decrease in my seasickness after one dose of this vile drink, I wouldn't be convinced to drink a second. I did place the cotton ball back in my ear, though.

My stomach lurched, almost rejecting the drink, but I held steady.

Svid would be someone to keep an eye on during my time here. All it would take is the crew to revolt, and Arn would be stripped of his captain status. Surely whatever he hid wasn't worth losing his ship over.

My stomach lurched again.

Right now I didn't have the energy, nor the stomach, to ponder the matter further. I collapsed into my bed and bit down my nausea and prayed for sleep to find me quickly.

6

EMME

Sleep wouldn't come.

Midday was no time to be sleeping, no matter how badly I longed for an escape from this rocking ship and the way it made my stomach roll over. At least I was no longer on the verge of vomiting, but as much as I turned in the bed and punched the thin pillow, Arn's cot wouldn't feel comfortable, and I couldn't get over the fact that I was *on a pirate ship*.

The ocean is the place for you. My mother had whispered these words into my hair as she tucked Emric and me into bed. He'd stare at her with wide eyes and ask for the same tales again. *You'll never feel anything like the thrill of sailing.*

She'd been so certain that Emric and I belonged on the waves with her, even when I claimed I'd never leave home. It'd always be a mystery how my father won her heart or convinced her to give up years of her life on the ocean to start a family with him on his humble sheep farm. But soon my mother longed for the waters again, so she left her young children and returned to her ship where she thought little of her family back home.

I shouldn't be here. I should be back at the Banished Gentlemen spending my final months with Bart. The Elmber

Nut might not exist, or we might die before getting there. I never should have left the security of land to follow a myth.

I wouldn't find sleep now, not when my mind was so restless. It was too late to turn back now, no matter how badly I wanted it. This tiny cabin would be my home for the next few months.

Perhaps Arn's secrets were hidden in its walls.

Arn's captain quarters weren't too different from my room above the Banished Gentlemen; both were small with a single window facing the door, a narrow bed, and walls made of pinewood. His cot was raised from the ground and hardly had enough room to sit up without bonking one's head on cupboards above. I didn't have a table as he did, or the slender bench along the other wall with storage underneath, or the intriguing chest under the porthole.

And of course, my bedroom didn't move as the ocean rolled beneath it.

Curiosity led me to open the cupboards above the bed, where rolled papers and a rusty telescope sat within. Once started, it was difficult to stop myself from poking through the rest of Arn's meager things in an attempt to better understand his life of piracy. All I had were a few of his stories and lots of my mother's, but so far it hadn't lived up to the excitement about which they spoke.

Arn was a difficult man for me to understand. He spoke little about why he left the king's navy, but I knew he hated the Julinbor monarchy. He was smart and insisted on keeping up his education, even though he chose a lifestyle that required little brains and more brawn. He'd stop in the road to pick up someone's fallen handkerchief, but he'd just as quickly rob a sailor of their goods. He'd ink his skin but refused to pierce it. Every time I thought I understood Arn, I realized that there were layers to him I didn't understand.

We were good friends, but he kept himself closed off, never

allowing me to see much of the man under the dark vest and gold tattoos.

Perhaps his room would tell me the tales that he would not, or why he looked caught in a lie when I asked him where his crew was. There was something he was keeping from me, something that made Ontario's eyes skirt away when we were on deck and made the men whisper behind doors, and I desperately longed to know what it was they kept hidden.

The chest by the wall was held shut with a lock, but upon shaking it, only the soft sound of fabric shifting came from inside. Likely his clothes. I moved on.

Under the bench sat a few worn-through pairs of shoes and boxes of clutter. Some dull necklaces, parchment and ink, a gold key with a chartreuse ribbon, bottles of thick liquids labeled *Squid Paralyzer* and *Shark Poison*, and a compass with a loose clasp. I searched for the letters I'd written him, but they weren't there. My heart unexpectedly sunk. He wasn't expected to keep letters that spoke of little more than my full life at the Banished Gentlemen, but part of me thought he had. After all, I'd kept his.

I'd read too much into his constant visits. He likely had many maidens in different ports who smiled at him as they poured him drinks and also wrote him letters.

I shut the top of the hideaway rougher than intended.

The floorboards showed no signs of a hidden compartment, and the bed concealed nothing under its sheets. I felt around the edges of the porthole for a little hole to a secret area but found nothing. Water lapped up near the window, and outside, land was nowhere in sight. My stomach flopped again, and I gripped the rim of the porthole for balance.

As I did, something shifted under my thumb. With newfound energy, I slid my fingers under the plank and found something wedged between the slits in the boards.

Please, please, please.

Yes.

A small key rested in my hands, and I dropped to my knees to slide it into the hole of the chest and twist. The lock made a satisfying click as the latch loosened, and I eased the top open. Arn's plain vests and jackets and breeches sat inside.

All the excitement ebbed out of me. That wasn't thrilling at all. I shuffled deeper only to find his wool socks. There were no diaries or hidden plans or mysterious photographs of long-lost family members here. Nothing to tell me more about Arn or why he'd been acting slightly unusual. There was really no reason for this chest to be locked.

The socks made a strange noise as I moved them, and I sucked in my breath. My hand searched for what had made the noise and discovered a sock stuffed with papers. With anticipation, I pulled it out to discover what Arn was hiding.

It was my letters.

Warmth waved over me, and my hand closed over my mouth. He'd kept my letters. He'd cared about them enough to lock them in a chest. We exchanged them once every few months, even when there was little to write about. Kaffer Port had skilled messenger falcons who delivered the letters without fail, no matter where he was.

I thumbed through them until coming upon an envelope that wasn't mine. My hand froze as I read his name in curly writing on the front. The border of the envelope was stained black, and there was a black sun stamped on the corner. The parchment inside felt thick.

My fingers hesitated over the seal as I was struck with a sudden conscience. These were Arn's personal belongings that I shouldn't snoop through. Guilt pinched me, fighting against the curious parts that longed to tear the letter open.

You're going to do it anyway.

Just as my fingers pried at the opening, heavy footsteps in

the passageway startled me, and I shoved the notes back inside the sock. Someone knocked on the door.

"Just a moment."

One glance at the room and Arn would know that I went through his things. As quickly as I could manage, I placed the sock back where I'd found it, straightened the garments inside the chest, and shut the lid. I barely had time to lock it or return the key before the knock came again.

I flew to the door and pasted an innocent smile to my face before opening the door. My mouth formed an *O*. "Ontario."

His shoulders sagged. "Were you expecting Arn?"

I was but was also relieved this gave me a chance to further straighten up the room before Arn came back. "No, I'm happy to see you; come on in."

He carried some bread with him, which he handed to me. "Nibbling it usually helps me when I feel sick."

"Do you get seasick a lot?" I asked.

"No," he said, then added, "but sometimes."

He rubbed the back of his neck as he took a few steps into the room. Three silver earrings shone from his left ear. The sides of his dark hair were shaved, and the top was pulled into a bun at the back of his skull, while midnight-blue tattoos covered where the rest of his hair ought to be. He shared the same physical build as Arn, but they had contrasting personalities. While Arn got stressed often and lost in his thoughts, Ontario was calm-natured and quick to talk his captain down from a frenzy. In all their time spent with me at the tavern, he'd never said one bad thing about his captain and never questioned his leadership. Arn treated Ontario well and trusted him with everything, so I suspected he knew how lucky he was to have a first like that.

Over the times he'd accompanied Arn into the tavern and joined us for a game of cards, I got to know Ontario well. A man of few words but a sharp mind. The other crewmates were prone to exploring the town and the other taverns it held, but Ontario and I knew each other.

Now I'd see if I knew him well enough to know when he was lying.

If something was amiss with Arn, Ontario would know it. Maybe he knew what the black envelope with the sun in the corner meant. He would tell me what Arn wouldn't. The dimples in Ontario's cheeks creased as he studied the maps on the table. Keeping a close eye on his expression, I asked, "What's going on with your captain?"

His head jolted up and eyes widened slightly. The surprise fell quickly, and he dropped his attention back to the table. With a calm voice, he answered, "Everything is fine."

I pointed the bread at him. "I knew something was up. Tell me."

He shrugged. "He's merely excited about his opportunity. We've been waitin' for old Barnacles to die for quite some time."

He was bent over in apparent captivation with the papers, even tracing his finger along the path they planned to take, but I didn't forget the look on his face a moment ago. "Ontario, I know something is wrong with him. Not sailing with a full crew? Getting drunk? That's not Arn. He paraded into the Banished Gentlemen practically shouting his plans to go after the treasure. Something's wrong with him, and I want to know what."

His brow rose at the part about the Banished Gentlemen.

"I know he's low on money." I moved to stand across the table from Ontario where I could look in his eyes, daring him to lie to me. "How bad is it?"

A war raged behind his eyes, and I kept mine boring into him to wear on his guilt. Finally, he sighed. "It's bad. But it's not something you should have to worry about."

"The other men are worried about it too. I heard talk of mutiny."

Though this should upset him, Ontario smirked. "Who? Svid?"

I nodded, and he chuckled. "He's trouble, that one. Svid speaks of mutiny all the time, but nothing will ever come of it. See, here's the thing about Arn." He circled the table to stand by me, until I could smell the rum buried into the fibers of his shirt. "He's different. And the crew knows it. When we fished Svid and his brother from the water, they couldn't read. Couldn't write. Couldn't count. Arn taught them to do that, and by doing so, he removed the anchor holding them to the sea. They could go inland and get a decent job with the education he's forced upon them. They are lucky to have him, and they know that. No one will demote Arn. Ever."

That was all very well. But that still didn't take away from the fact that Arn hid something.

The ship lurched, and I stumbled into Ontario. His steady arms caught me. He grinned. "Don't fret, you'll get used to the ship's movements soon. I'm surprised you don't sail more, considering your mother was Arabella the Ruthless."

My nose flared at the name.

"Stop trying to protect me from whatever is going on with Arn. I want to help."

His hand stroked my elbow before letting me go. "I'm not trying to protect you, there's just not much to tell. He needs money, so we are getting some."

A matter as simple as that wouldn't be enough to elicit the look in his eyes a few minutes ago, but his firm expression told me that I'd pry no more information from the faithful first mate. He leaned back to the maps, drawing my eye with him. Arn had spared no detail in his drawings, from the snowcapped mountains to the small marshes and cluster of islands the size of a pin. He'd studied every curve of the shores and every bend of rivers from previous maps to be certain he got his exactly right.

He was smart, I reminded myself. Arn was logical and realistic and educated. How much trouble could he really be in?

"Ontario, how much do you know about this island we sail to? I've never heard of a man who had reached its shores."

"Not a man, perhaps. But I heard your mother did it."

I brushed this away. "My mother did many reckless things. How certain are you that the island is safe?"

He took a few moments to reply. "It worries me," he admitted. "I've heard . . . rumors. More than just that Bernabe De is dead. I've heard that he's alive." His face tightened. "I've heard of traps set up all across that island designed to kill any who dare dock at its port. I've heard Bernabe De himself waits with a pistol loaded with never-ending ammunition, that he never sleeps and never eats, but watches, ready to kill any living thing." He looked unseeingly at the maps on the table. "That man was a ruthless creature when he sailed these seas, killed more of his friends than his enemies. I can't fathom what the heat of that island has done to his mind. Dead or alive, taking that treasure won't be simple."

His words haunted my mind. It was a darker story than Bart had told me. To venture to this island, one must be truly desperate. I knew why I was, but I couldn't figure out why Arn was. "Then why go after this treasure? How badly do you need this?"

Ontario's face cleared, and he straightened. "Your mother successfully sailed to that island. We can too." His fingers tapped the table with hesitancy. "I'd quite like to know more about your mother, if it's a story you don't mind telling."

If it was anyone else, I'd deny the request, for the years of questions from pirates in the Banished Gentlemen who recognized my relation to my mother had grown tiresome to the point where I pretended not to know who she was. But Ontario was different. "What would you like to know?"

His question was immediate. "What was it like having her as a mother?"

When asking about my mother, people wanted a romanticized

tale about growing up at the helm of a pirate ship, watching my mother conquering the seas and living richly. They wanted to know if she really was as beautiful and fearless as they'd all heard.

She was. She was beautiful, and she was fearless. But she was a lousy mother.

"She was theatric," I finally responded. "She lived large and loved large and wanted to give us the whole world. Most of her days were spent on the sea while my father raised me and Emric on a charming inland sheep farm. It was a quiet life, but I enjoyed it. No swashbuckling tales here, I'm afraid."

His eyes watched mine, and something new swirled inside. Most people listened to me speak of my mother with awe or excitement etched across their faces, but Ontario was without any of these emotions. His expression was different, and it was challenging to put a name to it. Sympathy, I finally realized. Not amazement nor wonder, but sympathy for a young girl who'd never known the affection of a mother.

His tone lowered, almost sounding like pity. "And she spent more time on the ocean than with you?"

So there was an understanding in that sympathy. "Yes," I told him. "But she brought lots of money with her each time she visited, so we lived comfortably. Many families around us didn't have that." I should be grateful for that. That should have been enough.

"I'm sorry to hear that. She missed out on getting to know you." His dark eyes were set on mine, until I lowered my head. The boat rocked again, throwing me against him once more. I laughed uncomfortably, but he was slower to release me this time.

At that precise moment, Arn opened the door. Like wave retreating from the shore, I flew from Ontario. Arn's lips pulled tight as he looked at the newly vacated space between the two of us, then cleared his throat. "Just checking to see how Emme was doing. Glad you're all right."

Then he turned back, leaving me with a flushed face and an uneasy stomach that had little to do with the rocking ship.

7
ARN

I was keenly aware of every time Ontario was near Emme. Every time he gave her a grin as he passed, every time he brought her food, every time he patted her back as she leaned her head over the rails in sickness—I saw it all.

I'd witnessed Ontario smitten with a lass enough times to know what it looked like. Unfortunately, Emme proved more difficult to read. She'd smile back, but her attention never lingered like his did for her. It didn't linger on me either.

Stop torturing yourself. Focus.

Emme suspected something was amiss; her constant questioning told me that much. When did I let the other part of my crew go? When did I plan to hire more men? How much financial trouble was I in? She'd gotten creative after those questions ran dry. It'd be best for us to buy some newer pistols for the men, have you rationed enough money for that? Her relentless desire to understand the situation I'd gotten myself into was unyielding, and while I did my best to answer the questions, her dubious expression remained.

If I told her what I'd done, she'd have more questions than answers.

The tale was a dark one.

At that time, we had grown so thin on money. I ate hardly

more than stale bread every day. We were desperate. The hunger in my men's eyes grew with each sunrise, and the coins in our purses dwindled.

Then the miracle came, or so I thought.

I thought myself to be so lucky when my old crewmate led me to a man who could solve our problems. He promised us wealth and happiness in return for a signature on parchment. I'd given it little thought before agreeing, blinded by my hopelessness.

I'm a bigger fool than any other man, surely.

There was nothing else for me in this life. I'd given up everything to be a pirate, and it was too late to go back to the man I once was. How idealistic I had been. How naïve. Home didn't want me anymore, and workers weren't quick to hire someone who deserted the king's navy and lived on the high seas.

Admiral Bones appeared to be the answer—a thin man with narrow eyes and deep pockets who offered to loan us money last year. Stories of him circulated the seas, including how he dealt with those who didn't pay him back. They said that all the bones are taken from their bodies until they are found as nothing but skin and entrails along the shore.

It was a fate I was determined to avoid.

But now it was time for him to collect, and we had naught. None could say how long it'd be before he came after us.

I'd almost forgotten to remove the invoice from Admiral Bones from the chest in my room. If Emme had seen that, if she read the amount I owed him or the threatening promise he made of what he'd do if I didn't pay him, she'd demand to be returned to the Banished Gentlemen. Back where she'd be working another four or five years in hopes of buying back her childhood home. Back to the lonely life she lived in a town she disliked with the smell of the sea in the air.

She deserved better than that, and I could help her get it. This treasure would offer her a new life.

After three long days and longer nights of sailing, the distant, low-lying Arwa Isles came into view. The two islands sat beside each other with a wide channel running between them where smaller ships could travel between the two piers.

They were named Norwa and Souwa, for one was further north than the other, but besides their names there was little to differentiate between the two. Though small, they were their own nation belonging to a young king after he slayed a dragon who terrorized the hills. The lands were rich in gold and perfectly positioned between several countries to serve as a trading outpost.

Along the shores ran seaside homes and shops, most adorned with swallow-tailed banners that added vibrant color to the pale, sandy streets. A shipyard sat outside Norwa with fresh maroon paint on the sign, while fishing boats and small barges lined the wharf outside Souwa. As we drew close, the crew flocked to the deck to watch with merriment as the land drew nearer.

Emme bobbed on her heels as we steered toward one of the piers. Her fingers picked at the ropes she'd been mending with a bone needle. If she picked hard enough, she'd need to mend them again, but I didn't say anything.

Last I heard, Emric worked as a smuggler for a man named Farrold on the coast of Souwa while he saved money for a ship of his own. That was a few months ago, and he might have moved on by now.

If he wasn't here, someone ought to know where he went.

We arrived at the pier, and Ontario jumped out to tie us in. On the docks, workers hustled about hauling chests or rolling barrels and inspecting inventory before loading it into a vessel to be shipped out. A few of the men ran to help Ontario dock the *Royal Rose*.

I descended from the helm of the ship and met Emme at the side. "We made it." I grinned and squeezed her hand. "We made it." She didn't pull away. It was the first physical touch between us since I saw her so close to Ontario in my cabin three days prior.

That's what stung the most, that they'd been together in my cabin where I'd so often imagined Emme being with me. And they stood so close. The thought of something happening between them before I walked in, or what might have happened had I not entered, tormented me.

She took a shaky breath as they pushed the gangplank overboard so we could disembark. I thought she'd flee from the ship, but she clasped tight to my hand and stared over the land.

"It's been three years since we saw each other. There's so much to tell him . . ." Her voice drifted off like a sliver of wind leaving me to guess if her words were for me or for herself.

She tucked the rope and bone needle away with tight lips clamped shut between her teeth.

I didn't have siblings, so I couldn't understand the relationship between them, but I knew the tension of seeing a relative again after years of distance. I felt it when I thought of my father, who I hadn't seen since leaving the king's navy. "You don't have to come."

She shook her head. "And stay on this old ship? No, thank you." Her distant expression broke into a wink and grin.

"Remember what this is for," I said, leaning in. "*Baaaaa.*"

She laughed, but there was a burden in her smile. I desperately wanted to ease that burden, but nothing I came up with could make this moment easier for her.

Her hand slid back into mine as we went down the gangplank, stepping over the rough spot in the middle. The tightness in her grip increased with each movement, as if I was her lifeline. Despite her worried eyes as she scanned the faces, she still held the courage to continue on.

She was a marvelous being, and she didn't see her own strength. Her brother was a fool for leaving her behind in Kaffer Port.

The sun dipped behind the mountains, lending a gold hue to the air that illuminated the black-and-gold tattoos across my arms. I'd gotten those tattoos because I thought the pirate branding made me appear fearsome.

As we crossed on the pier, a worker's face turned white as sand, and his body froze.

But it wasn't me he was afraid of.

With our next steps, he trembled backward. "Arabella the Ruthless. Back from the dead." His voice quivered, and his body shook as he stared at Emme, who had gone still. Her skin was as white as the man's, and the muscles in her neck were tight.

The man continued to wobble in fear, lowering himself onto the planks. "Please spare us."

Her head tilted at that, and her eyes narrowed. I moved forward to shield her from his sight. "Be on your way, mate. You're mistaken."

His hand trembled as he pointed toward Emme. "Is that not Arabella the Ruthless? The one who was said to have died?" A few others had stopped as well, some curious, others as terrified as the first worker. Some reached to their cutlasses and shifted back.

Their troubled whispers reached my ears. "I knew we shouldn't have allowed her son here. Nothing but trouble, that one."

Jolly good, he was here, then. A bit of good news for our journey. Now we only had to find him before someone with jittery hands got too eager with their blade.

Wary eyes watched us, taking in Emme's linen dress and simple weapon belt before glancing to see what flag she sailed under.

Emme frowned at the crowd and raised her voice, "No, I'm not her. I don't know who that is."

I'd seen this happen many times. A pirate would come through Kaffer Port and note the resemblance between Emme and her mother, usually a scoundrel who had interactions with the late pirate. Some would want to talk to Emme, others wanted to sneer at her out of dislike for her heritage. Ones who felt especially scorned would want revenge for whatever Arabella the Ruthless had done to them, and Emme was the perfect way to let out the anger. With a dagger in her pocket and her quick feet, she'd fended off many attacks.

Her mother may have taught her to fight when she was a child, but I'd been the one to teach her to fight as a woman.

One particularly dark night, an angry visitor managed to pull her out of the tavern when Bart wasn't looking, cursing her mother's name the entire time. Emme stabbed him, but the man didn't falter as he pulled out a pistol and aimed it at her heart. I, on mission for my captain, came upon them on the docks and sent a bullet through the man's side, then another into his chest. That was how I first met Emme, with her eyes wide in terror and some scoundrel's warm blood dripping over her eyes. My steady hand wiped the tears from her cheeks as she stood in shock. Once recovered, she didn't flee back inside. She stayed to help me hide the body, and though we both ended up covered in blood, our friendship began. As did our lessons in self-defense.

I knew better than most how much she loathed the thought of her mother and all the trouble it brought upon her.

"She's the daughter of a candlemaker, not a pirate." I stepped in to save her now.

Emme didn't wait to reaffirm the fact. She turned on her heel and hurried away, beckoning for me to follow. I checked back to the workers who still stared at her. As we reached the causeway, I took the lead, turning around to face her.

"Are you quite all right?"

"I'm fine." She glanced back toward the muddy road. "It's my brother we are interested in right now, not my mother. Perhaps I should have asked them where he is."

I gave her another look, but her eyes were elsewhere. "I know the establishment he once worked for. Follow me."

We set off again, this time without her hand in mine, though I could still feel the warmth where hers had been.

"I know about your dislike for your mother, but you don't speak of Emric often."

Emme kept her face downward as we walked so her identity wouldn't be mistaken again by the few people who passed by. She'd pulled out her braid and arranged her brown hair in a way that it covered her face and swept against her long lashes. Streaks of caramel contrasted the darkness as result of the sun's rays.

She took a few minutes to reply. "There's not much to speak of. Emric has always been my best friend, and I love him more than anyone in the world, but life hasn't given us an opportunity to see each other in years. The time apart makes it feel like I don't know him anymore. According to his letters he works in a pawn shop as he saves up money to purchase a ship." She flashed me a mischievous glance. "He wasn't so lucky to score one in a game of cards like you were."

There was little luck to do with that. The previous owner was notorious for gambling, and Ontario made it his mission to get the other pirate as drunk as possible while Timmons dealt the cards in my favor. The man soon passed out, and I'd sailed off in the *Royal Rose* by morning.

"If your brother wants to be a captain someday, then why doesn't he sail with other pirates?"

She kicked a pebble ahead of her a few times until it skipped out of reach. "He claims it's faster to work on land and buy your own ship than sail for another pirate." She glanced at me. "He's an interesting character. You'll see."

As the sky continued to darken, we wound through the town toward a small antique shop with a seashell sign. The windows were darkened, the door loose on its hinges, and the steps up to the door were covered in sand.

While we were still a good distance away, I pointed to it. "That's the one, with the blue flag out front."

Suddenly the door flung open, and a heavy-set man with a snarl on his face stormed out and glared both ways down the street. We stopped when he shouted, "Where is he?" He waved his fists and shouted again. "Where is the scoundrel?"

"That's where Emric works?" Emme asked me, voice low.

I nodded. "Don't worry, I'm sure it's not about your brother." I wouldn't want to be on the other end of that rage.

The man growled. "Emriiiiic!"

Emme and I exchanged glances. "Well," I said.

Just then, a figure slipped out the door behind the man and took off down the sandy street toward us. "Sorry, Farrold!" he called out as he ran.

"Aaarrgg!" The angry man waved his hands and chased after Emric, who jumped over a cart, rolled to his feet, and looked back.

"It was good pay!" Emric shouted before taking off again.

"It was my *daughter!*"

Emric sped up, but Emme stepped in his path. He jolted to a halt, and his mouth dropped open. His brown curls stood out in every direction, and his eyes bulged from their sockets. "Emme?" He took a small step forward. "Emme, is that you?"

"Hello, brother."

Her tone was difficult to analyze. I searched it for anger or pain or remorse but found none of these things. She spoke so plainly, like it'd only been a few months since she laid eyes on her sibling. Not years.

But I glanced down and saw it. The slight shake in her fingers.

For a moment, Emric was still as sails on a windless day, but a growl from Farrold made him jump. The large man couldn't move fast on his short, chubby legs, but he wasn't giving up his pursuit. He'd be upon us soon.

"How are things?" Emme tilted her head.

Emric glanced back, then grabbed Emme's arm. His eyes went back and forth over her. "You're real. You can't know how often I've thought of you over the years. It's marvelous to see you, but 'less you fancy being whipped, we'd better go."

She sighed, glancing to me with a wink while ignoring the man running toward us. She spoke in a deliberate slow tone. "I don't know. I might rather stay here and see you get whipped."

He uttered a nervous laugh, then looked back at Farrold. "Go."

They took off as I followed behind. Emric threw out over his shoulder, "Have to do better than that, Farrold!"

"My daughter!" Farrold waved a plump arm at us as he huffed. Emric led us through the town and down small alleys and over barrels until we were all out of breath, Emme especially. Her face was red with effort, and her breath rattled in her chest. Emric only stopped when he'd reached the pier and bent to steady his breathing. "Got anywhere to hide? He knows all my best places."

I gulped for air as I looked behind us. We'd lost Farrold a long time ago. "I don't think he will catch back up."

Emric shook his head. "He's mighty angry; he won't stop until he's found me."

"The ship?" Emme panted.

I raised my brow. "Are you sure? You just got off."

"I'll be fine," she said between gasps.

Emric's mouth dropped. "You came on a ship?" His eyes swiveled to me as if he'd be less surprised to find out Emme traveled here by magic carpet. "How did you get her on one of those?"

Emme laughed. "Did you think I'd tunneled my way here? Yes, we came on a ship. Now come on, unless you want to stay here and tell us the story about his daughter . . ."

His face turned red. "Ship will do. Lead the way."

The pier was less busy on our return to my ship, and no one stopped us with comments of Arabella the Ruthless along the way. Almost everyone greeted Emric, and he tipped his head at them and asked for his whereabouts not to be given to Farrold if he came around, to which they'd laugh and oblige. His popularity was what made him so easy for me to locate.

He inspected my ship, pulling on some ropes and tapping on the wood. He nodded his head in approval, and pride swelled within me.

Emme claimed to have forgotten something, though through her mumbles I couldn't hear what, and she promised to be right back. Her weight favored one leg as she descended below deck. Emric continued to inspect the boat, now standing at the helm and grasping the wheel. "Good ship. Solid design. Clean. Say, how'd you get those sails so clean?"

"I washed them."

"Fascinating." He stroked his short, dark beard. He looked like Emme—sharp nose, point in the ears, a full, curved upper lip. Both strong frames and thick brows. But Emme moved about the ship as a wind, quiet and soft, while Emric was a crashing wave demanding to be noticed. The wind flapped open his jacket, where a nice pistol sat buckled to his side. Emric had the look of a pirate, with gold earrings in his ears and tattoos on his hands. And if the muscle under his sleeves knew how to fight, then he'd be a fine addition to our crew.

"How'd you convince my sister to sail with you?" he called down.

"I asked. Repeatedly."

He continued inspecting my ship. "I could have asked her

a thousand times, and she never would have said yes." He looked at me. "Why do you want her on board?"

The answer wasn't one I was willing to admit to her brother. Her presence calmed me, and with a mission of this magnitude combined with Admiral Bones's threat hanging over me, I needed all the calming I could get. Already, having her aboard had helped settle my worries.

Plus, she'd once confessed how much she made at the tavern and how much she'd need to move back inland. To save her from years of work in a place that she didn't love, a crew's portion of this treasure would grant her those desires in considerably less time.

Then there was the added bonus of her brother, who would never agree to join us unless his sister was on board. I needed all the crew members I could find.

And she was quite beautiful. That could not be overlooked.

"She's smart," I said, choosing my words carefully. "Her knowledge of the sea is not one that's easy to come by. And she's already taught my men some of what your mother taught you in swordplay. Brilliant little tricks she knew. Emme's a sensible girl who is quite valuable to me."

Emric descended the stairs and stood so close that I could smell the rum in his breath. Finally he grinned. "Good. She's valuable to me too." Then he turned away. "Now if you don't mind, it's been years since I've seen her, and I'd much rather be in her presence than yours."

8

EMME

I made an excuse to fetch something from my room as soon as we boarded so I could recover from the run in private. My pounding heart would never calm. It banged against my ribs while my lungs roared and my legs complained of the fire that raged within them. Arn's cot felt like a slab of stone that only angered my body further, but I was too exhausted to move. I didn't have the energy I once had.

The doctor had warned me this would happen. This sickness was beginning to slow me down.

It started as a dull ache in the bones, the kind that made one sore all over, even after a day of rest. That's the stage mine was in now. After a few weeks of soreness I had fearfully called upon a doctor, who conducted a complicated test involving soaking my plucked eyelashes in pig urine for several days before confirming my suspicions. I had Paslkapi. The weary death.

He explained the next stages for me, but I already knew what to expect. I nursed my father into the grave with this same sickness, though his broken heart sped up the decline.

Soon, it would hurt to move. Every step would be unstable, every movement shaky. My breathing would get shallow, and my body would slow down. Eventually, it'd be too painful to get out of bed, and a few days later I'd be dead.

It wasn't that bad yet. But slowly, day by day, my body would fail me.

It was unusual for someone my age to have Paslkapi. I had ignored the doctor's twinge of excitement as he scribbled notes into his pad and requested to examine my body once deceased.

Emric's voice came at the door, and I groaned. I didn't know how to tell him about this—*if* I would tell him about this. His eyes would look sad every time they found me, and he would smother me out of doing anything for myself. People treated my father like a fragile teacup after they found out, and I loathed the idea of being treated the same way.

This was my secret, and Bart alone knew it. I vowed to keep it that way. I didn't want to be treated as broken while I was still alive. According to the book we found, the Elmber Nut on the Island of Iilak should be able to heal me, and no one needed to worry in the meantime.

Emric called out again, and I forced a smile as I sat up in the bed and pretended to be busy fixing my belt. "Come in."

His head poked into the room. Behind his newfound height and strength were the familiar titled eyes, sharp chin, and goofy smile that I remembered. He had Papa's face. Likely no one stopped him in fear of Arabella the Ruthless.

"Tell me, how'd he convince you to sail aboard a pirate ship?" Emric wore tight pants and a loose white shirt with a pendant necklace hanging on a chain that he played with as he moved through the room. The attire of a true pirate. He'd always known that was what he wanted to be.

"Tell me, what's the story about the man's daughter?" I asked instead.

He threw back his head and laughed. "It's a funny story. A mysterious man came into the shop looking for someone to do a job for him, but it was a two-person task."

"Job?"

"Smuggling."

"Emric!"

He shrugged, showing no remorse. "That's my job. I need the money if I'm going to buy a pirate ship. Anyway, the shopkeeper's daughter heard and wanted in. So I let her. We pulled it off too, but old Farrold found out and wasn't pleased. Odd, because he's my boss, but it's not my business."

Ah. That wasn't as bad as I thought it was from the way Farrold shook his fist at Emric. Emric looked amused. "What did you think I'd done?"

I blushed. "I don't know. I don't know what manner of trouble you've been getting yourself into."

He sat on the bed beside me. "I'm sorry for that. I truly am. You cross my mind all the time, but work keeps me busy. Good ships don't come cheap. Are you terribly angry with me for not visiting more?" He cocked his head to look in my eyes.

He deserved to have his own life and not be forced to stay at a small seaside town to raise his little sister when his heart called him elsewhere. It felt selfish to wish he'd stayed at Kaffer Port for me. And yet I wished it all the time.

"I know how important getting a ship is to you," I told him.

He looked relieved. "I hope to have one as good as your friend's captain someday."

"My friend *is* the captain."

His face showed pure envy. "He owns this beauty? He can't be old enough. Where are his whiskers?"

I laughed. "He doesn't have them. But he has a ship, so . . ." I weighed the two out in my hands.

Emric stroked his own short beard with pride. "Still, seems wrong. Does he know if he grew out his beard, he would look fiercer? All the good pirates do it. Someone ought to tell the fellow."

I grimaced. "If you hope to be in his good graces, I'd

recommend not mentioning that little detail to him. He's sensitive."

"Seems I'll be in his good graces anyway, by being your brother," Emric said. It took me a moment to understand what he meant by that.

I blushed. "We aren't like that. Merely companions."

His eyes narrowed as he examined me, but I had nothing to hide. Arn had never once crossed that delicate line with me, and I doubted he cared to try. Undoubtedly, he had finer options than the simple girl who longed to herd sheep, and my future held no place here on this ship with him. Our many years together provided ample opportunities to progress the relationship, but by now it seemed this was as close as we were meant to be.

It wasn't fair of me to wish for any more from him when he was already giving me so much by taking me to this island.

Like a bolt of lightning, one fact struck me with hard force. If I didn't get that healing nut, I would die without knowing what it felt like to be kissed.

"Guess I misread the situation."

From the door, someone coughed. Arn hovered in the doorway with a tight smile and a pink hue prickling his cheeks. His unbuttoned white shirt was tucked into tan pants held up by a wide belt and partly covered by a dark blue jacket that he tugged on. "Sorry, I just came by to check on you."

My face felt hot, and I stood quickly. "It's fine." I glanced at Emric then back at Arn. "Have you asked him yet?"

"Asked me what? If I want to captain this exquisite ship?" Emric hopped up. "You've come to the right man."

Arn frowned. "I manage just fine, thank you. No, I have a business proposition for you." He gestured to the maps. "Take a look."

Emric said yes within moments. We actually had to ask him
to settle down to explain everything properly to him while he
kept bobbing his head and declaring yes. Arn kept trying to
explain the map, but Emric shoved it away.

"I know how to reach those islands. My mother told me
of that secret channel. Splendid. That treasure will easily buy
me a ship."

Arn's face was unreadable for a moment. "You'll only get a
share of the treasure, but it should be a hefty amount."

Emric bounced on his heels. "Beats smuggling. I doubt
Farrold wants me to come back to work, anyway."

Arn straightened the maps, then gave Emric a long look.
"You really want to come?"

"You couldn't stop me at this point."

The corner of Arn's brow lifted to me, looking for my
thoughts, and I shrugged. He stuck his hand out to Emric.
"All right. Tomorrow you will both be initiated."

My forehead furrowed. He hadn't mentioned any initiation
to me. Emric had the same question. "Initiated?"

Arn grinned. "You'll see. It'll be fun."

Initiation turned out to be the sleepy crew members congre-
gating on deck while Arn stood outside the cabin with a boyish
grin. Outside, the world was waking up, and the sky held hints
of pink and orange as the sun wandered toward the tops of
the mountain peaks. Arn had set something up in the cabin
where his makeshift bed lay, then closed the door while Emric
and I stood before the crew. Ontario was the only one who
looked excited for the initiation, which we still hadn't been
given more information on.

"Before we start, proper introductions are called for," Arn

said. Emric and I stood on portside near the stairs to the helm, while Ontario ushered the other men into a misshapen line. "That works. Look alive, men."

He went down the line, making the introductions for Emric.

Ontario, his trusty first mate. Bishop, the cook with the persistent smile, even as the others groaned and rubbed their eyes around him. Bo, who took several swigs of his flask and toasted it to us. Emric raised his flask back, and they took a drink together. Percival, the tallest of the crew by a whole head with blond curls almost as wild as Emric's. Malcolm, who I'd never heard say a word. The twins, Svid and Sims. Timmons, the self-described flute player and chess expert. Collins with the red hair. Zander with the eyes so dark they could be black. Henrik, the strongest of the bunch. And little Lewie, not more than fifteen years old.

At the end, Emric nodded as if he had all the names committed to memory already. "And now?" He cracked his knuckles, eyes eager.

"When each member joins the crew," Arn began, "they go through an official initiation." He swept his foot back and tapped on the closed door. "In there is an old pirate's boot. Legend says he had the largest crew of any other pirate, thanks to his power with words."

Large crews were difficult to come by. The more sailors, the more chance for mutiny.

Emric and I shared a glance. "Words?"

"Yes, words. Some say he used hypnosis, others say he was just so kind that no one wanted to leave him. No matter how he did it, the fellow lived to a very old age, until one day his first mate went into his cabin to find him gone. All that remained was his boot." He tapped the door again. "That boot is your initiation."

Emric and I eyed the door. A slight breeze brought in the smell of the ocean as Arn continued to explain.

"When you go into the room, the boot will tell you one word. That word will be your mantra during your time on my crew. Bravery, knowledge, ambition, stealth—it will be the word that defines you on this ship. It will be what you strive toward and what motivates you, and it will keep us unified."

Emric leaned toward me as he kept one eye on Arn. "He's a different sort of pirate, eh?"

I leaned back. "He reads a lot of books."

"Ah. All right, Arn. I'll do your initiation. What was your word?"

Arn's chest puffed slightly. "Leader. And my first mate's was loyalty. These words define who we are on this crew."

"Yes, yes." Emric waved his hands. "Let's get on with it, shall we? Just right in there, and the boot will speak to me?"

Arn's smile faltered at Emric's lack of patience, but he nodded and pushed open the door. "Should take just a moment."

He was right. Emric closed the door for only a few moments before he came back out and stretched his arms to the side. "Done."

"Your word?" Arn asked.

Emric smirked. "Captain."

Arn's face drained of color, and Emric allowed the silence to hang for a few moments before laughing. He slapped Arn on the back. "Just kidding, matey. It was strength. Not surprised there." He flexed his arms and laughed again at Arn's stunned expression.

The other crewmen chuckled, and Emric grinned at them. Ontario struggled to hold his face straight, but a sharp look from Arn sobered him. "Emme? Your turn, love."

I could guess what the boot would say to me. Simple. Sensible. Afraid.

Sick, perhaps.

With a bow for Arn's sake, I entered the cabin and shut the door behind me.

The boot stood tall on the table as if the owner's leg still rested inside. It wasn't a particularly fancy boot, the brown leather looked old and the clasp dulled, but as I approached, it began to hum.

I waited. It said nothing.

Was I supposed to speak first? Arn hadn't mentioned such a thing. What would I even say?

A few weeks ago I was serving drinks at the Banished Gentlemen, and today I was on a pirate ship prepared to hunt down a healing nut and speaking to old boots.

Just as I opened my mouth to ask for my word, the boot hissed, the buckle shivering like a snake. "You should not be here."

That was more than one word, and I didn't like any of them. I licked my dry lips and took a step away from the hissing boot. "I know."

"You're not safe here," the boot spoke again. It sounded angry at first, but now its tone held concern.

Again, I nodded. "I know that too. It's too late to turn back now."

Another low hum came. I thought that might be it, but as I turned away, it spoke once more. "Then I offer you this advice. Tread lightly. The danger comes from unexpected places."

Did that mean that Bart was right when he said we walked into a trap at the Island of Iilak? Or was there a different danger we faced? I asked the boot, but it remained silent.

"Magic boot?"

Still no reply. It seemed if it wanted to be helpful, telling me what the danger was would have been more appropriate than mentioning there was one, but after three times of asking and receiving only silence as a reply, I accepted that I would get no more information.

Danger comes from unexpected places.

Arn would be expecting a word. With my head swirling, I stepped back out.

"How long was that word?" Emric asked when I reemerged on deck. Everyone waited for my answer.

I glanced at Arn, who raised his eyebrows. "Aware," I said finally. "I don't know what it means."

Something between confusion and surprise crossed Arn's face. "Interesting. We'll figure it out." He clapped his hands. "All right boys, time to sail!"

They scattered to pull in the ropes and open the sails. Arn kept his eye on me for a few more moments, but I stilled my face. "Where to now, Captain?" The strain in my voice was painfully clear to me, but he only turned and gestured over the sea.

"Straight on 'til the Seas of Lost Land."

Emric threw himself at the helm of the ship and grabbed the steering wheel. "You heard him, straight on! Heave and ho!"

Arn sighed and whispered to me, "You never told me how spirited Emric was."

I gave him an apologetic look. "But you should see him with a weapon."

A mumble escaped his throat. "He better be good." Then he called up, "Thank you, Emric. I'll take it from here." He ascended to the helm and wrestled the wheel away from my brother, who stayed put at his side and laughed.

Emric winked at me. "This is going to be a jolly good trip; I can feel it."

9
CARN

What in the name of the dark seas does "aware" mean?

Was she aware of my deceit? Of Admiral Bones's intent? Emme had hardly looked my way since she received the cryptic word from the boot, and I began to wonder how much that old piece of leather knew.

I wasn't worried about Emric finding out about Admiral Bones—his excitement about being a part of a pirate's crew blinded him to any hidden intentions on my part. It boded well for me to have an experienced sailor and skilled swordsman aboard, but if he tried to take the steering wheel from me one more time, I was going to throttle him. If he hadn't been Emme's brother, I'd have tied him up and thrown him overboard by now.

As the sun began to set, Emme climbed down the riggings from the crow's nest while little Lewie took over the next shift.

She was used to the seasickness by now but occasionally asked to sit down and rest. Still, she insisted on helping as much as any of the other men. She swabbed the deck, aided with navigations, acted as lookout, and trained some of the eager crew members in swordplay. Her mother had taught her well, and the men were eager for the tricks she and her brother knew.

As the days turned into weeks, Emme stopped grimacing as the boat swayed and pinching her nose as the seawater splashed her. If I didn't know any better, it seemed she was beginning to enjoy herself.

I told her as much, and she grinned. The sun brought out the green flecks in her light brown eyes and made them shine. "Being on this boat isn't the worst thing in the world."

I leaned against the railing. "Who would have thought ye enjoyed being a pirate? It's a good look for ye."

She laughed. "I'm not a pirate. But I'm not exactly miserable either."

I hoped I was part of the reason she was enjoying herself. Reconnecting with her brother appeared to have been good for her, as well. If I didn't know them, I wouldn't have guessed that they hadn't seen each other in years, but sometimes a tense look crossed her eyes when he was around, so perhaps things weren't entirely patched. She hadn't broached the topic with me yet, so I made the attempt myself. "Emric is certainly having fun."

"He does seem to fit in nicely." Her eyes trailed him across the deck as he chatted with other men, who chuckled at something he was saying. "He's always been like that. Wherever we were, people fell in love with Emric's loud laugh and animated face. He's never struggled to make friends. He'll be a loved captain one day."

The idea of enjoying Emric's boisterous presence over Emme's calming nature seemed ludicrous to me. I'd choose Emme every time. But as she watched her brother, a different expression crept over her face.

In wonder, I crossed my arms. "You're jealous."

Her face flushed, but she didn't deny it. Instead she said, "It'd be nice to be loved like that."

"He's not as sensible as you are," I told her. That felt like a safe compliment. Not too much sentiment in it. Not like what I really wanted to say, which is how adored she was.

She laughed humorlessly. "Perfect. My brother is charming and funny and charismatic, but at least I'm sensible."

And beautiful. And smart. And kind.

"He's so much like my mother was." Her voice was no more than a whisper, catching on the wind and floating away. The wind must have taken her emotions with it because I couldn't decipher them. Was that pain in her voice? Or indifference?

"Do you want to talk about why you told those sailors you don't know Arabella the Ruthless?" I asked.

"Not really."

Her words brought an unexpected, sharp sting to my chest.

I'd never met someone as closed off as Emme. She was like an island, full of riches and beauty but never letting anyone close enough to see it. Through the years I'd known her, I'd slowly seen pieces of her, always small and always calculated, so I never saw more than she wanted. If she had a secret, I had no doubt it'd never be revealed unless she wanted to show it.

I could respect that. I only showed her pieces of me. The best parts, not the darkness. Not the parts that lied and cheated and killed.

A ribbon of wind teased her wavy hair as she turned to me. "Fancy playing some more dice? I'll try not to beat you too terribly. Wouldn't want your sensitive ego damaged."

I'd rather hear the answer to my question, but the sly look in her smile as she played dice was not one I'd pass up. "Ha, you beat me one time, and now you think you're invincible. Don't tempt me to keep a tally of all the times I win."

Before we could open the door to the main deck cabin, Lewie's voice pierced the salty air. "Sail ho! Look there."

"Stars and seaweed," I muttered. I called out to men below deck, and we all flocked to the starboard side to stare across the tumbling waters. Silence settled like a wool cloak as we squinted our eyes and leaned out to sea. Lewie pointed a long arm over the waves.

"A ship." Emme's eyes grew wide.

In the distance, a ship sailed toward us. All we saw was black: black prow, black sails, black mast, black flags. Even the water around the ship seemed to roll darker. It kept back from us, too far to see the markings of the flag or if men stood on board, but stayed on our path.

The sky itself darkened at the ship's arrival.

"Where's your telescope?" Emme asked.

I shook my head. "It broke."

Her eyes peeled from the ship to narrow at me. "And you haven't purchased a new one?"

I kept my eyes on the ship. "No," was my short reply. We were saving all our coppers for the debt I owed. A moment later she turned her attention back to the ship, bending over the railing to better see what followed across the waters.

We were traveling toward the Seas of Lost Lands and were already further north than most men ventured. Beyond this point lay little civilization and few ships, save those traveling to Qrew Ir to mine the mountains or explore the Moving Islands for magical objects. The lands beyond here were . . . uncertain. Better suited for feral beasts and creatures of the world. Most mortal maps stopped at these seas; only a few included the lost lands or Qrew Ir or the Never-Ending Land. It took a clear mission to bring a sailor this far.

A ship didn't come to these waters by accident.

Whoever captained this ship—he either sailed after old Barnacles' treasure, or he was tracking us. Either way, our next move seemed clear. I raised my voice. "All right men, let's show him how fast this beauty can go. To the oars. Emric and Emme, stay above with me to man the sails. Lewie, stay up there."

With hoots and hollers, everyone else dropped below deck

to row us faster while Emme and Emric adjusted the sails' angles to better catch the wind. The sea had been quiet for us recently, with a steady breeze to keep us on our path. Once finished, Emme joined me at the helm and peered into the distance. "He's still there, but he's not getting closer."

"We'll lose him soon. Not many can outrun the *Royal Rose.*" From below deck Ontario's strong voice echoed as he led the men in rowing.

Emric called out from the other end of the ship, "If we turn thirty degrees east, the wind will take us faster."

My mouth tightened, and Emme must have noticed. "It's what you asked him here for," she reminded me.

I tried to think quickly. By turning the helm to match the direction of the wind, it'd bring us to maximum speed. However, that'd take us off course. "It'll be faster, but in the wrong direction. If he's after the treasure, we'd be giving him the lead," I shouted back.

"How fortified is this vessel against an attack?"

"Supplies are not the problem. It's hands. I haven't my quartermaster, so I'd prefer to avoid a fight."

Emric laughed, tightening a knot. "Most men wish to avoid a fight. That's not always possible. And by the looks of it, one's coming to you. Consider turning if you hope to outrun him." He checked the riggings again and went below to help row.

My wheel didn't turn. We could outrun this black vessel on our own, and I wouldn't give him an opening to the treasure.

"He's still there," Lewie called out.

"Aye, I see him."

Things continued in this fashion; the ship stayed behind us at the same pace, never coming closer, never falling back. Hours passed, and he stayed as if on an anchor dragging behind us. His black sails glistening with the moonlight were the only things visible as the night fell dark around us.

The darkness blanketed us in unease. All pirates know it's best not to be caught in an attack at night.

But the black ship made no move to get closer, and finally the weary men abandoned the oars and trickled off to bed, keeping their pistols close in case we fell under attack. Even little Lewie crawled down from the crow's nest and tiptoed below deck. Only Emme stayed at my side, facing backward to watch the ship.

"I don't like this," she said. "It scares me." Her teeth clattered together.

"Are you cold?" I stripped my jacked and placed it over her shoulders. She thanked me and pulled it closer around her body.

So far, the Sea King Valian had chosen to bless our voyage with smooth waters and calm winds. We hadn't faced pirate foes, crossed any navy ships, nor met a creature from below. "It'll be fine," I reassured her. "Ships pass on the seas often."

My words sounded fake to my ears, though if she could hear my nerves, she didn't say. The larger ship continued to keep up with our pace, though it made no sound. No crashing of waves breaking at its hull, no shouting of orders from the crew, no crack of sails in the wind. Only silence and darkness.

It bled its darkness into the sea, sending ribbons of black swimming to reach my ship and lap against the planks, asking to be let in. Soon, the waters were darker than the settling night.

A coldness pricked my skin, tracing its way along my arms and up to my neck. As my teeth turned to ice, I clenched them together, keeping a curse in. This ship wasn't natural. It must hold a piece of coveted magic aboard, and right now that magic was aimed upon us.

Emme took in a quick breath beside me. "Something moved."

"From the black ship?"

"No. There." Her fingers dug into my arm as she pointed

to the water next to the boat. "Something's there. See, it moved again."

My eyes followed to where small waves broke against the starboard side as the *Royal Rose* skipped through the water with no signs of unusual movement beneath. Emme cautiously stepped closer to the side and peered over the edge.

"I thought for certain—"

With a great splash and a roar to follow, a large creature the colors of blood and bone burst through the surface of the water and flung itself into the air.

She shrieked, and I gave a startled cry, taking in the three rows of sharp teeth lining its mouth and scales the size of an oar covering its long, thin body. Large fins flapped as it propelled over the middle of the ship and back into the water on the other side. The last thing to sink beneath the waves was a wide, forked tail.

It was like an eel, but massive. Deadly.

I shouted below, "Wake up, men! We're under attack."

10
ARN

"Nimnula," Emme shouted, jumping over the railing of the helm onto the deck. "It's coming back around." Her braid flew behind her as she pulled out the barrels of gunpowder and popped their lids open. She thumped her heel against the boards to alert the crew as she loaded her pistol.

If Emme wasn't on board, I wouldn't have identified the creature as a Nimnula until I checked my books later. Not many pirates had faced this particular beast with scars of white across scaly skin and teeth so sharp they could chomp through bone, but I recalled one thing from their stories.

If the creature jumps over the ship once then swims away, you'll be safe.

But if it jumps again, it's preparing to attack.

The way the creature bent as it slid into the water indicated it would still be on the port side of the ship, so while Emme ducked behind the starboard railing, I ran to the other side and leaned out to the sea. *Please swim away.*

"Wake up, men," I shouted a second time. They'd have to be drunk to sleep through the piercing call of the Nimnula. My hands shook ever so slightly as I loaded my pistol with powder and my flax sack with more.

A few moments later the creature's snakelike head

appeared again at Emme's side and then arched over the ship. Water splashed against her face as it once more jumped.

He's attacking.

Emme fired at its body. The bullet clanged against the Nimnula's rough scales, leaving no visible mark, before the creature plunged back into the dark waters on the other side of the ship.

Adrenaline coursed through my body. I roared, "Come on, men, to your stations." I took up a fighting stance, planting my feet on the deck, which was dripping with seawater. The splash from the Nimnula's flight over our heads left me chilled in the night wind, despite fear spreading tendrils of heat through my limbs.

From below deck came a rampage of shouts followed by footsteps as the crew scrambled to alertness. A moment later, they appeared above board and scanned the ship with frantic eyes and disheveled clothes.

Emme spoke before I could, in a calm voice but strong as the wind. "It's a Nimnula. Use your pistols; the cutlass won't reach the spot you need to hit."

The men obeyed and loaded their guns from the barrel of powder we kept under the quarterdeck stairs. A few murmured with lowered brows. "Nimnula? What's that?"

Emric, with his pistol loaded, stared into the water. "How many times?" he shouted.

"Twice already," Emme told him.

That meant nothing to me, but Emric called to the crew, "All right, fellow swashbucklers. Listen up. The beast must jump the ship nine times as he warms up his belly. It'll attack with fire, burn the ship, then pluck us out from the water once the ship is destroyed. We have seven more jumps before the fire. However, it has a weakness, which is good news for us. Look beneath its head to find a black spot."

"We aim there?" Bo asked as he hurried to load his pistol with powder.

"Nay. It's a decoy. Aim for two feet right of it. Here it comes now."

The men listened to Emric as they would a captain and stood behind him with steady hands on their guns. The creature jumped again, propelling himself into the sky up and over the ship. His orange belly glowed brighter now, a sign of the fire growing within.

Shots were fired.

The Nimnula was only in the air for a few seconds before its long body slid into the water again, which didn't give us much time to aim. Emric swore. "I was so close. It'll take a few solid shots to get him down"

"Lewie, go bring the men up from the cannons. Those won't do any good here," I instructed. The boy nodded and fled below deck to inform the other men while we crouched to take our positions.

A moment later the creature jumped again.

We all shot. The creature's high-pitched screech vibrated through the air while his red eyes burned. Then he dropped into the water. Five more times before the fire would come.

"I think I hit the weak spot." Emme's eyes held a hint of excitement as she loaded her pistol again. She flung her head to swing some of her damp hair over a shoulder.

Emric hollered, "Great shot. One or two more, then we've got him."

We all lined up for the next jump. This time I anticipated when it'd appear, so I was prepared to shoot right on time. With the three masts, it only had a few locations it could jump through without ramming its scaly head into one of them, and each prior jump it had chosen between the two rear masts. But the next jump came at the front—a move that none of us predicted. It got away without a hit. To my delight, dark red oozed from the spot in its neck where Emme had hit it.

But as it sank into the water, the fire in its belly glowed brighter.

Four more jumps.

The deck was a scramble of activity to reload weapons and reposition our feet to get a better shot at the beast. The moonlight offered plenty of ability to see the creature, but it jumped with such speed that aiming was difficult.

It jumped again, this time on the other side of the boat. "Spread out," I yelled, directing men into a line along the side. We couldn't know where it would move from next, and we were running out of time.

Three more jumps.

The crew scattered across the deck, some kneeling and others standing on the railing with a hand braced against a line to aim at the beast. Ontario's lip turned up in a snarl, while Bo bit down on the collar of his shirt and clutched the pistol with white fingers. Curses came from all directions.

Another roar came from the creature as it leapt from the waters. It threw itself over the ship near me. I barely had time to load my gun before I fired. King Valian blessed my shot. I stared in frustration. "I hit the spot, I'm sure of it. Why won't this creature die?"

The Nimnula glowed red now from the top of its nostrils to the end of its tail. The next jump came faster than we anticipated, and it got away with only paltry shots to the side. The air grew warmer around us each time, preparing us for the brutal sting of flames.

"One more chance. Make it count," Emric shouted to the men.

That moment seemed to last forever. But finally it sprung up, moving quicker than any of the previous times, and flew over the ship. In a flurry of shouts, we all fired, and my bullet flew to the neck.

The Nimnula dropped into the water with a splash.

"My bullets are striking true, I'm certain of it," I shouted. We all scrutinized the water, and our hands twitched with fearful anticipation.

Emric spotted him first. "Move back, he's ready to fire. Their flame is no wider than a man's body but deathly precise, so be quick on your feet, men."

The men scrambled to the sides as the creature prepared to attack, while Emme ran to the riggings. My stomach dropped to the deck. She shouted, "I should be able to get a good shot from a little higher." She pulled herself onto the railing and grabbed hold of the line. She barely glanced at the water before climbing with the pistol secured in her belt. I called for her to be careful, but over the noise of the men's shouting, she didn't turn her head.

"Here it comes," I warned the crew, still keeping half my focus on Emme. "Be ready. And by Valian's Crown, get away from that barrel of powder."

The Nimnula rose from the water with a wicked flare in its eyes, swaying from side to side as the rest of its long body twitched under water to keep it afloat. It moved just enough that getting good aim was difficult, and most of our bullets clattered off its scales. A low hum rolled from its belly. Red eyes scanned the ship before locking onto something over my shoulder.

Emme screamed, the sound biting through the gunshots and turning our attention to her. I frantically searched for what was wrong as she tugged at the skirt of her dress where it was caught in the pilot ladder, trapping her to the deck.

"Run, Emme," I cried out to her. I fired at the Nimnula in vain. Emme jumped down from the railing and yanked at the dress but it wouldn't be freed. My body forgot how to function as the creature hissed, then opened its mouth and prepared to send fire directly toward Emme.

She was trapped. And it aimed for her.

"Shoot now," Emric shouted. "Kill it." His own eyes raged with fire as he aimed at the beast.

All the men obeyed and began to fire at the neck. I didn't shoot. Emme's hem began to tear, but she wouldn't run fast enough to escape being burned.

She once told me I was too impulsive. Right now I didn't care.

My gun dropped to the deck with a clang as I slid my knife out, darted to her side, and slashed the hem free. Behind us, the air was filled with the sounds of pistol shots and men yelling.

Then came the unmistakable feeling of heat on my back. Without thinking, I grabbed a line in one arm, Emme in my other, and hurled us both overboard and away from the treacherous flames that licked my shirt.

"No," Emme cried as she fell, clawing her nails into my back, sending darts of pain through my skin. I almost let go of the rope but clutched it tight against my chest. That rope was our lifeline. If we let go, we'd be lost in the dark seas.

With a splash, Emme and I plunged into the water.

The coldness stabbed us with a shock I hadn't braced myself for. My teeth clamped together, and my arm squeezed around Emme, who wrapped her limbs around my body and held tight.

Her fingers fumbled to find the rope and grab hold with me. The rope yanked as it reached its end, jolting us forward.

As the ship sailed with the wind, we were dragged through the freezing water. We clawed our way higher up the rope with numb fingers until the waves lapped at our chests, eventually finding our way to the side of the ship. We hit against the wood as we struggled to get any higher, but to no avail. All we could do was clutch the rope and bite through the cold.

"The Nimnula," Emme said in my ear, spitting water. "We are in the water with the Nimnula."

The thought of the beast drove me to attempt to pull our bodies higher up the rope, but the shock of the cold was quickly having its effect on me. I suddenly wished for the heat of the fire to be back, even if it burned my skin.

At least the ship wasn't ablaze, and we could make out the distant shouts of the men. "The other side. Do you see it?"

Beneath the black surface of the water, something red appeared. The glow of the fire in the Nimnula's belly swam beneath the ship and closer to us.

"Men! Shoot!" I yelled. Any fear I'd ever encountered was nothing compared to the terror of the Nimnula's long body preying through the water for us.

From above they shouted something, but all my focus was on the red eyes as they rose in the water and scanned the surface. Emme's legs tightened around me, and I held my breath, keeping as still as possible.

Pistol shots still filled the air. The Nimnula screeched.

From his neck streamed thick rivers of blood. Another shot. The Nimnula didn't scream this time but instead swayed in the air for a few moments. Then, with a pitiful whine, it dropped into the water.

Its glowing body sank beneath the waves.

Cheers filled the air, and Emme's deep sigh heated up my neck. "He's dead," Emric shouted from the ship. "Well done, lads."

My heart didn't recover so quickly, as it still beat against my chest with rapid speed. My trembling was as much from fear as from the cold, and my head rang with fright. I'd almost died. I'd almost lost Emme.

I called up to the cheering crew to remind them of our presence.

"Arn," Emric shouted. "Hold tight!" He instructed the

other men to pull, and we were dragged against wooden planks as we were lifted from the icy waters.

Everyone applauded when we sprawled onto the deck. Ontario clapped me on the back, and I lurched. Emme stopped him. "No, don't touch his back, he got burned." She reached to inspect my burn, but I shook my head. "Are you all right?"

I grunted under the pain. "Better me than you." My teeth still rattled from the cold. "It's not that bad. It only got me for a moment before we fell into the water. I'll heal."

Emric was beside us. "Right you are. And that's the only strike it hit before we took it down. This fine ship is unscathed. Well done, everyone, good work all around." He hopped up to the wheel and turned it. "Let's carry on. I can steer while you rest up, Arn."

My mouth opened to argue, but my eyes caught on something, and I gasped. "The black ship."

Emme's face whitened, and everyone turned to look at the ship that still followed us. The excitement of the Nimnula had distracted from the potential threat that loomed behind, and our struggle to defeat the beast left us slow on the water, giving ample time for such a foe to catch us.

But he hadn't.

The black ship stayed in the distance, no closer and no further than it had been before we were attacked. It lurked on the water, silent as the night around us. We could hardly make out its frame, but its presence prickled my skin, as if it were right beside us in the sea demanding to be noticed. Mocking us for forgetting him. How could that be, that the ship followed us through the night as we moved at top speed, yet grew no closer once it had the chance? The answer felt painfully evident to me, and my stomach went into knots tighter than the ones on the riggings.

"It's not trying to attack us." My voice felt thick. "It's tracking. Someone on that ship is watching us."

Ontario slipped to my side with a face drained of color. He spoke under his breath. "Do you think it's him?" I knew who he meant. My debt was due.

"No. He can track me through the oathbinding. Someone else watches our movements, and we better pray to Sea King Valian we don't lead them directly to the treasure. For all our sakes."

Ontario clamped his jaw, looking ready to hurl. His change in expression reflected the clenching in my stomach. I admonished him, but I was also speaking to myself. "Wipe that expression off your face, mate. Fear is not the pirate way."

11

EMME

"Arn, there's something very important I must ask you," I said. We stood in my, or rather his, cabin below deck after Arn had begrudgingly handed over the wheel to Emric for a few hours so he could look over the ship. It appeared that he deemed his old cabin, where I was, the most pressing place to inspect first.

"What is it?" Arn asked.

"Now, this is crucial. If I'm going to do this, you mustn't look at me any differently than before. I'm still me, the practical girl who wants to get back to dry land and her beloved sheep."

The corner of his lip rose, but his eyes remained puzzled. "All right, I won't look at you differently."

"I'm afraid I'll need you to promise it."

He cocked his head.

"It's important to me," I said.

His fingers crossed and he twirled them in the air with his symbol of a promise. "I swear it."

Arn had changed from his previous shirt and jacket which were little more than charcoaled, tattered remains. Even with his new tunic on, his pants bore the black mark of fire. His golden hair dripped with water, pulling at the curls until the tips brushed his dripping eyelashes and he tightened a fleece blanket around his body.

I didn't look much better.

After my dress got caught in the riggings, it was evident that Arn had been right; there was no place for dresses aboard a pirate ship. As much as I hated thinking it, trousers made more sense. I repeated that to myself numerous times. That didn't make me like my mother. It made me sensible.

I sighed. "I need pants."

After a delayed moment, his face burst into a smile, and he laughed. "I'll go fetch some." He bounded from the cabin in long strides. In less than a minute he was back with brown pants bundled up with a white tunic. "You'll need a top if you intend to wear pants. Here." He tossed the clothes to me, then stepped out of the room.

With the clothes in hand I almost changed my mind. My mother used to wear such things, even as the ladies in town gawked at her. She couldn't be talked from her tight breeches and tied-up shirt, even when she married Papa. He loved her spirit, her tattoos, and the way she could swear more colorfully than anyone in town. Perhaps his complete acceptance was why she loved him.

What would be left to distinguish me from my mother if I didn't have my dresses? Would I be no better than her, a pirate who loved nothing but the sea, not even her own children?

It was almost enough to keep me from changing into the pants, but the image of the Nimnula flashed into my mind. Its mouth wide, fire burning from its belly, and Arn placing himself in front of me as a shield from its harsh flames.

The agony on his face as fire licked his back. His tattered shirt. The smell of burnt flesh.

I couldn't miss the slight cringe as he walked. He hid his wounds from me, but I saw his pain. The pain he took to save my life.

Emric shot at the Nimnula instead of coming to me. That was the smart move; take down the beast before it destroyed the ship and killed each person who sailed on it. But Arn had turned to me.

That was why I would wear these pants—so he'd never again be forced to pick between saving me and saving his ship.

I let the linen dress fall to the floor and pulled on the long pants. They fit nicely around my legs—not as tight as my mother wore them but tighter than a skirt. Even still, they were clearly made for a larger human—a small treasure chest could fit in the extra space the pants allowed around my waist. That wouldn't do at all. I wore a sash with my dress, and I restrung that around the loops of the pants and tied it tight. The flash of yellow pleased me, the color brightening up the dark pirate attire.

"That's not half bad. Fitting. Comfortable. Easy to move in," I mumbled while stretching my legs out. The hems would need to be rolled up, but this would be suitable.

The shirt came next, creamy white cotton with long sleeves and strings to lace up the collar. I tucked the front into my pants so the yellow bow could still be seen.

All right. This was the best I could do. I used my old dress to dry out my hair before calling to Arn. "You can come in now."

With a slow creak the door opened, and Arn stepped inside. He circled around me. "Emme," he said, "you look incredible."

"Not too much like a pirate, I hope."

"No. Certainly not. More adventurous than before I daresay, maybe even dangerous once you put on your cutlass. But nothing like a filthy pirate. It's the practical choice, though," he added. "There's a loop in the back I stitched myself; it holds a dagger. It's a tad uncomfortable, but if captured it's not a spot they'll quickly check." He patted his backside where he kept a dagger hidden that I'd never noticed. I moved my own blade from my boot and into the loop. It put stiff pressure on my back, but I could get used to it.

"Perfect. Well, just about." Arn reached up to the peg where I'd hung my cutlass and belt. He winced at the motion.

"How bad is it?"

"Could be worse. Remember when I stumbled into the Banished Gentlemen a few years back with those burns on my arms? It's not like that."

I remembered that night well. Amid the drunken crowds, Arn pushed through the back door with a gritted jaw and bare chest as he held his arms out to me. He'd hardly been able to move them. He'd spent the night in my bed, as I paid a pretty copper on ointment for his wounds. When the pain got so bad that tears brimmed in his eyes, I distracted him by telling him stories of my mother.

"May I see?" I timidly reached for his shirt. He didn't protest as I gently peeled the fabric off his skin. I gasped. From his shoulder blades to his lower back the skin had turned pink with white blisters dotted throughout.

"Oh, Arn."

I rolled the shirt up on his shoulders. "Hold this." He did so as I went to fetch honey and calendula from the small herbal cabinet in his new living quarters. I reprimanded myself for not having thought to apply this salve as soon as we were pulled back on deck.

With the two ingredients and a roll of gauze, I hurried back to the cabin where Arn waited. He'd removed his shirt entirely, and I willed myself not to be distracted by the gold tattoos on his bare chest.

"Will this hurt?" He sat on the edge of the table with his fingers dug into its side until his knuckles were white.

I'd forgotten his low pain tolerance. It made it even more heroic that he placed himself in front of the fire for me. "Just hold still."

I stretched the gauze out over the table while I poured honey over it. Then I took the colorful flower and ground it into the table and sprinkled the petals into the honey. "All right," I warned, "this may hurt."

I looked at his face and hesitated. I set down the gauze and untied the ribbon from my hair, handing it to Arn. "Bite down on this," I ordered. He let me place the ribbon in his mouth.

As gently as I could, I wrapped the sticky gauze around his back and across his stomach, keeping it in place. His body trembled under my fingers, prompting me to work faster. His hand flexed at one point and twitched for mine, but then he pulled it away and clasped it against his other one.

"Finished." I helped ease his shirt back over his body, and he let out his breath. "You'll have to let me change that every two days. And we need more dressing."

He ran his hand over the wrapping beneath his shirt. "I'd rather not stop for provisions until we get through the Moving Islands."

"Then you better hope it heals without infection." I screwed the lid back on the jar of honey.

"I've survived worse than infection, but I thank you for your help." He leaned against the table and brushed back his hair. His tired eyes studied mine. "It's nice having you on board. You add a gentleness to this ship that wasn't there before. And my men smell better now too. I think they are trying to impress you."

"Ha! Glad I can be a good influence on the crew's hygiene."

Arn focused intently on the ribbon. "Ontario seems to be working especially hard to win your favor."

My face flushed. I had noticed the extra attention from the first mate, but he gave similar attention to all the lasses who came through the Banished Gentlemen, and it never meant anything. I also noticed how the suspicious letter with the black emblem from Arn's chest went missing right after Ontario came to the cabin, confirming that whatever Arn hid, Ontario was part of it.

Arn watched for my reply. What could I say? That Ontario was intriguing, but I couldn't care less? That it wasn't right for me to think of any man when I didn't have a certain future to offer anyone? That I thought of a man anyway, but it wasn't Ontario?

Unsure how to respond, I said, "Ontario is delightful company."

Arn's smile faltered slightly but quickly returned. "That's why I keep him around."

At that same moment, Ontario pushed through the door. "Captain? The ship has stopped following."

Arn stood from the table with a grimace. He picked up his jacket and slid his arms through the sleeves. "Truly? Where did he go?"

Ontario nodded as his eyes shifted between the two of us. "He pulled back. We don't know where he went but he isn't on our path. Between that and our defeating the Nimnula, the men are eager for a celebration. We have proper nighttime festivities set up on deck, if you care to join."

Arn clapped once. "That's just what we need. I'll finish inspecting the ship, then I'll join you."

Ontario nodded again. "And Emme? The new outfit looks great."

I'd almost forgotten my new attire. "Thank you," I said. Arn was frowning as he left the cabin. I followed closely behind until he turned one way toward the cannon room and I turned the other to scale the ladder. Sounds of laughter drifted from above.

Crates had been brought out to form a wide circle near the main mast. Toes tapped the floor, and several hands clapped in rhythm while Timmons, a tall and quiet man with a full beard and teardrop eyes, played a little tune on his flute. Each man held a flask in hand and poured rum into his belly.

Most impressively, they'd brought out a large iron bowl where they pulled some small planks of wood and created a fire to sit around. I hadn't seen a proper fire in months and had missed the way it tossed light across faces. For once, the air smelled of something other than fish and salt.

As I fully emerged, the men eyed my trousers, and there was a variety of low whistles and light, mocking comments.

"You must be new to the crew; I don't believe we've met."

"Say lad, have you seen Emme?"

I laughed and allowed them their fun. "Why, no, I haven't. I daresay we won't be seeing much of her or her dresses any longer."

Emric's attention remained on me the longest with a stoic expression that proved difficult to read. Eventually he grinned.

"We'll make a proper pirate out of you, yet. You look just like Mother."

12
ARN

Emme visibly tensed as Emric mentioned their mother, but by his smile and dancing eyes, her brother was blind to her reaction. *Interesting.* While Emric spoke of Arabella the Ruthless in high praises, it hadn't occurred to me that he didn't know the level of animosity his sister carried for their pirate mother. Her shoulders relaxed after a moment, but the strain in her hands did not. As I closed the hatch to the deck below, Emme forced a smile to her face. Ever so slightly, the tightness in her hands lessened.

"Captain," my crew greeted me.

Their voices simmered until we could hear the waves lapping against the hull. Despite the rhythmic sway beneath her, Emme found a seat next to Timmons with a steadiness that wasn't there a few weeks ago. Her hands fidgeted with her tied-up trousers. They suited her, though I missed the warm colors of her dresses and the way the fabric clung to its sweet scent of flowers, even amid the ocean spraying its scent across the deck. At least her smile was the same, even as thoughts of her mother dulled her eyes.

Behind her, the moon attached to the sky, leaving streaks of silver that danced off the rolling waters. My crew sat to either side of me. In this quiet moment, I looked around at each of them, caught up in their own thoughts or conversations. Unwashed hair pulled into buns, low-cut shirts with loose strings hanging from every hem, scars on every arm from dangerous voyages sailed together. Percival with his wooden leg that left him with a limp, Collins with three missing fingers, Bo missing an entire hand. Though my crew was small in number, they were plenty in spirit.

I was a lucky captain.

Emric hopped atop a crate and cleared his throat. "Well, boys," he announced, "we've escaped the clutches of a Nimnula and outrun a mysterious black ship. All with a crew of only fourteen. I'd say, time to celebrate."

The men hooted, and I allowed Emric his moment before putting up my hands. If I weren't careful, he would win over their hearts, and I'd lose my crew. When he spoke, every tongue hushed to listen, and when he moved, all eyes followed. Their enthrallment with him was not subtle.

I straightened my back, despite the pain, and gave a speech of my own.

"Pirates. When I left the navy three years ago, a young lad at seventeen years old, I dreamed of this life. Sailing the high seas in search of a treasure large enough to make me rich. Answering to no man. Living under no rules but the pirate's code. But without a great crew, I would be nothing. Today, you again demonstrated yourselves to be the crew I knew you were. Henrik, your aim has improved tremendously since you first arrived. Percival, you didn't hesitate to retrieve the gunpowder and help slower men load their pistols. And little Lewie, you didn't cower at the beast. You proved yourself a strong man. All of you were brave in the face of danger. The *Royal Rose* is lucky to have such sailors aboard. Tonight, we celebrate you."

I unclasped my flask from my waist and raised it. The crew cheered, and Timmons picked up his flute.

He played us a tune under the night sky. One by one, each crew member took a swig from their flask then began moving to the melody, incorporating their own music with timed claps or taps of the feet. Emric was the first to stand and begin dancing, looping Ontario's arm through his own and flinging him around in circles. Ontario laughed and grabbed Bo, until almost all the men were dancing around the fire while the others kept beat with their hands.

Emme didn't wait to be asked to dance. She hopped up and swayed under the moonlight.

All the fears from the Nimnula, all concerns of the black ship that trailed us for half a night, all worries for what waited on the Island of Iilak, it all drifted away like morning fog.

Then I was surprised to find Emme's hands taking mine, and I completely forgot about my troubles. I forgot about everything except her and the way her tongue peeked between her teeth as she smiled and how she always saw the best in me where others saw only a pirate. With her hand in mine, I almost forgot my own name.

Timmons played a livelier tune, and our feet moved faster on the cedar boards. Emme's hands left mine as we looped arms with new partners, spinning away from each other. But even after she'd skipped around the fire and spun around with Emric, she returned her to me and we reconnected. Another two spins and she was whisked away again. Each time we switched partners it never took long before her arm was back in mine.

It was such a little thing to notice, and perhaps mere coincidence that we ended up in each other's path so often. Or maybe she enjoyed being around me as much as I enjoyed being around her. I chose to believe the second.

I wasn't the only one enjoying the night. Across the deck everyone laughed carelessly, especially when Bo raised his flask to the glow of the moon and began to sing.

> *Through high seas and dark nights we sail*
> *With a hearty crew and a belly full of ale*
> *To find my luck and a loot too*
> *Yes, that's what pirates do.*

Soon others joined in, their voices ringing out over the empty waters. Emric leaned against the mast and threw his head back. Timmons stood up and continued to play as he trotted around the fire. We formed a circle with him and skipped together.

> *Lower the sails and away we go*
> *To steal the keys, to find the gold*
> *Avast ye sails and heave and ho*
> *Yes, that's what pirates do. Ey!*

The rum began to get to men's heads, creating a merry atmosphere amid many stumbling feet. Emme looked as I'd never seen her before, dressed in a pirate's garb and joining in with gusto; if I didn't know better, I'd say she'd been a part of the crew for years. My heart sped up as I watched how she moved, how her wild hair bounced as she danced, how the corners of her eyes wrinkled with her laughter, how the curve of her hips twisted from side to side. As she moved toward me, she grabbed both my hands and spun me around. Then she paused, and her face faltered. "Is your back feeling all right? You aren't hurting it further, are you?"

My back was the last thing on my mind right now. "Oh, is that why you keep coming to me? Concern?" I asked. The corner of my mouth tilted up. "I guarantee you, love, I can handle pain."

She threw her head back and laughed. With the firelight reflecting in her eyes and her scarlet ribbon pulled through her braid, she looked like she owned this sea.

The girl from the land was now queen of the water. If she didn't hate sailing so much, she'd make a fearsome pirate. She'd handled the attack from the Nimnula with a bravery that not many inland girls possessed.

I dared to put my arms around her and pull her toward another song.

Her body tensed, and I inwardly chastised my forwardness. But her focus wasn't on me. It pointed toward the sea.

"What's that sound?"

It took a few moments of my ears straining to hear what she did. It began as a delicate whisper, like butterfly wings brushing against a flower, then grew into a trickle of airy notes drifting through the night sky in a haunting melody. As far as I could see into the blanket of darkness was emptiness, only rolling water blanketed in moonlight, but the voice continued to echo louder across the waves.

I'd heard this once before. It was just as beautiful as I remembered.

The men gradually stopped their dancing to listen to the enchanting song coming like a fog across the water, encompassing us in a melancholy tune that seeped into our skin, soaking our very bones in beauty.

Soon more voices joined, until the susurrant sounds of the sea and the flaps of the sails were drowned out by mesmerizing music.

"What is that?" Emme repeated with less fear and more awe. She moved away from me toward the side of the ship. Her hands rested on the rails, and her eyes scanned the sea with wonder written across her face.

"Mermaids' songs," I said. At the slight sadness in my tone, Emme glanced back at me. I continued, "It means one of their own has died today. They're mourning. This is a funeral."

Her lips turned down as she peered into the waters. Slight ripples moved in the distance, barely within eyesight. We wouldn't catch a glimpse of their fabled beauty, but the singing was freely shared.

Music was a specialty of the merfolk. Though few heard their song, once it reached one's ears, it was difficult to enjoy the music of humans again. After this, Timmons's flute would sound flat. These notes carried such purity with them that it brought tears to my eyes.

It was a lovely way to mourn someone, with such splendor.

At the mermaids' beckoning, the stars themselves reached down to the waters like magnificent rain, draping the sky in twinkling lights that shimmered when they met the sea. Before long, the entire sea around us was covered in glittering stardust. Some fell on the ship, leaving behind a white glow to infuse the air with a sense of magic.

Emme didn't move, but she took in a breath at the star shower, eyes skyward and mouth slightly open. As the song began to fade, the starlight dimmed, leaving us all feeling hollow, as though their lack created an emptiness inside us. Each man leaned forward a bit to catch the last whisper of music and the last glance at the stars now rising to retake their place in the sky.

The night was soon still, and the waves could be heard again.

Murmurs of approval drifted through the crew. Emme didn't speak; she kept her face toward the vast darkness of the horizon. Then she said, so quiet that I almost missed it, "That's why Mother fell in love with the sea."

Hope stirred in me. She was beginning to love the waters. Perhaps one day she would love them as much as I did.

Our eyes clung to the sea, hoping for a last piece of beauty, until Bo's loud voice broke us from our trance. "No, that's not how it goes." His voice slurred. He towered by the fire with crossed arms and a puffed-up chest as he spoke with Percival, who bobbed his head rapidly.

"Is too! You're the one who's got it wrong. Sit down, I'll tell it right. Go on now, sit down all of you. I'll tell the tale of the Black Avenger." He waved his arms and pointed to the seats. With reluctance, I tore myself from the portside railing. Percival signaled us to move faster. "Come on now, I tell it real good."

"You tell yours, then I'll tell the real tale," Bo huffed as he squatted on a crate. It wasn't surprising that those two had broken from the trance first. Bo especially was never taken by pretty things.

Emric swung around the mast before sitting next to Bo. Timmons put away his flute and perched atop another wooden crate near the fire. The other men settled in around them.

Emme's eyes lit up. "Ghost stories." She gave one last long look across the water before sitting beside me.

With all our attention on him, Percival finished the last of his flask before beginning with a dramatic clearing of his throat. "Long ago, in a time when a wicked king ruled and pirates had none of the honor they do now, a young lass appeared on the shore of the sea. They say she came from the sea itself. Upon arriving at port, she was refused passage aboard a ship from a band of pirates."

"Stupid men," Bo grunted.

"Stupid, stupid men," Percival agreed. He leaned forward on his knees as firelight crept over the sunken hollows of his cheeks.

"That refusal enraged her like none other. So this lass vowed to take the sea from those who denied it to her. All across the high seas she raised her own caravan of damsels, each with fire in their bones and blood on their teeth. They called themselves the Nightlock Thieves, and together they stole a boat in the night. Thus began their reign of terror. With their wit, their pretty faces, and their dark hearts, they killed every man they came across, skinning their bodies and gnawing on their bones until they were nothing but dust. They took over the high seas. Merchants were too afraid to sail, families suffered, and none who met the women survived. Even the whales in the sea feared them, and the mermaids closed their great golden gates and never came to the surface of the water. Soon, the Nightlock Thieves' quest for vengeance and taste for greed brought them off the seas, and they plundered the lands. Villages burned, and none were spared from their hungry desire for power."

He paused before continuing, letting us lean into the story.

"One day, they sailed away and were never heard from again. But they say the Nightlock Thieves live in the stars and will one day return to reclaim the sea."

There was silence for a moment after Percival finished. Then Bo snorted. "You told it all wrong."

"Did not."

"Did too. They don't live in no stars; they were killed. Their spirits live in the dolphins."

As they argued, a familiar sound squawked behind me. Most of the men were too caught up in which version of the tale was the right one, or too drunk to notice the sound, but the haunting noise sobered me up.

I eased myself backward to the helm of the ship where the large bird always landed. It perched on the wheel with an evil gleam in its eye as dark as its master's. Before drawing nearer, I glanced behind me to be sure none followed. I was alone.

If I'd been a more daring man, I'd toss the bird into the ocean and not deal with the matter, but my head would be the price paid for such an action. Patience was not a strong quality of the bird's owner, and neither was forgiveness.

The bird offered his leg for me to untie the rolled-up parchment. Then it took off, flapping its wings into the night until it was gone.

With trembling hands, I broke the black seal and unrolled the letter.

There was no introduction and no signature at the bottom. No greeting, no pleasantries, no embellishment. None was needed. Just one sentence that turned my blood cold.

Come by the port, or I kill your father.

Blimey. I should have known better than to strike a deal with the devil.

13

EMME

Arn didn't notice me. But I saw him. Stealthy feet led me closer to watch as he opened the furled note and a chilling darkness seeped into his eyes. His teeth clamped on his lips, and his body went rigid as stone. The fire reflected off his skin, whiter than a ghost.

Fear crept over me.

His hands finally broke free from their stillness to crumple the note and throw it into the dark sea.

I fled to rejoin the crew before he returned from the helm. But with glazed eyes he strode past us all and shut the door to his cabin.

I ought to have ripped open that black letter I'd found in the chest when I had the chance, especially if it had anything to do with this cryptic night message. Whatever was in it, it was enough to darken Arn's mood and push him away.

I started as a finger tapped my elbow. Licks of the flame sent light curling around Emric's sharp nose and illuminating the frown etched in his face as he pulled me to the side. "Something doesn't feel right." His breath reeked of ale, but his eyes were sober and staring into the fire.

"I'm in agreement with you there." I glanced at Arn's closed door.

Emric's crinkled brow deepened as he whispered, "They got the tale wrong. The Nightlock Thieves didn't sail away, one of their members became filled with remorse for the destruction they caused, so she turned on the rest and killed them all. They say she still sails the sea watching for any who might grow too powerful, so that no one with a dark heart can bring that sort of destruction to the world again. A ghost upon the waters."

"That sounds horrifying." I glanced around his shoulder to the cabin where Arn had gone. The door remained closed, and no light was lit inside.

"It's a precaution," Emric responded. "Look at you, for example. You're smart and you're beautiful. Men have a weakness for that sort of thing. Some would give up everything just to be near those like you." He glanced at me. "Not me, of course. I'm immune to such effects. But never underestimate what being a woman can do for you."

There were no right words to say when your brother said something like that to you.

Emric's nostrils flared as he huffed out. "See, something's still not right. I've heard this tale before."

It wasn't an unusual thing to exchange ghost stories. But this specific tale certainly had put Emric in a strange mood, pulling at his beard and rubbing his nose in thought. Even as Timmons played another tune on his flute—undeniably grating compared to the mermaids, but the drunk crew danced all the same—Emric didn't move.

"Mother," he said quietly. "Mother told me the tale, and something about that story terrified her."

In the morning, while half the crew slept off the night and the other half slugged through their work, Arn burst through the cabin doors. His eyes were red, and wrinkles marred his clothes. He crossed the deck and turned the wheel. "We need to stop at Aható for provisions," he said sharply. "We should reach there by nightfall."

Ontario removed a flask from his lips to protest. "But Captain, that's out of our way."

Arn's voice was like a cutlass against steel. "We have no choice."

A look passed between him and Ontario that I couldn't identify, but it confirmed a suspicion.

This change of plans had something to do with what they were keeping from me.

Aható sat in the foothills of mountains that overlooked the rippling blanket of blue sea. The sky was a clear curtain of silk that cast a calm rain down to the country. As we drew nearer, the sea's horizon was replaced by copper mountains and rich wildlife.

This was the last point of chartered civilization before the Seas of Lost Lands. Even with my distaste for being aboard ship, I'd rather hoped to avoid this island altogether.

Civilization may be a strong word. In truth, what inhabited Aható was either men searching for what this part of the unknown world held, or men who didn't want to be searched for. No merchant ships came this direction, no king claimed land, and no women came to bear children. Instead, the land lay free and feral and untamed.

What business Arn could have here, I could only guess. But each guess made me fear more than the last, so I abandoned any attempt and just watched him closely. Eventually, his secret would be revealed.

When the *Royal Rose* reached shallow waters, we dropped our anchor. Arn suited himself with no fewer than four weapons: his cutlass, pistol, and two daggers. By the bulge in the side of his boot, I suspected another knife hid within. More weapons than one ought to need for simple supply replenishment.

Collins, Lewie, and Bo—who was still quite drunk—remained aboard the ship while the rest of us loaded the three rowboats and set out for the rocky shore. As I sat down, the knife I kept in the back loop of my pants shifted, almost piercing me. I adjusted the blade and glanced at Arn. Droplets of sweat glistened from his brow. His jaw clenched, and his complexion paled with each pull of the oar, despite the sun, until he was ghostlike by the time we stepped into the low tide and dragged our boats ashore.

About a half mile inland sat a speckle of shops and homes, toward which Arn pointed. "We will find what we need there. Some food and drinks, and Collins said we need more rope." He looked at Emric as he spoke, who nodded.

"Yes, Captain."

Emric had never called Arn captain before. Perhaps he could sense that something was wrong too. Arn fidgeted with his jacket every two seconds and cast wary looks in every direction, but the rest of the crew chatted on happily, oblivious to the war inside his eyes.

Sharp rocks along the uneven path prodded at the soles of our feet as we trekked inland. I maneuvered myself nearby Arn. He kept his gaze fixated solely ahead. "Are you all right?"

He didn't turn toward me. "Quite." The word was so short I might have imagined it was there at all.

He picked up conversation with Ontario, leaving me out purposefully. I slowed and let them pass by, noting the tight grip the first mate kept on his cutlass.

The situation grew more suspicious as we entered the town and Arn and Ontario disappeared. I'd looked away for one moment to see Emric wander into a shop, and when I looked back, they were gone.

Sneaky pirates.

I left Emric behind and tried to follow them. There were two paths ahead, so after a quick pause I picked the northern trail that led further inland and hoped for the best.

The sounds of the sea faded as the quiet of the town surrounded me. Wind rippled against broken wooden boards and picked at chipped paint along faded signs. Rampant weeds clawed against the walls, and the scent of dead fish clung to the humid air. Livestock moaned, but there seemed to be no one to tend to them.

A proper ghost town. Chills trickled up my spine. It wasn't often that I longed to get off land and onto a ship, but I found myself looking toward the ocean more than once.

I swore I heard footsteps behind me, but it was nothing but the scurry of chickens. I'd lost Arn and Ontario. Whatever their secret was, I wouldn't be discovering it today. With one last hope, I ducked off the path to poke behind shops but could see no trace of Arn's gold tattoos or Ontario's dark hair.

I stopped. Between two shops and twenty paces to the east, a sign made my blood run cold—the same black sun that marked the mysterious letter was carved into the wood. In a town of dry colors and broken glass, the well-maintained dwelling stood out. Dirt sifted beneath my feet as I got closer to its polished gray door and the narrow windows and stones on the roof.

My gaze sliced back to one of the windows. Arn and Ontario stood inside.

A shout of excitement caught in my throat as I pushed my back against the nearest ivy-covered cobblestone wall and cautiously peeked in. Arn's mouth was moving, but he wasn't looking at Ontario. Someone else was inside. I had to know who.

My position wouldn't allow me to see anything. I risked

another few steps forward, taking me from the safety of the vines' concealment.

As I took a third step, something sharp pressed into the arch of my back. "Scream, and I kill you."

He could have said anything. He could have said, "I'll slice Arn's throat while you watch if you make any noise," and it wouldn't have made a difference. When a sharp knife suddenly presses against my back, I can't prevent the scream from leaving my throat.

A gruff hand wrapped around my waist while another clamped over my mouth before I could cry out. I thrashed my feet and raked my nails across their arm, but more hands grabbed my legs and hoisted me into the air. I bit, but my head was yanked back so hard that my vision spun. The last thing I saw was Arn's back as he stood oblivious before a flax bag came over my head. Their grips tightened, rendering me helpless as rope was tied around my arms. Soon my feet were tied as well.

"Take her back. Boss will be pleased," a deep voice said, a hint of pleasure riding in it.

No, I pled silently. Someone help me.

I was thrown onto a hard surface that began to move a moment later. From the sound of rickety wheels, I guessed it to be a wagon of sorts. Someone sat next to me with their hands firmly on my arms, keeping me still on the bumpy ride. A gag in my mouth prevented screams from being effective, but it didn't stop me from trying. I screamed until the knife reappeared at my back. "Cut it out."

I screamed anyway and instantly felt a sharp pain draw across my side. *He cut me.* Not deep enough to bleed much, but a few red droplets were sure to stain my tunic.

"We're almost there, no need for unpleasantness," a new voice said, shaking as we bounced down the road. I couldn't tell if that was meant for me or the one with the knife. I thrashed again and felt the blade once more. There was no cut this time but it remained pressed it against my side as a reminder.

The wagon came to an abrupt halt, and I lurched away from the blade. The man cursed, and a moment later his arms wrapped around me once more and pulled me from the wagon. I resumed my smothered screaming, and he kneed me.

"Quiet, you," he snapped, jerking me forward to some unknown end.

I should have stayed with Emric. How long before they realized I was gone? It shouldn't take more than a few hours, and this town didn't appear large enough to hide me for long.

My kidnappers didn't know they would soon have a band of pirates after them. That thought alone gave me confidence I so desperately needed.

My feet struggled to gain footing as they dragged me over sand. The light that came through the sack dimmed, and my feet bumped over what might have been loose boards. When I was pushed down, I found a splintered chair beneath me that caved inward as it met my weight. With a rough force, my bonds were released and the sack removed from my head.

The captors kept strong arms around me, despite how much I thrashed. My hands were pulled through the posts in the back of the chair and tied together, so I could stand if I wanted but would be stuck to the chair and therefore incapable of a successful escape. The twine they used prickled my skin. Once knotted, it was difficult to move.

My surroundings offered little hope.

Tall walls met at a high, wooden ceiling to create a space as large as our ship's deck, and a roughly boarded-up window to the right let in shards of sunlight that caught on the dust in the air. The foul smell of tobacco burned my nose. A scratched oil lantern sat atop a narrow, cluttered desk pushed against the back wall, illuminating the numerous shelves of trinkets that adorned the room. An antique shop, I realized.

Unless the tales of this forsaken island were false, there ought to be no need for such a place here.

Three grizzly men stood with their arms folded and eyes boring into me. Two wore gruff expressions partly hidden under poorly shaved beards, one had a crooked nose and the other bushy eyebrows. But the third examined me with proud squinty eyes, as if pleased with a job well done.

At his expression, anger coursed through me.

The source of my anger was difficult to place, for part of it came from disappointment in myself for letting down my guard, while another part was frustration with Arn who, by keeping secrets, had unknowingly led me here. Which one infuriated me more, I couldn't say. Both, no doubt. As the three men studied me, rage grew in my chest.

Followed by a deep fear for what would come next.

I dug my heels into the floorboards and willed myself to focus. If I didn't find a way to escape, I'd be at the mercy of these foul men. Now was the time to summon any strength and find a way to free myself.

I blocked out anything that wouldn't be useful—the fear, the anxiety, the crippling worries clouding my mind—and only allowed the brave parts to band together and form a plan. In the transition to the chair, they'd ungagged me, and I debated the benefits of more screaming. They couldn't have brought me far—the ride took only a few minutes, which placed us on the outskirts of the small town. Screaming might bring someone to me, but I couldn't bet on that. I needed something to save myself.

"Where is he?" Crooked Nose muttered to the others.

"He'll be here soon," Squinty Eyes said, his smile foolishly wide.

I dreaded who "he" was.

My breathing was like fire in my throat, hot and dry, licking up every ounce of energy just to take the next breath. This blasted disease in my bones was going to be an even earlier death of me. Even if I escaped, my legs might not take me far. Already they ached from my ankle to my knees because of the walk up the shore and to the suspicious building.

If I wasn't careful, I'd work my body to death before reaching the Island of Iilak.

Hints of dreary colors filtered through the boarded-up window—browns and tans and grays—nothing to indicate where we were. I wouldn't know the town well enough to recognize it even if the window were wide open, but at least it would give me an escape path. Then I'd pray to the Fates that I could reach help before the men reached me.

A heavy lock adorned both the front door and a second near the back table, but both appeared sturdier than the boards over the window. If I could get my bondages loose, I could barrel through.

As I was watching, the back door unlocked and opened.

A tall, wide man entered. At first, I thought it was Bart, but that was the dim lights and mental exhaustion of the day dulling my mind. They did bear similarities—the same muscular body, dark skin, wide eyes, and sway as they walked. But this man wore an expression that Bart never did. Greed. Hunger. Pleasure.

With each step that brought him nearer, my eyes narrowed into a feral expression. I was thinking of something frightening to say, but before I could, the newcomer spoke.

"Strong, healthy looking." He circled around me at a close distance, bringing a sharp smell with him. His eyes took in every detail of my body, not missing an inch. I inspected him too. Though quite strong, he wasn't much older than me. All four of the men in the room were young, except for Bushy Eyebrows, who was about forty. One-on-one they shouldn't prove too difficult to beat, since they didn't know the tricks my mother taught me.

But all together, and with my disease already slowing me down, I stood no chance.

The large man stopped, glancing at the cutlass at one side and pistol at my other. "Weapons—did you not think to remove those?" He looked back at the other three, who swallowed. The smile left Squinty Eyes's face. They were afraid of him. He must be the one in charge.

My tired brain tugged at me. *Weapons.* Of course. The dagger Arn had told me to keep in the back of my pants. When I pushed my hands against my back, I felt the slim hilt there. They weren't aware of that one, which would give me one moment of surprise to make my move. If I could get it free and saw through these bonds, escape might be possible.

All there was to do was find the prime moment to fetch the blade.

"Will she do?" One risked speech.

A rough hand reached for my cheek, but I bit at him.

"Spirited. Yes, she will do nicely." The man in charge reached for me again, and a low growl came from my chest.

"Touch me, and I'll kill you," I hissed. I couldn't know how savage I looked with my hands bound behind my back and hair loose around my arms, but I hoped I was fearsome. I wanted them to cower like the men on the docks of Souwa had. Perhaps if I told them who my mother was, it'd strike fear into their chests.

No, I'd free myself. I didn't need any help from her.

The large man threw back his head in an amused howl, sending locks of hair over his shoulders. "I'd like to see you try. Perhaps we will set that up someday, it'd be a fun sport to watch. But not today. I'm merely removing your weapons, but I shall endeavor to not touch you as I do so." His hand approached again, slower this time. He took out my cutlass and pistol, then reached for my boot and pulled out a small blade. He patted down my legs.

"Just one hidden blade?" His tongue clicked. "You wouldn't have survived out there for long."

To hide my relief that he didn't find the other one, I snarled through my teeth again, but he just smirked. A light prowled in his eye as if this were a game to him, one he enjoyed playing. How many others had he played with before?

My mind still churned with what purpose they might have for me.

Crooked Nose took a small step forward. Shards of light from the window caught his skin, revealing a tanned complexion and half-shaved head. "Might she feel more comfortable if Pearl comes out? Assures her everything is all right?"

At the name of another girl, my curiosity piqued, but the large man groaned. "I don't trust her, but if you think it will help. Keep her in check."

Crooked Nose bobbed his head and darted behind the door to fetch the girl. It took several minutes while we waited in silence. Their hungry eyes hardly left me, offering no chance to retrieve my dagger and cut through the twine undetected.

"I'm Aroth," the man in charge said. I hoped the daggers from my eyes were as piercing as I intended them to be. He got no reply from me. He smirked again. When his eyes turned to the door, I found my chance. I moved as slow as the night moon over the ocean to bring my bound hands to my waistline.

The smooth hilt of my dagger slid into my palm just as Crooked Nose came back with a young woman with skin as pale as Arn's sails and eyes as round as a pirate's wheel. He led her by the hand, not by rope or by chain, which comforted me more than I thought it would. She didn't try to take her hand from his. Upon seeing me, she turned her face away and made it a point to look at the windows or the walls, anywhere but me. She pressed her slender body against Crooked Nose's side. "Why am I here?" she whispered.

"To make her feel comfortable," Aroth spoke. He grinned at me. "Now, daughter of the sea, we welcome you to our clan."

14

ARN

High ceilings rounded to a point towered above us, mirroring the design seen in cathedrals. The irony amused me. The devil himself would think twice before entering this home.

Closed glass boxes framed the walls with nothing more than bones inside them. A tribute to the admiral's name, and a tribute to those he'd killed. If I didn't find money for him soon, my beloved ship would be his and my bones would be set up with these others to be mocked by those who saw.

He owned many homes like this through the seaside continents, each with these delightful decorations.

Admiral Bones grinned through pearly white teeth. His jade dagger twisted in his mouth with a tip as sharp as the gleam in his expression. Five men stood at each side of the room with pistols in one hand and a knife in the other, as if a fight could break out at any moment. If I thought we could win, I would try it.

Admiral Bones's pistol remained in its holster, but the blade between his lips sent a clear message. He wasn't afraid of us.

A quick scan of the room showed no sign of my father. Admiral Bones contacting my father disturbed me as much as his being taken—if the admiral had spoken with Father, then he has been made aware of things I'd prefer he didn't know.

Facing his disappointment sent unease squirming through me almost as much as dealing with Admiral Bones.

With luck, this nasty business would be over with before two full moons could glow over the sea.

Ontario's feet jittered with nerves, but I stiffened my body to keep mine hidden. Though the gruff guards may not detect my wilting fear, only a fool hoped to deceive Admiral Bones. Rumor had it that he can read the thoughts of those he did business with.

He stalked around us, particularly interested in Ontario, whom he prodded at from all angles. "You've grown into a strong lad. Your father is quite proud, I'm sure." His thoughtful eye traced a line down my mate's face while he clamped on the dagger in his mouth.

Ontario's nose flared. The little he'd told me of his father was that he hated the man, and the subject was to be left at that. He could be deceased, for all I knew. "My father is dead to me," Ontario growled. *Ah, so not deceased then. But certainly not a strong bond there.*

"Pity. Care to sit?" A smile toyed on Admiral Bones's lips as he removed the dagger's tip from his lip long enough to point it toward the chairs opposite his desk. I could imagine men sitting there in the past, tied to the seat and tortured. I'd not sit in that chair unless forced.

"Where is *my* father?" I asked instead, ignoring his invitation.

"Safe for now, since you obeyed in coming. Now my question: where is my money?"

Dealings with Admiral Bones could not be handled meekly. He wouldn't find me weak.

I spat the words at him. "You'll get the money. We are on our way now. If you doubt my word, you can track us." I nodded to my foot, where beneath my leather boots and old, frayed socks lay my binding oath. The tattoo that marked me as his.

That mark proved I was a fool after all.

I'd never oathbound myself before. It was something taught to each child as a common rule—like don't wander too close to deep waters, and spread vinegar on your doorstep to keep spirits out. Never oathbind yourself to someone. Never.

But I strayed from caution and broke the sacred rule when I oathbound myself to Admiral Bones.

As soon as an agreement was made to the oathbinding and the promise was uttered, a squid-ink tattoo inscribed itself along the top of the promiser's foot, trapping them in the vow. That tattoo wouldn't go away until the promise was fulfilled, and if you tried to escape it, the ink would slowly poison you.

The only way out of my debt to Admiral Bones was death.

Since the tattoo appeared on the top of feet, one may only be oathbound to two promises at a time, which served as both protection and limitation for desperate souls. But I didn't need the other foot; I'd never oathbind myself again. Nothing made me feel as powerless as this binding.

It tracked me.

It tormented me.

It pierced my skin and seeped into my mind until I could hardly forget about it, each tap of the foot, each step I took a relentless reminder of the debt I owed. The debt to this vile being.

Admiral Bones grinned at me as if he could read my thoughts and found the darkness therein to be appealing.

"Have no doubt, I have tracked you the whole time. You sail after Bernabe De's fabled treasure. Have you considered that island is not what you think it is?"

Ontario's head jerked, and my back straightened. What things could this man know about such a place?

He chuckled. "Your expression tells me you haven't. That

island brings more death than victory." His dagger returned to his teeth while a glee paraded in his gaze.

With great effort to keep my face calm, I repeated, "Where is my father?"

"That's not for you to worry about, lad. My money is what matters, and that tricky island you sail to. Many seafarers with desperate hopes as high as yours will be after such a treasure. How do I know you'll get it? Or will you be back in six months asking for more time?"

He wanted an assurance I could not honorably offer. If there was one thing the pirate life taught me, it's that the sea makes no promises.

But Admiral Bones wasn't an honorable man, so it bore no weight on my conscience to offer him pretty lies in return for my own neck.

Just as I opened my mouth, a sharp sound bit the air behind me, almost like a woman's scream, but the sound faded quickly. Though many wild animals roamed this island, hairs on my neck stood up, and every muscle cried out to check. But if Admiral Bones thought anything was amiss, he'd run me through with his cutlass, so I didn't move.

"We will get the treasure," Ontario spoke up, and slowly the noise slipped from mind.

I nodded once. "We've something other sailors don't have. They won't be getting this treasure before us; I'll promise you that."

The brow on Admiral Bones's leathery face rose. "And what might it be that you've got?"

To his credit, Ontario didn't look nervous, even as I lied. We had naught. The children of Arabella the Ruthless were already proving useful with their extensive knowledge of the sea, but that wouldn't impress Admiral Bones, and his ears didn't deserve to hear Emme's name. Instead I slipped my hands into my pockets. "A good pirate never reveals his secrets."

His beady eyes narrowed. "I call bluff."

"Don't care," I said with more resolve than I felt. I tried to stay steady under Admiral Bones's glare, and the solders with their cocked pistols beside us. "My secrets are my own."

A conniving smile crossed Admiral Bones's face. "But we are in business, son. And according to the code, if I call bluff, you provide me with some proof that you tell no lies."

Stars, I'd forgotten the blasted code. The victory in his expression caused me to scowl until I came up with an idea. There was something he respected more than the code: money. Now it was my turn to smile. "You're right. And breaking that code results in death. So, kill me. I die, and our transaction is nulled. You'll get none of the money, nor my ship." I took a bold step toward him. "So let us be on our way, and we will go fetch it."

He stroked his dagger against his chin. Finally, he waved his hand. "Be off with you. Get me what I'm owed."

My lungs breathed again. We turned to leave, and one of the men opened the door for us. As he did, he kept his head low, revealing the gray sun colored into the black bandana that covered most of his face besides his eyes. Red hairs curled from under the cloth at the back of his neck, and long eyelashes shielded his eyes from mine, but my mind made up the bright blue color underneath.

Hairs tingled on my arms. I'd seen this man before.

Slick, navy gloves covered his burly hands, and a crisp jacket covered his arms, but a sliver of light skin showed between the two.

That was all I'd need.

I feigned a carefree demeanor and theatrically bowed to the room. "Thank you all very much," I slurred. "Quite nice doing business with you." Admiral Bones grunted and turned away, but I stuck out my hand to the man holding the door. "Truly an honor."

After a moment's hesitation, he accepted the handshake. My fingers slid up to his wrist. If I was right, there should be a bubbled scar here. When he raised a brow at my hand, I laughed. "Handshakes, always a tricky thing to get right."

He pulled his hand from mine, and I felt it. The two snake scars embedded on his wrist.

This was the man. This was the man who convinced me to hire on more men than I could afford, and who later led the way to Admiral Bones to strike our deal.

He'd set me up.

Anger surged within me, and my face grew hot. The crisp wind did nothing to cool my temper, and my teeth clashed together at remembrance of the friendship once between that man and me. How blind I'd been.

As calmly as I could manage, I slipped my hand down to my cutlass. I drew it out, and in the same fluid motion I sliced it across the man's neck. His head fell to the floor, followed by his body.

Ontario yelped, but I jumped through the doorway and held my cutlass in front of my face. The other guards pulled their pistols, but I spoke quickly.

"Kill me, and lose your chance at your money."

It was a threat I'd just used, but it was still valid. They glanced to Admiral Bones, whose eyes narrowed to dangerous slits that examined the pool of blood around my feet.

"Nasty business between us. It was personal." I slid my cutlass back into its place, as if it was the most natural thing in the world, and waited for what Admiral Bones would do, ignoring my wildly thumping heart.

After a moment, Admiral Bones's teeth gleamed. "Good to see you are tougher than I thought you were. Seems you might have a chance to get this treasure after all."

I tipped my head before shutting the door between us, while dark blood cascaded down the steps.

"Captain?" Ontario walked with an eagerness to separate himself from this place.

"Remember Kareem? The man who I thought returned home to nurse his mother into the grave?"

Ontario cast a weary glance behind us and nodded.

"That was him."

He halted on the stone path. "Are you sure?"

"I felt the scar."

Ontario swore. All this trouble we were in now was because of Kareem. The man who had once been my second was nothing more than a deceiver who'd brought me to ruin. Ontario and he had been close friends as well, and the betrayal was bound to sting him just as much as it stung me. It was costing us both everything. "I knew we should have stayed far away from Admiral Bones."

We wound back through the dead town raining curses upon Kareem and his mother until we spotted the crew with hauls of supplies. As Emric spotted us, he frowned. "Where's Emme?"

I froze. "Is she not with you?" He shook his head. Immediately all of us turned various directions to scan shadowed streets and call out Emme's name. Only a seagull called back.

"I thought I heard a scream," I muttered under my breath. I raised my voice. "I don't trust this place. Bishop, Percival, Timmons—load the provisions into the boats, and prepare for us to set off. The rest of you search the town. Keep a partner with you, and shout if you need help. Go, men. Run."

Uneven rocks dug into the leather soles of my boots, as the idea of Admiral Bones getting to Emme propelled me even faster. This small town suddenly felt like an entire kingdom.

One worry filled my mind, making me forget all others.

I couldn't lose her.

15

EMME

Cut twine. Don't cut myself. Run. Stab anyone in my way.

To accomplish that, I needed a few moments to saw through the bindings, so my string of questions began.

"Your clan?"

Aroth picked a speck of dust off his lapel. "The mountain-dwelling clan. We live in the valleys of the mountains here on this island. It's a beautiful place, isn't that right, Pearl?"

Pearl's responding smile stretched too wide, and her eyes carried far too much complicity within them. Gullible. Naïve. As she rested against Crooked Nose, her hand stroked his chest, and her head tilted in toward him. She wore a violet satin dress with tight, long sleeves and a hem cut off at the knees, showing sturdy boots underneath. Each time our eyes met, hers skirted away.

"It's remarkable," she said. "The sunrises are especially stunning. You'll love it here every bit as much as I do." Her words rolled from her lips like honey dripping from a tree. She carried no mark of being kidnapped and no sign of rebellion. If she was taken as I was, she didn't show it.

But her words did bring one comfort—they didn't plan to kill me.

Aroth's arms went wide. "See? You'll adore living here. Now come, let's bring you home."

"Wait," I spoke quickly. The dagger in my hands pressed against the twine, ready to snap it. My next sentence had to be timed to cover the sound. There was a sharp sting on my wrist as I drew the blade across the ropes, but there was no way around nicking myself in acquiring freedom. I'd take a cut over whatever awaited me here.

"I must know what's to become of me here," I said.

The ropes loosened on my wrists, and I pressed them against my body to keep them from falling to the floor to give me away. One final tug would free me. I needed to choose my moment.

"What's to become of you?" Aroth stroked his beard. "Well, that's partly up to you, lass. Simply put, this is your home. You'll live here, work here, *breed* here, die here."

I didn't like the emphasis he put on breed. The sick, dark feeling in the pit of my stomach urged me to make my escape. Now.

The last of the twine snapped, and my arms swung forward.

The room exploded into motion. Aroth reacted first, jumping toward me the moment I left the chair. My dagger slashed at him, but he was quick to dodge and pull his own blade.

The other three men crossed the desk toward me, leaving the girl standing by herself. I only had a moment before they reached me, so I grabbed the chair and swung it as hard as I could into the planks on the window. The wood cracked, and the chair shattered in my hands.

The window boards cracked as well, but not enough. Their edges still clung to the rusted nails, threatening to impale me if I attempted to jump through the narrow crack. If I were a waif, I could fit through, but my rounded hips needed a bigger hole than that.

Pearl ducked under the desk while I smashed the chair. To my surprise, when she came back up, she held two curved blades in her hands.

"This way," she yelled. There was no chance of me getting through the window and fending off four large men on my own, so I took the opportunity she offered. If Pearl was tricking me, I'd turn my blade on her.

As she waved her hand at me, I sprinted toward her, grabbing my stolen cutlass and pistol along the way. She shoved the desk over into Aroth, who collapsed on the ground under the weight of it. He'd be back on his feet quickly. Crooked Nose reached her before I did and put up his hands.

"Love, put the blades down."

I swung my cutlass at him. It caught his side, and he let out a sharp scream that echoed through the room. Pearl's eyes lingered briefly on him before driving her own blade through his chest. His eyes gaped as he sunk to the floor where blood was already splattered.

I had no time to quell my stomach before Squinty Eyes swung at me, but his stance was weak and his hands easily let go of the blade after I twisted mine around his. Mother would laugh at how easy he was to defeat. Once more Pearl stabbed through the heart, and he crumpled beside Crooked Nose.

Bushy Eyebrows dropped his cutlass to the floor and held up his hands. Aroth swore at him and started to rise. I took out my pistol, and at the sight of the barrel, Aroth raised his own gun. Mine went off first, embedding a bullet into his shoulder. At his angry yell, Pearl grabbed me by the sleeve and pulled me toward the back door. "Follow me. And hurry." She took off through the doorway and into the darkness behind it. I threw myself after her. A gunshot went off behind us, making us both duck, but nothing struck. Fear pushed me faster. Behind us, the men shouted. If they followed, we couldn't outrun them for long.

Pearl pulled me along as she ran with an unnatural speed. Running for her life, I thought. I tripped through the darkness, but her hand yanked me up roughly.

Suddenly she turned to the side, and there was a creaking noise. A door in front of us was pushed open, and we stumbled outside where the building was surrounded by rocks and tough grass. Pearl released my hand and shouted in my ear, "Run!" Without looking back, she scrambled over the nearest boulder and away from the building.

Now in the light, I ran with more certainty. Fear ought to still be coursing through my veins, but I now didn't feel it. Instead I felt very much like Mother in one of her adventures that she used to tell us, on the run from lurking danger with the thrill of the experience pushing me forward. The disease in my body called for me to slow, but I ignored it. Soon I caught up to Pearl and beckoned her to the side. "I have a ship waiting at the shore. You'll be safe there."

She nodded as she gasped for breath. Her cheeks were rosy, and her eyes brightened with the fresh air and freedom. I pointed her in the right direction, and she navigated us through the winding streets until the small-town shops greeted us and the smell of the saltwater filled our lungs.

The sea had never smelled so beautiful.

At last, over the roofs of shops I saw the *Royal Rose*. "Almost there," I panted through my dry throat.

We turned the corner by a rundown building with a sign of boots on the door and ran right into Emric's arms.

Pearl uttered a cry, but I threw my arms around him and clung tight. His arms tightened around me. "Emme, where have you been?" Arn arrived beside him chest heaving. He looked rapidly between me and Pearl.

"Are you in trouble?"

My breathing was shallow. Now that I had come to a stop, the disease mocked me for ignoring it, and the ground swayed beneath my feet. My bones felt frail as twigs that quivered beneath me.

I'd gotten free, but at a cost.

This disease was not merciful, and my wild sprint across the island would cost me in time. Weeks, perhaps months.

I sucked in enough breath to speak. "We need to go right now. There are men after us." At my words and the fear in Pearl's expression, their eyes darted around us, and their hands went to their pistols.

Then Arn cupped his hands by his lips and bellowed into the cloudy sky. "Return to ship!" I took another gulp of air before willing my limbs to run again. It would be impossible to keep my illness a secret if I didn't mask it.

Arn paused several times to shout down the streets for men to return to the beach as the landscape of rocks turned to coarse sand.

Our boats waited by the shore, and we pushed against them to ease their hulls into the crystal water. As we loaded, the rest of the pirate crew appeared, first the twins Svid and Sims with a red-cheeked Zander in tow. Then Henrik and Ontario from the western side of the town. The sand kicked up as their feet pounded toward us while we ushered them faster. Together we clambered into the three rowboats and paddled into the frothing waves.

The oars hitting the water and men asking questions were the only thing that covered the raspy sound of my breathing.

I'd been such a fool. My effort to follow Arn might have cost me my life.

Emric told the other men to keep their questions to themselves until we'd loaded the *Royal Rose,* while giving me a worried look. I turned from him.

Pearl was curled up in the bow with her hands clutched to her collar and chest heaving as she watched the island pull away. The wind blew her hair over her face, but she appeared as miserable as I.

Just as I was about to speak to her, Arn's hand found mine, and the warmth closed over me. "Are you all right?" he asked, voice low. A sadness lived in his expression, as if he carried the blame of what happened on himself. In truth, I had blamed him partly too. But now removed from the island and the short-lived danger, the blame fell solely on me.

Arn's eyes were much kinder than any of the men back in that town, and his hand encouraging as it held mine. He grunted as he pulled his oar through the water using his chest and other hand, keeping his eyes set on me.

"I'm fine."

The biggest worry on my mind was how much of my life had been taken away from the excursion, instead of what had just happened. It felt wrong somehow to not be more afraid of the encounter, but at least fear hadn't crippled me. I'd been taken, and I got free.

A year ago I would have been too afraid to pull that knife out and risk my life, but today I had fought my way out.

Arn's brow rose. "Fine? You were being chased."

Despite myself, I gave a shaky laugh. "I know. And if you would have told me that would happen when you first asked me to sail with you, I would have pushed you over the pier. Don't get me wrong, I was terrified at first, but I held my own. I don't know. It sounds a little vain, but I'm proud that I'm braver than I thought I was."

Arn's hand squeezed mine. "I always knew you were brave, but I'm proud of you too."

This trickle of confidence made everything, for now, seem okay.

Pearl was a different story. She kept frightened eyes on the island while gnawing on her lip. Arn followed my gaze toward her. "She looks petrified of that forsaken place. What happened to her there?"

"Honestly, I'm not quite sure," I told him. "She'll have more answers than me."

I was right. We loaded the ship, raised the anchor, and made quick work of sailing off. A storm was coming as evening settled in, and we worked quickly to lift the sails. Emric fretted over me a bit more, a short tale was told to the others about running through the island, a nice flask of rum was poured for Pearl, and the men got in their questions, until at last Arn hushed us all and everyone settled down enough to hear the proper story. The clouds were quite thick by this point, and several of us clutched blankets around us.

"Emme, you start." Arn kept a hand on his cutlass and an eye scanning the ocean as Aható island grew smaller behind us. I'd rather him sitting by my side holding my hand as he'd done in the rowboat, but the crew was waiting intently for me to speak, and he had a ship to steer.

"There isn't much for me to tell," I confessed, deciding it would go better if I left out the bit of trailing Arn and Ontario through the town. "A few men grabbed me and brought me back to their shack where they informed me that it was my new home." I recounted how I cut my bonds and how Pearl seized control of the situation to get us both out. I concluded, "Then we ran into you." It was only the bones of the story, and I hoped Pearl could fill in the details that confused me.

Emric paced back and forth as I spoke and ran his hands through his hair. He scowled. "What were you doing away from the group?" he demanded. "Do you know how dangerous these lands are? From here on to the Island of Iilak, there's nothing but treacherous waters and forsaken islands. You can't venture through places alone."

His concern touched me, but his tone wasn't pleasant. "I can take care of myself."

"You got yourself kidnapped," he reminded me. His expression was similar to our father's when he worried, with his cheeks turning red and his brows set low.

"I freed myself and helped someone else, and"—I waved my hand over Pearl, who sipped her rum as she watched us—"we helped each other."

Emric growled and kept pacing. Then he abruptly turned and stomped up to the quarterdeck where Arn stood behind the wheel and thrust a finger against his chest. "Where were you? You're always with her. You should have been there to save her."

"Hey." I frowned.

Arn brought his focus away from the waters. He looked straight at Emric and spoke levelly. Both men were matched in height, but Emric's tanned skin, long dark curls, and dark eyes made him look like a brewing storm next to the lighter shades of Arn. "This isn't my fault, mate. And she told you she can take care of herself."

"She shouldn't have to!" Emric stomped down the stairs.

Pearl cleared her throat and spoke up. "Are you all pirates?" Slight concern trickled in her voice. At the chorus of ayes that followed, she said, "You're the oddest bunch of pirates I've ever met." Her eyes, shining blue like the water, examined the mast and sails. "With the cleanest ship. And the soberest crew."

I was almost comical to see Arn's chest puff up as she complimented the cleanliness of his ship, while the other crew members looked about in slight confusion. "Soberest? Are we allowed not to be? Captain, are we allowed to be drunk in the early afternoon?"

"Nay, men, you are not."

A series of grunts followed, and Pearl grinned. "You're nothing like the men on that island, I'll tell you that. Nor the pirates I used to sail with." She reached up to begin braiding her loose hair. "I was left on this island a few weeks ago by my earlier crew. It didn't take long for those men to find me and drag me in the same way they took you." She looked at me. "You handled it better than I did; I was a terrified wreck. But they didn't hurt me."

She had no idea how terrified I had been. "What did they want with you?"

"To marry me." At our stunned faces, she went on. "See, there aren't many ladies that come to these waters, and those men aren't eager to leave that island. Some rocks they've found in the mountains keep them rich. They have a man who trades with them. Anyway, to maintain families, they need women. They need wives. So when one comes to their shore, they take her. They think they are being kind, allowing us to choose our husbands and decorate our own homes, but it's nothing more than a fancy prison that demands you produce children to keep the bloodline going."

My brow creased. "It's an open island—surely you had chances to run? You seemed pretty comfortable when I arrived." The words came out more accusing than I'd wanted, but she didn't recoil at their tone.

Instead a small laugh floated from her chest. "Run where? To the water? To swim to freedom? I had no way off that island and no hope of survival outside staying with them. So I played the part. I blushed and I flirted and I acted as if I was so grateful to be there. It worked like a charm. Just yesterday they trusted me to go to the town on my own. In the next week, as the trading boat came, I was planning to sneak away upon it. Luckily, you came earlier."

It was smart. I wouldn't have had the stomach to play that game.

Emric's expression had turned from anger to being impressed at Pearl. "Well done. And welcome aboard. You might be wishing for that trading ship soon, though. We plan to go to the Island of Iilak, and we won't be turning back now."

Her face whitened again. "The Island of Iilak? In search of Bernabe De's treasure?"

Arn stiffened, and Emric's mouth dropped. "How could you know that?"

She clutched her braid. "The ship I was on two weeks ago? The *Dancer?* It sailed there too."

The men either cursed or groaned, but Arn paled. "The *Dancer?*"

"Aye. You know of it?"

His hands clenched the spokes of the wheel as he sucked in his lip. "Aye. I knew its captain once. I knew him quite well. Landon and I were mates in the king's navy together as lads." He tensed his jaw. "I hate that man."

16

ARN

Will my past forever haunt me?

"What did he do to you?" Pearl asked me. The rest of my crew looked at me waiting to hear the tale.

I scowled. "A story for another day. If someone gets to the treasure first, we will need a new plan." There was a clap of thunder, and the clouds released their hold on the waters and let it pour around us. The cold in the air was made worse as water seeped into our skin. "Go below deck, mates." I had to shout through the pounding rain. "I don't need any of you catching a cold."

They went below, leaving me to fume over what today had brought. First the betrayal from Kareem, and now a race against Landon. My only solace was Landon didn't know we were sailing after Bernabe De's treasure behind him. But his head start would be a hard challenge to overcome. Two weeks. He ought to be close by now. If he got it before us, we'd take it from him on his sail home. I'd kill him if I had to.

This treasure meant more to me than it did to him. If I didn't acquire it, I'd lose my ship and my life, my crew and father would be in danger from Admiral Bones's wrath, and I'd never be able to help Emme reclaim her sheep farm.

Landon couldn't get the treasure first.

Landon and I had been more than mates in the king's navy—we'd enlisted together. At fifteen we were placed aboard the same ship and sailed under His Majesty King Unid's flag. We were the best of friends. *Brothers*. He had the good looks and silver tongue, and I had the sharp mind.

The day we uncovered the truth about the king, both our hearts turned against him. His hatred and disgust ran just as deep as mine did. It'd been his idea to leave the navy. When we rebelled, we did it together. And when we freed the pirates, we both joined their crew. Memories still plagued me of that night with the scent of smoke and burning flesh as we'd tossed overboard the charred bodies of the navy men and stole the ship from those who'd guided us into manhood.

We became pirates of the high seas. Together. Landon was with me through it all. We were to captain jointly one day.

But we both fell for a pretty lass with the colors of the night in her hair. Merelda Ann. After I poured out my heart to her, she chose Landon, who then pulled a cruel trick to send me away from them. It was a horrible thing to not be loved in return, but what'd they'd done to me would leave a scar straight to the bone. Resentment turned to hatred for the man I once called my brother. Now we were captains of our own vessels and hadn't spoken in years.

From the look that had crossed Pearl's face at his name, I wasn't the only one Landon had hurt. To spare Pearl from reliving the ordeal further, I hadn't asked for more. I needed to create a new strategy in case he got to the treasure first. One thing was for certain, we'd need more men if we hoped to succeed in an attack.

After Pearl had several nights to recover from her trauma and fill her belly with our food, I worked up the courage to ask her the questions I longed to know about my old friend and the lass he sailed with.

"So, you sailed with Landon."

She'd come to the quarterdeck to sit away from the noise of below and watch as we advanced toward the Moving Islands. We should be upon them by now, but they shifted over the waters, so there was no telling what placement they were in today.

Pearl frowned at Landon's name. "You've finally asked me about it. I've been wondering all week when you would."

"Did you know him well?"

"Aye, I did." She hesitated. "He and I were lovers."

My brows shot up. Lovers. He wasn't with Merelda Ann, then. Pearl's eyes showed no sign of a lie, and she'd have no reason to do so. Where was Merelda Ann? Did he break her heart, or did she break his? What was she doing now? It'd been a long time since I thought of the girl with the hair as dark as midnight and the smile as bright as the stars.

"You seem surprised." Pearl was regarding me. "He is known for his slew of ladies, but he and I were different. We met at the Golden Sun Tavern on Ktoawn where he goes after every victorious voyage. We sailed together for a year until he left me alone on that . . . island." Her face blanched.

Surprised was hardly the word for it. Disgusted suited my emotions better. "Quite a devilish thing to do, leaving a lady alone in a place like that. What reason did he have for it?"

She shrugged. "Lost interest, I guess. He didn't give me a reason. We came upon the island, some of us got off, then later they set sail without me."

She said it casually, but I'd seen the terror in her eyes as she watched the shore of Aható fade away. My words couldn't fix what he'd put her through on that island, but I spoke anyway. "I'm sorry."

Her smile was faint. "It's okay now." She bit her upper lip as she looked over the water that rolled beneath us. From ahead, Lewie called out for land, signaling we'd found the first of the Moving Islands. It was still a speck in the distance, but I adjusted my wheel slightly to avoid running into it.

Pearl leaned over the side of the ship and filled her lungs with the ocean air. "I can't continue with you."

For a second, I thought she was going to jump, but she took a step back. "I can't sail after the treasure and after him. If one of these islands looks friendly, I'm getting off." She braced herself against the edge of the ship with a great sadness in her eyes. "I'm sorry, I just can't."

"I understand. I would never force someone to stay aboard my crew if they didn't wish it. And the Island of Iilak won't be for the faint of heart. But are you certain you wish to dock on one of these islands? No one knows what they hold."

"I know what they don't hold, so I'll take my chances. I know how to take care of myself," she said.

Says the girl who was kidnapped.

There were stories, as there often are, about what creatures called the Moving Islands home, but none of those stories felt appropriate to repeat when Pearl looked so determined. She might have a jolly time there, perhaps stumble upon a magical item or two. Many seafarers hid things upon these islands, either personal things they naïvely believed they could find again later, or dangerous items that should never be found. Some said there was a weapon there that could send an entire island to the bottom of the ocean.

"The island up ahead is small but doesn't look to hold much that you could survive on. The next island past holds more lush colors; perhaps it carries some fresh springs, coconuts, and papayas."

She leaned further over the side to scope out the land in the distance. "That'd be plenty to survive off until another ship comes by."

Until another boat comes. With the unpredictability of the Moving Islands and the distance we were from common waters, it could be months before another ship passed, but most likely years. In that time she'd be reliant upon her ability to make fire and find food while surviving whatever creatures lived there. Was that truly a more terrible fate than seeing Landon again? "Pearl, we will try to retrieve you on our way home, but there's no guarantee that we'll be back this way, or that anyone else will come."

Her shoulders squared for the island. "I know, Arn. Don't worry about me. Having an island to myself sounds really nice right about now." But that was what worried me—that she wouldn't have it to herself.

Emme came from below deck and scanned the area. She waved when she saw us. Her braided hair wrapped around her head like a crown, with her ribbon tied into a bow at the back. She'd bandaged her wrist, and I felt guilty each time I looked upon it, knowing that if I'd been with her, I could have protected her. She hadn't needed help being rescued, and she put on a brave face when talking about it, as if it was nothing more than a slight occurrence, but I saw the way she tensed as Emric placed his hand on her shoulder from behind, and I knew fear ruled her mind.

I should have been there.

"She's beautiful. Does she know you love her?" A daring smirk played upon Pearl's thin lips as she wiggled her brows.

"You've misread," I answered with a flat tone. That was the way of the seas, hide what you love, or else it might be used against you.

But Pearl chuckled to herself. "She's lucky to have you. Friend or more." Pearl winked.

Emme came up the stairs, and I willed Pearl into silence. "Good morning, Arn; morning Pearl, how are—"

She stopped speaking, and the color drained from her face. She raised a trembling arm out to the sea. "The black ship. It's back." Her words carried a wisp of chill that settled over us like a heavy cloak.

A distant shape moved toward us. The same black ship that trailed us earlier was following us once again. It moved across the Seas of Lost Lands with silent speed, breaking at the crests of small waves and plunging forward to meet us. As it approached, my mouth turned dry. Would it come closer this time? Would we finally see who captained this vessel?

Any thoughts of Landon and of Merelda Ann disappeared from my mind.

Behind me, Pearl let out a gasp and stumbled backward. Emme and I exchanged glances. She was not on the ship with us before when it followed us. She had no reason to fear this ship.

"Pearl, what is it?"

"Tha-that ship. It's following m-me." She flailed for the railing to steady herself. Her voice quivered. "What does he want?" She collapsed to her knees to bury her head in her lap and began praying.

"To your stations, men. The devil's ship is back," I roared to the crew, sending them into a flurry of motion.

Emme knelt beside Pearl and put a hand on her shaking back. "Pearl, it's okay. But we must know, in your experience with this ship, did it ever get close enough to attack?"

Her head shook in her lap as her muffled voice replied. "But we saw his flag. I'm certain the devil himself sails on it. It haunts my dreams; it haunts my mind. I can never be free of it. He'll never let me go." She began praying again and tightened her body inward.

Emme looked up to me with bewilderment. This lass must have seen this ship more often than we had. From the amount of concern it brought me after only one encounter, it was no wonder she felt this way after many. Something about this ship could drive a man mad.

"Prepare the cannons," I shouted to the crew. "Stand ready!"
This ship might not attack, but we'd be ready, if need be.

Emme stayed with Pearl for a few moments, though her own hands trembled. She tightened them into fists to still the shaking, and her jaw clenched.

Pearl didn't move from her crouched position. She wanted to be left alone on an unknown island but was terrified of this ship?

I put my back to them to watch the vessel and could make out a marking on the flag, black and gold, just like mine. There was some design there, but it was too far away to decipher, riding at the perfect distance to be certain we saw him but not close enough to be identified. That could be no accident. He was toying with us like a predator plays with his food before devouring it.

I'd had enough of games.

"Fire the cannons," I ordered the crew.

Emme looked at me with wide, questioning eyes, but I nodded to Emric. He nodded back and dropped below deck to instruct the men. We had enough ammo to engage both this ship and Landon; neither would take us down. I wouldn't let some dark ship haunt me.

The first cannon shot, then the other. With a loud boom both cannonballs whizzed through the sea air with deafening speed before plunging into the dark waters, meters away from the ship. The sea protested with waves that broke against the hull of the devil's black boat.

"Hold fire."

Now that we'd made moves to attack, let's see what the devil would do about it.

He drew no nearer. As we continued sailing north, the black ship began to seem farther away.

"Can you see his flag?" Emme stood by the wheel, facing back as I steered us forward.

I glanced behind me and squinted. "Almost. It's a small flag, I think he means to keep it a secret."

"Your sight must be better than mine, because I can hardly see it. But he's not following."

"Perhaps we scared him off."

"He's also not going away. He's just there."

A shiver ran up my spine, accompanied by a coldness, as if someone dragged an icy finger up my back. Each muscle it passed froze and refused to move further. What sort of trickery was this? The coldness spread until my entire body was rendered useless.

I struggled, but I couldn't move.

Despite my best efforts, my body stayed paralyzed while fears took over my frantic mind. I needed to move. If I couldn't steer us away, then the ship would catch us, and the lives of my crew would be on my hands. Admiral Bones might not need to kill me—this ship would do it first.

With great force I pried my jaw open then bit down hard on my tongue. The sudden pain jolted my body back into motion, and it took all my strength to pull my arms free from whatever dark magic had taken ahold of them.

My breathing came in quick strokes. A visible shiver shot through Emme, starting in her toes and moving upward. When she looked at me, I saw the questions swimming in her mind.

This boat was fighting back, and he had unnatural weapons.

"At least the boat is still keeping a distance." Forming words felt as difficult as pulling a heavy crate along the bottom of the ocean.

Emric's head emerged from below deck. "Those are some cannons you have down there. Did we get the scoundrel?" He swept his long hair back behind his head as he searched the water.

"Nay," my words felt thick. "But he's stopped his pursuit. Well done, matey."

If anything was amiss, Emric didn't notice. "Splendid, I don't suppose I can play with the cannons a bit more?"

My face gave him the answer, and he gave a quick grin. His hands moved to lower himself back down but he stopped. His head slowly looked up and his lips stiffened. He tried to speak.

"It's happening again," Pearl cried. "He will never leave us alone. We will be haunted forever."

"No one is haunted, Pearl. We are safe. He isn't advancing." Emme tried to comfort Pearl, but her words lacked resolve.

One look back at the ship and my body froze, this time from terror.

"Emme."

At the urgency in my voice, she stood up and gasped.

The ship was approaching.

It flew toward us with a speed unseen on the high seas and unmatched by any animal on land. The south wind did nothing to slow the dark sails. It appeared spurred on by a wind of its own and danced over the waves effortlessly. As it drew closer, I realized the water itself moved aside for him. He skipped along the surface, closing the gap between us.

"Fire again," I screamed at the top of my lungs. Pearl screamed as well, and I hurled against the wheel to turn us away.

There was dark magic at work here.

There was no time. He'd come at us too fast. Emme threw herself over Pearl as I called out, "Brace yourselves!"

The crash didn't come. As the devil's ship drew toward us, it pulled upward. The ship expanded until it was as large as a whale made entirely of dark mist that clouded my lungs. An earsplitting sound erupted from the boat as it drifted over us then burst apart. Dark vapor settled over the *Royal Rose* as a voice filled the sky.

"You should not be here."

Then the sky cleared, and it was as if nothing happened.

It took several breaths for me to be certain I was alive. I'd never gotten close to dark magic before, and I never wanted to again. This was some sort of trick to drive us away from these waters.

There was a reason these seas weren't often sailed. This must be one of them. These seas weren't meant for man.

You should not be here.

Had his warning been for me? I was meant to be a navy man, not a pirate, and after only a few years, I'd brought myself close enough to ruin to oathbind myself to Admiral Bones in desperation. Other pirates likely laughed at the idea of me.

Perhaps King Valian himself, fabled ruler of the seas, knew I didn't belong on his waters.

You should not be here.

"Is everyone okay?" Emme found her voice. Poor Lewie gripped the edge of the crow's nest and looked ready to hurl. The ship's vapor must have enveloped him. Perhaps next time he wouldn't fall asleep at post. I glanced around. Emric looked as white as a ghost and hardly moved as the rest of the crew came barreling from below deck, demanding to know what just happened.

"Something truly terrible, lads. There's devilment in these waters that mustn't be played with. Keep your heads about you—this sort of darkness can make a man go mad," I cautioned them.

None of them failed to note Emric's pale face or Emme's shaking hands or the way Pearl was sobbing in a curled-up ball at my feet. A surprising part of me was glad they could see this. It would help them heed my warning to guard their minds from trickery.

"Something terrible indeed."

17

EMME

Pearl asked to be let off at the nearest island after the encounter with the black ship, saying the waters were no longer the place for her. So on an island with pure white sands, rich pine trees, and a damp atmosphere, Pearl left our crew. As her feet hit the ground, she exhaled as if she'd found the solace that she long sought after.

She was the only one who looked at peace.

It wasn't half an hour later before Henrik started screaming. His deep, bloodcurdling cry brought everyone to the deck. He claimed to have seen his brother who had drowned at the age of five after their fishing boat overturned and Henrik hadn't been strong enough to swim them both back to shore.

With sweat dripping down his face, he pointed to the cabin under the quarterdeck and repeated his brother's name over and over. "He was there. His ghost is upon this ship."

The other men shifted their gazes across the ship while Bishop and Arn exchanged glances. "I'll go make some tea," Bishop said, lumbering below deck.

"Guard yourselves, men," Arn gave warning again. "There is a darkness here that preys on the weak-minded." He took his blanket from the cabin and wrapped it around Henrik's shoulders, then steered him to a barrel to sit upon. Bishop brought the trembling man tea with calming herbs.

Emric sat on the steps leading to the helm, his hands against his face and his jaw clamped in thought. Some of the crew sat by Henrik, while others watched for the black ship to return, muttering that it would no doubt be back soon.

"Who is he?" Arn's question drifted away in the wind, for no one had the answer.

Arn was the most troubled by the encounter. He put Ontario in charge of steering and retired to his cabin for several minutes to calm his mind. I longed to go in there and see how he fared, but I had my own swirling thoughts to sort through.

The coldness hadn't bothered me as much, nor the way my feet turned to lead.

But when that ship came at us, and the words came—*You should not be here*—that chilled my heart more than anything. The old boot had said the same thing to me. What did it mean?

After watching how piracy ruled my mother's heart over her love for her kin, I vowed to never be a pirate. I wouldn't join the ranks of the heartless thieves who plundered a wealth that wasn't theirs and killed blindly. They cared for no one besides themselves.

Until Arn, I'd hated all pirates.

I thought that was what the boot meant when it told me I didn't belong here. But it felt different when the ship uttered those words. A heavy weight rested on my heart, and I wanted answers.

"Mother spoke of a ship," Emric's voice drew our eyes to him, to where he sat on the old boards of the steps. "She spoke of one that followed her through the day and sent her nightmares during the night. She knew who captained this ship, though she wouldn't say who. All she said was it was someone who wanted her off the seas."

His voice was scratchy. "My mother made many afraid, and she boasted many enemies. But none put fear into her until this one. She grew so troubled that she ran from the seas. She fled all the way to Julinbor, where she met a poor sheep farmer and fell in love. She had us." He gestured at me. "But her love for the sea finally overruled her fear, and she returned to it."

That story was new to me. But it wasn't a surprise.

My mother had always been clear about her love for the sea, and it'd always been a mystery how she met Father and fell in love. But now I knew—it was fear that drove her to the land, not love. Part of me had clung to the belief that she really did love her family the most, and her trips on the high seas were to provide for us, even though we never came first to her.

She'd been in love with the waters until the day they drowned her.

Beware the waters. Guard your heart against their call.

I hadn't guarded my heart well enough. I'd allowed myself to enjoy this time among the pirates and among the sea. But these waters would lead to nothing but destruction. They'd already taken my mother; they didn't deserve to take me.

"I'm no pirate," I said under my breath, hoping the sea would hear me. Hoping this nameless sailor would hear me and leave us alone. Hoping I would hear myself.

Arn had stepped out from the cabin. A breeze caught his mussed hair and drew it back from his worried brow. "You believe it's this same person who's following us? But why?"

"I don't know," Emric replied. "I don't know. But I won't let it haunt me as it did her." He stood up. His hazel eyes looked at me. "And I won't let it get to my sister." Emric stood from the stairs and placed a hand on the rail. The sky to the west held hues of orange spreading over the sea and bringing out the gold flecks in Arn's flag.

"I won't let him get to you. I vow it," he said. "I would

oathbind myself to you as a promise that I will save you, no matter the cost."

The sincerity in his eyes was enough to prove it to me. Though Emric left me as Mother had, his love for me was never in question. "Don't be silly, Emric. You should never oathbind yourself to anyone. I believe you. We'll keep an eye out and guard our minds against his nightmares."

"Imagine that," Percival spoke with a hint of awe in his voice. "A haunted ship is following us. Those are the things of tales."

The others agreed as if they had a lack of concern for the potential danger. "We'll have a good story for when we get to port, that's for sure."

"Besting a ghost ship—that'll earn us many ladies, I think."

Arn ran his hand through his hair before glancing out to where the black ship had been. The sun dipped below the horizon, and the stars began to take their places in the sky. "All right. Let's get dinner started. There will be no more talk of haunted boats tonight." He cast a quick look at Henrik, who hadn't moved.

As the rest meandered off to begin their chores, I placed a hand on Emric's arm.

"Do you really think it's the same ship that haunted Mother?" I asked him. "How could that be?"

I searched his eyes for any signs of fright, but he had always covered his emotions well. "Don't fret, Emme," he merely said. "Your fate is not bound to this ghost sailor. You have a long future ahead of you; I can feel it."

My lips smiled but my heart ached. Tell him. Tell him now. He deserved to know that I was sick with Father's illness. He deserved to know his sister would die.

But he had moved away before I could tell him, leaving me behind with a heaviness inside that I feared would never go away.

A sound woke me from deep sleep, and I sat up with a start. Starlight bathed my small room in a silver glow, but shadows remained dancing in the corners. My heavy lids drooped as I clutched the wool blanket closer around my neck so sleep could find me again.

"Emme."

It came as a drawn-out whisper, a hushed sound that drifted into existence, brushed across my ear, then drifted away. Here one moment and gone the next. My breath caught in my throat, and my body went numb as the voice came again amid the soft waves outside the porthole.

"Emmeee."

Each hair on my arm stood up as a breath brushed against my skin. That couldn't be right. There was no one in the room. But there it called again, and the warm air against the back of my neck settled over my body like the ocean's mist.

This cannot be.

Terror took hold of me as the voice called my name a third time. It beckoned me to find it. And as much as I wanted to stay in the safety of the cabin and hide from it, I couldn't resist getting out of bed. My body moved against my will toward the cabin door and into the darkness of the passageway. The breath swept across my neck again, pushing me toward the ladder and up to the deck.

Two odd things about the voice gripped me. First, this voice that spoke my name in the dark of night was female. And we had no other females on board.

And the second fact, which terrified me the most, was the familiarity of the voice. It'd been so long since I heard that tone, the tone of one who used to sing me to sleep and read me stories. The one who taught me to be strong and brave. The one who told me to love the water.

That voice could only belong to my mother.

I shivered. Are these the seas where she drowned? Was her body here in the waves, her ghost sent to haunt me? If I peered over the ship's edge and looked deep enough, would I see her decaying body on the sandy floor?

The moonlight lit up the sky and coated the boat with silver. I crawled from below deck in a daze. The voice grew stronger as I stood on deck, until it sounded like it came from directly behind me.

I turned around, and there she was.

My mother.

A gold dress clung to her body as it dripped water around her bare feet. As the light caught the fabric it shimmered with colors of the rainbow. It was as if her dress had been sewn to her body and morphed into fish scales.

I'd never seen my mother in a dress before. I think I preferred her in pants over this ghostly garment.

More startling than her attire was the unnatural green color of her skin and the seaweed snaking through her toes. Barnacles grew along her fingernails and from the corners of her eyes, and her lips looked like a fish had eaten from them. A foul stench stained the air, and an eel slithered through her soaked hair, I stepped backward in disgust.

"My daughter, how I've missed you. So you answered the call to the water."

Her voice rang clear now—no more breath against my neck, no more whispers in the dark. She examined me with eyes of black and a smile as if it pleased her to see me afraid.

The ship deck was strangely empty, so this fright was mine to experience alone.

"Is this where you drowned? Is this where your body lies?" The words came from me, though I hadn't thought I could speak anything coherent right now.

She threw her head back and laughed. Her hair floated

around her in a wide circle, the eel still navigating through. He would loop in and out as if that was where he belonged, as if my mother was his home. A pool of water at her feet continued to grow, soaking the deck in shimmering green liquid.

"Dead? I am not dead, love. These waters cannot hold me. I rule them. And someday you will join me." Her hand reached for me, and my feet froze. "You will join me in the water. That is your destiny."

I struggled away from her reach, but my body refused to obey. Just as I opened my mouth to scream, her hand brushed my cheek.

"Hush, dearie. I will not take you yet. It is not your time."

Then her form crumpled to the floor, leaving behind the seaweed and puddle of water in her place.

A laugh echoed across the water. "Join me, Emme. Join me as a queen of the sea."

I fled from the deck back to my room below, I pulled the covers over me and prayed my mother was really dead.

Beware the water. Beware the seas where your mother drowned.

18
ARN

"Stars and seaweed," I exclaimed.

Half of the crew was there and standing back as I knelt beside Lewie's bed. "How long has he been like this?"

He was shivering despite the three blankets around him, and sweat formed along his brow. Each sway of the boat caused him to wince. It was clear he was sick.

Ontario wrung out a rag over a bucket of water before dabbing it along the boy's cheeks. "He woke up in fits of madness and has been shivering ever since. Feel his head, he's burning up. He needs a dose of something."

"Then let's get him some. Henrik, come with me. We'll see how you are with medicine." I pushed past Bo and Percival as I moved toward the upper cabin in search of something to bring the boy's fever down. Henrik followed behind.

I'd been teaching Henrik to read and write, but we'd not had many lessons in cures. That would need to change—not only for him, but for the rest of the crew as well. I wouldn't be doomed to a fate of falling ill and dying simply because I was the only one on board who knew herbs. If you sailed on my ship, you learned medicine.

Plus, Henrik needed distracting from his visions. He claimed to have seen his brother again last night.

"So, what can be used to cure fever?" From atop the old bookshelf I pulled down a large book and opened it for Henrik to inspect. He squinted at the pages, then at the jars lining the shelves behind me.

"Thyme?"

Henrik was a large man, adorned with muscles and a courage that couldn't be dampened and a willingness to follow orders. But he wasn't too bright.

"Rose. See?" I pointed to the page. "We will also use ginger and basil. Let's get a few rose petals down to Bishop in the kitchens and see if he can get an oil and a drink prepared."

I grabbed the ingredients from the shelf and started toward the door, but Henrik didn't follow me. When I glanced back, he stood with his hands fidgeting before his chest.

"What is it, Henrik?"

He hesitated before answering. "Do you think King Valian is punishing us for something? Sending us these nightmares and this sickness?"

Seeing such a big man afraid of such a thing caused me to laugh, but I quickly stopped. Henrik's eyes held no humor. "No, mate. I don't think the sea king is punishing Lewie with this sickness."

Henrik didn't look convinced. "Yes, Captain. But if it's all the same to you, I'd prefer not to go back there, 'less I have to. Last night gave me bad dreams of my own, you see, and I don't need any more darkness around me." He gestured. "I'll stay here and practice my letters."

Since Henrik would be of no use at Lewie's side, anyhow, and educating himself would be a better use of his time, I allowed him to stay. Down in the kitchens I explained to Bishop what was going on and asked him to make a drink from the basil and ginger to serve Lewie now, and both a drink and oil from the rose to give him later.

"Aye, I can do that." He pushed his sleeves up over his

hairy arms and set a small pot over the fire. "I heard the lad up last night with those nightmares. Seems he wasn't the only one to have them. He was the only one to wake up so sick though. Wonder what he did to earn it."

His words stopped me at my exit. "Earn it? Bejabbers, why does everyone aboard this ship think sicknesses are earned?"

Bishop shook his head. "The sea king must be punishing him for something. No one goes to bed fine and wakes up that sick. It's not natural, I tell ya." He continued working, but when I didn't reply, he peeked up at me. "Ye don't agree?"

"Nay. A fabled pirate king doesn't have control over anything that happens on this ship, and neither does that dark vessel that follows us."

"As you say, Captain." Bishop shrugged. "Here's the basil and ginger drink. He won't like it, but make him drink it all. I'll send up the rose medicines later."

"Very good, thank you."

Ontario stayed by Lewie's side while the rest of the crew wandered off to do their chores. I knelt by the boy's bed and raised the glass to his trembling lips. "Drink."

He hardly opened his eyes as he sipped the liquid. His face scrunched, but he made no complaint. When he was done, he settled back into the pillow, and I pulled the blankets to his chin.

I turned to Ontario and kept my voice low. "Do we know what it is?"

Ontario draped the rag over the boy's head and sighed. "Not yet. There's not enough information to guess."

"You don't think it's King Valian, do you?"

To my relief, Ontario grinned. "Nay, but I know some of the shipmates do." The grin fell. "Though I rather hope the king is real."

I gave him a look. His face was somber. "He's going to

need someone to pray to. Because whatever ails him, it doesn't look good."

Ontario stayed by Lewie's side while I went above deck to checked on Emric. He held the wheel with pride as we continued out of the Seas of Lost Lands. The winds favored us today, and we made good distance. I could only guess how close Landon was to the treasure at this point, but if we continued to sail at this speed, we might catch him. With all my might I wished he'd run into trouble along the way to slow him down.

"Everything going smoothly here?"

"If you've come to take back your wheel, you can't have it," Emric told me with a glint in his eye.

"You can steer all day," I assured him. "I ought to rest. But there's something we need to figure out first. Call Emme down from the crow's nest, and I'll round up the men."

Emme had risen early and crawled into the lookout, where she had stayed all morning, scanning the seas diligently. There was something odd in how she watched, she kept her eyes fixated not on the horizon but on the water right below the boat. The keel of the boat was barely visible, but she pressed against the rails and gazed intently at the endless waves.

"Has she been like that the entire time?" I asked Emric.

He glanced at Emme and nodded. "Something's gotten into her. I think the story of Mother from yesterday messed with her head. She'll be all right."

Hmm. I'd speak with her later to be certain she fared well. For now, we had an important decision to make, and I quite needed us to make the right one. I called the men who weren't busy tending to Lewie up to the deck. Most of them were below the helm gossiping about what Lewie could have done to deserve this sickness before I cleared my throat.

"At this point we are two to three weeks away from reaching the Island of Iilak and the treasure. But, as we have discovered, another sails before us with intentions of taking our loot. Because of this we've already decided to not fetch the weapon we planned to trade for. Now, there is a shortcut we can take, around the Disappearing Islands through the Sea of Valor. It'll save us a week's travel."

The men looked at each other and nodded. "Aye, let's do that." A bit of good news for the rough day, they no doubt thought. Before I could say more, Emric shook his head and spoke up from the wheel at my side. "No." He looked at me as if I were crazy, and his grip tightened over the spokes. "Do you know of those waters?"

"I was getting to that," I raised my voice. "There's something to be known about that sea. Only the truest hearts may sail through. Any others—if any corrupted or untrue souls sail among us—we won't be granted passage. Our boat will get lost in those waters, and we will never be heard from again. So I ask you: which way do you wish to go? Test our luck on the Sea of Valor, or take the safer route?"

They blinked, each uncomfortable in their own way. Some looking to the floor, some pulling at their hats, some sucking on their lips. It was almost comical to watch them, none wanting to claim to be impure of heart, but none confident enough to go through the sea.

The comments began.

"Erm, let's not be rash here."

"Perhaps safety is best."

"You can never be too sure."

"Wouldn't want to risk anything."

"We are pirates, after all."

I held back a smile with difficulty. "So it's agreed then? We stick to the route and avoid the Sea of Valor?"

"Aye!"

"Thank you, that is all." They dispersed, and Emme headed back to the crow's nest.

Emric snorted. "You couldn't truly have been willing to go through the Sea of Valor, could you? You're dafter that I thought."

Ignoring the insult, I placed a hand on Emric's shoulder. "Certainly not. Here is your first lesson if you're to be a captain one day. Always make the crew feel like they are in charge. I had no intention of going through those waters, but if they learned there was a shortcut and we didn't take it, they wouldn't care why. They'd only care that they didn't get a voice. Always keep the crew happy."

He nodded. "I'll remember that. Thank you, Captain."

Perhaps I'd judged Emric too soon. He and I might get along nicely someday.

"Why didn't *you* want to go through?" he asked as I climbed down the stairs.

"What?"

"What secrets do you harbor that make your soul unworthy of passing through those waters?"

His question startled me. His gaze flickered from the sea to me as if to see how honest I would be. There were many reasons I had for not being worthy: the men I'd killed as I left the king's navy, the men I killed in battles as a pirate, the items I'd stolen, and the secrets I was keeping from my crew concerning Admiral Bones. Plus there were the sins I planned to commit: stealing the treasure and using it to pay my debts to Admiral Bones and for Emme, instead of paying the crew or Emric.

The Sea of Valor had many reasons not to accept me. I merely shrugged at Emric and said, "I am a pirate, after all." And left it at that.

He accepted my answer with a smirk, and I went to check on Emme.

She stood in the small crow's nest with her arms wrapped

around her. Her father's scarlet ribbon held back her hair, but the wind up here had pulled a few strands loose that whipped around her face. She heeded them no mind as she kept her eyes to the sea. "If you're here to relieve me of my post, I am fine."

"You are the most diligent lookout I've ever had." I stood beside her. Our arms grazed each other, but she kept her eyes forward. "Are you all right?"

"I'm fine," she told me. But she didn't look fine. Now close to her, I saw the creases in her brow and the sunken skin beneath her eyes. She looked exhausted.

"Have you been sleeping well?"

Her mouth formed a straight line as she glanced at me for the first time, revealing the tears in her eyes. My hand reached for hers. "What's wrong?"

She not only kept her hand in mine but moved in closer to me.

"I saw her last night. My mother."

If there was a proper response to that, I didn't know it. My own mother died when I was young, and my father raised me with love, leaving me uncertain how to talk about Emme's mother who loved the sea more than she loved her daughter. There was a deep pain here that she tried to keep hidden, and I didn't know how to address it. So instead I wrapped my arms around her and pulled her to my chest.

"I'm sorry. Do such dreams come often?"

"That's not what I meant." She pulled back slightly. "I mean I saw her. On the boat. She was here."

Again, the proper response was lost on me. There was nothing I could say to that. She was seeing visions, just like Henrik.

With gentleness, I reminded her, "Emme, your mother is dead."

Emme retreated. "I know that," she said impatiently. "But she was here. She was here. She was on deck wearing a dress, and there was an eel and all this water, and she was here, Arn. She was here, and she wanted me to go with her."

The intent of the black ship was clear—to kill us off by haunting our minds. It sent visions of Emme's mother to her, calling her into the waters. Had Emme obeyed, had she stepped off the quarterdeck and into the deep, she'd have drowned. Just like that, gone because of a vision that wasn't real. Luckily, the black ship hadn't accounted for the fact that Emme didn't love her mother enough to follow her anywhere. But it might try again.

I was now more concerned about Emme than I was about Henrik or Lewie. I drew her into me again to check her temperature against my cheek, but she pushed away. "You don't believe me."

"I do." I didn't, but that felt like the right answer. "I believe that you saw her. Where exactly was she?"

Emme sounded defiant. "She called me from my room, and we stood right there and spoke."

I looked to where she was pointing.

I'd guessed too soon. Perhaps the black ship wasn't meaning to drown her by sending that vision, because while Emme claimed to have come above deck, I knew that couldn't be true.

Matters like this must be dealt with carefully. "Emme, whatever happened last night, you didn't come to the deck. I was awake all night at the wheel, and there was no one with me."

Her eyes widened and searched mine, and whatever she found left her looking more confused than before. She buried her head into her hands. "I don't understand. It was so real. It was so real!" she repeated.

"I know. But it's over now, Emme. Your mother is gone."

With hesitation, she nodded and looked back to the sea. But a moment later her eyes grew panicked, and she gave a startled cry. My hand grasped hers again, and she squeezed back. Then she turned her head to me.

"Can you hear? It's her. She's calling me again."

19

EMME

My mother's voice drifted against the back of my neck, bringing the smell of the sea with her. I gripped Arn's hand tighter as I swiveled my head to look behind me. His familiar scent of books and rum masked the awful smell of the sea.

"I'm right here. You're safe."

My eyes must have looked feral, because his held an ocean's worth of concern.

He spoke again but his words sounded distant to my ears, and beneath the warmth of his touch, a chill spread across my skin. A feeling settled in the air, the sense of something dark coming that I couldn't avoid, something terrible and hopeless.

Suddenly Arn vanished. My hand reached to the air where he had just been.

It was empty.

The sea fell quiet, and a gloomy veil settled over the ship. Emric was no longer at the wheel; it turned as if controlled by a ghost. Percival wasn't sweeping the deck, and Henrik wasn't sitting with a book. As far as my eye could see, I was alone.

This isn't real, I told myself. It's just a dream.

A sound broke through the silence, the turning of waves beneath a hull. A boat drifted near. Not just any boat, but the devil's ship. Though it was still at a distance, I heard the crack of sails as if I were aboard and the turn of oars as if I pulled them.

He came toward me, the nameless sailor on the black ship. He wore a long silver garment with a hood that covered the darkness of his face. As the ship came nearer, a foul smell punctured the air.

Death. The ship brought a sense of death with it.

Eventually I could feel arms closed around me, shaking me back and forth. "Emme, what's happening?"

Arn's voice brought me back to reality, and the black ship disappeared.

"Stars, Emme. What was that?"

I blinked a few times as I struggled to make sense of what had just happened. Another vision? This one had nothing to do with my mother. Was it warning me of something? That my presence on this ship would only bring death? Even though the illusion was gone, the weighted feeling stayed with me like a pendant around my neck, holding me down until it felt like I couldn't move, couldn't breathe.

"Something bad is going to happen," I managed to tell Arn. "I shouldn't be on this ship."

Arn held me closer. "I swear on my life and my mother's grave, I won't let anything happen to you. You are safe with me."

It was a promise he couldn't make. He was a pirate; this life was filled with uncertainty. But I took hold of his words and strained to find some comfort in them. Anything to keep from drowning in my fears.

"Come, I have herbs to keep you from evil spirits." He turned me toward the ladder. He descended first, keeping a hand up and careful eye on me.

I never should have set sail with Arn. The seas bring nothing but destruction. My last few months of life should have been spent on dry land where safety was certain. Dying to the illness would have been better than living on this ship with whatever horrors awaited this cursed crew.

Arn brought me to the cabin where he rummaged through shelves to find the right herbs. "This one wards off nightmares, but what you just had wasn't during sleep. Let's try parsley. Here." He sprinkled some of the green herb into a small cloth and rolled it until it was a tight sphere, then tied the top shut with long twine. He knelt before me. "It must be worn around your ankle. May I?"

I nodded. "Thank you. I hope this works."

He lifted my pant leg and fasted the orb to my ankle. "I hope so as well. Emme, may I ask about the vision? Was it your mother again?"

My eyes closed as the memory replayed in my mind. "No, this was different. It was cold and dark. The *Royal Rose* sat empty on the waters, and the black ship sailed toward me. There was something about it, it's hard to explain, but I felt death. My death or someone else's, I can't be certain, but death was in the air. Then you spoke, and it all vanished."

Worry was etched on Arn's face. "And you're certain it was the black ship?"

"Aye, what else would it have been?"

His eyes skirted away. "I'm not sure. This must be what Pearl meant when she said the ship was haunting her. Let's pray she found peace on that island. We'd better make these enchantments for each of the crew members to keep nightmares away from us all."

"I'll help. It'll keep my mind from wandering."

Arn set out the parsley, and we got to work folding it in pieces of cloth that the crew could fasten around their legs. My own hit against my ankle as I moved and was terribly uncomfortable, but if there was a chance it would ward off these nightmares, then I'd never take it off.

A trail of wind came through the porthole to shiver across

my neck, and I dropped the parsley. But it wasn't a vision. It wasn't her voice. It was only the wind. Arn pretended not to notice my fright, which was kind of him. "Sorry, I'm just a bit on edge," I said as I scooped up the herbs.

"It's understandable." He helped me gather the parsley and pour it back into the jar.

Instead of returning to his work, Arn wrapped his strong arms around me again. We stood without saying anything, and his warmth filled the parts of me that felt afraid. I told myself that the visions weren't real, but this was. Arn was real. He was here. I was safe.

His head pulled back but remained close enough that his breath tickled my nose.

"I don't know how much this means to you," he started, "but I'm here for you. For as long as you'll have me, I'll be here for you."

His words brought a deep comfort. For a moment it felt as if everything would be all right. We'd find this treasure. I'd get the Elmber Nut. This black ship would leave us alone. With Arn's assurance came a solace that I craved more than words could say, and I smiled at him.

"It means a lot to me. It truly does."

His face brightened and inched toward mine. Slowly, gently, he dipped toward me. My breath caught in my throat. What would those lips feel like on mine? Would they wash away the rest of my fears and leave me with nothing but happiness?

What does a kiss feel like?

I didn't find out. His body hesitated, and his beautiful blue eyes searched mine. Then he squeezed my arms and turned back to the table, leaving me to guess if he wanted the moment as I did. Perhaps it was nothing but the rock of the boat that led me to believe he'd bent toward me, tricking my heart. The fear of the visions had dug a well within me that longed for some beauty to fill it and cast away the darkness. But such feelings were nothing more than foolhearted wishing for something that would never be mine. Arn would never be mine.

It surprised me how much that thought hurt. Where did these feelings come from? I exhaled, letting my built-up emotions escape with my breath.

"Have you ever been around death before?" Arn asked me, voice casual. I knew his heart wasn't conflicted as mine.

I attempted to mimic his eased tone. "Yes. Once. My father. He passed in his sleep, and we buried him that afternoon."

It'd been an emotional day when I lost my father, but a peaceful one. He was ready to join our mother in whatever afterlife awaited him, and he'd fought a hard battle with his disease. Emric and I cared for the farm as long as we could before our inexperience couldn't keep it afloat anymore and we had to sell for a low price. It was just enough money to get us to Bart's home, where he took us in. He'd been like a brother to our parents and became a father to us. He made it easy to forget that we were orphans.

Arn knew something about loss; his own mother was dead. But he had a loving father still alive. His life wasn't marked by death as mine was. First the death of my mother. Then the death of my father. Soon my own death.

"Death is not a pleasant thing to be around."

"Nay, it's not," Arn agreed as he tied another anklet of parsley closed. The tone in his voice caused me to glance up, it was riddled with familiarity and sorrow. If I wasn't mistaken, a tinge of regret as well.

"Have you been around much death as a pirate?" Pirates encountered many seafaring battles, but Arn had not spoken about such things with me. It was a fact that I appreciated, but it made me curious. What manner of violence had his cutlass seen? Was his time as a pirate more gruesome than his time in the king's navy?

Arn slowly set the parsley down and raised his head. "I

have." His voice was flat, and his cheek twitched in thought. He said no more than that.

A new thought came to mind, one darker than before. Had Arn caused death?

The picture of Arn standing over a body, driving his cutlass into the flesh and tearing the heart out was a painful one, but now that the idea planted itself in my mind, it proved impossible to shake.

"Arn?" I had to ask. "You've killed before, haven't you?" He kept his mouth clamped shut and picked up some more parsley.

"Arn? Have you killed someone before?" I pressed.

His lips drew tight, he glanced at me, and his eyes told me the answer.

"You know I have. That's how we met."

I'd never forget that chilled night with the clouds so low they touched the ground and blanketed the port in a heavy mist. A man had asked me to help his elderly father inside, but I'd found no man waiting outside. Instead, he dragged me down to the pier. He had drawn out his pistol. Then his eyes went wide, his body lurched, and his blood dripped onto me. Arn stood behind him looking handsome in his navy outfit as he saved me from certain death.

"I remember. But how many others have you killed, Arn?"

Silence met me. His lips were a trap door, slammed shut and angled down while his eyes closed.

"Five?" I asked. "Ten?" What started as a curiosity was beginning to worry at me.

Again, silence.

My knees shook a bit, though it might have been pain from standing too long. I couldn't bring myself to move, even to give my weak body relief. I stayed planted in that place staring at the man I thought I knew. "More? A hundred? Arn, how often do you kill?"

His eyelids slowly opened to reveal blue eyes as dark as a stormy sea. "I don't keep count. Many." He kept his gaze on me as the air between us thickened and my stomach clenched. As I stood in disbelief, Arn's shoulders rose, then fell again. "I'm a pirate."

That was all it took, that one moment, for Arn to transform into someone else. When Arn informed me he'd given up his life in the navy and become a pirate, I thought that was the end of our friendship, but he quickly proved himself to be different from the other pirates that came through our port. He was smart. He was kind. He was sensible. He didn't bring a new lady with him every time. And his cutlass never had dried blood upon it.

I always believed that though Arn was a pirate, but he wasn't cutthroat. He didn't cut throats.

But was that all a façade for me? Did he keep parts of himself hidden that he didn't think I'd like? Was the person I cared for one that didn't exist?

I wasn't bothered that he'd killed a few. Piracy wasn't for the feeble. But by the stars, I'd truly believed Arn was different. Softer. More compassionate. The kind who would avoid killing as much as possible.

He sighed with his whole body and shook his head, letting some of his blonde waves fall by his downcast eyes. "What do you want to hear? That I'm sorry?"

That might help a little.

"Emme, this is my life. I steal. I lie. And when it comes to it, I kill. But I can assure you it's never my first course of action, nor my second. Only when it's needed—when there's no other reasonable path—will I load my pistol."

I stayed quiet. In my confusion, words only failed me.

"Emme, please say something."

All I seemed capable of doing was picturing Arn killing. He was a weapon in nothing but skin.

"You know I'd never hurt you, right? I'm not like that."

He tried to approach me, but I held up my hand. Ironic how a few minutes ago I wanted him closer than he'd ever been before, and now I didn't want him to touch me.

His shoulders slumped. "I don't care for killing. But you asked. I have done it, and you know it."

I had no right to be surprised by this information. As I sorted my feelings, they showed me what hurt the most, and I had to admit to myself it really wasn't anything Arn had done or not done. Something else gnawed on my bones.

A week ago, I wanted this. As we listened to the mermaids' song and watched the stars kiss the sky, I fell in love with the sea. I fell in love with this crew. I thought, if I could get the healing nut and stay alive, I could live with them forever.

I thought I could be a pirate. I'd allowed those ideas to frolic in my heart, tempting me.

The Fates punished me for my thoughts, because then I was kidnapped. Then haunted. And now I was reminded of what a pirate really is. Someone who kills. Someone who wasn't afraid to lie and steal and trample those around them. My foolish heart had almost believed in the allure of this life, while forgetting the wicked.

I couldn't be upset with Arn for being who he was. But I could be livid with myself for forgetting who I was.

Arn leaned forward, his eyes questioning me. He wanted me to say more, maybe to say it was okay. But those words wouldn't come. We stood in the cabin staring at each other when Ontario appeared in the doorway.

"Captain? Lewie has gotten worse. You'd better come."

Arn gave one last helpless look to me, but I lowered my head and said, "Go. I'll finish these." After a moment, he left me alone with my conflicted thoughts as he cared for our sick mate.

20
ARN

The look in Emme's eyes was not one I'd easily forget. Like I'd physically hurt her. I might as well have taken my cutlass out and run it through my own chest, because that's how badly it hurt to see her so upset.

Before today, she'd been coming around to life on the water, and I wasn't the only one to presume so. Many of the crew members mentioned how natural she looked on the ship, and how comfortable she appeared. Emme no longer clung to the rails or looked ready to hurl when the violent waves circled us. She'd developed good legs for the sea and could verbally hold her own with any of the crew.

She was slowly becoming a good and proper pirate.

I hadn't missed when she said "aye" earlier. Even our dialect was becoming common on her tongue.

But that cursed ship came and threatened to ruin everything. The way it haunted her mind would do nothing but further reinstate her resolve against pirates until she begged to leave the ship. Leave me. The light in her eyes was already beginning to fade away like a candle being blown out, not even a flicker left to revive.

A bit like the way Lewie looked now. The poor chap was getting worse, and it'd only been a day. His hair was drenched in sweat, and he shook dreadfully. He kept muttering undistinguishable words. Ontario and I exchanged glances.

"How is he getting worse so fast?" I asked.

Ontario drew his finger along the crease behind his ear in thought. "Wish I knew, Captain. It's not looking good for the lad."

He had the decency to keep his voice down, but I doubted Lewie could hear us even if we yelled. He was here, but he wasn't.

Ontario looked to me for orders.

"We'll have to dock somewhere for more medicine," I said. "I don't have the supplies here to heal him at this point. There's an island we should be coming upon within the next few days that might carry a plant to possibly help him."

"Might?" Ontario asked.

"I can't promise anything. But at least we can get him more water." My hand brushed over the boy's burning forehead. He didn't react to my touch.

Lewie was the only crew member aboard that I had paid for, though it wasn't as savage of a tale as that made it sound. He was born aboard a ship and worked alongside his father until the age of twelve, when his mother died and his father stole loot and abandoned crew, leaving his son behind. The remaining pirates were prepared to kill Lewie when I came upon them at port, and I managed a low price for him instead. It took a year of being on board for him to finally speak more than a sentence, but he'd been welcomed into our family since the first day.

He was fifteen now, and far too young to die.

A crew member of mine had never died aboard my ship. I wouldn't let young Lewie be the first.

"We'll head straight to that island and get more herbs. Just keep him alive for three days. That's all I need."

Lewie went into a coughing fit, and Ontario knelt beside

him to soothe him through it. He nodded up to me. "All right. But hurry."

I thought the idea of docking would appeal to Emme, but she didn't react when I gave the news to the crew that we needed to stop soon. The rest of the crew wasn't thrilled with the prospect, each set on making haste for the treasure, but they quieted their complaints when I mentioned it was for Lewie.

Lewie wouldn't survive the trip to the Island of Iilak without medicine. I shut myself in the cabin and researched herbs that might be on He'tu.

By the time the sun rose two days later, the island of He'tu was upon us, and Lewie's forehead was as hot as a fire.

I distributed among the crew several pictures of herbs to collect, and we left Ontario, Bishop, and Lewie on the *Royal Rose* and set out to find a miracle.

From the dark circles under Emme's eyes, she'd slept poorly, but she gave me little more than two words when asked how she fared. Emric watched us interact with keen interest. "Bit of trouble, eh?"

"Get in the boat, Emric." I held the rope for him to slide down into the rowboats, and he chuckled.

He gripped the ropes but chose to stroke his beard instead of descending. This habit of his to stroke his chin seemed only to surface in my presence, leading me to believe it was a subtle way of reminding me what I didn't have. "Out of curiosity, if she gets mad enough to kill ye, who gets this nice ol' boat of yours?"

"Ontario." I pointed below. "Down."

"And say he dies?"

My hands went to my hips atop my cutlass and pistol. "Emric, are you planning on killing my first mate?"

He waved his hand. "Nay, wouldn't think of it. Just

wondering who needs to die before I get this fine vessel." He patted the oak rails.

I humored him. "If I die, and Ontario, and Percival, then you may have the *Royal Rose*. But if we all die within the same week, then ye can't have it, because it'd likely be you who ran us through."

He grinned. "That's all I needed to know. Now come on, we best not dally." With a salute, he grabbed hold of the ropes and swung down. I followed him, and we paddled toward He'tu.

To call He'tu an island was to call a whale a fish. It stretched as far as we could see in either direction, mimicking a country more than an island. Like the other islands nearby, it was uninhabited by civil folks, but none could say it was free of other roaming creatures. We'd be on high alert.

Beige beaches met us as we dragged the boats on the shore. Beyond the sand loomed heavy forests filled with an eerie silence and distant mountains marking where we needed to go. Everything sat so still that we could almost hear the waves crawl up the sand and litter tiny shells before cascading back down the slope.

Get the herbs and be back by nightfall. It should be simple.

"All right men, you know the plan. Half will go that direction." I pointed toward the closest mountains. "The rest of us will seek these plants on the other side of the hills."

"Last one to make it back must swab the decks for an entire month," Percival declared.

"Ayes" met the challenge, and the others headed into the forest. They kept their hands on their cutlasses and moved with stealthy feet, prepared for whatever may jump out at them from the thick trees. From the silence around us, it seemed we were the only ones on the island.

Silence was not to be trusted.

I stood with the second group among Emric, Emme, Bo, and Collins, but before we began, Emme placed a hand on her brother's arm. "I think I ought to return to the ship," she said in a soft voice.

"And miss all the fun? We could have a real adventure here." His bright eyes scanned the island hungrily.

"It's just that . . ." She paused, peeking at me. Her glance made it too obvious that I was the reason she preferred to remain on the *Royal Rose,* and I tried to control the disappointment that gripped my chest. "I hadn't realized how far we'd have to travel to get the herbs, and I'm quite tired today."

With a nudge I directed Bo and Collins onward while I stepped over to Emric and Emme.

"You're a better fighter than most of the crew—we may need you," I said to her.

She held the end of her braid in her hands, and her mouth twitched. She only did that when she was uncomfortable, and I hoped it wasn't my presence making her so. "I'm only half as strong as the men and have spent the last few years working in a tavern, not fighting at sea like them. I wouldn't be much help in a fight, certainly wouldn't be capable of killing anyone."

Emric scoffed. "These baboons haven't been taught to fight from the age of two. You have. Your instincts are better than any of theirs, and your reflexes are incredible. If caught in a troublesome situation, I want a pirate like you at my side."

Her brow drew down at his words. I cleared my throat. "Is it me?"

Emric's eyes shifted in understanding. "I'll leave you to this," he said as he backed away. Emme was still a moment before she turned to me.

I searched face, but it held like a fortress against my gaze. "Have the nightmares been wearing on you, or are you still mad at me?"

Those eyes looked into mine with such familiarity that for a moment it felt as if nothing had transpired between us. I was back to the carefree swashbuckler who wandered into her tavern at various times, and she was the smart girl with the kind smile.

"I'm not mad at you, Arn." Her words brought an ocean of relief to me, but she wasn't finished. "I'm mad at myself. Furious, honestly. I've been forgetting who I am and who I ought to be. I shouldn't be getting swept away in all this."

"Who you ought to be?"

A breeze came from the hills and swept her braid behind her back. She turned her head and studied the *Royal Rose* floating in the distance. "I'm the girl who raises sheep inland, not one who sails with pirates, fights Nimnulas, and gets captured by rogue men on islands. All of this has caused me to lose focus on what I'm meant to do." She turned back to me. "Speaking with you the other day reminded me of why I shouldn't trust pirates and why I can't allow myself to become one."

I said nothing, trying to comprehend her frustrations. Her hand flickered my direction before it dropped. "I'm not mad you've killed people. I'm mad I was ignoring it was part of the pirate life. That's a life I don't want."

It began to make sense now. "Do you not want to be a pirate because you hated them as a girl, or because after sailing with us you are now confident this isn't what you want?" Though it seemed apparent what she'd say, I waited on my toes for her answer.

She twisted and fidgeted with her belt, her focus everywhere but directly on me. "This isn't what I want."

I bit back my tongue. Why did my stubborn heart always fall for the lass who didn't want a life with me? Here I yearned for Emme when she cared so little about that part of me which made her pull back in disappointment. Or was it revulsion? "There then," I spoke casually, quite different than the way I felt. "That's it. You say you don't want to be a pirate, so don't be one. We'll get this treasure, and you can have your sheep farm. None of the crew is asking any more from you, and I don't need to keep hearing you say you don't want a life here with me. I believe you." My words tumbled out harsher than intended, and she recoiled.

"I mean you no harm."

I chided myself. "I know, Emme. Look, the other men are already up there. Are you coming with us or not?"

She cast a weary look to where Emric, Bo, and Collins stood waiting at the foot of the hills. "No, I need rest."

"Fine. I'll see you when we get back."

"Arn—"

"I have to go, Emme." I turned and strode across the sand to where the men waited. I didn't look back.

Emric was staring into the woods upon my arrival. The trees cast a shadow over his face as he spoke. "We best be off. There's something wrong about this place."

21
EMME

As Arn walked away, my heart bled after him.

How could I explain to him what I could hardly make sense of myself? Though necessary to save my life, I'd expected to hate every aspect of this voyage. The harsh waves, the pungent smells, the crass pirates, the similarities to Mother's life—these were all things I despised.

Everything that made me think of *her*, I loathed.

But the sour taste in my mouth sweetened with each day aboard the *Royal Rose*, until moments came when I forgot what I was meant to be hating.

Am I foolish for clinging to this aversion? What would happen if I let my anger go? Was I even capable of such a feat?

"She hurt you, but you need to cast it away," I told myself. I breathed out. I closed my eyes and focused on the word *forgive* as light waves lapped against the leather of my boots. Forgive. A breeze swept by, and I tried to cast my anger within so it would be taken from me, but the breeze was not strong enough to carry my resentment away. Or I was not strong enough to let go.

"You cannot be free of me." My mother's voice made my eyes open. It was an unwelcome sound in my moment of

self-reflection. Would I never be free of her? "You are meant
to join me. Throw yourself into the waters. Let me in."

Though her voice came to me, an image of her did not. I
closed my eyes again. "Go away."

Her crackling laugh paraded through my mind. "Dear
child. You can never be rid of me. You are me." She laughed
again, but the sound grew quieter until the waves could be
heard once more, and her presence drifted away.

I would not be my mother. I would not be a pirate.

Foolish girl. Find the healing nut and be rid of these pirate
fantasies.

Beware the call to the waters. You do not belong here.

The waters whispered to me, reminding me of what my
mother wanted me to forget. This battle might continue to
rage within me during my time with Arn since he might be the
only one who could make me reconsider my distaste for the
sea. When I returned home, the desire would surely go away,
and I'd be free of my mother. This was a hope I could cling to.

He and my brother had vanished from my sight into the
rolling hills of the island. I'd not be able to make it halfway
to the plants before the disease slowed me down, and Emric
would certainly notice something was wrong. As it was,
it would be a struggle to row back to the ship by myself. It
did pain me that Arn mistook my desire to keep my sickness
hidden as not wanting to be near him, but he had a kind soul,
and I hoped he could forgive me if I moved inland and never
saw him again once this was over.

I decided once back onboard, I'd polish the helm of the
ship for Arn. That would cheer him up.

Before I took a step toward the rowboats, a cry came from
behind me.

My body stilled.

It came again, a drawn-out cry that spread through the
land mist and settled in the trees.

The voice was unmistakably female. We were not alone on this island.

My mother had taught Emric and me to recognize a variety of creature sounds and calls. I recognized this one. This particular creature would always call out a warning sign before hunting its prey, as if to give a head start on surviving. It was all a game; she always caught her target. She had a distinctive call, one that Mother claimed to imitate perfectly. Two low pitches followed by a high tweet.

The call of the Huntress. A tall, thin, womanlike being that moved stealthily through the trees and killed with the venom in her left claws.

The cry came again. Two low notes followed by a high one.

It was as if hearing my mother's voice in the air. She was right, she did imitate it perfectly.

The Huntress was on the move.

My blood turned cold as I realized what that meant. She was hunting my crewmates.

Emric would recognize the call. Mother taught us a sure way to defeat them, and he'd know how to keep the others safe. But the group that went to the side of the mountain wouldn't know that they were being hunted.

If I didn't warn them, they'd be dead before tomorrow's light.

The thought surged strength to my legs, and I took off through the sand and into the thick of the trees.

Soft dirt sank beneath each step, while overgrown plants grabbed at my ankles and branches whipped my arms. Moisture clung to the air in a way that made it feel hotter than it was, and before long, my face dripped in sweat.

My lungs heaved with such intensity that I feared they'd give out at any moment. Curse this blasted disease. A child could run faster than I did now. Each step wobbled, and I grasped at branches to brace myself.

"Zander, Percival!" I cried into the thick trees in hopes they could hear me. "Svid!" One by one I shouted their names.

No reply came, and I trudged deeper into the misty forest. My feet faltered, and I fell onto my face. I hadn't the energy to get up immediately. The taste of dirt filled my mouth as I gasped for breath.

If I couldn't get to them in time, perhaps I could beckon the Huntress to my scent and save the crew that way. I'd be an easy target for her. I struggled to my knees and called out for them again.

From the side came a soft rustling among the thick trees. I barely had time to turn my head before a lithe figure barreled into me. Blast, I should have drawn my dagger sooner. Her hands slammed down on mine, and her weight crushed against me. Two slender eyes stared at me from behind a narrow nose, and short blonde hair tickled my cheeks.

This wasn't the Huntress. She tilted her head as she examined me, sniffing my scent.

Questions swarmed my mind, but the one that stumbled out was, "What are you doing?"

"Saving your life," she said. Then she hit me so hard that light began to fade, until darkness overtook it, and I passed out in the middle of the forest.

My senses returned slowly, the first being smell. Cinnamon. I hadn't smelled such a scent in months. It prompted my eyes to open, while my mind struggled to make sense of what was happening.

A roof made of branches and tall grass and bark woven together stood above my head, and a bed of dirt beneath me. Neither gave off a cinnamon smell, so my eyes moved on. The structure, while obviously lacking for materials, was large—tall enough to stand in, and separating two ways to other rooms.

A figure moved in one of the rooms, and I gradually remembered what had happened. I drew to my feet and felt for my dagger at my waist, but it was gone. As the girl stood with her back to me, I took the opportunity to check my dagger in the back of my pants.

Arn was right, people truly never checked there.

I slid the dagger out and tiptoed toward the girl. She wore tight leather pants with a wool tunic over top and had light blonde hair that swept against the tops of her shoulders. Pieces of twine held together a few small braids on one side. The most interesting part of her appearance was the tattoos that covered almost every inch of her skin. Her elbows, her heels, the side of her neck. Her face was the only thing untouched.

Despite her rough exterior, she didn't appear terribly strong. I could knock her out and run.

"Not the proper way to thank your host, now is it?" The girl looked over her shoulder with a little smile. "I mean you no harm, you can put that away." She turned about with rolls in her hands. "Fresh off the fire. Please, come sit."

"You have a funny way of not meaning harm." I touched the tender patch by my temple.

"Would you have quieted if I asked?" She didn't wait for an answer. "I saved you from an unpleasant death. Now sit." She motioned toward a log rolled against the back wall. A few pillows were tied around the wood to make the seat comfortable, and a vibrant cloth hung behind it. I lowered my dagger without sheathing it as the girl handed me the cinnamon bread. Her eyes stayed firmly on me, and her hands didn't waver. She wasn't afraid of me, and she wanted me to know it.

Perhaps she was stronger than I guessed. I put away my weapon. Despite my mixture of frustration and curiosity, I only had one thought on my mind.

"I have to go, if you haven't ruined things already." I dug

my heel into the soft dirt and made for the door. The Huntress took her time tracking her prey, prone to play tricks on them before capturing them. If I was lucky, she still toyed with the men and hadn't taken them yet. The Huntress would drag her prey back to her lair where she prepared dinner in front of them before killing them as the main course.

The sun was several hours past where it had been before I'd been knocked out. I'd lost too much time.

"You shouldn't go out there alone. A Huntress roams these woods. She got close to you already, but she won't bother you if you stay with me. We have an agreement of sorts." The girl set the rest of the cinnamon bread down.

"It was the Huntress I was after."

The girl snorted. "I've only seen one person kill a Huntress. You'd best either stay with me or leave the island. Eat the bread before it gets cold."

The way she spoke indicated she cared little for this place, but the detail she'd put into creating this home told a different story. "Do you live here?" I asked as I took some of the bread and scoffed it down as fast as I could, stealing glances outside.

"Not by choice. Banishment holds me here."

I looked at her, alarmed. "Banishment for what crime?"

She gave a half smile. "Falling in love with the wrong person. A prince of the merfolk. He loved me, too, but his arranged marriage kept us from wedding. His bride-to-be wanted me dead, so he stripped me of my fins and banished me here to keep me alive. I can't touch the waters, or they'll know."

I listened, riveted as I swallowed the last of the bread. She turned her face away. "He sends provisions from time to time to make my stay comfortable and has ordered the Huntress not to touch me. If you stay with me, she might spare you too."

With her curvy hips and entrancing eyes, it was no wonder a prince fell in love with her, but there was no time to feel sorry for her. "I have a crew here on this island that I need to save."

Her skin paled. "You have friends here?"

Just as I was about to answer, the Huntress's cry rang again through the air. Four high-pitched calls.

The girl looked across the trees. "Ahh, so she's caught another one."

No. I spun around. "That's her victory sound! She has them. I have to find her."

With surprising speed, the girl grabbed my arms before I could run out. "Wait, you'll never save them on your own." I tried to pull my arms from her grip, but she held me fast. "Please, let me help."

"Help?" I was nearly frantic.

"I know where the Huntress lives. I can escort you there."

I stilled and she loosened her hold on my arms. The remains of the Huntress's call still echoed through the forest from the direction of the hills where Emric and Arn had wandered. That shouldn't be right. My mouth felt dry. "You said she caught another one."

"Aye. She gave that first cry shortly after I saved you. How many friends traveled here in your company?"

My legs felt wobbly beneath me. "Several. They were in two groups."

The girl's tongue clicked. "Unless there's other lost souls on this island, she has both groups. So sharpen your blade, girl, because if we want to save them, there isn't time to waste." She plunked down her bread and tightened her belt.

Blindly trusting this mysterious girl to help save my friends made my stomach knot, but she was right. We had but a few hours before the sun set, and then the Huntress would feed.

I stuck out my hand for her to seal the agreement. "Fine. Take me to her lair."

"Not so fast." There was a gleam in her eye. "Before I help you, I need something in return."

What could she possibly need that I could offer her?

"Oathbind yourself to me. Or else I don't help you, and your friends die."

I stepped back. "You're insane." I turned to leave.

Only fools oathbind themselves, and only bloody morons oathbind themselves to a stranger. If she asked something I couldn't grant, and I refused to fulfill my oath, the ink in the binding would poison me, and I'd be dead. It was more power than one should have over another being, and I'd not be anyone's puppet.

"I'm not insane," she said. "I'm desperate. And you know you'll never find her lair in time to save them."

I glanced over my shoulder as she titled her head. The thought of oathbinding myself drew a shiver from my spine, but her next words hit me like an ocean's wave.

"What will it be, daughter of Arabella?"

22

ARN

A voice drifted through the air. "Arn, wait. I'm coming."

My heart perked up, and I halted. "Emme? Over here." I tried to see through the tall grasses and meager trees we'd come through, but the rolling hills interfered with my vision.

"Careful mate," Emric warned. "There's something I don't trust about this island."

I pulled from his grasp. "She's not a trap."

Bo and Collins continued slashing through the overgrowth as Emric's narrowed eyes scanned the horizons. "I thought I heard something earlier. The wind is carrying strange sounds. We need to be on guard," he insisted

"Everything all right, Captain?" Bo took a swig from his canteen.

"All's fine. Emme is coming after all."

Emric put an arm in front of me to stop my movement. He stared into the trees. "No. It's been hours. She wouldn't be coming now."

I pushed his arm away as I listened for Emme. Her voice called out, "Arn, help me."

I bolted in its direction as Emric yelled for me to stop. I barely heard him above Emme's screams. The next thing I knew, Emric was slamming his body into mine. We went crashing to the ground, and he quickly maneuvered to hold a knee against my chest. "Think, mate. It's not her."

A new voice spoke. "No. It's not."

Through the dirt in my eye and the buttery sunlight, I squinted past Emric to find a tall, slender woman approaching from behind a crooked tree. Nay, not woman. Beast. This creature had blue scales for skin, iridescent eyes, and legs that stretched longer than the rest of her body. A thin tongue forked from between her lips. "No time for games today, I'm afraid. Dinner waits for us."

I clambered back, giving a swinging glance for Emme, but she wasn't here.

Emric was up on his feet. He lunged at the beast woman while Bo and Collins yanked me up.

The creature didn't move as Emric went for her, pulling a blade from his side to swing at her arm. Metal clashed together. She smiled wickedly. One hand grabbed Emric's, and she raised her forearm to show a plate strapped to it.

"That won't work twice."

Emric collapsed to the ground.

We shouted in surprise. Bo and Collins turned to run as I charged at her.

She snapped her fingers, and ropes from below our feet sprung up, entangling the three of us in a knotted mass of vines, boots, and grunts. Emric's blank eyes stared up.

She glided forward and reached for me, sinking her nails into my hip.

"Sleep, pretty one. You'll be eaten first."

My body stopped its thrashing, my mind slowed, and darkness overtook me. The last thing I heard before I lost conscious was the creature's lyrical voice.

"Now, let's see if we can set a trap for this Emme."

23

EMME

I staggered back. "How do you know who I am?"

I should run. Now. But the devilish grin in the girl's eyes was too tempting to turn away from, and the sound of my mother's name on her tongue stilled my feet.

The girl replied, "You look exactly like her. I knew it the moment I saw you. So, daughter of Arabella, what will it be? Will you let your friends die, or will you oathbind yourself to me?"

"How do you know my mother?" My hands itched for my blade, but I restrained myself.

"I met her. I said I'd only seen one person kill a Huntress. T'was your mother."

My mother had been here? What was she doing so far from the high seas?

I pulled back my shoulders and narrowed my eyes. I put as much strength into my voice as I could and hoped for the best.

"If you knew my mother, then you know to be afraid of me. I won't hesitate to kill you, and I'll easily find the Huntress's lair on my own."

I surprised myself at how much like my mother that sounded.

But it wasn't enough to frighten the girl. She didn't quiver. Instead she stepped back and crossed her arms. "Go ahead and try to find her home. You won't. But what will you do if you locate her? Think you can kill her?" Her eyes looked me up and down.

She was taunting me. "Aye, my mother taught me how to defeat these creatures."

"By slicing their left wrist so they have no poison?" She laughed. "I was with your mother the day she killed the other Huntress that way. Set her on fire and threw her over a cliff. Trust me, it won't work again. That was this Huntress's sister, and she's now well guarded against that move. So, daughter of Arabella, how will you defeat her?"

Blimey. If she was right, that explained how the Huntress was able to capture Emric—the tactic we learned wouldn't work on her. "When were you with my mother?"

"About five years ago. So, daughter of—"

"My name is Emme," I snapped.

She only uncrossed her arms and stuck out a hand to me. "Mine is Sereena. Now, if you want me to lead the way to the Huntress's lair and provide you the method of killing her, all I require is an oathbind. Do we have a deal?"

I stared at her hand like a dangerous puzzle that I had to solve. Choose one way and my crewmates die. Choose the other and I'm bound to a stranger. Either way cost me more than I was willing to give and offered little promise of getting off this island easily.

My mother had many enemies, but a person who considered her a friend was someone I trusted even less. What sort of evil must dwell in your heart to be friends with someone as conniving and ruthless as my mother? How much could I trust the word of such a person?

The sun beat down upon my neck as a reminder that time was passing, and each moment of hesitation could mean the men got killed.

The crew was my first priority. My fleeting life meant little compared to theirs.

I agreed to sell my soul. "Fine. State your claims."

I expected her to once again smirk and get that gleam in her eye, but instead her shoulders relaxed. "A favor. That's all I ask. When I call upon you for a favor, you must say yes."

It sounded too simple. "What sort of favor?"

"The nature of the request, I do not yet know. There are many things I cannot do from this island. You will be my eyes and hands in the world, to be used when I call upon you. One favor, then you'll be free."

"And if I die first, or you?"

"If I die, the ink will fade from your skin, and you'll be free. If you die, then naturally our oathbind is no longer valid. What is your answer? I will show you how to free your friends if you agree to an oathbound favor."

Her hand hung in the air again, and this time I took it.

For Arn's sake, I told myself.

"I, Emme Jaquez Salinda, bind myself to you in this oath, that when you call upon me for a favor, I will obey."

Her hungry eyes watched my mouth utter the words, and as the last syllable left my tongue, a searing pain pierced my foot.

I ripped off my boot and old sock to see the binding etch into my flesh. The charcoal-colored ink swirled along the top of my foot near my biggest toe in a delicate crescent before plunging downward and opening into harsh strokes toward my arch. It traced the design of a crashing wave along the edge of my foot, then curled up as if the waves reached for the stars of the sky near my toes. With flourishes and swirls it marred my foot, leaving me with a dark tattoo that told of my promise to the girl from the sea.

The edge of the tattoo curled up to my heel, barely low enough to be covered by a sock.

It stung sharper than I thought it would, and my foot was hot to the touch as I pulled my stocking back on.

"Let's not waste any time. Tell me how to defeat the Huntress."

Her thick lips pulled back into a smile. "That's the fun part. We will trick her."

"All right. Trickery it is." I tried to push the oathbinding from my mind as I focused on how to free Arn, Emric, and the rest of the crew. They didn't know that I was coming for them and that there was still hope. I could imagine the Huntress now stoking her fire, licking her lips at the sight of humans to feast on. "What's our game?"

Sereena pointed at me. "You are. If there's one thing this Huntress fears, it's Arabella the Ruthless. You pretend to be your mother, and it will scare her enough for us to make a move. We'll have to be quick."

Of course my mother was the only answer out of this. I would never be free of her.

"So I scare her, you slice her neck."

Sereena shook her head. "No. Her skin is too thick. She must burn. Lucky for us, if she's preparing her dinner, she'll have a fire going." Sereena imitated a pushing motion, then the explosion of flames, and my head turned away. She laughed. "What, don't have the stomach for it?"

"I'll be fine," I muttered. "Shall we go?"

She shook her head again. I glared at her in exasperation. "What now?"

"You don't look enough like your mother to fool her. We've got to dress you up first,". Hearing that I didn't look enough like my mother should have brought me solace, but my patience was wearing thin. The sun continued to lower, and the vast island darkened, leaving little time. If we couldn't accomplish this rescue soon, Arn would be dead by tomorrow. Ironic how I've been so worried about my own ticking clock and how he might fare when I die, never thinking he could die first.

"If you think you can dress me up like her, go ahead," I said through gritted teeth. "Then let's be on our way."

"Not your clothes." Her hand waved over my body. "Your skin. Your mother had tattoos, aye?"

My heart stopped as I realized what she meant. "No."

"Then you've oathbound yourself for naught, because we aren't going to fool the Huntress without your mother's iconic tattooing. I don't have paint, but I do have the tools to tattoo. You may pick your own designs, but there must be some."

I wanted to flee and leave her there. But my mind told me, *for Arn.* "How long would it take?"

"I have mermaid tools. It'll be done in a few minutes."

I bit my tongue. "Fine. Do what you must."

She clapped. "Splendid. This is a hobby of mine. Come. Let's get you tatted up."

Her once-lover mer-prince sent her supplies for tattoos, she explained to me, knowing how much she enjoyed the art. She had run out of room to do it to herself and had taken to staining leaves and blankets to pass the time.

My mother had boasted many tattoos: a long shark down her arm, a stingray on her back leading to her neck, names of her enemies along her wrists, her ship on her finger. Countless others that peeked out from the hems of her clothes. She was always so proud to display them to any who asked.

"So, what shall we do? The waves? Coral? A shark?" She mixed a black powder with water inside a wooden bowl. A salty smell wafted through the air as if the whole sea lived inside the bowl.

This called for more thought than just a whimsical decision, but time was the one thing I did not have. Tattoo ideas came to mind, and I filtered out any that too closely resembled my mother's. I needed something that looked like what her tattoos might have been but were mine instead of hers.

"An octopus," I said. Just like the nickname my father had for me as a child. "Put it on my back where she had the stingray. Then a band of coral on my wrist."

She nodded in approval. "I like it. And for your arm? She had a tattoo along here." She traced a line down the back of my forearm, and I stared at it in an attempt to visualize what I wanted there. What meant something to me that I wanted to remember?

"I'll start with the octopus," Sereena said. "You can think about the other design for a bit."

A memory clung to me, and it felt perfect. My mother's tattoos were always dripping with death and evil, but these would be of beauty and hope. "Can you draw a calm ocean with starlight resting on it? The kind that comes at the beckoning of a mermaid's song?"

Her sharp tool faltered in her hand. "It's been a long time since I heard one of our songs. Yes, I can draw that."

"Good." I stripped off my shirt so she could draw the tattoos. "That was a night I want to remember." Now when I saw it, I wouldn't think of my mother. I'd think of dancing with Arn and of the mermaids' song and how the starlight rained around us. I'd think of being reunited with my brother and how for the first time I went hours without thinking of the disease. I'd think of happiness.

Sereena brought the sharp pen to my back. "Hold your breath, love. This may sting."

The quill pricked, and I bit down on my tongue to combat the pain that the ink left behind as it soaked into my skin. She made quick work of it, etching in the face of the octopus then wrapping his tentacles around my body. One curled up to the nape of my neck, and another wrapped over my shoulder, then under my armpit and back around. A third came toward the front before curling up under my chest. The others wrapped around my side or down to my hips. Finally, Sereena announced that she was done.

I craned my neck to see. My arms didn't seem to be my own. She'd added gold accents that glimmered throughout the tentacles and added dimension to it. Sereena didn't give me much chance to take it in before dipping her tool back in the ink and beginning the coral bracelet around my wrist. This one took significantly less time, and in no more than a minute, she had finished both the coral and the waves on my arm. A cool feeling oozed over my skin from the rich cream that she applied, soothing the irritation. Once finished, she stepped back to inspect her work.

"There you go. Almost done. We haven't much time, but you need a little more."

The sky was dangerously dark outside as she opened up a chest. "Wear these. And this." She held up a brown tunic and a handful of jewelry. This will make you look exactly like your mother. The Huntress will be so afraid, she might throw herself in the fire."

I'd already gotten full tattoos, might as well throw some bracelets on too. The sleeveless tunic was made with a soft brown fabric and fastened at my waist with a twisted belt and buttoned to the middle of my chest with golden buttons. Gold rings adorned my fingers, and copper bands rounded my ankles and wrists. Sereena twisted a band of pearls through my hair.

"Perfect. Now we can go. Here's your dagger."

"This better be worth it," I grunted as I took back my blade. I regretted leaving my other cutlass and pistol aboard the ship. Sereena marched through the doorway, and I followed, but I got a strange feeling that the girl I once was stayed behind in the hut, and a new girl came out—one that I didn't know. One that looked an awful lot like a pirate.

I could only hope she was strong enough to save her friends.

The stars were out by the time we reached the Huntress's lair. While I would have searched further into the forest, it sat nearer to the beach. Had I not oathbound myself, I never would have found it in time. An especially thick wall of trees guarded an entrance to a clearing in the woods where a barricade of bones surrounded a deep pit as wide as the *Royal Rose*. The crew's bones could soon be in that pile as well. A stairway dug into the ground down to the pit. We hid behind the bones to get a look at the situation.

It was a dire one.

The Huntress had a fire roaring in the center of the pit with flames so high that they reached the ground level from where we watched. In the middle of the fire was an iron bar with clasps to tie up food. Nothing could last long in that heat. She tended to a large pot on a table, stirring the contents and smacking her thin lips as yells from the crew tied in the pit sounded through the woods.

They were bound to the wall by ropes, hanging by their hands with feet dangling, scrambling to get a foothold to relieve their shoulders from the pressure. Some, like Bo, called out relentlessly to be freed, while others like Emric spouted threats. Percival yelled for them to all be quiet. Arn, who hung at the nearest end of the row, said nothing.

At first, I thought he might be dead, with how his head hung low and his body didn't move. But when the fire popped and sent sparks to his feet, he kicked them away. Relief rushed through me.

"I'm here," I breathed, though he couldn't hear me. Their weapons were arranged in a circle just out of their reach, taunting them. If I could cut one free, he could loosen the others.

"What do we do?" I whispered to Sereena.

Sereena studied the pit. "You distract her, I'll cut the men free. When we get a chance, we push her into the fire."

It wasn't a proper plan. It wasn't even thought through very well. But it was all we had, for just then, the Huntress looked up at the men, her gaze settling on Arn.

"Who cares to die first?"

Without thinking, I pushed through the bones. My strong voice projected over the night.

"Huntress. I killed your sister. Now I plan to kill you. Fear me, for I am Arabella the Ruthless."

24

ARN

When Emme's voice rang out, I almost didn't believe it. I thought it to be my mind playing tricks on me, but I looked up, and there she stood, surrounded by those bones. Hope pinched me, but it was a fleeting feeling, for the next emotion to overtake me was dread. This Huntress would capture Emme, and she'd die along with us. Because of me. Because of my foolish ambition and my audacity to drag Emme along. I should have left her in the portside tavern where she was safe.

But then something odd happened.

Instead of attacking, the Huntress screeched, dropping her spoon and stepping backward. Emme marched down the stairs, voice raised at the Huntress. "You let them go, and perhaps I'll spare you." The fire cast its light across her face, and, in that moment, her eyes flickered to mine.

I tried to shake my head, but she had already looked away. Run. Save yourself. But I couldn't even form the words, so stunned at seeing her here and looking like *that*.

She wore a low-cut tunic and gold jewelry that caught the red of the light, intensifying her sharp eyes as she stared down the Huntress. Tattoos covered her skin—down her arm, across her wrists, by her neck; the black ink matched the pupils of her eyes, both demanding to be noticed, both impossible to tear away from.

The Huntress had moved behind the iron pot and cowered close to the dirt. "You should be dead. They said you were dead." The name Arabella the Ruthless clearly meant something to her, and Emme was taking full advantage of that.

"You're going to wish I were dead." Emme bared her teeth and stormed further down the stairs, never taking her eyes off the Huntress. The beast woman stumbled back further. Emme looked tougher than I'd ever seen her, but it wasn't until she reached the bottom of the pit and pulled the dagger from her hip that my breath caught in my throat.

She looked like a pirate.

My eyes weren't the only ones fastened on her. The entire crew had fallen into a hush as Emme punched her feet into the dirt with each step, bringing herself closer to the Huntress.

"It won't work, she protects her wrists. She still has her poison," Emric shouted, the first sound any of us had made. Emme didn't acknowledge him.

"I will not kill you the same way I killed your sister," she snarled at the Huntress. "Tell me, do you still hear her screams at night? The sound she made when I threw her charred body off the cliff and into the fjord? When you close your eyes, do you still hear how she begged?"

Her words came cold. Heartless. The Huntress hissed at her. Emme continued her methodical steps, until she was close enough to the Huntress to spit on her. She glanced at me again, but the Huntress's low groan drew her attention back.

The Huntress dug her heels in the ground in preparation for attack, but as her bright eyes drank in Emme, a rumble came from her throat. "Lovely tattoos, Arabella."

The first taste of nerves flickered across Emme's face. Fearing something to be wrong, I yanked on my ropes, kicking against the wall in attempt to wrench my binds free, but it did nothing except tear at the skin of my wrists.

"Tattoos," the Huntress hissed. "I wonder . . ."

She spun around and pointed a scaly finger at the stairs. "Ah, Sereena. You know better than to fiddle with my games."

In my focus on Emme, I'd failed to notice that someone else lurked under the cover of night—a girl with short hair who crawled down the last of the stairs. Now spotted, she cursed and flicked something out of her belt. The steel of a blade caught the light, but instead of throwing it at the Huntress, she dove for me.

The Huntress screeched and flew toward us, but Emme managed to throw a knife at her. Though it only scraped along her cheek without drawing blood, the Huntress faltered in her steps long enough to look back at Emme with her red eyes and scream in fury.

The girl latched her legs around my hips and hoisted herself up to reach the binds that held my arms. A shot of pain darted through me as she wasn't careful in cutting my wrists free. The ropes severed and we both fell to the ground.

The Huntress screamed again, and within moments she was upon us. This time I knew to watch for her poison claws, so, as she swiped at us, I rolled to the side. The girl darted the other way, forcing the Huntress to choose which of us to follow. She chose me. Unfortunately, I didn't have anywhere to run but toward Emme, who was now on the other side of the men with her dagger pulled out. I barreled past her, bringing an angry Huntress behind me.

"Watch out," Emric yelled, as Emme joined in after me.

"Do we have a plan?" I asked as we leapt over the long table.

She looked back at the Huntress. "Not quite."

"Splendid."

I turned and shoved the table over just as the Huntress neared us, sending vegetables flying as it knocked into her.

We had but a few moments before she'd regain her footing and come after us again, and very limited options on what to do next. If I could get to the weapons, I could find my pistol, but it was loaded with only one shot, and this creature's skin seemed immune to penetration.

There was an angry cry as the girl who cut me free was pinned to the dirt by roots wrapping around her ankles. Iron bars protruded from the walls of the pit to arch over the girl at a rapid speed, plunging back into the dirt at her feet, trapping her in a cage. Her breathing came in rasps.

The Huntress gave a gruesome grin, then took slow steps toward us, hissing through her teeth. We had nowhere to go and could only press our backs to the wall.

Emme's chest rattled as she gulped for breath, and sweat dripped from her brow. "We have to burn her."

"Will you be okay with that?" I asked my question quickly, for the Huntress advanced. "Me killing someone?"

She nodded toward the trapped girl. "Yes. It's more beast than human."

The Huntress stopped in front of us, red eyes sparking. She had us trapped, and she was taking her time to kill us. Letting us fret about whatever lay ahead. Emme's hand reached down and squeezed mine. "Watch my back. And when you find the right moment, push her into the fire, even if she's holding me."

Wielding her dagger, she threw herself forward and straight into the Huntress before I could respond. In a tangle of limbs, they both tumbled to the edge of the fire.

"Watch the left hand!" Emric shouted as the rest of the crew cheered.

"Now, Arn," Emme yelled. But I hesitated. I couldn't push Emme into the roaring fire.

Perhaps there was a way to do this. I charged at them, bending low as I ran into Emme's back and shoved them both toward the flames. Heat engulfed us all as the Huntress roared with rage. My hand tightened around Emme's belt, and I flung her away from the fire.

Flames closed around the Huntress's body, crawling over her skin and eating her hair. The rage in her eyes matched the color of the flames. A foul smell filled the air as her flesh began to burn.

Then she took a step forward, then another one. She was walking out of the fire.

I scanned the area. When I knocked over the table, the iron pot had rolled off, now close enough to grab. I grabbed it and swung it into the Huntress, forcing her back in the hot flames. The pot fell after her.

She didn't get it off in time. Her cries filled the night sky as her body went up in smoke.

I didn't move until she was nothing but ashes in the wind.

"Untie us, would ya?" Bo tugged on his ropes. But Emric shook his head.

"Wait," he urged. "Check on Emme first. She's not moving."

My heart stopped as I peered through the smoke to where Emme lay unmoving. I sank to the ground beside her and cupped her head in my lap. Her chest strained to rise and fall, and her breathing was ragged. Something wet touched my hand. Four sharp lines stretched under her arm. The Huntress had got her.

I breathed a sigh of relief and rested my forehead against hers. "She's only been paralyzed," I informed the others. "She'll wake in a few hours."

Emric's voice was edged. "If she had died, I'd have killed you."

The men once more demanded to be freed, but I released the girl from the trap first, and helped her up. "I don't know where you came from," I told her. "But you have my thanks."

She took a large gulp of air and pushed her hair back from her eyes to glance were Emme lay. "Of course. Always a pleasure doing business with pirates."

That word settled over me unpleasantly. "Business? What do you mean?"

But she was already scurrying back up the stairs. "Keep the girl safe," she shouted over her shoulder. When she reached the top of the stairwell, she turned. "I'll be needing her alive."

Then she took off into the night.

Her peculiar words played through my mind, but the threats from my men if I didn't free them drowned the words out. I cut them down, and they rubbed their sore wrists and gathered their weapons, helping themselves to the Huntress's food. I drew Emme into my arms and stroked her cheek, wondering again what the girl's words meant.

For the second time that day, I truly regretted bringing Emme along with us and the danger that I put her in. Once this business with Admiral Bones was through, I'd let her be off and never bother her again.

She didn't wake until met with the mist of the seawater and rocking of the rowboats as we paddled our way to the ship. None of the men found any herbs, so we would have to spend the night here and find some in the morning, while praying to every god we knew that Lewie survived the night. Emme's eyelids flitted open, and she let out a moan.

She strained to speak. "Did we do it?"

"Aye, love. She's gone."

A smile tugged at her lips. "Good. Good."

I examined the claw marks on her arm—the price she paid for freeing us.

"It'll heal, but it'll be sore for weeks." I frowned. "Emme, how did you find and convince this Sereena to assist you?"

Her face froze. "I let her draw these blasted tattoos on me." She smiled, but the corners of her eyes didn't match her smile.

Instead they looked sad, like she'd lost something. Or like she was lost herself.

"I happen to think they make you look fierce. No one will mess with you now."

Her smile was a little more genuine this time. "Let's hope so. Perhaps old Bernabe's ghost will take one look at me and hand over the treasure."

"One can hope." We bumped against the side of the ship where the ropes waited for us. "Can you climb?" I asked Emme, holding out the rope for her.

She swallowed but nodded. I stayed below her just in case and, while she did move slowly, she managed to pull herself onto the deck.

The main deck was empty, and it wasn't until we dragged the rowboats aboard that Ontario surfaced from below. He twisted his cap in hand and kept his arms close to side, not greeting us or asking how we fared.

"We've had quite the adventure, mate." I moved to clap him on the back, but his eyes stopped me. Tears brimmed within.

My chest sunk with realization of what this must mean, and his words confirmed it. "Lewie died a few hours ago. I'm sorry, Captain."

25

EMME

"We give this body back to the sea and to King Valian. May ye find peace in your next life."

Lewie was wrapped in a thinly knitted blanket, allowing us to see through the black yarn to his closed eyelids and the freckles on his white cheeks. I lowered my eyes as Arn and Ontario slid the body into the sea, and soon all our heads were bowed in respect. I flinched as the lifeless form splashed into the water.

Rest well, Lewie.

Arn didn't wait long before returning to the wheel, his focus on the sea. We had two weeks left before coming upon the Island of Iilak, and many possible dangers awaited us before then. The sea was an unpredictable beast, and this trip was taking a toll on us all.

While the rest of the crew dispersed, I stayed near the quarterdeck in case Arn needed me.

The pain of losing Lewie cracked him to the bone, and I feared what would be left of him when the sorrow faded. His knuckles whitened as he gripped the wheel, and his lips were set in a line.

The only good thing about Lewie's death, *and King Valian*

forgive me for thinking such a thing, was that it distracted Arn from further questions of how I convinced Sereena to assist us.

The oathbinding weighed on me like an anchor, tethering part of me to that cursed island and to that girl. I'd gone against the one rule I thought I'd never break; I'd sold my soul to another. She owned me. This favor that I owed her kept me a prisoner, this ink on my skin reminding me that I was no longer in control of my own future. When she needed me, despite where I might be or what I might be doing, I must do her bidding.

No matter what it was. If she wanted something brought to her, I must bring it. If she wanted something done, I must do it. If she wanted someone dead, I must kill them. That is the power of oathbinding; it rendered me helpless but to the bidding of who I was bound to. The promise must be fulfilled, or the ink in my tattoo would kill me faster than the disease in my bones.

It didn't feel as they said it would. The fact that I now owed something to someone wasn't the worst of it. The worst was losing a part of myself. Part of my future was in her hands.

It was the price I paid for Arn's freedom. And for him, I'd pay it again.

"He looks like a wreck." Emric planted himself next to me and gestured to Arn.

Arn hadn't moved. He was like a ghost captaining the ship, capable of drifting away with the next breeze and drowning under the pressure of high waves. "His friend just died; he's mourning," I said with a shrug, as if I wasn't equally concerned about him. The other men were certainly less jolly: Timmons no longer whistled, and Percival didn't make his jokes. Even Bo kept himself from merry drinking, though he held his flask close. But Arn? He was broken.

"He's taking this too hard. It's not his fault the lad got ill." Emric tightened the knot of his hair and shook his head. He looked at Arn again. "When I'm captain, my men will never see me fall apart in such a way."

My gaze wandered to the other crewmen. As Henrik mopped the decks, he exchanged glances with Percival, who inspected the riggings. They both kept looking sideways at Arn. It hadn't occurred to me that Arn's leadership might be questioned if he fell into a pit of sorrow and lost his ability to think clearly.

"I'll go speak with him."

Emric's face lightened. "I bet you know how to cheer him up."

I pushed at his arm, and he laughed. "Listen, I can't claim to understand what might be going on between the two of you, but he's a swell lad. He truly is."

I frowned. "Did Arn tell you to say that?"

"Nay, love. Honest, he didn't. But you ought to know this. The Huntress trapped us by impersonating you. Arn didn't hesitate to run to you. He may be reckless, but he's reckless for you."

A flutter captured my heart, one that was difficult to push away. The image of Arn abandoning all reason to chase after me made my cheeks flush, but such ideas could bring nothing but trouble. "He's a pirate, Emric. I'm not."

He looked me over. "You sure look like a pirate to me." He tipped his head and let me be.

I climbed the stairs to Arn, who gave me a small glance. "How are you?" I asked as I came to his side.

His chest rose and fell four times before he answered in a voice etched with pain, "If I were a better captain, I'd have had more medicine on board that could have saved him. It's my fault the boy died. I should have done better."

I placed a hand on his forearm. "Arn, you did not kill Lewie." At the sound of the young lad's name, Arn's eye squeezed shut. I'd come to try to clear his head and ease the worries of the crew, but one look at Arn, and different words spilled out. "You are a wonderful captain. The crew respects you for mourning him so deeply."

He looked at me fully for the first time that day. The dazed expression shook from his face, and when he spoke, his words came clearer. "How are you?"

Arn's unrelenting concern for others was what made him a good captain. Emric's words repeated in my head. *He's reckless, but he's reckless for you.* I wouldn't give Arn any cause for extra worry, especially about my oathbinding. I leaned against the railing. "I'm doing fine. The Huntress was a vile creature, and her death was necessary to save us. I'm not haunted by it." I met his eyes and gave what I hoped was a reassuring smile.

Arn's face brightened, and that alone felt like a victory. "Splendid. I must say, you're stronger than I first fathomed you to be. I'm impressed. And the tattoos do look incredible. The girl did a remarkable job."

I raised my arms to inspect them. "I keep catching a glimpse of the ink and thinking these arms belong to someone else. It'll take a while to get used to such a thing."

Arn's eyes ran over the length of my skin. "They suit you. What's this one here?" He pointed to the drawing along my forearm of the mermaid's song, and I grinned.

"Remember that night of telling ghost stories and dancing and listening to the beautiful mermaids' singing? Then the stars reached from the sky to kiss the waters?" The memory of it felt as crisp as the sea's breeze, forever etched into my memory. "It was the first night I felt like a part of this crew, not like an imposter. And it was the first night I saw the beauty of the waters instead of something to be feared. Everything about that night was perfect."

A light in his blue eyes sparkled like the sea at sunrise. "I'm honored to have been a part of your favorite night here. Once we get the treasure, we will dance again."

"That's sounds lovely."

I clutched his arm as something over his shoulder caught my eye—the dark colors of the ship in the distance watching us. It lurked on the horizon with sails pointed toward us, and the sea trembling beneath.

"You all right, love?" He turned his head to where I was looking and cursed. "Blimey. That foul ship is back."

A tremor ran through my body. "Should we attack?"

"Nay," Arn spat. "Let him watch us. Go get new parsley for your ankle enchantment and cook some twine with lavender and keep it in your pocket. We won't let this ship haunt us any longer."

I nodded, but Arn stopped me before I left. "Emme? Thank you for coming with me on this voyage. I knew your sensibility would be good for me."

That brought a smile to my face. "I think your adventurous spirit is good for me too. I'm glad to be here."

I spent the rest of the day in the kitchen with Bishop boiling twine in lavender and water, then passing the twine out to the crew to wear as protection from nightmares. All the while the black ship waited—watching us. Taunting us. Playing with us.

As if we hadn't seen enough death this week, he sent more visions of death to crewmates, sending half of them huddled into balls on the floor.

When it came time to lie down that night, I was well fortified against any nightmares the ship might cast my way, yet my mind still struggled to fall asleep. I clutched the sides of my cotton jacket and buried my head under the blanket, checking to feel the twine in my pocket. The overwhelming smell of lavender pinched my nose, which had almost forgotten what sweet smells were like during this time on the sea.

Click, click, rattle, tap.

My breath stopped. I yanked the blanket off and stared at

the oak cupboards across the small room. The doors jiggled and the handles vibrated with some force behind them, as if begging to be free.

Fear would no longer control me. I swung my feet from the bed and quietly stepped across the boards to the cabinets, grabbing my dagger off the table along the way.

Three deep breaths. Then I swung open the doors.

I was not prepared for what was within. I expected a rat, or a small animal of sorts.

Instead, yellowed bones fell out. They flooded on the ground, knocking against my feet and collecting along my ankles—an endless stream of skulls and femurs and long fingers until the floor was covered in human remains.

The lifeless sockets stared at me, and I screamed.

Bones crunched under my weight as I tripped backward, landing on a skull. I shifted to the side, pushing my back against the wall and kicking the bone out from underneath me. It rolled across the others before hitting the table, shaking the candle that burned there. The candle tipped over the edge, and the bones caught fire.

It spread instantly. The whole room was suddenly engulfed in flames that licked my toes and singed my arms. Heat surrounded me as fire slithered up the table and curled around the porthole, turning my room into a curtain of dangerous red.

I screamed again. There was no way to put this out. I would die here in this room.

The rest of the cabinets began to rattle with the same sound the bones had made, and I covered my ears. My head buried into my chest as hot tears ran down my face.

"Look. See your destiny." Deep voices hissed, beckoning me to raise my head. "Look!"

Through the ash and smoke stood a figure on the opposite end of the room—a girl with curved thighs, strong arms, and wild curls around her head. Iron armor was strapped to her body, and a cutlass hung at her side. In one of her hands she held a skull.

This is just a nightmare, I told myself. This isn't real. Still, I called out to the figure. "Mother? Is this your doing?" My voice rose. "Leave me alone."

A laugh came, but it wasn't my mother's. The bones were mocking me.

"Leave me alone," I screamed again.

The door swung open, and Arn ran into the room, his linen shirt halfway unbuttoned. With a hiss, it all disappeared. The bones, the fire, the form—it was all gone. The candle remained flickering on the table, and I cowered by the shelves with cheeks soaked in tears.

"Emme? What happened?" Arn wrapped his arms around me. I curled into his chest and wept. His hands caressed my hair as my tears ran down his shirt.

"I'm right here. You're safe," he said over and over until I'd calmed down enough to peel myself away from him.

He took my hands and searched my eyes. I kept myself close to him as I used my shoulder to dry my cheeks. "It was another vision. I didn't even have time to fall asleep before it came."

"Was it your mother again?" His breath swept across my nose as he spoke.

I took a shaky breath. "I think so. But there was something more. Death. It was a horrible sensation. Arn, death is coming."

His blue eyes appeared darker in the dim light as he listened to me. At the word "death," he gripped my hands tighter. "I promise you; I will do everything I can to keep you safe."

A troubled feeling curled in my stomach. "It's more than my death. I fear death awaits us all."

Arn's brow wrinkled before he placed it against my own and cradled my hands to his chest. "It's only the nightmares. We'll create more enchantments for you to wear. I won't let anything happen to you. I vow this, I will fight for you." His voice grew husky as it dipped into a whisper. "Above all else, even my own life, I will make sure you are safe."

That promise clung to the thick air between us—so fragile, so desperate—just like us. It mirrored our relationship, something that I wanted to make sense of. Wanted to be certain of. Wanted to hold onto and be reassured of. But this promise he made couldn't be guaranteed to survive the hardships ahead of us, just like we couldn't be sure to last, once the sails dropped and the voyage was over.

There could be no promises. There could be no assurances. Nothing I could cling to and know would be mine forever.

But for the first time, I didn't need that.

This would be enough for me—this moment here, this spark between us. Knowing that for a moment, everything could be perfect.

Arn was comfort. Arn was familiar. Arn was a little bit of home in a world where I was losing a sense of who I was. He was the safety I didn't know I needed.

If I stopped pushing against that, what would it bring me?

I leaned in, and his breathing slowed as our noses brushed together.

I held my breath.

Suddenly he pulled back a little. His lips grazed my forehead where they lingered before he said, "Let me help you back to bed. I'll be right outside the door if you need anything."

It suddenly occurred to me that he must have slept outside the door to have heard me cry out in the first place, and my heart swelled. Arn may be a pirate, but he was a good man.

"I mean it, Emme," Arn said. "I will always do what I can to protect you."

My breathing felt easier as I lay down this time.

I let that promise lead me to slumber.

26

ARN

I sat in the shade of the stairs on deck when a shout came from inside the main cabin. The door swung open, almost knocking me in the face, and Henrik ran out yelling at the top of his lungs. A gunshot sounded, making us all jump.

"What's going on?" Emric leaned over from the helm.

"Ahh!" Henrik screamed.

Ontario and Bo fled the cabin a moment later, followed by another gunshot. From across the deck, Svid and Sims craned their long necks to see inside the cabin.

Percival came storming out with wild eyes and a pistol raised to the clouds.

"I won't die." He was nearly crying as much as he was howling. "Someone will die, they keep telling me that. I won't let it be me. If someone must die, it won't be me." He looked right at me and leveled the gun. His hand shook so badly that his aiming wasn't exactly pristine.

It boded well for me that he wasn't a good shot. As the gun went off, the bullet went through the stairs next to me. Unfortunately, the gunpowder was kept behind me, so if he shot again, he had a good chance of hitting it.

Stars and seaweed. He was going to destroy us all.

I jumped up and ran, as much for the sake of my own skin as for drawing his target from the gunpowder.

The wild hysterics continued. "I have to escape these visions. They demand a life is paid." Percival holstered the pistol against his narrow hips and drew out the cutlass, which he started swinging violently through the air. "You hear me? It won't be me!"

The visions were obviously getting to his head.

Emme popped her head up from below, her eyes bulging at Percival. I ushered her down quickly. Svid also hopped down, almost slamming into her.

"Easy, mate," Emric called down. While he stood shouting into the chaos, the rest of us ran around like fish on the run from a shark.

"I won't be the one who dies," Percival hollered again. He swung for Ontario's head. Ontario ducked with a yelp and ran up to the helm.

"Hey, don't come here," Emric protested. "I don't want him coming after me." Ontario only scurried to the other side and knelt to peer at the main deck through the beams.

"Percival, no one is going to die," I began, but Percival swung at me, embedding his sword into the mast.

"Easy there." I held up my hands. "Don't hurt my ship."

"Ahhh!" He ripped the blade free and aimed for me again. I pressed my back against the railing and glanced over into the rolling waves, debating my chances against Percival versus the deep sea.

Bo crept up behind Percival and struck the back of his head with his flask.

Percival's eyes rolled up in his head before he slumped to the deck. His cutlass clattered to the ground, and I kicked it away.

"I've always wanted to do that," Bo said. The rest of us eyed Percival's limp body. His chest rose and fell, and we all gave a sigh of relief.

Emme had poked her head up above deck again. She tentatively stepped out. I took Percival's pistol from his holster. "We must be careful, men," I spoke to the unsettled crew. "These visions are meant to drive you mad. Don't let the dark ship steal your sanity."

As I spoke, I glanced over the waves where the ship loomed, almost as if it were laughing at us. My teeth gritted together.

One day I'd find a way to kill whoever roamed on that ship. I'd kill him before he brought us all to madness.

A few weeks later, I woke early to relieve Ontario from his post and take over at the wheel. He nodded to me and rubbed his weary face. "The ship left sometime during the night. Don't know when he'll be back."

It was no longer a question of if the mysterious ship would show itself. It was a question of when.

"And this came for you last night." Ontario held out a letter to me, one that I didn't fail to notice had been opened. It bore Admiral Bones's crest.

With a grumble I took hold of it. "Which enemy bothers you the most, Ontario. Admiral Bones, the black ship, or Landon?"

"Well, Captain. I'd have to say the one that's threatened to kill us. So Bones."

I grunted. "Don't be mistaken in thinking they wouldn't all like to slice our throats at the first chance they get, mate."

The crisp paper unfolded, and I read the words within.

> *When you get the treasure, bring it straight to me. If you take any detours, I'll kill you all. Including that girl you sail with.*

I crumpled the note and threw it in the water. Ontario's

eyes widened a bit, and I clasped his shoulder. "Go get some sleep, mate. I'll wake you if there be any problems."

Admiral Bones wouldn't distract me this fine morning. We'd soon be coming upon the secret strait that would lead us into the sea that held the Island of Iilak.

We were so close I could practically smell the treasure. The lure of it filled my lungs with the scent of desire, the chance of power within my grasp.

Emme woke not long after and came above deck with a sleeveless shirt that showed off her tattoos. Her eyes were bright as she looked up at the sky. Emric emerged later and began his routine chores, but his attention repeatedly went to the water, checking every few moments to see if land was near.

Everyone knew what today was meant to bring. Everyone was eager.

At high noon, Emric bounded up the stairs and pointed. "There, mate. There it is." He cupped his hands over his mouth and hollered, "Land ho!"

A slow stretch of land came into view with vibrant colors that stood out against the deep blue of the sea. After the bright shades came gray hues of cliffs tumbling toward the shore where sharp rocks jutted out of the cliffside.

"Steer there. You'll find the pass between those cliffs." Emric pointed, but I saw nothing. This didn't look like the map I'd been given. I saw no cliffs and no jungle on the drawing I possessed, but both loomed before me. The land here was titled the Never-Ending Land for the fact that it stretched as far as any knew in both directions. For the longest time it was believed that this was the edge of the world—this distant land mass that none cared to visit. But then someone claimed to have found islands beyond, and intrigue grew.

I didn't care if the land truly did stretch both ways forever. I didn't care if there was more beyond. All I cared was that the Island of Iilak was real and that we were on the right path to find it.

"Are you certain?"

Emric nodded with confidence. "Aye, my mother showed me a detailed drawing of this pass."

Of course she did. This time I would have to trust Arabella the Ruthless to lead us the right direction. "If you say so. Let's pray to King Valian that the pass is wide enough to keep this ship from those rocks, or we'll find ourselves at the bottom of the sea."

Soon the strait came into view. The waters crashed against the high rocks and pulled us in closer, propelled by a rough wind that danced through the pass. The way looked wide enough to fit us, but just barely.

A darker part of myself wished to see Landon's ship smashed against the cliffs somewhere.

Emme came on the quarterdeck. "We are so close now." Excitement tinged her voice. Looking at her, one would never know she was continually haunted by nightmares.

"A few more weeks and this will all be over," I told her. "You'll get your sheep farm." The brightness in her eyes lessened, but only for a moment.

"And I'll get my own ship," Emric said, patting Emme on the shoulder. "It'll be a great victory for us all."

My smile faltered. Depending on the size of the treasure, I wouldn't have much left after paying Admiral Bones. It was my hope that the crew would forgive me and pardon my using their shares to pay Admiral Bones, especially if Ontario helped talk them down. Worst case they'd throw me overboard, but I doubted it'd get to that.

Emric might not hesitate to throw me overboard, however. Or challenge me for leadership and take the *Royal Rose* away.

My fingers tightened on the steering wheel. Those were worries for another day.

The cliff's shadow blanketed over us as seawater sprayed onto the deck after crashing against the scree. A narrow opening broke through the rock and stretched about one hundred meters before opening on the other side and spilling into sparkling water. Holes were punched into the walls where large lanterns burned with flames, indicating either someone lived here to light them, or they burned with everlasting oil.

I prayed for the second.

My calloused hands gripped the splintered wood of the wheel. Too far to one side, too far to the other, and this ship was never making it to the other side in one piece.

"Need me to stand at the side and tell you if you're too close?" Emric offered.

"No." I answered quickly. That might be helpful, but I wasn't about to admit it to him. Emme kept watch over the edge.

"You're good," she informed me.

We sailed without hindrance into the strait.

We'd gotten no more than a few meters before the cliffs shook with a ferocity as if King Valian himself trembled beneath the surface. With a deafening roar, sharp rocks erupted from the bed of the sea and rose as tall as the cliffs, layered too thick to get past. We cried out in surprise and held tight as waves rocked the boat. The cliffs continued to rumble until the rocks had reached their heights, then they settled quiet again.

Our boat stilled as if an anchor held us.

"What's going on? What are those?" Emric jumped from the quarterdeck and rushed to the bow.

The sudden rocks had walled us out. There'd be no getting by them. And there was no other way around.

"You seek to pass our waters," a chipper voice sang through the air, sending us all reaching for our weapons and turning in circles to see who spoke. "You must play our game." I searched the rocks until a figure leapt up from below, flicking water upon us with her tail. It dove below with a laugh. Another figure appeared a moment later, one with deep purple fins.

"Mermaids," Emme breathed.

"These can't be friendly ones, to live so far from their people."

"We are friendly if you agree to play," the voice called again. I looked up and saw a mermaid sitting upon the cliffs. She had a coral tail and long blonde hair braided in an intricate design over her shoulder and daisies forming a crown around her head. Seaweed covered the skin of her chest and wrapped around her arms, showing off where her muscles bulged.

She'd be pretty if it weren't for the sharp teeth she bared at us.

"What's your game?" Emric called out.

Other mermaids came from the water, some swimming alongside the boat in a blanket of radiant colors while more leapt from the waves to perch beside the first on the gray rocks. They scaled the cliffs using the strength of their arms, and I was amazed at their power.

"It's a simple game," the coral-colored mermaid sang once her sisters had settled beside her, each as beautiful as the next. "You want to pass? You give us three secrets. If they are juicy enough, we let you through."

This could be much more serious than it sounded.

"Blasted mermaids," I swore. "Always too eager for gossip."

They merely waited with hungry smiles upon their faces.

We all shifted our eyes between each other, wondering who would give up a secret first, until to my great surprise, Bo stepped forward. He put up his hands and shrugged. "I'll confess. Sometimes at night I steal some rum." He turned to me. "Sorry, Cap'n."

A few of the crewmen snickered.

I couldn't even summon an angered expression as Bo turned back to watch the mermaids huddle their heads together in a mass of curls and flowers and seaweed. Before the ship rocked from one side to the other, they separated.

"That's not enough. We want more. Give us three good secrets, or you don't get past." She smiled, flashing her sharp white teeth.

The tight walls of the cliff provided no room to turn the *Royal Rose* around, and even our oars couldn't fit out without breaking against the scree. The fortress of cliffs ahead of us was impossible to penetrate. There appeared no opportunity to get by without giving the tricky mermaids what they asked for, and as captain, it was my duty to oblige.

I hadn't saved my crew from falling into deep debt. I hadn't protected the men on He'tu, nor Emme on Aható. I hadn't kept Lewie from dying.

I knew what the mermaids wanted. But I had to offer up a secret that was deep and dark. This was a secret I'd protected for years, and the words felt like acid as they came to my lips.

"I have one." Eyes turned to me. For a moment all that was heard was the lap of water against the hull. I drew a breath. "My father encouraged me to join the king's navy. He'd been so proud of me, his only child. But four years ago I left the comfortable life to pursue piracy and hadn't the ability to tell my father. He still doesn't know. He believes me to be an honored man among the navy ranks, and I have no intention of telling him otherwise, nor ever seeing him again."

There. The words were out. They cut me to the heart, and I closed my eyes for a moment to bear down the sting, biting my teeth so hard I thought they might crack. I longed for my father to know the truth, but he was the only remaining person I had from my childhood, and his love was not one I cared to lose. He'd been so proud to wave me off toward the navy—he'd renounce me as his son if he found out what I'd become. Then I'd be truly alone in this world.

Ontario knew that my father wasn't aware I was a pirate. What he didn't know is I planned to tell him I died at sea.

When I opened my eyes again, the mermaids were huddled together in whispers. Emme came to my side as we waited.

The mermaids sat back on the sharp rocks and flicked their tails to and fro. "We accept this secret."

My men cheered, though their voices sounded like mocking to my pained heart. But my troubles were my own doing, and I didn't deserve to pity myself.

Quiet befell us once more as the two final secrets hung in the air, waiting for someone to grab them and share the inner parts of themselves. I held a larger secret, of course, that of Admiral Bones, but I'd rather be sent away by the mermaids than killed by my crew. Sharing that secret would take me from my men's good graces at a time where we needed to be unified.

"Oh, did we forget to say this?" At our silence, the coral mermaid sang out, "If you fail to deliver, none will be left alive."

This met with an instant clamor as the crew protested violently. I heard Emme's sharp intake of breath beside me. I glanced at her and realized she was about to speak.

What sort of deceit could this innocent girl possess?

"Emme, you don't have to—"

Her voice floated up to the waiting mermaids. "I've oathbound myself to a stranger."

She stared back at the mermaids as my jaw dropped open and my mind struggled to find the words. It was Emric who spoke first. "What?" He leapt up to the quarterdeck and cocked his head to glare at her. "You mean to tell me that you oathbound yourself to someone? *Oathbound*? Did Mother not warn us against such things? Were you forced into this binding? Who is it?" he demanded. He stared down each of the crew members, until he came to me with a feral expression.

Emme put a hand out to him. "It was the only option I had."

He turned on her while the mermaids chatted together. "Only option you had? Only option? You could have come to me."

Her shoulders drew back, but her voice shook. "I did it to save you, you big oaf. I made a deal with Sereena to free you all from the Huntress."

A deal with Sereena. So that's what the girl had meant about doing business with pirates. She swindled Emme into oathbinding herself. Rage furled within me, and I swore if I ever saw that girl again, I would kill her.

Emric quieted somewhat, but his voice remained hard. "You still could have told me. Am I not your brother?"

The mermaids laughed, taking delight in this little game they were playing. "We accept the secret," they declared. "One more."

Emme glanced at me, and I wanted to say something. I wanted to tell her I was sorry she had to oathbind herself, sorry that I couldn't have been there to do it for her. Sorry that she'd sold a piece of herself in that way. That I would do whatever I could to help her when it came time to fulfill the terms of the binding. But the words felt too easy, too meaningless compared to the magnitude of what she'd sacrificed to save us.

Never oathbind yourself to someone. That's what we were all taught. I knew as well as any what desperation could lead someone to do.

Emme didn't look broken, though. Her posture remained strong, and her chin was tilted upward. Either she wasn't afraid, or she hid it well.

Emric was still seething with anger. His dark eyes were almost black as he set his jaw. Then he hurled himself around. He leaned over the quarterdeck railing and shouted to the mermaids. "The next secret is mine. I am the son of Arabella the Ruthless. After she was presumed dead, I remained in contact with her for six months before she actually died. No one knew this, but she sailed for the same island we sail to now. She died on the way."

Even the mist in the air seemed to still at his confession. The only one who moved was Emric himself, who turned to look at his sister once before walking away.

Emric did that for more than fulfilling the mermaid's request—that was meant to hurt Emme. To keep a secret like that from your family, to watch them mourn someone who wasn't dead, and then tell her like this—no one deserved that.

Emme's fists clenched so hard that her knuckles turned white. Tears swelled in her eyes as I drew her to me.

"I hate him. I hate her." Her voice was fractured. "I hate them both."

"I know."

The crewmen had congregated around Emric to ask him questions, but he pushed through them to stand at the bow and yell, "Do you accept our secrets? May we pass?"

The coral mermaid leapt from the rocks and dove into the water with a twitch of her tail. She swam through the water with more speed than my ship could match and flung herself into the air.

The crew backed up, but Emric didn't. The mermaid settled herself on the edge of the ship next to him and stared at his face, close enough that if she leaned forward, her lips would graze his. He didn't pull back. She grinned, her bright eyes twinkling like stars against a night sky.

The tension appeared to ease away from Emric. His hand flickered toward hers. In that one look, she'd transfixed him.

Her voice was lyrical and less demanding. It was more like a soft breeze. "I like you, son of Arabella. Yes, you may pass through our waters, just as we let your mother through years ago after she defeated a foe of ours. We owed her a great debt, and we would like to repay that now."

Her dainty hand reached into her fin and drew out a

small box with silver fittings. She handed it to Emric, her hand closing over his. "This can capture a ghost. But listen carefully. He must pick up the box of his own free will to be taken prisoner. Use it against Bernabe De on the island."

"Thank you," Emric said. When she pulled her hand back, he tossed the box to me, and I narrowly caught it.

The coral mermaid stroked Emric's cheek. He didn't flinch under her touch. "Such a pretty thing." She sighed. "Try to stay alive, strong one."

She whistled, and the rest of the mermaids threw themselves down from the rocks in a flurry of colors and splashed in the waters. Emric leaned over to catch a last look. As soon as they landed, the cliffs began to shake again, and the rocks lowered back into the deep.

"Sail on, pirates," the mermaids sang out. "Sail on, and try to survive the island."

27

EMME

"Emric, we need to talk." I had swallowed my anger to approach Emric, though the sight of him made me want to throw myself overboard. Or throw him overboard.

He pretended to be very interested in the rigging. "Listen, we both know I'm prone to dramatics. I'm sorry I got so upset about you oathbinding yourself. Now that I've had time to think on it, it was quite brave of you."

I leaned against the railing and crossed my arms. "Nay, that's not what I'd like to talk to you about. The other thing."

"The Mother thing?"

"No, I wanted to know your thoughts on Arn's father. Yes, the Mother thing. How could you keep such a thing from me?"

He crossed his arms to match mine. "You really care to know?"

I truly might throw him overboard.

"It tore Father up when she died. So yes, I'd like to know what made you so cruel as to keep the fact that Mother was alive hidden from us."

"Father knew." His voice carried no empathy.

The deck swayed beneath me, and I gripped the rails for strength. "What?" I breathed.

"When Mother died—the first time—do you remember what you said to me?"

I thought back to that day. I was in the field with the sheep when a messenger came running down the path with his hat in hand and red cheeks puffing. The candlemaker, also the town gossip. He barely had time to catch his breath before the words tumbled from his mouth.

"Your mother was killed when her ship got taken down. Arabella the Ruthless is dead."

I remembered crying unconsolably that night. I remembered holding Father's hand all the next day and gently forcing food into his mouth the days after. I remembered the confusion and uncertainty that followed.

It took a moment, but I remembered what I said to Emric as soon as the candlemaker had run back off.

Emric echoed my words. "At least now we don't have to hear of pirates anymore. That's what you said. So if you want to talk about being cruel, think of how little you cared when she died. You became happier when she was gone. You smiled more. You laughed more. You took to caring for the farm in Father's place and were delighted to do so. So when Mother's letter came a week later that she was alive, we thought it best if you didn't know until she was back from her mission. But that never happened."

I had been happier. Being the daughter of Arabella the Ruthless had labeled me as something I wasn't. Other children feared me, and Mother pressured me to perform at levels that I couldn't reach. I was constantly on guard for which of her enemies would come looking for retribution for one of her sins by killing her family.

The woman cared little for us, and our life was easier with her gone. So yes, part of me was happy. But now guilt curled in my chest. I swallowed it down. "What business did she have in these parts?" I asked Emric.

He glanced out to the sparkling water as the Never-Ending Land drifted away behind us. "She sought the Island of Iilak as we do. There is a fabled Elmber Nut there that she believed could have healed Father."

My brows shot up, and my anger left like an ebbing wave, leaving me dry and empty inside. I swallowed. "She was trying to save Father?"

Emric scoffed. "Valian's Crown, Emme. You say it as if you're surprised. Did you truly hate the woman? Of course she was. She loved him."

I licked my lips. "Did she ever get the nut?" My breath was still as I waited for his answer, even though I knew how this story would end. Mother never came home. Father died, and Emric and I were left alone.

He shook his head. "Nay, her letters stopped after she reached the island, and I don't know if she made it off or if she died there."

My next question seemed obvious. "How do you know she's dead?"

Emric's dark eyes briefly scanned my own. "She would have written to me if she lived. She loved me too."

She loved Father, and she loved Emric. But did she know that I wasn't aware she was alive, and did she care that I thought her to be dead? How much of her mourned each time she left us for her trip, and how much cared if she ever came back? I thought of my mother, carefree and wild, living on the seas as if she didn't have a family elsewhere.

She taught us how to chase what we loved, but she didn't teach us to stay and fight for the ones we cared for. To be there when it mattered.

"I don't care what happened to her. But I do care about the nut."

"The Elmber Nut? What for?"

I'd kept this secret from Emric for long enough. If I wasn't going to be like my mother, then I couldn't hold secrets from those I loved.

"Because I'm sick too."

After the longest conversation Emric and I had ever shared together, complete with tears shed and plans made, the sun hung low, and Emric's stomach growled with the loss of the dinner we'd skipped.

Before leaving for the kitchens, he gave me one more sad look. "Are you certain you don't care to tell Arn? He'd want to know."

"It would hurt him more than anything. You see how he already worries over everyone. He has enough on his mind right now." With a nod, Emric left the cabin, leaving the door open.

I went up to where the decks were swabbed and glistened like the sea around us under the fading daylight. The waters were so clear here that one look overboard revealed the vast coral reefs below and the small fish that skirted in and out of the rocks. They hid as our shadow passed overhead.

We'd be upon the island shortly if Arn's map was accurate. I'd have the Elmber Nut soon.

"You didn't have to do that for us," Arn's voice came down to me. Though he didn't specify, we both knew what he spoke of. His blue ribbon held the top half of his blond hair while the bottom half remained too short to reach the knot, and his unbuttoned blue jacket flapped over his white tunic shirt.

I looked around. "Is the rest of the crew below deck?"

"Aye," Arn replied.

I nodded and climbed the few stairs toward him. "And yes, I did. If I hadn't, you'd be dead."

He gave a short grin. "I'm grateful for that. What are the terms of the binding?"

I peeled off my shoe and sock to show him the tattoo. With how carefully I'd taken to keeping it hidden, I hadn't had much time to examine it myself, and it too looked like someone else's rather than my own. "I owe her a favor. Whenever she needs me for it, I must go."

Arn knelt and took my foot in his hands to study the tattoo, rubbing his thumb over the darkened skin. His touch carried warmth, and the binding didn't look as terrifying in his hands.

"I'll go with you when it's time to fulfill it. You won't be alone," he said, meeting my eyes.

"Thank you." I reached my hand down to him as he stood up. His fingers laced between mine.

"I can't believe you oathbound yourself to save us."

Unlike with Emric, it wasn't accusation or anger dwelling in his tone, but gratitude. He never would have asked me to oathbind myself to save his life, and that's what made the decision so simple. All the fears I had over my binding and all the uncertainties for my future drifted away as Arn leaned his head against mine, refilling me with a river of peace. I forgot the oath, I forgot my disease, I forgot everything but my own name as all I thought of was Arn's hands in mine, his head against my own, his body close to mine. The presence of him was intoxicating, and for once I didn't tell myself to take tiny sips. For once I wouldn't tell myself how it wasn't worth the pain that was sure to follow.

This time I would let myself drink.

I guided his hands to my sides where I let go, moving my own hands to his shirt to tug him closer. Encouraged by the touch, he wrapped his arms around my sides, pulling us together. He steered us toward the polished railing.

My heart beat wildly in my chest.

"I don't deserve you," he whispered, voice thick.

I glided my hands up his back and smirked. "You don't."

His breath swept over my lips, and his nose brushed against

mine. Every ounce of my body lit on fire with anticipation—half of me wanting to lean forward and the other half savoring every moment.

He moved tenderly, drawing his hands up my sides and down my arms, then back up to find the corners of my jaw.

I would finally know the taste of a kiss. The taste of him.

But as his strong hands lifted me up to sit on the railing, the dagger—the blasted dagger that Arn told me to keep strapped in the back of my pants—slid outward and caught the railing just right to chip into it.

The sound of wood splintering made us both look down to where I'd cut a nice little chunk out of the side of his ship.

My face flamed, and I hurriedly slid back to my feet. "Oh, Arn, I'm so sorry." I rubbed at the spot as if that could make it disappear. "I am so, so sorry. Your precious ship. I know how meticulous you are about it."

Arn threw back his head and laughed. He took back my hand. "It's fine, Emme, it's just a scratch." He grinned. "Now I have something to remember you by." He moved close again, but the door to the hatch opened and Emric climbed up with dried meat in his hand, drawing Arn away from me.

"Blast," Arn muttered as Emric waved to us. I waved back, but the moment was properly ruined.

I should have leaned in.

After Emric came Henrik and Ontario, and the chance to get lost in each other floated away.

"It's been a long day, I'm going to try to get some sleep," I said, squeezing Arn's arm. He gave me a nod.

I may not have gotten Arn's kiss, but I still replayed every sensation as I drifted off that night.

Though I went to bed with such fond thoughts, the nightmares still found me. Once more I stood in a pile of bones as a girl laughed. I didn't see her face or ask her name, but the vision left me with such a fear that I woke up to my own scream.

Arn stumbled through the door. I raked a hand across my damp cheeks. "Death," I said. "I fear death is in our future."

Arn rubbed his tired eyes. "It's okay. I'm here."

A golden light bathed the room as the sky outside the porthole transformed with the first light of day, the dark fleeing. I faced the window and let some of the buttery rays melt over my face, praying they were strong enough to banish the darkness inside me too.

I might wear my mother's tattoos, but I only held a sliver of her bravery.

"Are you all right?" Arn asked gently.

"I will be," I said. "Very soon."

Outside the window, the world offered a taste of hope. For the first time in a while, there was something other than endless seas. It was distant, hardly more than a fragment of green against an orange sky, but it was what we'd been waiting for. The pounding of footsteps above confirmed it.

Ontario stepped in. "Captain." He raised his hand in a salute. "We've reached the Island of Iilak."

28
ARN

It wasn't a large island, which boded well for me and my tired men. Out of all the places we'd sailed to, the Island of Iilak was the smallest. One forest spread over three small mountains, which met together at a fjord with the brightest blue water I had ever seen. We sailed around the small bend toward it.

"Landon's ship?" I inquired. The shores appeared to be empty of pirate ships, rowboats, or other crews.

Ontario replied, "Not anywhere to be seen," as we looked over the island from the *Royal Rose*. Strange, but I'd take the miracle. Perhaps King Valian had blessed us today.

I glanced behind us in case the black ship was near, but we were the only vessel on the waters.

"Look there," Ontario pointed. As we pulled closer to shore and the entire fjord came into view, we could see Bernabe De's ship smashed to pieces against the rocks. "So that much of the tale was true." He tucked in his cream shirt and buttoned his red jacket, then retightened his belt with his weapons inside, eyes never leaving the island.

"Let's pray it all was. This treasure is our last hope." I checked that my own weapons were secured at my side and the strings of my black leather boots laced. "All right men, we drop anchor here. Let's find this booty and capture the ghost."

The men cheered, but it wasn't quite robust. We'd spoken of this island for so long, it felt odd to finally be here. Like a dream instead of reality. Yes, these sands ahead could lead us to the treasure and bring me to redemption.

I could only hope Landon hadn't gotten here first.

The anchor sank into the sand below, and the rowboats were lowered.

Before we loaded them, Emme paused at my side. Her hazel eyes scanned the island so thoroughly that she could have taken in every little detail—every mountainside cave, every fallen pine tree, every sandy cape on the shore.

"Arn, there's something I must tell you." She lifted her rounded chin up to stare at me.

Nerves were already flying through me at breakneck speed, crashing into my bones and making me weak inside. To keep her from seeing them, I forced a grin upon my face. "Is it how much you adore me, and how if I die, you'll never love again?"

Her crooked brows drew down, but a moment later her expression broke into a smile that dimpled her full cheeks, and she laughed. Her hand squeezed mine as she replied. "No, it is not. But this island . . ." Her face grew serious again. "I've heard Bernabe De created the rumors of his death as a trap to lure those who sought his treasure to this island where he can kill them."

"Ah, yes. That. I've heard those rumors as well. There seems to be only one way to know for sure." I gestured toward the shore. "To the island we go."

"To the island we go," Emme repeated less certainly. She rolled back her shoulders, which were speckled with freckles from days in the sun. Her deep-cut tunic showcased the octopus tentacles wrapped around her back and arms, and while those made her look rogue, it was still the tattoo of the starlight kissing the sea that I loved the most. The one that made her think of me.

Giving her an encouraging nod, we climbed into the boats and set off to claim the treasure. The men were debating about how many chests there would be, somewhere between five and five hundred being the span. Five hundred would be splendid. It would take many trips to carry it all home, but it'd be enough to pay Admiral Bones and the crew.

Our feet dug prints into the sand as we lugged the boats ashore and tightened our pistols at our sides. We surveyed the island.

"Where first, Cap'n?" Ontario asked.

A slight breeze brought the smell of pine to my nose and tousled my hair. "I say whatever we do, we all stick together. There's no use for half of us finding it and the other half being too far away to help. And I'd bet anything that the treasure lies in one of those caves." I indicated the mountains. "The question is, which one?"

"Might as well start with the closest one," Ontario suggested. "And work our way from there."

None offered a better plan, so we started treading through the side of the fjord. The nerves inside me grew until I thought I might burst, sending bits of me scattered over the mountain. Today I would prove myself as a captain. Today I would earn back the rights to my boat. Today I would help Emme buy back her childhood home. Today I would show everyone that I wasn't a fool for leaving the navy and giving up a life of certainty.

Perhaps I'd make my father proud if I returned home with enough money to make his life comfortable. I'd stay long enough to help fix the roof that always leaked in the spring and buy him new clothes so he didn't have to continue stitching up his old ones. I could bring Percival as well, the only man on crew with neither piercings nor tattoos, to show Father that not all pirates were the same. Emme might even come with me.

It was a lot to ask of this day, but I allowed my eager heart to wish, all the same.

With each step, my dreams took off until I'd convinced myself nothing wrong could happen today.

I was so lost in thought that I almost didn't hear the rustling in the woods.

We paused, my legs weary from the steep incline of the mountainside, and glanced around.

"Animal?" Emric wondered.

I shrugged as my eyes traversed the area more slowly.

"Hello?" a man's voice called out.

In an instant, we'd all drawn either our pistols or our cutlasses, depending on our strengths. I pointed my pistol through the dense trees and narrowed my eyes, sidestepping in front of Emme.

"Hello?" the man called again. My hand lowered. I recognized the voice.

"Say it isn't so," I hissed under my breath.

From above us on the mountainside stumbled down a man with short black hair and thick eyelashes who wore a navy tunic with the hem split and black pants smeared with mud as if he'd slept on the ground for a week. He tripped toward us with most of his weight favoring one leg.

Blast it.

"Arn," the man whimpered. "Arn, my old friend, is that you?"

I glared at the man, pistol up.

"Landon."

"Help m-me," he stammered. "Please." Vulnerability vibrated within his voice as he reached a feeble hand outward. I ground my teeth together to keep from spitting at him.

The men looked between the two of us as Landon came nearer, stopping far enough away that none of my crew could reach him with a cutlass swing.

Ontario broke in. "Shall we kill him, Captain?"

I didn't hesitate. "Aye."

Landon cried out for mercy, and Emric stepped in front of him and faced us. "Hold your weapons."

"No," I commanded, flaring my nostrils with my seething anger.

But Emric didn't budge, even when a few of the men leveled their pistols again. Emme cried out for them to stop and put a hand on Landon's shoulder. I cringed.

"He is weak and alone. At least let us use him for information before deciding to kill him." Landon pulled away from Emric, who chuckled. "You want to survive? Help us. Or else my captain won't hesitate to kill you, and I won't hesitate to follow his orders."

Landon cowered, and for the first time I felt a hint of pity for my once friend, but I swallowed it away.

"What will it be?"

Landon sank to his knees. "I'll give ye all I have. I'll point ye to the treasure. Just help me."

I studied my former crewmate a moment, then at my signaling, the crew formed a circle around him. I put my pistol away and crossed my arms. "And how do we know you won't take this treasure for yourself?"

"I don't want any treasure," he pled. "I just want off this place of horror."

After I begrudgingly allowed him to drink from our flasks and eat a share of the meager food we'd brought ashore, Landon leaned his head against the tree he was tied to and grinned. "It's good to see you again, old friend. I see that facial hair still hasn't come in."

A growl came from my throat. "Kill him."

He did his best to put up his hands that were fastened to his sides. "I'll tell you where the treasure is. We arrived a few weeks ago to this island amid a storm so rough that it shook the ground. We came ashore anyway and began our search. For three days and nights we did not sleep. We only searched until at last we found it."

He stretched a thin finger to the upper portions of the mountainside. "It lies in that cave."

"Which one specifically?" Emme challenged.

I didn't like the way Landon's gaze rolled over her. "The one with an entrance shaped like a heart." His eyes lingered.

I intervened. "So you found the treasure. What happened next?"

"The island turned on us. The ground quaked until it split, swallowing up one of my mates. New rain brought fierce floods that swept away two more. Rocks falling from the caves crushed another. And then there was the ghost . . . we weren't strong enough to defeat him. The remaining crew ran, but this wound slowed me down." He lifted his pant leg to reveal a deep cut along his calf that oozed yellow. His tone grew bitter. "My crew took my vessel and abandoned me here." He spat on the ground and cursed their names.

I ought to feel sorry for him, but instead, victory surged through my veins, as if he and I had been playing some game, and his loss meant that I was the better pirate. I set the terms. "You get no ration of the treasure. You don't join my crew. You show us to the treasure and help in any way needed, then we bring you to the nearest civilization where we leave you."

He nodded. "Agreed."

"Good. Since you've been inside the cave, you will help me create our plans. We rest and leave in the morning. Are there any objections?" I looked at the crew, but they all shook their heads.

"Very well, then. Load your pistols and fill your bellies, for tomorrow we prove ourselves as pirates."

My anger needed a moment to cool, so I distanced myself from

Landon for a few hours while leaving Emric in charge of watching him. A few minutes later Emme appeared at my side.

"What did he do to make you hate him so much?" she asked, leaning her curved frame against a tree across from me and pulling her braid over her shoulder to twist the end of the ribbon between her fingers.

My insides felt as twisted as that ribbon. "Are you certain you care to know?"

She nodded.

"All right then. There was a girl. Her name was Merelda Ann, and she was the doctor's daughter in the town where we grew up. When Landon and I freed the pirates from the naval ship and joined their crew, she came aboard with us. We both fell in love with her."

There it was. A little grimace that proved she cared.

I hurried on with the story. "We made plans, she and I, to run away together. Start our own crew. But in a change of heart, Merelda Ann chose Landon. That would have been enough for me, but Landon couldn't stand that Merelda Ann once had feelings for me too, so he created a plan. When we next captured a ship, it was meant to go to me, but Landon took to slandering my name to the pirates, filling them with such lies that one morning I awoke in port to find the pirates had sold me to another crew, abandoned me, and Landon had run off with my ship. I was taken as a slave aboard another vessel where I met Ontario, who was their other slave. Over time they acquired more slaves. Ontario and I freed us all within two months and rebuilt a crew together from the saved men."

The things I endured during those two months were not ones I ever spoke of. Once freed, it took a long time to build back up a name for myself, and even longer to get over the betrayal from a man I once called my brother. Upon seeing him now, that betrayal rose back to the surface of my skin with such heat that I thought it would burn me.

Emme stayed quiet for a while with her eyes fixated on the ground. At last she raised her head. "Was this during those eight months that you didn't come by the Banished Gentlemen?"

"Aye. Much changed for me in those eight months." Emme was the only friend I had kept from before the betrayal, though I had never told her the circumstances. It'd been early on in our friendship. We were still at the point of friendly conversation each time I docked at Kaffer Port, and it wasn't until a year later that I began to think of her often when I was away.

Her eyes regarded me. "It seems that now he needs your compassion."

I snorted. "It would appear that way. Though I'm finding it difficult to give that to him."

Emme was a better person than me in every way, and if someone treated her the way that Landon had treated me, she might be able to forgive them. But I couldn't. And I didn't want to. She placed a hand on my arm as if she could transfer some of her kindness into me, but the only person that my heart softened for was her.

"What if you take an early night?" she suggested. "Get some sleep, get Landon off your mind. You'll feel better by the time we head out in the morning. I imagine you haven't been getting much sleep in anticipation of all this."

I glanced back toward the camp where Landon sat fastened against a trunk. The men had gotten a fire going and some went to fetch water to boil. "It might be good for me."

Emme nudged me back toward camp. "Emric and I will take care of everything. You rest."

It was hard to argue with her. "All right. I'll go. Tomorrow we get that treasure, then we drop Landon off at an island and I never see him again."

Emme found a shaded area for me to rest my head. "Sleep well, Arn. And don't worry about a thing."

29
EMME

Once Arn was asleep, I confronted Emric. "I must fetch the Elmber Nut now. There'll be no time tomorrow."

"I know, it's all I can think about." He put his hands on his hips and surveyed the crew. He'd tied back half his brown hair in a high knot and left the bottom curls loose, and a freckle over his upper lip twitched as he thought. "Here's our plan. I'll go find it tonight, you stay here with the crew."

"No." I wouldn't even entertain such an idea. "This is my sickness, I ought to be the one to find it."

"But you'll tire easily. It'll be faster if I go."

"And if you get into any trouble, no one will be there to save you. I'm not letting you go alone."

His cheeks sucked in, and he blew out a breath. "Fine. Get your pistol and make sure it's loaded." He tightened his own belt and beckoned to Ontario. "Ontario, my good man. You've got a keen eye. Can you keep watch over Landon while my sister and I explore the area?"

Ontario raised a brow. "You heard what he said about this place. Land quakes, floods, falling rocks and the sorts. I think it better if you stay here."

Emric smiled wide and placed a hand on Ontario's shoulder. "You're a smart man; it's no wonder the captain has kept you around so long. But wouldn't it be nice to know a bit more about the area? Be sure there's no trap awaiting? Emme and I have good instincts—we will be fine. And we won't go far."

At Ontario's silence, Emric continued. "I'm sure Arn will appreciate waking to find his crew was useful while he slept."

Ontario rubbed the shaved sides of his head and glanced over to where Arn slept. "He would like that."

"Splendid," Emric said, giving Ontario a slap on the back. "We'll be back soon." He gestured to me, and we began walking.

No one stopped us, though Landon's dark brows glowered as we passed. I saw him differently after the story Arn told me of what this man had done to him. The pain of rejection intensified by the humiliation of being sold into slavery.

I wasn't convinced we should let Landon come with us to get the treasure. Arn clearly couldn't focus through his hatred. His thoughts had to be hindered by Landon's presence.

How much of his mind dwelt on that girl too? When Arn heard Landon sailed after this treasure, he must have thought Merelda Ann would be here too. It was hard not to wonder how much she filled his thoughts over these past few weeks.

"Do you know what the Elmber Nut looks like?" Emric interrupted my musing. He walked with one hand on his pistol and the other on his cutlass.

"It grows upon a thick bush with golden leaves, found at high altitudes. That's all the book said."

Emric glanced to the sky through the pine trees. "So atop a mountain."

I nodded. "But which one?"

Emric paused to look at the three mountains. The one to our right held the cave where Landon claimed the treasure to be, while the one to the left sat closest to the fjord. The one in the middle was the furthest away, and it'd take us until night to get there and back, even if we hurried.

"As much as I want to go that way"—Emric pointed to the right—"it's best if we keep our distance from the treasure until tomorrow. I don't want to awaken any dangers that might lurk inside. Let's climb the one to the left and hope it holds what we seek."

"Fair enough." We pushed through the heat and overgrown island. Roots pushed through the ground and threatened to trip us while fallen leaves and wild bushes made it difficult to see where we placed our feet.

Though months away from autumn, the island paid no regard to nature's laws as it was alit with vibrant colors of fall. Something Mother once told me echoed within. Mind beauty, for it is the disguise of evil. Now thinking of it, I wondered if she spoke of herself, for many had said her to be beautiful. Is that how she trapped her enemies?

Something else came to mind, and it sent a chill through my blood despite the heat. "Do you think Mother died on this island?"

Emric's feet paused. "I don't know. But the last letter I ever got from her was when she reached these waters."

Silence came as we were both lost to our thoughts, but my eyes stayed a little more alert now, scanning for possible signs of her. The *A* marking she carved into trees. Her bones under a tree.

I didn't know if I wanted to find anything or not. Would it bring me peace, or just upset me?

"Do you hate me as you hated Mother?" Emric asked suddenly, and my head jerked up. The fact that he had to ask such a question struck me like a knife. How could he think such a thing? I looked at him, but his eyes were serious. He planted one foot up on a moss-covered rock and rested his hands against his knee with his dark eyes fixated on mine.

"Of course I don't hate you," I said. "She was our mother and went away from us to live a fantasy on the sea. That's why

I disliked her, and I felt all pirates were like her. But you're different. And Arn is different. You care about others."

He began walking again and chopped at tall weeds as he brushed past. "But I abandoned you too." Guilt tinged his voice—a guilt that I didn't know he possessed.

I shook my head vigorously. "That was different. You left me in the care of Bart while you tried to make something of yourself. It wasn't your responsibility to care for me, and I think no ill thoughts toward you."

I was relieved to see his familiar smile. "Good. Because I couldn't stand it if you hated me."

It wasn't often that I saw what went on in Emric's head, so the small amount of sentiment in his words was enough for me.

Truth be told, I had felt bitter toward Emric for leaving me alone with Bart. Father hadn't left us by choice when he died, but Emric's departure was his own decision. While I saved every penny I earned from working at the Banished Gentlemen to try to get back the farm, Emric had abandoned his old life like it was easy and left me behind with it.

But I felt no animosity toward my brother now. And I was determined not to die and leave him without any family at all.

Emric drew in breath and froze. Every one of my senses heightened as I shifted my eyes around, but I saw nothing.

"What the devil?" he said under his breath.

I still saw and heard nothing. "What is it?" I eased closer to him.

"Do you not see the bodies?" he asked. His stood like a ghost with his face drained of color and his body wavering in the wind. He gestured a shaky hand in front of us, but my eyes still saw nothing.

"The bodies," he repeated, voice cracking. "Their bones hanging from the trees. There's so many of them. An entire army of dead bodies."

I knew some of the other men on our crew were having

nightmares, but I hadn't realized Emric was. I felt a twinge of gratitude that it was not me this time, but that was dulled by the ghastly expression on Emric's face. It wasn't a small feat to make him afraid, and whatever he saw made him terrified.

"I'm right here," I repeated Arn's words to me as I placed a hand on Emric's arm.

The moment my skin touched his, a jolt of energy went through me.

Suddenly I saw it too. The army of bodies, their skeletons hanging from the trees with frayed ropes, their bones creating an eerie sound as they clattered in the wind. The music of the dead. It sang from around us, growing louder with each passing second, threatening to swallow us up with them and turn us into another dead ornament trapped on this island.

"It's not real. It's just a vision," I said, though my voice shook.

Emric swallowed. "These may not be real, but their warning is. Death is coming."

That scared me more than the bones themselves. I'd spoken those same words to Arn a few days ago. Warned him that death was coming for us all.

If we didn't keep moving, it would be my death. I needed that Elmber Nut. I grasped Emric's hand and urged him along.

The skeletons' jaws bounced with laughter as we passed by, but I kept my eyes straight on the prickly brambles ahead. This seemed to be my normal now, seeing visions and pretending that I didn't. My mind was haunted by bones and death and I was doing all I could to stay sane.

"They are trying to tell us something." Emric's head twisted as we passed more skeletons, revealing his dark curls plastered to his neck with sweat. "A warning. They are warning us."

I forced my feet into the ground with each step and tightened my grip on my brother. The disease in my body caused my lungs to roar with pain. My legs cried for relief. This sickness frightened me as much as the bones hanging in the trees. My breathing came in shallow huffs. "If we don't find the healing nut, it's my death they will laugh at," I said grimly.

His glazed eyes drifted to me, and he shook himself. He said nothing, but walked on with more certainty, passing me on the mountain.

The music of the dead played behind us, until I couldn't know if it was the bones in the trees or the wind in the air that made the ghostly sound, but the dark feeling lifted, and the vision released us from its grasp.

We kept silent. By the time the trees thinned out and the top of the mountain didn't look a day's journey away anymore, I finally spoke. "Have you had these visions often?"

He nodded. "Ever since we first saw that cursed ship."

"But that's—"

"Before anyone else got visions, I know," he grunted in a way to show that he was not pleased about this fact. "Perhaps the ship thinks I need more time to be persuaded."

"Persuaded to what?" I wiped sweat from my brow before it could fall into my eyes.

Emric began to show signs of exhaustion himself. He breathed deep before glancing back to me. "Persuaded to leave the seas."

It took a moment for my feet to move again. "You're convinced these visions are coming from the black ship? And that it's the same one that haunted Mother?"

"I do. I don't know what magic item it holds that allows it to haunt us so, or what reason it has for doing it. But Mother spoke of someone who wanted her off the waters. I can only assume it has the same thing in mind for us. Maybe he is greedy to own the seas. Maybe it is King Valian himself."

I found no response to that, but Emric had stopped moving and peered across the sun-dappled thickets. For a horrid moment, I thought the skeletons were back to plague his mind, but his face broke into a beam as he said, "Is that it?"

He pointed an arm toward a patch of dense trees, and I shook my head. But as the wind moved, their wide leaves opened, and flashes of gold came through. I peered closer. Behind the trees sat golden shrubs. I began to cry.

We found it. We found the Elmber Nut.

We ran toward the trees with renewed energy, not stopping until we dropped ourselves on the hard soil. I gently encircled the leaves with my hands. They grew in golden lumps like a rose cupped together in layers that peeled back, one by one, until the brown shell of a nut appeared within.

Emric turned to another of the plants. "Let's take them all. These could come in handy."

"No." I stopped before he could pull at the tree. "We can only take one. We are permitted only what we need. If we take more, the nut won't heal, it will kill."

I tenderly plucked the nut and held it against my heart. "Besides, we only need this one."

I wiped at my tears. I'd left the Banished Gentlemen and the safety of land and traveled to an island many didn't believe existed to find the Elmber Nut. Now I wouldn't succumb to the disease.

First, I'd need to mash it into water and drink a dose every day for a week. Then I'd be healed. My life restored

"Thank you, Emric." I was filled with gratitude for his help as I slid the Elmber Nut into my pocket. "Thank you."

"Anytime." His eyes skirted across the mountain. "We best get going; the sun has already dipped below the mountain peak, and we need to be back before it rises again." He helped me up. "There's still one more task at hand."

30
ARN

I dreamed of death that night. Of a sea so dark that none could see through it, and the stench of blood in the air. It was a relief when Ontario woke me with a rough shake as he called out my name, but when I opened my eyes, he was several meters away from me.

"Wake up, Captain."

He wasn't shaking me; the ground was moving.

It rumbled again, and I sprang to my feet. All around me the crew was awaking with a start, grabbing hold of trees to steady themselves as leaves fell from above. Landon pushed against his tethered bonds and eyed the ground warily. I searched for Emme. She was nowhere to be seen.

"Emme!" I called out.

The ground stilled, and though the sun was not yet up, none of the crew looked eager to return to sleep. Instead they gathered their weapons and rolled their cots. We were used to the waves moving underneath us, but not so on solid land.

"Has anyone seen Emme?" I asked the group.

It was Landon who replied. "As the ground began to quake, she and another one took off." He spat into the grass.

"Save your spit," Ontario told him. "You won't get water from us."

I searched for Emric but didn't see him either. A quick count revealed the rest of the crew was accounted for.

I looked at Landon. "Took off?"

Landon jutted his chin toward the cave. "Toward the treasure. Said something about being sure nothing was wrong."

My brow furrowed as the men tied up their bags and waited for my orders. The sky held the lightest of blues as it awaited its sun, leaving the mountain too dark to spot Emme or Emric.

I pulled out my knife. "Let's go get that treasure, boys." I cut Landon from the tree, then retied his hands behind his back and pushed my blade against his skin with more force than necessary. "And if you get any ideas, I'll kill you."

"Noted," he grunted.

Ontario led us through the mountain with me behind him, holding Landon on a rope to be sure he behaved. Landon made sure to tell us where the floods came that washed away two of his men and what size of rocks killed another, until all of my men treaded on their toes and darted their eyes about like nervous mice.

"That's enough from you." I pushed the blade against his back again.

He didn't reply.

We climbed at the same speed as the sun, so by the time we reached the cave, the bright colors of the mountain were seen in full glory. If we stood facing the ocean with the reds of the leaves and the greens of the tall mountain pines and the crisp apple scent in the air, it painted a tranquil image. But when we turned to face the cave, a chilled gust licked our faces, and the bright colors turned to black rock and unknown darkness until my stomach twisted into knots tighter than any on the *Royal Rose*.

"Well, here's ye cave. In there be the treasure. What are ye waitin' for?" Landon prodded.

"Quiet, you." I tugged his ropes to remind him who was in charge. "Where would Emme and Emric be?"

"Probably getting the treasure for themselves," Landon said.

I had to admit, I wouldn't put it past Emric. But not Emme. Something was wrong.

"It'll take all day to go back to camp and find them, then come back here and get the treasure," Ontario said. "Let's get the treasure now, then find them. You have the box from the mermaids, right?"

My mind was still with Emme and Emric. Perhaps they went searching for clues of their mother. Wherever they were, if we went in without them, Emme would be saved from whatever dangers this cave held. I pulled the mermaid's box from my pocket. "Aye. We just need the ghost to pick it up of his own free will."

Landon eyed the contraption. "Ah. So you've come prepared."

If I knew anything about Landon, he hadn't. He was probably so focused on being the first to the island nothing else mattered. Still, I was curious. "What was the ghost like?"

His cheek twitched as he peeked into the cave. "He's fearsome. Our cutlasses and pistols wouldn't hurt him. He chased us all the way out here, where falling rocks crushed one of my men, sliced my leg, and sent the rest of the crew running."

Large rocks sat on the inside of the cave, and each one of the crew glanced nervously at the entrance. There was no choice for me; either I risk the rocks or I risk Admiral Bones. I'd take the rocks. But my crew shouldn't have to.

"I understand if none of you feel brave enough to enter. I'll think no less of you, and it won't be spoken of again. If any of you care to stay out here, you're welcome to. The rest of you, follow after me."

"If we're choosing, I'd like to stay out here," Landon said. But I tugged him after me.

"So you can slip your bonds and bury us in there? No. You come."

To my delight, the others followed as well. Bo put up a few

complaints, but in the end he waddled into the cave, and we were all lost to the darkness.

All we could do was put one foot in front of the other and hope the ground found us. Our footsteps echoed against the stone, as did Bo's nervous click, but none of us asked him to stop. It was nice to be reminded that someone else was nearby, that someone else was as nervous as we were.

My hand traced the damp cave walls over all the bumps and sharp edges and turns that they made. My head struck once against the low ceiling, and I warned the others about it. Stale air filled my nose, and I gagged.

"No rocks have fallen yet," Bo pointed out. "At least we're all still live."

True. So far, we'd fared better than Landon's crew had. Despite the small land quakes, we hadn't faced the floods or falling rocks that he claimed plagued them. I would doubt his claims if it weren't for the long gash in his leg that made him hobble behind me.

As I grazed my hand along the wall, the surroundings eased into view. First, small shadows of the crevices within the stone, then bit by bit, the cave ahead became less dark, until we didn't have to squint to make out each other's silhouettes. Bo's nervous clicking died down, and we all breathed a little easier. This time when the ceiling lowered, I didn't have to bash my head to know it.

The changing light was no indication that we moved in the right direction, but I chose to take it as a good sign. Something was ahead.

We walked with bent knees until the ceiling rose once again and we found ourselves in a room with two paths ahead of us. I tugged at Landon. "Which one."

"Left," he said. I studied his face, and he groaned. "It's left, all right? I want you to get the treasure quickly so we can be off of this cursed place. No tricks about it."

"There better not be."

With his hands bound and his pockets empty of weapons, he'd have to be more than skilled to attempt anything, but I'd keep an eye on him all the same.

"It'll be just up ahead. Prepare to see more money than your life is worth," Landon said.

We climbed down a narrow path and spilled into another room, where we dropped our jaws to the floor.

Gold. Gold everywhere.

The cavern rivaled the size of my ship, with thick stalactites dripping from above, each sharp enough to impale a man. The musty smell from before morphed into a twinge of copper pooling from the treasure spread in mounds about the room. There ought to be a dragon sitting there, that's how much there was. I thought to see how the others were reacting, but it was difficult to tear my eyes away from the open chests of gold coins, the crowns sitting atop crates of jewels, and the heaps of weapons in the middle.

This would be enough to pay back Admiral Bones for sure, with enough to buy back Emme's farm, and perhaps some for my men as well.

The unrest that had been growing within my chest day by day, drowning my heart in oceans of worry, began to ease up as calm sands of relief came into view, and it felt like my feet were on dry land again. I almost forgot about the ghost until a voice called out, "You think you can take what is mine?"

A cold wind came over me, and my hand tightened on Landon's ropes as he pushed himself against a wall.

"Untie me, you fool," he hissed. "He'll kill me."

Landon was the last thing on my mind as the ghost came into view. He floated through the walls and appeared hanging above us, a gray form of a man with a full beard and big belly and sharp cutlass at his side—as translucent as the rest of him. We could see through his whole body except his eyes. Those piercing eyes lit up with a green glow and stared at us as we cowered beneath.

He drew his cutlass and pointed it at us—first me, then Landon. "I thought I'd taken care of ye."

"Bernabe De. Always a pleasure." Landon's voice quivered with fear, and I found myself stepping in front of him.

"We've come to take yer treasure," I declared. The rest of the crew gave a halfhearted argh.

The ghost's lips stretched taut over yellowed teeth. "Then come get it."

He flew forward with his blade aimed at my heart. I'd never been afraid of another man's weapon as much as I feared what that translucent cutlass might be capable of. As I put up my own cutlass in defense, they struck with the sound of metal clashing together, and I dug my feet into the ground to keep my balance. Bernabe De's eyes glistened as he pushed against me.

All my crew came to my aid, running with their cutlasses in the air. It was easier for them to be brave when the ghost's eye wasn't upon them.

Ontario reached us first, but as he swung, his blade passed through Bernabe De, who gave a toothy grin.

"That won't do nothing, lad." Pure pleasure shone on his face. "You can't hurt me." He leaned off his attack, giving me a chance to regain myself, and turned to Ontario. "But I can kill ye."

Their blades struck in the air as Landon whispered behind me, "I told you. Your weapons can't hurt him."

"Shut up," I said.

The crew was doing their best, but everything was worthless against the ghost. Our bullets passed through him, our cutlasses didn't leave a mark, and fear began to creep into the eyes of men around me.

Bernabe De fought against Ontario with stealth not often seen in men his age. Being a ghost must give new energy. He sliced at my mate, knocking his cutlass from his hand and cutting into the flesh of his forearm. Ontario yelled in pain and dropped to his knees.

Bernabe De raised his cutlass, and Ontario drew his pistol and fired, but his bullets only passed through the ghost, who laughed.

"How sad, none of your men are coming to rescue you," he taunted. His cutlass rose again.

"Arn," Ontario shouted, as he staggered backward on the floor. "I need the device. It's the only thing that can kill him. Give me the weapon."

The rest of the men trembled like cowards behind the gold as if it could protect them from the wrath of the pirate ghost. As if they were safe there. A few shot up prayers, and a few tried to tunnel themselves into the chests. Landon rolled his eyes at us, though his own hand trembled.

It was exactly as we planned, and they were playing their parts perfectly.

As Ontario called out for the box, I bit my lip. "We only have one chance. Don't waste it." Then I threw the box loftily into the air. Ontario crawled on the floor to catch it, but Bernabe De laughed harder.

As the box descended, Bernabe De stuck out his hand, and it landed in his grasp.

"You think you can use a weapon against me? I'll use this against you." He held it closer to his face to examine, and we all held our breath.

For a terrifying moment, I thought it wouldn't work. If those sneaky mermaids were playing a trick on us, we'd all die for it.

But then Bernabe De gasped, and his eyes turned to me.

His translucent body began to shrink, growing smaller and smaller until he was little more than a vapor in the air, leaving beady eyes looking around wildly. He'd find no help here. His body was sucked into the box, which clattered to the floor with a hollow sound, leaving a hushed silence lingering in the air.

No one moved. Not even Landon. We stared between each other and the box until Ontario spoke up.

"Did we do it?" He picked up the box. "It's heavier than it was," he declared.

"We did it!" Bo threw fistfuls of coins in the air. At his outburst, we all broke, letting the fear of the day flood out with the triumph that we had accomplished our mission. We defeated the ghost. We got the treasure.

I threw my head back and hollered into the air, letting my cheers echo through the chasms. My excitement felt too big for this cavern to contain, and I let out my joy by running though the gold. Like Bo, I threw it into the air with a happy shout. "We beat him!"

Landon rubbed his leg while waiting for us to finish celebrating. I stopped first. "Emme and Emric are still out there," I reminded everyone. "Let's start bringing the treasure out and find them."

"Aye, Captain." They were all laughs as they picked up treasure and began to walk out.

I glanced to Landon. "I still don't trust you. You'll stay tied up until we get to camp."

"Aye, Captain," he said in a mocking tone. But his sarcasm didn't bother me.

Right now, nothing could bring me down.

31

EMME

For the first time in months, when I opened my eyes that morning it was not to the smell of rum or the sight of wooden planks but to the sweet scent of fresh air and a blue sky above my head. A long gulp of air filled my lungs before I remembered where I ought to be, and I sat up quickly.

"Good morning." Emric had a small fire going and a rabbit cooking above it. "You hungry?"

My mouth watered, but I knotted my brows together. "We were to get the treasure this morning. Where are the others?"

"Do you not remember last night?" Emric asked as he turned the cooked rabbit onto its side. My brain worked to piece together the evening before, but it was too slow.

Emric waved his stick at the trees. "We made it down the mountain, but you were so tired that we camped here. You were clearly exhausted; you slept through the ground shaking this morning. Thought it might break apart."

"What of the others?" I gathered up my things and straightened out my clothes.

"I checked on camp a bit ago, but they were already gone. They've gone after the treasure."

Everything that might be going wrong right now came to mind: Landon betraying them, the ghost killing them, rocks crushing them—the thoughts made my hands work faster. I retightened the clasp on my hair and picked up my bag.

"We were supposed to be there for them."

Emric put down his stick. He rested his elbows on his knees. "Let me be clear: they are not my concern, and the treasure is not my priority. You are what I care for. Keeping you alive. You can't fight this sickness if you're tired. We can meet up with the others once you've eaten." He stabbed through the rabbit meat with his knife and brought it over to me.

His concern made me regret not telling him sooner about the disease. It weighed on me less now that he knew, and soon it wouldn't be a burden at all.

I pulled the nut from my pocket and my old wineskin from my bag. I pressed my knife against the nut until it splintered and ground it into dust. Then I put the dust in the sack.

"First day," I announced. "In seven days, I'll be healed." I poured a small portion of the bitter powder into my mouth and took a gulp of water. It took a few swigs to get all the powder down, and Emric watched until it was gone.

I swore I felt better already.

"Six days left," he said in a breathy tone as if it had healed him too. "Now eat."

We ate quickly, then set off toward the mountain with content bellies and a full night's rest under our belts. Though if we found Arn as anything other than alive, I'd never forgive myself for sleeping through the morning. I used that guilt to will my feet faster.

We made it only partway before we heard shouting.

We both took off into a run and eventually could make out Bo's whooping cheers. "We're rich! Filthy rich!"

"They did it!" Emric took off faster, and I struggled to keep up. We wove through trees shouting their names as we got closer. My feet stumbled over roots, and I almost planted into the ground, but I managed to keep upright. I listened for Arn's voice, for proof that he was alive.

Through the chorus of noise, I made out Arn's voice. "Emme? Emric?" he yelled. "Is that you?"

His voice was a relief. We shouted back, and soon their figures came into view through the trees.

Not just their figures but the treasure as well.

Arn, with all his limbs attached and no visible injuries, swooped me up in a tight embrace that crushed my bones. "Thank King Valian you're alive."

Emric spread out his hands. "Anyone miss me? Timmons? Henrik?"

They all laughed.

"You got the treasure." Arn set me down, and I gazed at the chests scattered along the ground like a blanket of gold.

"Aye, this is the last of the loot," Ontario proclaimed as he set down a pile of weapons. Most of the crew were gathered around the treasure, picking through the coins and jewels and examining them under the sunlight. Henrik was biting coins between his teeth, Percival was wrapping up weapons in twine, and Bo had on an emerald crown, parading through the wealth. Landon sat tied against a tree and glanced around us with shifty eyes. He was the only one who looked nervous. The rest of the crew were drunk off the treasure.

"Your plan went perfectly," Arn congratulated me.

Ontario snorted. "Almost." He turned his face to reveal a fresh cut down his cheek.

"Sorry mate, he needed to think we were desperate," Arn said as he scrunched his nose and cheeks to make an apologetic face.

"We were." Ontario wiped dried blood from his cheek. "No real harm done. Let's get this treasure to the ship and take off." He bent to pick up a chest with coins spilling from its lid, but Landon snickered, drawing every eye to him.

"Something funny, mate?" Arn brought out his knife and used it to push Landon's chin upward to look at him. "See, we came prepared, and your crew didn't. That's why we got the treasure, and you're tied to a tree. Perhaps I'll sell you as a slave at the next port we come to."

Landon jerked away from the blade, but the smile didn't leave his face. "You think you're so clever, but you won't be going anywhere with my treasure."

Emric grabbed his cutlass and set his feet firm, the first to understand. Before any others could react, a whistle pierced the mountain, and men bled from the forest to run at us. Everywhere we turned, there was another man coming at us: from the mountainside, from the beachfront, from all angles a pirate appeared, surrounding us with their weapons and showing all sign of intending to run us through.

Emric jumped in front of me with his blade out. "We don't want any bloodshed." His plea was ignored among the shouts, and the next sound was the clash of a cutlass against his own. Just like that, battle broke out. Landon was cut free by a lass with golden locks and tattoos by her eyes. He gave her a quick kiss as she handed him a knife. Before I could wonder if that was Merelda Ann, Ontario fired his pistol at Landon. Blood appeared on Landon's arm, but he hardly glanced at it. There wasn't time to reload, so Ontario drew his sword instead.

Arn, his face red with fury, charged at Landon. I glimpsed a pistol aiming his way and I lunged to grab the edge of Arn's jacket. It felt like my arm was yanked from my socket before I managed to tug Arn back toward me. The pistol fired, and a bullet hole appeared in the tree by Arn's head.

"Thanks. Is your pistol loaded?" he asked me, his eyes wildly dancing across the forest.

"One shot, guard my right." I raised my weapon and pointed it at Landon, but my finger hesitated on the trigger.

Could I take a life?

All the horrid things Landon had done to Arn came to mind in attempt to convince my troubled heart that it was okay to fire. But my hesitation lasted too long, and my moment was lost. The enemies drew too near, and I abandoned my pistol for my cutlass to block an attack from the girl. The force of her swing almost ripped my blade from my hand, and I was thrown to the ground. She twisted it to continue the momentum and came back at me faster than I could reposition my blade, leaving my head vulnerable.

Arn's quick blade saved me, and before I could react, he'd struck.

Her blood spurted over me, and I staggered back. Arn grabbed my hand and pulled me up to him.

"I promised to protect you," he said. He glanced at me as I tried to steady my breathing. "I'm sorry."

His words couldn't find me. I focused on the trees, on the glint of the treasure, on the scent of gunpowder—anything but the body at my feet.

Over his shoulder I saw Landon's eyes turn feral, and he charged for Arn with full speed. "Watch out," I yelled as I shoved Arn out of Landon's path. Landon adjusted quickly and swung at Arn, who dropped himself to the forest floor as the cutlass sliced over his head. Arn fumbled to get a solid grip on his own weapon as Landon bared his teeth and brought his blade downward.

A man came at me from one side, and I dug my feet into the ground to hold the force of his attack against my blade. His red beard shook as he huffed with his cheeks. Using a move my mother had taught me, I lowered my body, twisted the blade, and brought his sword dropping to the floor. He faltered, and I picked up his blade and swung them together, cutting his arm to the bone.

He let out a hollow scream as my stomach convulsed.

He clutched his arm and sank into the ground. *Kill him*, a voice inside me said. But I moved away. His head lowered into the earth as he screamed again.

Arn's and Landon's blades met by their heads, and they

wrangled to push the other's away. Arn brought a second hand up to his hilt to increase pressure, but Landon's went to his waist. A small knife slid out of his pocket.

Arn didn't see the blade, and his chest was unprotected.

"No!" I thrust my cutlass between them to block the strike aimed for his heart, and Landon cursed. In a fluid motion, he diverted his attack and sliced cleanly through Arn's wrist.

Arn's bloodcurdling scream vibrated in my bones as he dropped the cutlass and grasped the place where blood poured out at a sickening speed.

Landon was on his knees beside the girl Arn had killed, placing his hands on her head. Tears glimmered in his eyes. He glared at Arn and spat. "You'll die for this."

"Captain!"

Both Arn and Landon turned their heads, but it was Ontario with his back toward the beach who called out. He pressed a hand against his leg as red liquid oozed through his fingers. "There's too many of them, we have to retreat, Cap'n. We've lost too many."

My vision finally took in all the bodies on the ground. This fight had been too fast, we were too unprepared. My brother stood with his pistol in one hand and cutlass in the other, growling at two smaller men, while others were digging through the treasure and shoving some into their filthy pockets. Seeing my brother still standing filled me with relief, but my heart quickly sank into despair as I searched to find others in our crew.

"They'll kill us all, Arn." I could barely look at his anguished face and horrifying wound. "We have to leave."

The world felt like it stopped moving; the ground disappeared from my feet and my mind turned to water in my head, leaving me drifting away like a ship with no captain. There was only one thought on my mind. Get off this island. Get away from the death.

Death is coming.

I should have listened.

Arn gathered a shuddering breath and raised his voice, "Men, to the boats!" he cried.

Ontario ran. Emric ran. Bo ran. But no one else did. I spotted Timmons crouched on the ground and clutching his side, and I sprinted to his aid.

"Let them be," Landon demanded. "They aren't worth any more of our own lives." I eyed him. He still cradled the lifeless girl in his lap.

"I'll be okay," Timmons insisted. "Check on the others." He rose and hobbled through the trees and toward the fjord.

Despite Landon's orders, a thin youth no older than me rushed at Arn. Despite missing his left hand, Arn blocked the blade, twisted it, and disarmed him. In a move so fast I barely saw it, he thrust his cutlass into the other man's stomach and yanked it out.

Landon's voice thundered. "Leave them!"

His generosity might not last long. I scanned for more of our men, finding Zander in a pool of blood with two holes in his chest. I pressed my hand to my mouth as tears slid down my face.

Svid and Sims were almost inseparable in life. They were dead within inches from each other, though Sims's head was not where his body was.

Percival.

Henrik.

Malcom.

They were all dead.

Arn had bound up his own wound with his jacket and gritted his teeth as he helped Collins to his feet while Bishop crawled toward the fjord.

That was it, the four that were ahead and the four of us here. Everyone else was slaughtered.

I crouched beside Bishop. "Lean on me," I instructed. He grunted as he did so, his hefty weight dragging at my side as we went slowly together toward the fjord.

It felt like ages until we reached it, and I kept waiting for a bullet to rip through me, but the attacking crew stayed behind, drunk on their new treasure. Landon's voice was the last thing we heard before the familiar sound of ocean waves met us and the rowboats came into view.

The ocean once felt dangerous. Now I couldn't reach it fast enough.

Ontario and Timmons rowed one boat, while Emric and Bo waited in the other. At the sight of us, their faces fell when they realized no others were coming. There was no time to mourn. We helped Bishop and Collins into the boat, Collins nursing a gunshot to his side and Bishop a nasty gash on his calf. We didn't have enough crew left to row the third boat, so we abandoned it. With great difficulty and heavy hearts, we rowed back to the ship.

Getting the injured up the rope proved difficult, but they found a last ounce of strength to hang on while we pulled from above, until we were all sprawled on the deck.

It felt as if half our hearts were left behind.

"What's this?" Arn cradled his wrist to his chest and went over to the main mast. A paper and sack were nailed to the post. He pulled at the sack, and it exploded in his hand in a ball of purple dust that flittered through the air over the whole ship.

We all coughed and covered our faces, as Arn cursed. "One last trick. That's why he didn't want us all dead. One last trick."

The purple mist lit up like fairy dust, and a boom echoed through the air. There was a great flash of light and gust of wind, and the world went dark.

Only when the dust settled as ash on the deck did the sunlight come back.

I blinked. None of us was missing or more injured than before. I bent to roll flakes of dust over my thumb.

"What in the name of the dark sea?" Emric went to the edge of the ship, and our eyes followed. We were no longer by the Island of Iilak, but further out in sea. Land loomed beyond, and

Emric gazed at it. "That's not the Island of Iilak." He pivoted. "What was the dust?"

"Fairy dust." Arn's voice was dismal. "It sends a ship back to its berth." He stared at the coastline. "Blimey, I know these docks. We are near my hometown of Lemondey. We won't be getting back to that treasure anytime soon." He winced, clutching his jacket closer.

I gently touched his arm to examine his injuries. He relented, grimacing as he peeled back his jacket.

"I'm going to kill Landon," he growled. The bitterness he was feeling must be a thousand times more painful knowing he had been deceived by his former friend . . . again.

If it was anyone else but Arn, I might be able to convince him to abandon the mission and find smaller merchant ships to plunder to make up for the wealth we didn't acquire, but Arn wouldn't move past Landon's betrayal for a second time.

That didn't surprise me. What did surprise me was that I didn't want him to. I didn't want Arn to let Landon get away with what he'd done. I wanted to see Landon repaid for his cruelty and the men he'd killed. For the pain he'd caused Arn. I pushed the vision of the slashed girl out of my mind.

Landon was a ruthless pirate. And it'd take an equally ruthless pirate to get revenge.

"That's not normal." For a moment I thought Arn could see into my thoughts, but he was looking at the bloodied stub of his wrist where blackness began to seep across the skin beyond the edges of the wound. A sick feeling traced its way into my heart. Arn's head slowly came up, until his eyes locked with mine and his face contorted with fear.

"By stars," he said. "It's poisoned."

32

ARN

Pain.

Searing pain. If I were struck by lightning, it wouldn't hurt more.

The pain wasn't just in my wrist, it was in my head. In my heart. In the way that every tiny movement brought new discomfort that reminded me of Landon.

There weren't curses strong enough to use against him. With every fiber of my being—my aching, pitiful being—I loathed that pirate.

My lips snarled, and Emme saw my expression. "Is it bad?"

I grunted in response. She wrapped both her hands around mine, and I didn't have the heart to tell her that made it worse. I'd normally love her hands holding mine, but now the gesture mocked me. She had two hands; I'd forever only have one.

Stop it. You're being a child.

"How much longer?" I asked Emric, who steered the vessel with joy as if his comrades weren't scatted across the deck with injuries. No doubt he already saw my disability as a reason to step down as captain, leaving the position open to him.

I'd remind him that I was still in charge if I had energy left.

"The berth is upon us," Emric announced. "Drop anchor now."

Ontario nodded and released the wheel holding the anchor. We slowed to a stop, and I groaned again. I had to move.

I'd asked them not to take us toward the mainland. Across a large bridge sat a thin island where one resident lived with his wife and daughter. The town doctor. I knew them well as a lad, and if there was hope to survive this poison in my veins, it was there. After all these years, I never thought I'd return to the charming cabin with flower beds under the windows and brick pathways and the tall chimney where I spent many days growing up, running through the trees while the doctor studied the plants, or helping his wife plant herbs in her garden. This was where I met their daughter, Merelda Ann. This was where I fell in love with her. It'd been like home.

I hadn't been back since Landon and I convinced her to sail away with us.

Before I could stand up, Ontario swore, and Emric held up his hands. "Whoa, there."

"I don't need any of your kind here," a familiar voice shouted. "I've no interest in being a pirate's doctor, so you can turn around now before I run you through." The voice came from the end of the pier where I knew the wooden boards were slanted and riddled with holes.

"Put the pitchfork down, my lady. We're not here to steal ye away. We're in need of your help," Emric used his smoothest voice to reason with her.

She wouldn't be bridled. "Go away, I said." A tapping came against the side of the boat, and Emric put up his hands again. Emme had risen, but I took a few moments to find my feet. She wasn't supposed to be here. It was bad enough to face her parents but encountering her might kill me faster than this poison.

A new throbbing came from my wrist, and I winced.

Inch by inch I raised myself until I was standing with most of my weight leaned against the railing. The figure below kept an eye on Emric and waved her pitchfork at him as he tried to convince her to lower it. "I have sick men aboard."

I spoke up. "Merelda Ann."

At my voice, her pitchfork dropped and her face became white as a ghost. Her gray eyes sliced to me, and she gasped.

She looked as beautiful as I remembered. Hair dark as the night. Skin smooth as glass. Piercing eyes when she was upset. And the same pointed chin that now dropped open in surprise.

"Arn? Is that you?"

"Aye. Now may we dock? We need your father's skills." I lifted my bloodied arm, and she took a step back. Her eyes held mine for what felt like ages, as if she hoped to uncover my emotions from afar before inviting me in. To know if I still hated her for what she'd done.

I was in too much pain to hate her. All my energy went into standing. If the wind blew right now, it'd knock me over, and I wouldn't have the strength to stand back up.

"We haven't got all day," Emme said with tight lips. "Emric, let down that ramp." Her voice grew louder. "We are coming down, and you're going to help us."

Merelda Ann looked at Emme for the first time and nodded. When Emric dropped the ramp, she held it in place as the men began to descend. Emric let Bishop lean against him as he hobbled down the rickety plank with his right leg soaked in blood. Emric had a long cut down the length of his arm, but he didn't appear bothered by it. He was lucky to have gotten away with such a small wound. The others weren't as lucky. Ontario had a second gash on his face, leaving his features distorted. He limped as he came down the board. Timmons walked stiffly with his hands at his side where his torn shirt revealed a slice from a cutlass. He'd need stitches for sure. Emme offered her hand to him and gave Merelda Ann a sideways glance as she passed by her.

Collins suffered a side injury as well, but his was from a

bullet, and there was no telling what sort of internal damage that had caused. He crawled down the gangplank on all fours. Bo had a gnarly bruise over his eye and a flap of skin hanging off his arm. He must be drunk because he didn't seem to notice it, despite the damp blood on his shirt.

Emme was the only one unscathed. I'd paid a great price to keep her safe, and even though it hurt so bad I might pass out, I would do it over again.

With one thing different. I'd kill Landon.

Merelda Ann walked with Collins, though she looked back at me a few times as we crossed the pier and headed down the cobblestone path. The trees bowed in an arch over the pathway with large white flowers blooming. The air smelled of honey and lavender, and the bluebirds' song was just as sweet as I remembered it.

It was like I was thirteen again and spending my time on the island with the pretty girl, dreaming of when I would be captain in the king's navy.

My wrist sent a new surge of pain, reminding me of how times had changed.

Emric entered the house and made way for the rest of us to spill into the large entry room.

"Are Mathias and Mary here?" I searched for the kind couple but saw no one.

Merelda Ann bit her lip. "My parents passed a few years ago. I'm this town's doctor now." She didn't say it with sadness but more as a fact, and her eyes still hunted through mine. I turned.

"I'm sorry to hear that. Can you—" The pain in my wrist flared in intensity as the blackness spread further down the skin of my arm. "Can you help us?" My vision darkened, and the floor swayed beneath me. Stars and seaweed. What was that dagger laced with?

She took a timid step toward me and reached for my wrist.

Emme stiffened but didn't say anything. Merelda Ann's tender fingers hovered over my wound before she clicked her tongue. "You've been poisoned. This could be serious."

I knew that. "Do you know what it is?" I strained to get the words out, and my forehead dripped in sweat.

"I'll do a few tests. Are you—"

My knees buckled, and the world faded from my sight.

33
EMME

When Arn went down, I ran to his side. Merelda Ann backed up as I set his heated head in my lap. His hair was damp with sweat. "Can you help us or not?" My words were frantic.

She nodded quickly. "Lay him down. I'll do those tests and see what we are dealing with." Something changed in her, and she began to speak with authority. She pointed to the others. "Those with more serious injuries go to the tables over there. There are swabs and disinfectants on the wall with the wide window; treat your cuts with them. I'll stitch what needs to be stitched once I take care of Arn." They waddled over and began poking through her bottles.

I held Arn tighter. "I'm staying with him. Blast. He's burning up. He needs help fast." Hot tears pooled at my lids. Merelda Ann didn't comment. She left, returning a moment later with gauze and a blue bottle of something that she poured over Arn's wrist. It carried a foul smell to it. She dabbed at the wrist a few times and carefully wrapped it with bandages.

Then she lay her fingers against his throat. "His breathing is too slow," she said. "Whatever is in his body, it's killing him fast. I'm guessing viper poison." Her eyes were somber. "I have oil I can put on it, but this isn't like a bite; there's no telling how much venom has gone into his bloodstream already. And with how much blood he's lost . . ."

I didn't care for the way her voice drifted off or her eyes looked at him as if he were already dead.

"There's not much I can do for him at this point," she whispered.

My voice felt heavy in my throat. "Will he die?"

Her face hardened. "I'll be surprised if he lives through the night."

A deep pain vibrated through my chest and squeezed my heart until I thought I was dying with Arn.

The Fates, the gods, the Sea King Valian—whoever controlled the world was dark and twisted to do this to us. Just when I've found the Elmber Nut to save myself from death, Arn was going to die.

My heavy tears landed on Arn's cheeks. I soaked in every detail of him as if seeing him for the last time. If he hadn't been there today to stand in front of me, Landon would have killed me.

I couldn't lose him.

"Wait," I said to Merelda Ann. "I have something."

She wore a pitied expression as I fumbled for my pocket and drew out the worn leather sack. "It's the Elmber Nut." I held it out to her. "It can save him."

Her brows rose, and she took the sack from me to peer inside. "I've never seen one of these. I thought it to be a fable."

"It's real, I promise you. Is there enough there for him?"

She twisted a finger through the grains. "He must drink some for seven days, right? There's just barely enough. He might die before the seven days, but each serving should slow down his death. It might work."

My voice was tense. "It has to."

She fetched a dainty wooden spoon from the windowsill and dipped it into the bag, then mixed some powder into water.

"Use the blue bottle to clean your bandages, not rum," she ordered the others, who were applying the liquid to their cuts. She shook her head. "Pirates." Her tone was one I recognized, as I often used it myself a year ago when speaking of seafaring scallywags. Though from what Arn told me, she used to be one herself.

She brought the cup to Arn's lips and instructed me to lift his head. Bit by bit she allowed the liquid to slide down his throat until it was all swallowed, then she set the cup down and waited.

Color didn't return to his face, his temperature didn't lower, and his breathing remained shallow.

"It could take some time to work," she said. "I need to tend to the others." She rose almost reluctantly and hovered her hand over his arm, then pulled it back. "I'm so sorry," she whispered to me before walking away.

I was too worried for Arn to think about her or about what I'd just done. All I could do was stroke his forehead and hold his hand as his body trembled and pray that the healing nut was enough to save him.

34
ARN

Her soothing presence stayed beside me for hours. Perhaps days. I knew little of time and only of this agony in my blood. A warm glass was brought to my lips again, and the strange drink poured down my throat. I wanted to ask for something stronger but lacked the energy to open my eyes, much less speak words. I groaned, and Emme grabbed my hand.

"I'm right here," she whispered. "You'll be okay."

"We will see," Merelda Ann said. "It's been almost two days, and he's not awake."

"But he's not dead."

I fought to wake up, if only for Emme's sake. Merelda Ann was too straightforward. She didn't know that Emme needed a gentler tone or she'd drive herself crazy with worry. Emric wouldn't coddle her either. She needed me.

I struggled to move my muscles, but the effort seemed to welcome the darkness further in until I wasn't sure I was dreaming or alive at all.

35

EMME

Arn stirred in his sleep. His cheeks held a tint of pink to them, and Merelda Ann said his pulse was returning to normal. She didn't know why he didn't wake.

She kept as constant of an eye on him as I did, while the other men spent their days outside taking in the crisp air and stretching their tender wounds to distract themselves from the death of half their crew and the loss of the treasure. They pushed themselves hard to ease their sorrows, even taking to running laps around the island. Bishop had to get his stitches redone in his calf, but the rest of the crew minded Merelda Ann's orders well.

As I took a breath away from Arn's side, I studied Merelda Ann more carefully, and it was clear to see why he had been attracted to her. Her posture was upright, and she spoke with confidence. Her knowledge of medicine was impressive. Plus, she was absolutely beautiful. Delicate and fair, while my thighs were thick and my belly rolled as I sat down. It was hard not to imagine Arn's hand in hers, his kiss on her lips, his hands in her silky hair . . . If I weren't already on the brink of madness over concern for Arn, those thoughts alone would drive me over the edge.

But I'd never hurt Arn the way that she had. Perhaps that's why I didn't get jealous of her or pinch my cheeks in attempt to bring out any beauty.

"It's unusual to have the Elmber Nut. And it was already ground up." Merelda Ann stood beside me at the window as we watched the crew climb the trees like monkeys. "What did you intend the healing nut for?"

I owed her no answers. "It matters not. The important thing is it can save Arn."

Her lips twisted in a grin. "Hmm. I'm a doctor, you know. If you need any help . . ."

"I don't." If I thought she could help me, I might let her, but as my disease had no cure there was no point in sharing details with her. All there was to do was get back to the island and get another Elmber Nut. And hope that the one dose I took was enough to forestall death. I hadn't struggled to run across the island like I would have before, which gave me hope that I could live to nineteen. Maybe twenty. That one dose might have slowed things down.

"In any case, it was very noble of you to offer it to him."

Noble. It was hardly noble. It was the right thing to do. If what Arn told me was true, Merelda Ann wouldn't have made the same decision. Heat burned beneath my skin at the thought, and I dug my nails into the windowsill.

"How could you do that to him?" The words spilled out without intention, and she stilled before nodding slowly.

"So he told you about us?" She brushed her long, dark hair over her shoulder where it hung like a curtain of night. Her gray eyes flickered to him.

My nose flared at her use of the word "us," as if there was still something between the two of them. "He told me how you and Landon sold him and took his ship. It must have been a surprise to you when he showed up here as captain of his own vessel."

"What we did was terrible." She showed no hint of remorse. "We were so young, and the pirate life seemed so romantic. The grog and seasickness got to me, and I made a rash decision."

I waited, but she didn't say more. "That's it? A rash decision?

Spending your pocket money on a new linen, that's a rash decision. You sold Arn to pirates."

Her jaw tightened. "You didn't know what he was like. He was reckless and carefree. If he'd have gotten that ship, he would have taken on the high seas with abandonment, and his high spirit would have led him to his death. We tethered him back to earth. We saved him."

She didn't understand him. "Those are the things I love about him. He lives life larger. But he is thoughtful and carefree all in the same breath. Wild but smart. Ambitious and determined. Those are the best parts of him, and if you ever loved him, you wouldn't have tried to take that away from him."

Her eyes rudely moved past me, but then they widened. "He's waking."

I spun around and flew to Arn's side. His feet twitched for the first time since he went unconscious three days ago, and a low grumble came from his throat. Merelda Ann came behind me as his lids fluttered open.

"Hey, I'm right here." I placed my hand against his cheek and spoke softly in his ear. "I'm here. I'm here."

His arm reached for mine before pausing, and his eyes opened more. He lifted his arm and made a face. "I forgot I only have one blasted hand now."

His voice was music to my ears. I laughed, drinking in the sound of it. "I thought you were going to die."

"Not today, love. You're stuck with me for a bit longer."

With each hour that passed, Arn showed more and more strength until he could sit up in bed and drink his own soup. I finally felt safe enough to leave him and get some air, walking down the path under the trees to sit on the end of the pier.

As soon as I sat down, tears flooded from my eyes. An arm

wrapped around me, and Emric pulled me into him. "Sorry," I said, shaken. "I don't even know why I'm crying."

"Relief. Stress. You had to be brave for him in there, now you need to let the emotions out. It's okay." He patted my back as my tears dripped down his tunic.

I wiped my palm across my eyes. "It's so good to see him awake."

"It is a wonder though, with how sick he was." His knowing eyes burned into mine. "You gave him the Elmber Nut."

My head dropped. "I couldn't see him die."

He drew a hand over his face. "And I can't afford to see you die. I suppose we go back to get another one."

"I guess so." We stayed quiet for a while as my tears dried and birds sang their afternoon songs. They sounded merry like they knew it was a day to celebrate. Arn would not die, and that was reason to be joyous.

Emric lowered his voice. "Have ye had any more nightmares?"

I frowned. "No. I assume they were trying to warn us of the trap we sailed into. We ought to have listened." I didn't say the names of the fallen men. The ones who'd dedicated themselves to helping us reach that island, whose bodies would now never leave it. I felt guilty for not thinking of them more often, as worries for Arn had controlled my thoughts, and remembering their bodies scattered on the fjord would bring nothing but further sorrow that I didn't know if my distraught soul could handle.

Anything more might break me like a wave, and I'd sink to the bottom of the ocean.

"It's odd though," Emric mused. "I don't think the ship was warning us of Landon. Pearl said their ship had nightmares too."

I gripped the ends of the boards beneath my legs. "What were the visions of death about then?"

"To scare us off the water. Look." He gestured behind him. Out in the ocean, a ship lurked on the horizon. "The black ship is still there."

36
ARN

"You should go visit your father," Merelda Ann said as she changed the dressing on my arm.

I feared my father's disappointment as much as I feared Admiral Bones when he realized I hadn't got the treasure. Both might kill me.

"Have you told him anything?" I asked, grunting with pain as she tied the bandage off.

She shook her head and wound my old bandages up. "No. Of course not. But I know he misses you."

I missed him, too, but I'd rather him miss me than hate me. I set my wrist back on my stomach and stared up at the boards of the ceiling that had been painted since I was here last. "In a few years I'll have word sent to him that I died at sea. He can think my life ended with honor."

She gave a surprised laugh, drawing my attention back to her. "The king is no longer at war," she informed me. "Your father will think you died a foolish death when there is no battle to be fought."

I rubbed my tired eyes. This was not high on my list of concerns at the moment. "I suppose you can tell him everything for me, then. Care to tell him how you and Landon sold me as a slave? That's my favorite bit."

Her voice pulled tight. "I'm sorry about that. I thought it to be for your own good."

"I'm going to help you out. Selling someone as a slave will never be for their own good."

She studied my eyes for a few moments, but finally I grinned, and she grinned back. Years ago I would have liked to see her and Landon killed for what they'd done to me, but it was hard to hate her when she'd just saved my life. Her calm gray eyes settled on me as she sighed. Fingers tickled my skin as she slid them over my good hand with sure movement, like her hand belonged there entangled in mine.

I didn't pull away, and that was all the prompting she needed.

She swept her hair to the side and let it brush against my shoulder as her lips neared mine. How I'd craved those lips so many times. But having her here now with the sweet scent of honey coming from her neck and her lips inches from mine, it didn't stir my heart as it once had. My heart no longer yearned for hers.

"Don't," I said before her lips could touch mine.

She straightened. "I'm sorry. I've just missed you."

"There are other ways to miss someone without kissing them."

She laughed, but the sound was false. "I'll try one of those then. I really have missed you."

I moved my hand away from hers. "How did you end up back here?"

She leaned back in her seat. "Landon. After we left you—"

"Sold me," I corrected.

Her face flinched. "Right. After that unpleasantness, we had a good time together. But he soon grew enamored with other women. When I received the letter that my parents died in an accident, I came back home to pick up the business and haven't seen him since."

If I were a kinder man, I'd say how sorry I was for her. But that was a lot less horrid than what happened to me, so I kept my mouth shut and nodded. It worked out for the best for her; she didn't have to deal with Landon anymore. After what he'd done. Landon would be seeing me a lot sooner than he planned.

Merelda Ann sighed deeply. Her hands brushed back my hair as a small tear traced a line from her eye to her chin. "You don't have to kiss me. But please, can I sit here for a little bit and pretend that you are the boy I used to know? The one that climbed up in the old tree to save me and who almost drowned fetching my gold bracelet from the water? I've missed that boy very much."

Her eyes were so pleading that I let her stay perched at my side, studying my face for a few moments until she shook her head.

"The sweetness you once had for me is gone," she said. "I hurt you too much for you to care for me anymore." I stared at her blankly. Did she think I'd wait for her forever?

I shrugged. "It's been a long time."

"And yet, it feels like just yesterday." Her words were so soft, they might not have been for me. After giving me one more longing glance, she turned away and disappeared to her back room, leaving the door open behind her. A minute later she returned with a box in hand. "I have no use for this anymore."

She sat the box on my stomach where gold edging gleamed from all sides and faded brass showed hints of markings underneath dust and oils. It was larger than my hand but bore almost no weight against my skin. A low hum came from it, one that changed notes slightly with each passing second, like it sang a song to itself—one so deep and quiet that I had to strain my ears to catch the faintest hint of a melody. It sounded sad, but hopeful. Like the dawn after a long night.

"It can't replace the men you lost." Merelda Ann tucked her hands around her sides. "But it can help manage the boat until you get more pirates on crew."

"How?"

"It's magic." I'd guessed as much. "It can take you in the direction you wish to go. When you get on board, place it at the helm. It will propel the boat while you are missing the men to row for you. But it won't last forever. Maybe a month before it dies out, and that's all the magic it offers. It'll work right as new on other ships, but it will only serve each ship once."

"That's odd." I risked touching the box and was surprised to find it cold.

"I don't make the rules of the world," Merelda Ann said. "If I did, things would have gone a lot differently between us."

At that moment Ontario appeared in the doorway. The cuts in his face caused his features to be distorted, with one cheek sagging and the side of his lip pulled further than it ought to be. The once-tan skin was now colored as blue as his jacket that he straightened. "May I have a word with the captain?"

"Certainly." Merelda Ann took the box off my stomach to place under the bed. "He's all yours."

Ontario knelt beside me. "How do ye feel?"

I groaned in reply.

"Do ye feel capable of traveling again?"

I'd rather lie here forever than think of moving these aching muscles ever again, but the stiches in Ontario's face strained as it wrinkled in concern. From his pocket he produced an envelope. The black border and sun stamp were the last things I wanted to see right now. "The letter arrived from his bird this morning." He held it up for me to read.

You'll be dead in two weeks.

There was no command. No request. Nothing besides the promise that since we didn't get the treasure, we'd be dead. We had two weeks before he found us.

"He's truly not a pleasant man. Ye should have listened to my begging not to get involved with him," Ontario said. At my frown, he coughed. "How does he know we failed?" He stuffed the letter back inside his jacket.

With difficulty, I lifted my foot. "He's tracking through the oathbinding. My guess is he saw our sudden jump from one location to another and knows something happened to us." My chest rose and fell with a defeated sigh. "There's nowhere for me to run from him."

"I might have rather died on that island than die by his hand," Ontario said. "Perhaps our old mates had it lucky."

"Don't say that," I snapped. "Don't ever say that. No man is lucky for dying."

At the look on his face I chastised myself for responding so harshly. We'd just lost so many men; I ought to let him have whatever way he needed to make sense of it. As vulgar as it seemed, maybe those men were better off.

"What have we done, Captain?" Ontario whispered the question as he wiped tears from his cheeks. With each tear he removed, three more followed. He held up his wet hands. "These hands are soaked with more . . . with more than my tears." Another sniff. "They are soaked with the blood of my brothers. What have we done?"

Forsaking all pain, I placed my nub of a wrist on Ontario's knee. It burned at the touch, but my heart carried more agony that any physical ailment. "You are a good man. This nightmare is not of your doing. That burden is for me to carry alone."

He rubbed his nose. "There's no way to make this right, Captain. We can never undo what we've done."

"We can get that treasure back and save the other half of the crew from Admiral Bones's wrath."

"Impossible. It's too far. I'm not going back there."

"Not to the Island of Iilak. When we rescued Pearl, she told us of a tavern where Landon always goes to celebrate victorious plunders. He isn't aware that we know of it. We can reach it in a week and steal the treasure from his ship while he is drunk in the tavern. No cutlasses or pistols involves in the affair."

Ontario drummed his fingers against the frame of the bed. "I never want to see that man again. Truly Arn, I plan to kill him. But if you think we have a chance at getting that treasure . . . then yes, I say we go for it."

From my angle on the bed I could see the tops of trees and the ocean beyond, and while the men didn't often wander into sight, I heard them all day long. Whether they purposefully or unintentionally avoided my window, I couldn't say, but it left me to guess at how they were feeling. Did they hate me for leading half of them to their deaths? Did they plan to sail away and leave me here? What thoughts lay beneath their pitied smiles when they looked my way?

"Would the men be up for sailing after Landon?"

Ontario frowned. "I think so. They grow restless here, and their hatred for what he did swells within each of their hearts. If we have a chance at revenge, they may take it."

"Good. Will you ask them for me? I'd like to set sail in the morning."

His eyes lingered on my missing hand. "Are ye certain that's a good idea?"

"With Admiral Bones after us, we can't waste time. If Emric can handle captaining the *Royal Rose*, then I will manage sailing."

"Emric? I can captain."

I should have thought of my words more carefully. "Aye, I know you can. But the crew seems to like Emric, and he has a lot of knowledge about this matter. But you're right. You can both captain."

He was silent for a few moments. At last he said, "Aye, Captain. I'll ask the crew if they feel ready to sail."

He strode off, returning a few minutes later. Behind him

came Emric and Timmons, then Collin, Bishop, and Bo. Emme entered last and gave me a smile.

The sight of them brought tears to my eyes. This was the last of my crew. In their faces I saw the others, the ones who'd stood by our sides for months, some for years, now only to be carried forever in our hearts.

What I saw before me was a crew heavy-laden with sorrow but rich with courage.

"Captain," Timmons puffed out his chest. "We are ready to leave when you are. We will follow you anywhere."

We left at daybreak the next morning. Merelda Ann stood at the end of the pier and waved as sails were raised and oars were turned against the water, slowly propelling us away from the town where I grew up. I couldn't watch it fade away, even if I wanted to; my vision swirled when I stood for too long. Emme helped steer me to the cabin below deck and settled me in the bed.

"You haven't had your medicine yet," she said as she took out a leather sack and trickled some powder into a cup. "Two more doses left." She poured water from her flask into the cup and brought it to me.

I drank it in little sips. "What sort of medicine is this?"

"A powerful one that repels poison. Finish your drink."

The effort of propping myself up and drinking was enough to exhaust me, and once I'd finished, I lay back in the bed, wishing she didn't have to see me like this. I wanted to be her steady anchor; I never wanted to be a burden to her.

This connection between us wasn't defined, and I couldn't tell what she hoped for our relationship. Once we got the treasure, she might ask to return to Julinbor, and I'd never see her again, but I hoped she'd decide to become part of my crew. Whatever the future had in store for us was uncertain, but I would forever be grateful that she'd stood by my side for these past few months.

"Thank you," I told her.

"For what?"

"For what you said to Merelda Ann. About liking me just the way I am." The exact phrase she used was she loved me for who I was, but I didn't want to trap her into repeating those words to me, no matter how desperately I longed to hear her say it again.

She gave an awkward smile. "I hadn't realized you heard that."

"I'm glad I did. It gave me the strength I needed to finally wake up."

She sat herself beside me and laced her hand in mine, and I closed my eyes for a moment. I'd just left a place that used to be like home to me—the island with Merelda Ann. But to be back on the *Royal Rose* with the familiar turn of the waves and smell of rum buried into the boards and Emme by my side, this was home. This is what I wanted.

It was enough to make me forget the home I ran from.

My eyes reopened when something wet landed on my arm.

"Love, what's the matter?"

A river of tears poured from Emme's rosy cheeks. Her body shook as her cries grew rougher with each moment. Her sorrow brought me to tears as well, and I stroked her hair. "Is it the men who died?"

"I'm dying, Arn."

My hand froze. My heart froze. I ran her words over in my head again and again, certain I must have heard them wrong. Searching for the metaphor behind the sentence. Just as my feet steadied themselves on the ship, the world pulled itself from under me, and I plummeted into the ocean below.

I'd be drowning without her. Please, don't let me lose her.

"I've needed to tell you, but I didn't know how." She wiped

her tears on her sleeve while waiting for my reaction, but my body lost its ability to show emotion.

"What do you mean?"

"I'm sick. It's my father's disease. I may have months, I might have a few years. I can't know for certain."

I held her close to my chest as if at any moment the world could take her away from me. "Is there anything we can do to heal you?" The room felt too small to me, and the air too shallow to properly breathe. I refused to believe this could be true. "There has to be something that can be done." I caught her eyes. "Emme, I won't lose you." I tightened my fingers around hers. Not that way.

"If we went back to the Island of Iilak, there's a healing nut there that can cure me. But I know how hard it would be to go back there, where Percival and Henrik and the others lie." Her own voice cracked with a sob, and my chest grew damp with her tears.

"Iilak? Why didn't you tell me when we were there? Healing you is more important than finding a treasure. I would have abandoned that to find you help."

She pulled back to look at me. Her whisper tickled my cheek. "I did find it. But I couldn't keep it." I watched her, confused. Her eyes fell to the cup. No.

"No. No! This?" I reached for it. "Is that what you've been giving me to drink? That's what saved me? I don't want it. Here, there's still one dose left. You have to take it yourself." I pulled from her and grabbed the leather sack, but she shook her head violently. Some of her hair stuck to her tear-soaked face.

"It's not enough, Arn. It can't save me now. If you don't finish it, the poison will seep back to your veins and *you'll* die. You have to finish or else I gave it up for naught."

"My life isn't worth yours. Please." My voice broke. You can't die. Don't die." I pulled her back into me and dropped my face into her shoulder as droplets from my eyes fell down her back. She held me tight, and we cried together.

"I need you," I told her. My heart was breaking. "I love you."

She dipped her face to bring mine up. Her soft hands held my neck while my hand held her body close to mine. "I love you too."

She kissed me then, and everything else faded away until only she and I remained and the fragile future ahead of us.

It was delicate. It was uncertain. It would no doubt be filled with many more tears and blood and difficulties. But it was ours, and I was determined not to break it.

37
EMME

We congregated much like we had for little Lewie's funeral, but this time there were no bodies. This time Timmons didn't play a song on the flute to begin the ceremony, and Percival didn't say a few words. We all stood with white knuckles against the taffrails and eyes wandering over the ocean as the names of our lost crewmates sounded from our lips. We huddled close together as if that would make us forget the ones who weren't here.

Percival. Henrik. Zander. Malcom. Svid. Sims.

We each took turns speaking about our fallen friends, until there was not a dry eye among us.

That's how our days went, now—a rhythm of tears for our lost brothers.

The black ship watched us, his presence like mockery of our misery. *I warned you*, it seemed to say. *I sent you vision of death.* For once, we paid it little mind, and it sent no more nightmares over us.

I hated that ship. With all my heart, I hated it.

The funeral ended as we sent personal belongings of theirs into the glistening sea. Now it wouldn't be left up to us to remember them alone; the waters shared a piece of their souls.

We slowly departed from the rails, one by one, each to

return to their chores in solitude. I took my time swabbing the decks and mulling over my thoughts. I avoided cleaning the mates' cabins, for I couldn't bear to see the empty bunks. I couldn't imagine how difficult it was for the others to sleep there at night among the ghosts of their brothers.

I had to stop tormenting myself with thoughts of their deaths. It would bring nothing but sorrow.

Arn's presence soothed me, so once I finished my chore, I mixed the final drink of the Elmber Nut and brought it to the quarterdeck. He had a chair set up behind the wheel in case he felt tired, but he insisted on steering as often as possible. He kept one firm hand on the wheel spokes while resting his wound between the slots of the wood.

He eyed the drink. "Are you certain? I feel fine, and even one dose will help you at least delay the disease."

A large part of me did want to gulp down the last dose. I already felt less tired after drinking the first bit a week ago, but I wouldn't risk Arn's life. I pushed the cup toward him. "I'll be fine."

He pursed his lips but accepted the mixture.

I rested against the railing with my finger tracing the spot where my knife had left a scar in the wood. The touch brought with it a surge of emotions from that night. That felt like forever ago. Everything seemed so uncertain, yet I was so full of hope.

Look how things turned out.

"Are you all right?" Arn asked with a look over his shoulder. I gave him a small smile and nod. "Good. Because I'll need your help coming up with a plan to get the treasure back from Landon."

A cold wind blew against my back, though the day was hot and our sails lay still. I swallowed against my dry throat and closed my eyes. The wind came again, harsher this time until

I opened my eyes, and my hair lashed around to my face. Arn's hair remained unmoving.

It seemed the black ship wasn't going to leave us alone, after all.

"You don't belong here," the cold voice hissed, each syllable sending a new flicker of ice trailing down my back.

"You don't tell me where I belong," I whispered back.

"What's that?" Arn asked.

I plastered on a smile. "Nothing."

The voice didn't speak again, and the wind died down. I laced my arm through Arn's and rested my head on his shoulder. "Let's come up with a plan to get the treasure back."

His kissed the top of my head. "All right. Landon will probably be soused in the tavern, but there will be a few people guarding his boat. We kill them and take back the bloody treasure."

I had to smile. "That sounds terribly simple."

"And vague," he agreed. "Something's bound to go wrong."

I stared at the deck. Collins, who stood by the ropes on the starboard side, had burst into tears and collapsed into Bishop's side. The larger man patted his back kindly and shot us a helpless look. He almost fell with the extra weight on his injured leg, but he managed to keep upright.

This was our band of fearsome pirates. Broken. Wounded. Half dead. The men who were once full of energy and song could now hardly go a few hours without shedding a tear. No one tried to hide it. No one tried to pretend they weren't hurting. No one knew when we would be okay again.

Arn's jaw clenched. "That man will pay for what he's done to my family."

I went to bed late that night, and the dreams began to terrorize me. It'd been a while since I had one. I'd almost hoped they were going away. I woke drenched in a thick layer of sweat.

I didn't want to sleep only to dream again, so I thought I'd go keep Arn company. I slid my wool socks over my feet and my jacket over my shoulders and tiptoed out of the cabin.

Down the hallway and up the ladder I went, but the deck was empty. No one at the wheel. A flicker of light came from the cabin, so I inched closer to look.

Ontario and Arn stood facing the bookshelves with their backs to me. "We can't tell her," Arn said. "Emme can never know the truth."

My blood turned cold. He was a dirty liar of a pirate after all.

38
ARN

When the stars gathered in the sky and the wind picked up, Ontario and I met in the cabin on deck to discuss matters. We should reach Ktoawn and the Golden Sun Tavern that sat on its port by tomorrow evening, and from there we would sail back to Aható to bring the treasure to Admiral Bones if he didn't find us first.

If he found us, there was no guarantee he would keep us alive long enough to give him what he's owed. He'd sooner step over our dead bodies and take what he wanted than deal with conversation.

If I thought him to be a more civil man, I would sail to the Island of Iilak first and get the healing nut for Emme.

"We must return to the Island of Iilak as soon as we can," I told Ontario.

His eyes bulged, and he placed a hand over the cuts on his face as if the very mention of that place would rip the stiches open. "Never."

The emotions on his face were the same ones that ran through me. Dread. Agony. The desire to never be near the island again. We wouldn't be the only ones in torment about it, but we had no choice. I ran my finger along the rim of my wooden cup as I exhaled. "Emme's dying, mate. And she needs something from that island to heal her. I wouldn't return if I thought there to be another way."

He froze, and his expression turned from anguish into shock. "Emme, Cap'n?"

"Yes," was my short reply.

He straightened. "All right. Then we had better go back to the island if it will help the lass." He paused. "She won't like it, you know. Returning to Aható where she was kidnapped."

Stars. "I'd forgotten about that. In truth, I think she has too. She was brave enough to continue on the journey with us; she hasn't showed signs that it affected her poorly. I think if we promised to stay by her side, she'd return."

Ontario frowned. "Perhaps."

"It's for the best. We can't tell her," I said. "We can't tell Emme the truth."

"That's your call. But the crew will want to know why we sail to Aható. What will we tell them? We need more supplies?"

A headache grew in my skull. Protecting the men from the unpleasantries of Admiral Bones had become a bigger struggle than I anticipated. If I could go back in time, I'd tell them all. I'd give them a chance to stay and risk a deal with him or pack their bags and hope for a better life elsewhere. No doubt they would have found it. But it was too late to tell them now.

"They've just lost half their mates. If they knew a dangerous man was searching the waters right now, wanting to kill us, they'd lose focus and all their trust in us. We can say we sail to Aható for rest. Or to free all the other women trapped there. A gallant mission to raise their spirits. Once we deal with Admiral Bones, the sea will be ours."

Ontario shrugged. He opened his mouth, but it wasn't his voice that spoke.

"And the crew none the wiser, right?"

My breath stopped in my throat. Emme stood behind us in the open doorway with an ocean's worth of anger in her eyes.

The way her arms crossed and moonlight streamed from behind her made her look fierce.

And deadly.

"Ontario, give us a minute," she ordered through clenched teeth.

He bowed and left. He could have done so without the bow, but I suspected it was to soothe her anger upon him.

I wouldn't be a fool and ask how much she heard. By her expression, I could assume it was a lot. She took a fuming step toward me. Though ashamed to admit it, I took a step back.

"Tell me everything. Right. Now."

My head spun with a million things to say. "I didn't want to scare you," I started.

"But you did want to lie to me," she snapped. Perhaps that wasn't the best place to begin.

I took a deep breath. I had to tell her. "Back at Julinbor, I told you we were low on money. That was true. What I didn't tell you was we borrowed money from a very powerful man to continue paying the crew and buying enough provisions to continue pirating. Unfortunately, now that man has come asking to be repaid . . . upon penalty of death."

Her face flushed with anger. "Your death or all our deaths?" she demanded.

I hesitated. "That is uncertain. I'm the only one who is oathbound, but he's been known to come after the whole crew."

She took a sharp breath. "Oathbound? You're oathbound?"

It wasn't pity in her voice. It was pain.

"Aye. But if I can get that treasure back from Landon and pay Admiral Bones, I can fulfill the oath."

She had no sympathy, and I couldn't blame her. "The treasure that is supposed to go to the crew? You had no intention of paying us. I suppose you planned on announcing the treasure was stolen after you used it to pay off your debt." He eyes flamed. "It's a shame it was taken before you could use it."

It'd never once crossed my mind to say the treasure was lost, but it felt silly to claim so now as if I still had a sliver of morals to be proud of. I'd proved her right—that pirates were selfish and deceitful. She'd never trust me again.

"I did plan to pay you." My voice dropped. "But only you. I intended to beg for the crew's forgiveness once the business with Admiral Bones was dealt with."

She barked a laugh and ran her hands through her loose hair. The frustration she felt was clear in the way she bit at her lips and paced a few steps about the small cabin. Even the way she breathed was angry. As she turned herself around, she raked her fingers along the table and dug her nails into the wood. The muscles in her jaw feathered as she clenched it. Finally her gaze snapped to me. "And then what? Hope they are okay with you playing them that way? Do you think they won't despise you as much as I do now?"

A tear slid down her cheek, and it felt like a dagger to my heart. She'd shed enough tears this week—I didn't want to be the reason she shed any more.

"I didn't know how to tell you. Or them."

She glared at me. "How about when I told you of my oathbinding? That would have been a great time to mention you were oathbound too. Or when I told you I was sick? Another prime moment. But you—you with your big dreams— you made us believe that we would all have a better life once we got the treasure, when you were just using us to get what you wanted."

She drove her feet into the ground with every step, until I was certain she'd wake the rest of the crew. I couldn't ask her to quiet, though, and risk further anger. All I could do was raise my arms and let them fall back to my sides helplessly, ignoring the pain in my wrist as it bumped against my leg.

"I felt lost." I could only offer this true, but lame, reason. "I'm not trying to make excuses for what I did. I should have handled it better, but I didn't know how."

Emme shook her head at me. "You did. That's what makes this so sad. You knew the right thing was to be honest with everyone, but you didn't tell them because you knew they'd leave, and Arn the pirate would be a failure. You'd have to return home to your father and do something more with your life. And that terrified you enough that you were willing to mislead all of us to save yourself."

Her words were an icy wave. She was right. I was wrong. And I didn't know how to fix this.

"I'm sorry," I said helplessly. "And I will fight to make this right. I promise you, you're still going to get your sheep farm."

She gave a shaky laugh. "Are you crazy?" Tears pooled in her eyes. "I didn't need a sheep farm. I don't care about that anymore. I cared about you, and you've taken that trust and buried it at the bottom of the ocean."

She spun and walked off, but I called after her. "What happens now?"

She looked over her shoulder. "Do I have a choice? Apparently, we need to get the treasure back, or else we all die." She crossed the deck for the ladder to go below deck. "And Ontario? Don't think I'm not mad at you too."

She climbed down the ladder, and Ontario and I exchanged looks. Tomorrow I must come clean with the rest of the crew. Tonight I got to attempt sleep while thinking of all the ways I went wrong.

39

ARN

"You mean"—Emric pounded his fist against the side of the ship and slammed his foot into the first stair leading up to the helm where I stood—"to tell me that you promised the entire treasure to someone else?"

He reached the top and crossed his arms in my face. His dark eyes were barely visible underneath his lowered brows. My hand went out to steady myself against the wheel.

"A fair portion of it, yes." My voice traveled over the crew. Bishop and Bo copied Emric's strong stance with widely spread legs and their arms folded over their chests. Their glares burned into me. Collins cracked his knuckles, one by one, as if gearing up for a fight. Timmons stood with his arms limp at his sides and mouth hanging open. At least he didn't look like he wanted to kill me.

The morning cast its light over the ocean and illuminated the sweat on my body as I explained to the crew how I'd been low on money and had borrowed a great sum from Admiral Bones to pay them. I emphasized that part, how I did it for them. To provide this home for all of us.

Ontario leaned against the side of the ship with his head down and his ponytail undone so part of his wavy brown hair rested over his left eye. His wounds hadn't yet turned to dull scars, and as a result the bright red flesh marred his features. As I confessed my sins, I neglected to mention Ontario's involvement, allowing him the opportunity to do so himself. I did glance at him once, but he quickly looked away.

Emme sat at the other end of the ship wearing a high-fronted shirt with a low-cut back, so her entire octopus tattoo was visible. Her leather pants were tucked into her tall boots, which she crossed over each other as she watched the scene unfold.

Emric's voice was hard. "We worked hard to reach that island. Half the crew died for that treasure. And you meant to plunder it from under our noses because of this"—he gestured at my foot—"oathbind you got yourself tangled up into?"

Bo raised his fist into the air. "Chop his foot off!"

Timmons chuckled, but the others looked dead serious. Emme pursed her lips and knotted her forehead.

"Won't work, mate," Emric called down to the deck. "The oathbind would move to his other foot. Then to his heart. Unfortunately." His glanced darted back at me.

"Oh." Bo's fist lowered, just to pump back up again with renewed energy. "Chop it off anyway!"

Emric chuckled. His laugh was like the screeching of metal to my ears. "I like where your head's at. Any other ideas?" He turned away from me to lean over the railing and address the crew. "What shall we do with this scoundrel? Kill him?"

The crew shifted gazes between themselves while Ontario kept his head down. I narrowed my eyes at him but said nothing. Bo leaned to whisper something to Bishop, who nodded, but then Ontario stepped from the side of the deck and spoke. "I say mercy. He did it for our good and never intended any harm to come of it. We've lost enough brothers as it is." No surprise that he'd call for mercy for the sins he also committed. It appeared he didn't care to come forward for them.

At his words, Collins shook his head, and Emric stroked

his chin. "There's one idea. Who wants revenge?" From the excitement in his voice, I knew that he did.

The other four crew members raised their hands, leaving Emme and Ontario to watch with guarded eyes. "We want revenge!" Bo shouted. "Chop his leg off!"

The others laughed, and Emric retreated to the steps and addressed the crew from above. "I say no maiming. But surely he can't be captain anymore. My friends, I ask you, do you want a captain who lies to you? Who takes you on a long journey to accomplish his own personal work and cares naught for your interests? Or do you want a strong captain who fights for his crew over himself and who will lead you all to glory?"

All the air deflated from my body, and my stomach tightened as the crew chanted for a new captain. I'd never heard such a dire sound as that. Emric, encouraged by the moment, treaded down the stairs. His voice was loud and demanded to be heard over the chants. "Do you want a captain who knows the seas? Who knows how to fight? Who has pirate legacy in his blood?"

At this, Ontario moved forward and held up a hand. "Wait just a moment. I'm the first. If we are choosing a new captain, it ought to be me."

I found my voice. "There is no need for a new captain."

Emric didn't acknowledge me. "We need a captain we can trust. I leave that up to you men to vote. Ontario or me?"

"I know I was wrong, but I am still a good captain. There is no need for change."

"You led us to our deaths," Bo yelled. My mouth snapped shut at the fire in his eyes. "I'm prepared to vote for a new captain."

Their words pieced me as the others echoed his desires. Emme's hand was clamped over her mouth. At least she wasn't chanting along with them, but I doubted I'd hear her speak in my defense.

"Okay, men, who shall it be? Who is your new captain?"

Once more I urged them to reconsider, but my words fell on deaf ears.

Ontario wandered through the four men, looking each in the eye. "Bishop, didn't I rescue you from the waters after your old ship sank? Didn't I nurse you back to health? Timmons, didn't I use my money to purchase that pretty flute of yours for you? Collins, didn't I save you from the one-eyed pirate back on the Island of Iilak? You would have died without me." With each person he passed, their gazes fell to their feet.

Silence overtook them. "Men?" Ontario asked.

Emric watched with a knowing grin on his face. Bishop took a deep sigh. "I vote Emric."

"Aye," Collins said. Bo agreed.

Timmons shook his head slowly at Ontario before speaking. "Emric."

"I say Emric." Emric thrust his own hand in the air. "That's five out of eight. Sister?"

All heads twisted to where Emme sat at the edge of the ship. When her gaze fell on me it almost looked sorrowful. "I don't know."

Emric's lips drew in a line. "Fine. We have all we need, anyway."

Ontario didn't move as he looked at his mates who were all averting their eyes. He shook his head and went below deck.

Emric climbed to my side. "Good sir," he said smugly. "I can take the wheel now."

"It was one mistake," I hissed under my breath. "One mistake."

"Try to explain that to Percival. Or Henrik. Zander." He didn't name the other three whose bodies we left on the island, but he placed a hand on the wheel. I stepped away.

My men were angry and still grieving and eager to find someone to blame. But when the feelings settled, they would see that I was the best captain for the ship and give her back to me. I could only hope. For now, I accepted this temporary punishment.

"Fine. Let's talk about our plan," I said to the men. Startled, perhaps by my quick acquiescence, they hesitantly met my eyes. "Tonight we reach the Golden Sun Tavern where Landon ought to be celebrating his victory. While he's getting drunk, we will steal back our treasure."

"You mean your treasure," Bo said. "It means nothing to us."

"It does if you don't want to die," I said. Bo narrowed his eyes but shut his mouth to listen.

"Listen, crew, I'll make this up to you. But for now we must get back the treasure so we can pay Admiral Bones. Will ye help?" It took them several glances between each other and a few whispers, but in the end Emric agreed, and everyone else nodded. "Splendid. Then here's the plan."

Collins interrupted. "We don't trust you to make a plan. Your last plan got half of us killed."

My stomach tightened further. There was no love for me in my crew's eyes. No forgiveness. No mercy. Nothing but cold hatred.

It was a relief when Emme drew to her feet. "It's not his plan, it's mine. Listen up."

40

EMME

Ktoawn rose in the distance as a port full of life. Torches lined the streets as far as we could see to shed light on the busy town, and its sounds reached us far before we approached the long pier.

We all wore large hats to hide our faces, and from underneath their cover came the crisp whiffs of cedar and steamed dough. The black ship hadn't followed us as we closed in on this civilization, and when I glanced back, it had faded away.

Twenty other ships rocked in their berths, and Arn pointed a finger. "Third one in from the left. That's the *Dancer*."

Ontario steered us that direction. We rowed to an open place three spaces away that was close enough to transition the treasure between the two ships but far enough not to be immediately spotted by any of their crew.

"They shouldn't be expecting us," Arn said. "We have the advantage."

None sounded too enthused about it. I spoke up, "We can do this, mates." Emric helped me push the old gangplank until it connected with the dock, and the crew walked down, all except for Bishop who would guard the ship. His calf still slowed him down, so he happily volunteered to be our lookout.

Arn slid to my side. "Thanks for helping me back there," he said as we walked down the pier. A few men wandered to and from ships, but they paid us little mind. The sun had set several hours ago, and we were betting on crews being too soused to notice anything amiss.

"It doesn't mean you're forgiven yet," I whispered back to him.

His lips tightened but he nodded. "I understand."

It could be I was being too harsh on him. But the magnitude of what he'd kept from us was enough to warrant a few more days of anger, at least. Forgiveness would come once we were safe from the danger he'd unleashed upon us.

"It's a beautiful town," he said flatly.

If circumstances were different, this would be an enjoyable place to explore, but tonight I couldn't appreciate anything about it. "Let's just get the treasure."

He didn't pry for further conversation.

A tall board hung from hooks over a doorway with a golden sun painted upon it. Two windows revealed a crowded room around an oak bar and a fireplace burning bright. We lowered our heads and searched the mass for Landon.

"There. At the bar with his head down on his hands," Arn said. "Drunk already." Landon's dark hair tumbled over his shoulders as he rested his head on the counter while a man pushed a drink closer to him. He didn't move to touch it. "Anyone see the rest of his crew?"

"I thought I'd taken care of that one." Emric pointed to a woman with long legs sitting by the fire. She had a crowd of eager men around her. "Must not have stabbed as hard as I thought."

"I'm certain I fought him over there." Bo indicated a caramel-haired man with a cut on his forehead.

Arn nodded. "Good. They shouldn't be giving us any trouble. Let's get to the ship."

As planned, Collins slumped against the wall of the tavern and pulled his hat over his head. He would remain behind to watch the situation while we traced back to the *Dancer*.

The ship was larger than the *Royal Rose*, with another mast and three sails furled. Two cabins sat above deck, and they had plenty of room to store the treasure below. "Is this the ship that ought to have been yours?" I asked Arn.

"Aye," he said. "Isn't she a beauty?"

Perhaps one day it was, but now the paint was peeling, and the sails were dirty. Our ship was the most put together in the whole lot. "Not as glorious as your ship," I told Arn. He gave me a thin smile. Too late, I remembered my mistake. It wasn't his ship anymore. It was my brother's.

Once they discovered his deceit, I was glad the crew hadn't voted to kill him, but part of me hoped they'd throw him overboard just once. We'd fish him back out of the sea after we let him fret for a little bit.

I'd never imagined they'd take away his ship.

We passed by a few people before reaching the berth of the *Dancer*. Now closer, Arn frowned. "It should be lower."

"Ey?" Emric asked. We all hesitated before climbing aboard, shifting our eyes to any who might pass by and question the pirates inspecting other men's ships.

"If it's filled with treasure, it should be heavier. Look how it bobs in the water." Arn pointed to the hull. "Where is it?"

The men swore. "I say we check anyway," Emric declared. "I won't be a fool for not looking if it's there." Now captain, he didn't wait for Arn's permission before climbing the ramp. Others followed while Arn lingered to shake his head a few times and cast worried looks back at the tavern before joining us.

The deck was empty, which should have relieved us, but now the question was on all our minds. Was it empty because there was nothing here to protect?

Emric, braver than all of us, opened the cabin doors. Soon we were all going through the rooms and searching for the treasure as Arn stayed at the bow to be our lookout. Though the pistol was his weapon of choice, it was more difficult to manage with one hand, making him the weakest of us all right now.

"It's a large treasure, they can't hide it in pots," Emric grumbled as I opened cupboards. "Let's go below deck." He placed a hand on his cutlass and lifted the latch on the floor. If someone was below, they'd see the sudden moonlight coming from above and hear as Emric jumped through the hole. Bo hopped down as fast as Emric had, and together they turned to look at their surroundings. "Clear," Emric whispered. "For now."

I looked to Arn before I jumped. "Be careful," he mouthed. I nodded back.

The five of us slunk through the narrow hallway and peered through doorways. We pulled up the mattresses, pried at loose boards, and opened every barrel we could find. Nothing.

"Look in here," Emric poked his head out and ushered us into the galley. It looked almost identical to ours except for the large amount of crates stacked along the back wall. "It's not the treasure, but I think it once was. They are all empty save for this coin." He flipped a silver coin in the air and caught it. "The treasure must have been here, but they moved it."

The crates were only enough to hold half the treasure we'd seen. But if they'd moved that half, then they probably moved the other half somewhere as well.

"Where would they put it?" Bo asked.

Emric shrugged. "Hiding it inland? One thing's for certain." He tossed the coin again. "The treasure ain't here."

41

ARN

The crew's spirits were dropping, and that was saying something, since they didn't start out too high. "I say we return to ship and forget about all this," Bo suggested.

"The last person who crossed Admiral Bones was skinned alive down to the bones," Ontario reminded him. "Do you care to be a pile of bones, Bo?"

He stuck out his lip. "No, but I don't care to be caught snooping through another pirate's ship, neither."

Collins came running down the pier with his hat in his hand. "Get off the ship," he whisper-yelled. "Get off now!"

In a flurry of movement we hastened from the ship as he stopped to catch his breath. "Landon's . . . not drunk. He was crying, that's why his head was down . . . he's coming this way."

"Go, go, go." I urged us back down the pier and toward the townhomes that lined the docks. The narrow alleys between them provided patches of shadows deep enough to hide in, though not wide enough to hold us all. "Walk that way." I pointed Collins, Timmons, and Bo down the pier away from the Golden Sun Tavern. "And for King Valian's sake, be casual."

They took off just as the sound of boisterous laughter drew

near, and the remaining four of us pushed our backs against the brick walls. As we hid, my hand brushed against Emme's where it froze. After a moment she moved hers away.

My attention returned to the docks where the crew's voices turned in toward their berth. "You've never seen a ship like ours, I promise ye that," one boasted, receiving a flurry of giggles in reply.

"Captain, ye ain't coming with us?"

"Nay, mates." Landon's voice cracked. "I can't stand to be on that ship where she was . . ." Pain vibrated through his tone. An odd feeling pinched me, one that I never thought I'd feel for Landon. Regret. I'd killed someone who he dearly loved, and he had watched me do it.

Landon was my enemy who'd done terrible things. But I couldn't imagine the pain of holding the lifeless body of the girl you loved in your arms.

A moment of silence followed. Then a feminine voice spoke. "She loved you, Landon, and she died with honor. Let her rest in peace."

"You go enjoy yourself," was his only reply. "I'll sleep in the inn." Footsteps followed.

"All right, Cap'n."

The men began to converse again, and the ladies giggled some more. The gangplank creaked as they ascended into the ship, and footsteps on cobblestone clicked further away.

After a few moments, I peeked around the corner. The crew was congregated on the deck of the ship with their flasks in one hand and girls in the other. "We can't emerge now, they'll see us," I said. "And who knows how long they'll stay on their deck." I nodded toward the street behind the pier. "We can trace our way to the inn through back roads."

"The inn?" Ontario asked.

"You think he hid the loot in an inn?" Emric ducked his head over the corner to look at the ship.

I maneuvered my hand along the rough brick wall and gestured for the others to follow. "If the bloke is as selfish as I remember, then aye. I wouldn't be surprised if he's taking the treasure for himself."

"Sounds like someone I know," Emric grunted as he stumbled along behind me. The muscles in my back tightened at the insult, and I turned my head in time to see Emme jab her brother in the side. That little action was a sliver of compassion that I would hold onto.

We twisted through several back streets before emerging from the shadows a few buildings down from the Golden Sun Tavern. "Keep your heads down," I reminded them while searching for Landon. The other half of our crew rejoined us from behind.

"What now?" Collins asked.

"We think it's in the inn. Landon is staying there," Ontario whispered. The inn sat above the bustling tavern with all the windows pulled shut and lights out. We'd have to guess which room Landon stayed in, and hope he wasn't still in the tavern when we passed through.

"We can't all go in. Some should stay on the docks, some should go in the tavern, and I'll go up to the rooms to look around."

"I'm coming too." Emme placed her hands on her hips where her pistol and cutlass were strapped over her short tunic and leather pants.

"It's dangerous," I warned.

"And you have only one hand," she reminded me. "And Landon hates you. It's more dangerous for you than for me."

"We'd feel better if she went," Timmons said. The other crew members nodded. I tried to decipher if they'd feel better because I was weak or because they didn't trust me to go after the treasure alone. Neither option was appealing.

"Plus no one will look at a lad and a lass headed up to a

room at this hour," Emric wriggled his brows. Emme jabbed his side again, and he winced. "Right then. Be careful, now. And who wants to head into the tavern with me?" Bo raised his hand eagerly, followed by Ontario. Timmons and Collins stayed on the docks while Bo and Ontario headed inside, Emme and I a distance behind.

The strong scent of rum hit our noses as the bartender shouted his welcomes. A few heads turned to glance at us before looking away. In a place such as this, no one stared at pirates. In fact, most in this room probably were pirates.

Behind the back of the bar stood a narrow door leading to the inn, and I nodded toward it. We maneuvered past laughing gentlemen and tables of folks playing dice, and my hand stretched back to hold Emme's. She tugged it free and gave me a look, but I whispered in her ear, "Emric was right. We need to be as inconspicuous as possible."

Uncertainty passed through her eyes, but her fingers grazed mine and slid into place.

We reached the narrow door with the round wooden handle. The loud noises of the tavern dimmed as the door shut behind us and we found ourselves in a small room at the bottom of the stairs lit with a bright torch. A wide man sat on a tall chair behind a peg-legged table, and he grinned at us.

"Looking for a room, ey?" His mustache twitched as he leered in a foul manner.

"Aye," I said as I shifted closer to Emme. Her other hand slid over my arm and she flashed a smile.

"One copper, please." He waved a key in front of us until I paid him, then he flicked it to me. "Room seven. Enjoy."

We passed by to the stairs. "Now we know Landon isn't room seven," Emme said as soon as we'd climbed half the stairs. She removed her touch from me, leaving those places cold without her.

At the top of the stairs appeared a short hallway branching

both directions with doors on either side. At the end, each hallway turned east, where I assumed they turned once more to meet on the opposite end. A square-shaped hallway with around twenty rooms, and no way to know which held Landon or the treasure.

"What now?" Emme asked, looking around.

"I suppose we listen at doorways, unless you have a better idea."

Our feet tiptoed to the nearest doors, and we placed our ears against their planks in attempt to hear what went on inside. The night was young enough that many of the rooms may be yet unoccupied, and unless Landon was speaking out loud to himself, we had little hope of finding him.

"Do you feel sorry for him?" Emme whispered.

"Aye. I do pity him. I can't fathom watching your love die. If anything were to happen to you . . ." The idea hung in the air between us like sparks, small and tender, waiting to see if they would catch hold and burn. Did I still light a fire in her like I thought I once did? Did she feel any passion for me, where the thought of losing me would hurt her?

"Emme, I am so sorry for lying to you. I thought I was keeping you safe."

She was close enough to see the dimple in her cheek as she gave a sad smile. "I don't care about what troubles you are in, Arn. I'm willing to carry them with you. I do care about you being honest with me."

"I'm sorry." I risked reaching for her hand. She didn't pull away. "You know everything now. There are no more secrets between us."

Her hazel eyes gazed into mine. "To be fair, I'd been keeping things from you too. About my sickness and my oathbinding."

The softness in her tone felt like a peace offering, which I gratefully took. "Yes, but those secrets wouldn't kill me."

I smiled at her, and she smiled back. The ice that had been around us began to melt, until I dared to believe we could make it through this.

The soft creaking of footsteps on wood planks sounded behind us, and we both jumped. We looked at each other, then frantically around. "Find room seven," Emme whispered. A silver number twenty hung from the door to my left so I nudged Emme to the other end. Number one. We sprinted down the hallway and turned the corner, skidding to a halt in front of number seven. She fumbled with the key until it twisted, but I put my hand on her arm. She hesitated over the knob.

I held my breath and peeked around the corner.

A tall man with a thick black beard and cuts in the cotton sleeves of his tan shirt waddled up the stairs. He looked both directions at the top, and I pressed myself against the wall. A few moments later his footsteps resumed, growing quieter with each step.

A door creaked open, and I assumed it was he who spoke. "It's all here."

"Good." The voice that replied caused Emme's hand to grab mine. Landon. We'd found him. "Did you pay Ragnor?"

"Aye. He was quite pleased with the payment. Have ye decided what to do with the rest of it?"

"Not yet," Landon said. I guessed the "it" was the treasure. So he owed money too. "There are a few girls I had my eye on downstairs. And perhaps I'll purchase some new things for the ship. When the crew wakes in the morning we tell them some was stolen so the rest was moved to my room for safe keeping."

"Let's tell them it was all stolen, but we managed to get half of it back," the man suggested. "Makes us sound more like heroes that way."

Landon clicked his tongue. "I like that. Well done, mate.

You and I are now some of the richest men in all the land. This calls for celebration."

"Right you are, Captain." They both laughed. Emme and I stayed still as they walked back down the stairs, then waited a while longer to be certain they were gone.

"What if they see our men in the tavern?" Emme's tone quivered with worry.

"We'll have to hope they know how to keep their heads down," I replied. "And let's move fast."

We crossed the hallway to Landon's door and tried the knob. "Would our key work?" Emme asked when the door didn't open. I tried, but the key didn't fit. I handed it back to her and pulled out my sharp cutlass to wedge the tip of the blade between the door and the frame. With all my might I pushed until the door pried open.

The door swung, and we both exhaled. The marvel of the treasure sat in the dim room, waiting for us to take it. Behind the narrow bed were crates stacked on top of each other, with chests sitting at the foot of the bed and sacks lined by the wall. A few crowns lay out on the bed, calling for us to take hold and place them on our heads. They glistened in the moonlight from the window and looked glorious. They looked like freedom.

"It's here," I said, dropping to my knees in relief. "Thank King Valian."

"I'm as grateful as you are," said Emme as she brushed past me, "but we need to smuggle it out fast. Is there a back door?"

It took only a moment to scan the area. "Not from this room, but I bet there's one in the back hallway. Let's grab what we can carry and go check. They must have gotten it in here somehow."

Carrying things proved more difficult with only one hand to hold them, but Emme helped me gather a chest in my arms before picking up a sack of coins and rolling it over her shoulder. She placed a crown on her head and grabbed a second, smaller sack. Then she nodded to me. "Let's go."

My gaze stayed glued to her. "You're looking like a real pirate, you know? Dark tattoos and leather pants and stealing a man's treasure in the night. Bet you don't get this sort of excitement on a sheep farm."

"You also don't get your hand cut off," she retorted with a smile. "Come on."

At the other end of the hallway was a tall door leading outside to a rickety stairwell tracing the back end of the tavern. "It's not possible to transfer this to the *Royal Rose* without being spotted," Emme said, glancing down the alleys where laughter floated through the air. A hint of fear crawled into her voice.

I tried to sound as confident as possible. In a town like this, seeing pirates carrying crates wasn't something to raise a brow at. "It doesn't matter if someone sees us, as long as no one from Landon's crew does. We can take back roads to get to the dock."

She bit her lip but headed down the stairs. With only one wrong turn, we slipped through the shadows of torchlight and onto the docks next to my ship. Bishop pumped his fist in the air when he saw the crown on Emme's head, but his smile soon fell.

"Where's the rest of the crew? Don't tell me they're all dead too."

"No, mate," I assured him. "They are on post. Remain here and be on watch for anyone following us. We'll get the others and have this treasure out in no time."

We found Collins and Timmons casually walking down the docks pretending to be in deep conversation. They nodded eagerly at our instruction, and Timmons hurried off to fetch the others from the tavern where I could only hope they showed restraint at the bar. They met us as we passed on the stairway a few minutes later, each running their hands over the treasure with satisfied grins on their faces. We took shifts carrying the treasure and standing guard along the path to the ship.

"We saw Landon in the tavern," Emric said as he helped me carry a large crate through the streets. I bit through the pain of the weight on my injured wrist. "The way he was laughing with the lasses—there's not a broken heart in there."

"I'm not certain he has a heart at all," I rejoined. I wasn't sure if it appeased me to know that the girl I killed wasn't as dear to Landon as I'd believed, or if it made me feel worse for her.

I let the weight drop onto the ship where Bishop crouched at the bow watching the dock. Emric traded places with Emme on the street, and she and I went back into the inn for more.

"You ought to get the last of it," Ontario grunted as he and Bo passed us with their load.

"Perfect. Prepare the ship to sail." It was a very captainy thing of me to say, but they didn't correct me as I said it.

My heart pounded in my chest with nervous anticipation. We were so close. Landon would come to the room that night to find the treasure gone, but we would be long sailed away. We bounded up the stairs and into the dimly lit hallway to collect the last of the things when a roar stopped us short.

My blood froze in my veins. He wasn't supposed to come up until we were halfway across the ocean. Not now. It was too soon.

But the voice wasn't Landon's. The black-bearded man with a piercing in his lip stomped out of the room. His veins stood out on his forehead. He spotted us and roared again. The sound rivaled that of the Nimnula. He grasped an ax from its clip on his back and charged toward us.

Emme whipped out her pistol, but I grabbed her arm. "No,

it'll be too loud. Run." She hesitated, and she clenched her jaw. "Run, Emme," I repeated urgently.

She turned and raced down the hallway while I drew my cutlass and braced my feet for impact. The narrow hallway made it impossible to sidestep him and gave me nothing to look at besides the fury in his eyes. The ax left his hand before he reached me, and it took all my strength to bat it away. The vibration ran up through my shoulder. A second later the man slammed his body into mine, sending us both flailing to the floor. I swiped my cutlass around, but he'd already rolled to the side, and I didn't catch more than his sleeve. He grabbed the ax again and swung it at me, keeping both hands on the hilt and pressing down hard.

I got to my feet right as his weapon collided with my cutlass above my head. I positioned my injured wrist behind my other hand to withstand the weight, but my knees began to buckle. He didn't try a second attack; he maintained his current strike and grinned over me. I would break in a few moments, and he knew it.

Something wet dripped against my leg, and the man bellowed in pain. He fell to his knees to reveal Emme standing behind him with her cutlass tinged with blood. The muscles in his calf were lacerated straight to the bone.

He swiveled his head to glare at her. "You should have killed me," he growled. With a flick of his wrist, he turned his ax and swung at her. I brought my cutlass down and hooked the ax from underneath, but he struggled against me with a strength that would soon overpower my own, even from his knees. I tore my eyes from him to Emme, who stood breathing heavy with her cutlass trembling in her hands. We locked eyes, and I tried to get my message across. She had to kill him now, or else he would break free and kill us both.

Her lip quivered, and my grip on my blade loosened.

"I can't. I can't." But she raised her sword and brought

it down hard against the man's arms, slicing them partway through.

The ax clattered to the floor. Before he had time to react, I turned my blade and drove it into his belly.

He dropped to my feet, dead.

Tears ran down Emme's cheeks. "I'm so sorry. I couldn't kill him. I couldn't do it."

I stepped over the body to hold her. She wrapped her hands around me and buried her face into my chest for a few moments, then straightened herself. "We need to get the last of the treasure before anyone else finds us."

I let her go to step back over the body.

"And Arn?" she said. "Thank you."

42
EMME

Once Ktoawn disappeared behind us, we all breathed a little easier. But it didn't take long for men to realize the whole treasure wasn't there, and the fretting began.

"Landon has already used half of it," Arn explained. That earned several shifty glances between mates. Splattered blood decorated his cheek and the front of his navy tunic, the proof of how he'd let me run while he stayed to fight. Time and time again Arn proved he would fight for me, no matter how uncertain things were between us. No matter what it cost him, he was there for me when I needed him.

Maybe it was time I fought for him too. I backed up Arn's story with conviction, and he cast me a thankful smile.

"Is it enough to pay Admiral Bones?" Emric asked, peering into some crates.

"It better be," Bo snorted. "I don't care to be a pile of bones."

"I think it's enough," Arn said from the helm of the ship. "We'll sail directly there to bring it to him." He checked his compass, then looked at us. "Go get some sleep, you've earned it. I don't deserve to be among a crew such as yourselves." He treaded that line, acting as captain while not officially calling himself that. Emric frowned.

"You don't," Timmons shot back. But sarcasm filled his tone more than anger, the first hint that some of the crew was beginning to forgive Arn for his deceit. If we paid Admiral Bones without getting killed, it wouldn't surprise me if they all put this incident behind them and Arn gained his ship back.

Still, it was decided that the treasure would stay above deck where all could keep an eye on it, and with that settled, the men stepped over the cloth sacks and wooden crates and drifted toward their cots. Bo made a spectacle of counting the crates before he went to sleep, but Arn was the one who taught him to count and had to correct his numbers when he reached twenty, at which point Bo muttered something about it being good enough and went off to bed. I slipped past him and up the stairs to Arn at the helm.

"We got lucky tonight," Arn said as he watched the waters. Emric let him take the first shift of steering through the night so he could get some sleep. The wind pressed at our backs and tossed Arn's blonde hair around his ears. In a few months it'd be long enough to put in his ribbon again, though the blue fabric was now marred with droplets of blood.

"I'm sorry I couldn't kill him," I said, looking away from the blood on Arn. At least he hadn't been injured, though that man was twice his size. It was a wonder he managed so well against him.

"Most folks would have run away, but not you. You stayed to fight." Arn's gaze was steady on me. "It's okay. You still fought." There was pride in his voice.

"I actually wanted to kill him," I confessed. His brows shot up, "But there was something in me that wouldn't put that cutlass through his abdomen. I wanted to, but I couldn't."

He was quiet a moment. "The first kill is always the hardest. There's nothing to be ashamed about."

Shame wasn't the way I'd describe what I was feeling. When that man charged at Arn, I'd felt terrified.

No, perhaps I did feel a twinge of shame after all. I was ashamed that Arn had to finish the fight for me.

Next time, I wouldn't need him to save me.

Nightmares woke me from my sleep when the sunlight was barely seeping through the window. I rose to get dressed for the day in the tunic Sereena had given to me. It showed off my tattoos the best, and I was becoming quite fond of the way they looked. They made me appear tougher than I felt, and whenever I needed a boost of bravery I could look to their markings. I even thought of naming the octopus.

I surfaced above deck, giving my eyes a few moments to adjust to the brightness. Hues of pinks and blues adorned the morning sky, and a small wind still carried us west. Emric had taken over for Arn sometime between last night and this morning, but he didn't stand behind the wheel. Instead he leaned over the side of the ship and was speaking into the water. "I think we'll be fine. But fish my body out of the sea if he tries to drown us."

He's gone mad, I thought. But then a lyrical voice replied.

"I'll watch the seas for Admiral Bones's ship."

"Who in King Valian's name is that?" I asked.

There was a splash, and Emric spun around, face red. "Emme. I didn't hear you come up." He shifted at the railing, glancing over his shoulder.

"That's because you had your head dangling over the ship." I was at his side and scouring the water. I couldn't see more than a few meters into the murky depths, but a ripple drifted outward that wasn't caused by the hull breaking through the water's surface. "And unless I'm mistaken, the water was speaking to you."

He laughed uncomfortably. "That would be something, huh?"

I rested my side against the rail and crossed my arms. "Emric. Who was talking to you?"

His jaw twitched before he sighed. "A mermaid."

I blinked. "A mermaid?"

"Remember Coral? We met her at the secret pass between the Never-Ending Land?"

It took me a few moments to remember the mermaid with the light orange tail and the long flowing blonde hair who had given us the box. The one who'd perched herself on the edge of the ship where she stroked Emric's cheek. "Her! How?"

Emric blushed. I'd never seen him blush over a girl before. Girls were interested in him back on the sheep farm, but he always said he wanted more than a farm girl. He wanted a pirate. I wonder if he ever considered he'd be interested in a mermaid. "She sent me a note through a messenger clam. And I wrote her back. It's very practical, see, the clam keeps the parchment in his mouth and is given some enchantment that allows it to swim. It can deliver a note in only a few hours—"

He was rambling.

"Emric, are you in love with a mermaid?"

He'd been waving his hands, but now they dropped to his sides. "I don't know yet. But I like her. You'd like her too." He gazed over the water. "She's magnificent. Strong-minded. Intelligent . . ."

"Emric, she's a mermaid."

"There are ways for a mermaid to become a human," he said swiftly. "Ways for a human to become merfolk."

I'd never heard of such a thing. But then I remembered Sereena, stripped of her tail and stranded on an island. "Which way would you want?" I asked, not sure if I wanted to know.

He hesitated, and at that moment the hatch opened, and Bo stepped out. "One, two, three . . ." Giving up, he shrugged and placed a crown from one of the sacks on his head. "It all looks here to me. Morning, Emric; morning, Emme."

I waved, and Emric returned to the wheel.

"The black ship is back." Bo pointed across the water. "Is it closer?"

We rushed to the edge and made out the ship in the east that rocked over the same waves as us. Again, we saw no one at the helm, no oars moving, no indication that someone was on board. Only the ship on the waves as it watched us.

It's always stayed back at a distance. But Bo might be right—it did look to be closer that morning than it usually was. "It's hard to tell," I said.

"Look at its flag," Bo replied. "I can see a bit of the markings now."

I squinted. As the black flag whipped in the wind, we caught glimpses of a white design on the fabric in the shape of an ax. There was something else too, but I couldn't make it out.

"Who have you heard of that has an ax on their flag?" I asked.

Bo gulped. "I don't know. But I don't like that it's closer now. Makes me think it's getting ready to attack."

Between the black ship and Admiral Bones, it was hard to know which to fear the most. Both may be nothing: the black ship had never once attacked, though we suspected it of sending persistent nightmares, and Admiral Bones may leave us be once he had been given his payment.

But we might not have time to give Admiral Bones his money before he struck. And this ship could attack any day—and who knew what horrors lay there?

Bo and I exchanged nervous glances before I crossed the deck to Emric. "Can Coral find out anything about this ship?"

He frowned. "Nay. I've already asked. She doesn't see it."

My brows shot up. "How's that?"

"I don't know. She says she can't see it. There's some magic that keeps it from the mermaids' eyes. And Bo is right, the ship has never come this close before. We might be able to hit it with the cannons now, but I fear angering it." He bit his lip. "But I fear what happens if we don't do anything."

For three days the ship stayed at its closer position, lurking on the water like a predator watching its prey, sending us all visions of death and destruction and bones up to our knees. On the fourth day the ship left, and we found relief from the nightmares. On the sixth day we let out a cheer.

We'd made it to Aható. Alive.

43

ARN

"Do you think he knows we are here?" The crew kept their boots in the sand and their wary eyes on the sleepy town. Such a contrast from the expansive town of Ktoawn, Aható hardly covered the base of the mountains, and the only sound was the crack of flags in the wind.

"Aye, he knows. He tracks me through the oathbinding. He'll be here."

With Emme's help, I slung a sack of coins over my back. "You men stay here with the rest of the treasure. I'll find Admiral Bones and tell him his money is here."

"I'm coming too," Emme insisted.

My head shook fervently. "This man is unlike any you've encountered in your life. He has no heart. He'll kill you if he thinks you can't be trusted."

She grunted as she hauled a second sack over her shoulder. "I know. So you'll need someone to protect you. Come on."

All the crew snickered at her remark, except for Emric, who pursed his lips. "Be careful."

We marched to cross the stony path into the quiet town. I shifted my eyes through the streets and between the buildings to watch for any of Admiral Bones's men but found nothing more than a few quiet villagers sweeping their steps or stacking wood. They nodded to us as we passed.

"His place is right down this road and—"

"And to the left. At the edge of the valley," Emme finished. I stopped walking to gape at her. "I followed you there the last time we came." She kept moving, and I strode to catch up.

"You never said."

She squinted into the sunlight as we went around the bend. Admiral Bones's home lay ahead. "I thought I could figure out what you were doing on my own. Then I got kidnapped, then the black ship started sending us nightmares . . . your mystery meeting was the last thing on my mind." She paused to look at the black sun on the sign. "I feel foolish for not asking you sooner."

The gray door swung open in front of us, and two men stepped out. They had pistols at their sides and black bandanas covering all but their eyes. Each had biceps the size of my head and thick necks that would take several chops with the cutlass to ever cut through. I regretted allowing Emme to join us, but it was too late to send her back, and she'd never listen anyhow.

"Gentlemen," I greeted them. They crossed their arms over their torsos and said nothing.

With a glance at each other, Emme and I entered the dark room. Shades were pulled over the windows, and the air was crisp, as if it knew that warmth didn't belong in this place.

Admiral Bones stepped out from the shadows and leaned against a desk as we dropped our sacks on the ground. He flicked his wrist to one of his guards, who scurried forward to inspect the bags. Four more guards stood against the walls, watching while the other two remained outside. Admiral Bones and seven guards. If anything went wrong, we didn't stand much chance against them.

"You secured the treasure after all." The hollows of Admiral Bones's cheeks stretched back with what could only be surprised delight. It was odd seeing joy on such a heartless being. But then his expression hardened. "When you told me of this hoard, I thought there'd be more."

"There is." I straightened my back. Emme stayed still as a statue, a blank expression on her face. "We couldn't carry it all. There's more on the beach. Let us go fetch it for you."

"No." He circled the desk and kicked at the bags. They tipped over and coins spilled across the planks, rolling to the feet of the guards. Admiral Bones picked up a coin and placed it between his teeth. He spit it back to the ground. "I'll go to the beach with you. And my men will stay here to make sure no one comes to steal it back once it's been paid."

With exaggerated movements he loaded two pistols and strapped them to his holsters at his waist, then pulled on a long jacket, patting where the guns bulged under the fabric. "Lead the way."

Emme all but fled the house to lead the way back through the town with me just behind to keep distance between her and the admiral. If he planned to place a knife in anyone's back, I'd prefer it to be mine.

This nasty deal with Admiral Bones was almost complete. I'd get the oathbinding removed and never have to see this foul man again.

As soon as we approached the beach where the crew sat around the treasure, they leapt to their feet, and hands fluttered to their cutlasses when Admiral Bones appeared behind us. I gave them a reassuring nod. I didn't need anyone eager for their weapons today.

Admiral Bones stopped me at the stone pathway before the sand, his hands on his hips.

"I see there's something afoot," he snapped. "Fool. You should know better than to mess with me. Where is the rest of your crew?"

I opened my mouth, but Emme was the one who replied,

voice curt. "Dead. Because of all this." She waved at the treasure. "There is no trick. There is no game. You will take the treasure and let us be."

He looked at her as if seeing her for the first time. His eyes narrowed. "Interesting," he said almost to himself. "Very interesting. It's a wonder I didn't notice it sooner. You carry a strong resemblance to Arabella the Ruthless, little one. Could you be the daughter she kept tucked away?"

Emme's face fell. I should have left her on the ship. "Don't talk to her. Nothing but the treasure concerns you." The hunger in the admiral's eyes as he inspected Emme was enough to make my stomach churn.

He smiled with lips stretched so wide they might crack against his pearly teeth. "This treasure is not enough. You owe me more than what you have here. I paid your dues and your crew for half a year while you stumbled around pretending to be a real pirate, and you think this is enough to cover it? No. I still own you, boy."

With skin as white as a ghost, Emme spoke. "It's enough."

"The treasure of Bernabe De would pay any crew for years," I argued. But the admiral just laughed.

"Fear not, boy. You have something worth more than you know." A crooked finger stretched to Emme. "The daughter of Arabella the Ruthless would make a fine possession."

Her knees wobbled slightly, the first indication of dread. I stepped in front of her. "No."

He tilted his head. "This treasure isn't enough. But the treasure and this girl as a slave . . . that will satisfy your dues. You can be free of me, pirate. Give me the girl. Take your freedom."

His words slithered over us, and I could feel Emme recoil. I wanted to turn and tell her I'd never betray her to him, but the way the admiral's hand perched on his pistol, I knew that turning my back would be foolish. I stood my ground and shook my head. "If it's a slave you need, then take me. But you must swear to never touch one of my mates."

A dry laugh rippled from his throat. "I don't care about you, boy. You are worth nothing to me. Give me the girl, or accept the consequences of your inability to pay your debts."

His eyes bored into me, gleaming at this game he played. A game he thought he'd won.

He might have won. I had nothing else to offer. All I could hope is that after he killed me, the rest of the crew managed to get away.

As I opened my mouth to declare my defeat, a shot rang out. A second came moments later. I dropped to my knees. On the beach, the crew was grabbing the treasure and throwing it into the rowboats as fast as they could. Ontario stood stunned as he looked toward us.

Fools, I thought. *Those bloody fools. He'll kill us all.*

Emme grabbed at my sleeve and yanked me to my feet. "Go, Arn," she shouted in my ear. She holstered her pistol. My eyes widened. "Come on," she urged.

I whipped my head to the Admiral Bones, but he no longer stood in front of us. He lay on the ground, blood trickling down the rocks and into the grains of sand.

"You shot him?"

She grabbed me by my shoulders and shook me. Tears swam down her cheeks. "I did it for you, you idiot. Now go. His thugs will be here any minute."

I grabbed her hand and we dashed down the sandy slope to where the crew hauled treasure back into the rowboats. "That's good enough," I shouted. "We have to leave quickly." We abandoned a third of the loot and dug our feet into the shallow water to push off. Oars sank into the water and bashed against the rims of the rowboats as we sat atop the treasure and paddled as quickly as we could. I propped my wrist behind the oar and placed my one hand at the end, pulling with all my might to row as effectively as men with two hands.

We reached the ship, and I began barking out orders. "Tie that boat to the ship and climb up. Leave the treasure below. We'll pull the boats along until a safe distance away. No, no, leave me here. I can't climb up fast." I waved my wrist at them and ushered them up the rope, until they disappeared over the ship's edge. Then I bent down and used my teeth to secure the rowboat to the rope.

Emric's voice carried across the ship. "To the oars, men. Bring up the anchor, let down the sails." The canvas flapped as it was unfurled and stretched taut to the riggings. Oars began to move, and the wind caught the sails, lurching us forward. I braced my hand against the rope to hold steady as we began to sail from the island.

I stood on the rowboat with my feet buried in treasure as Admiral Bones's hooligans came out from the town. Their pistols rose, and shots echoed across the open waters, but their bullets didn't hit us.

My hand tightened on the rope to balance myself as I hiked up my foot and rolled the sock down with my wrist. The black tattoo that had marred my skin for the past two years began to fade, until the skin was clean once more. Washed away as if it had never been there.

I grinned. Admiral Bones was dead.

A short while later, the crew made their way down the ropes to drag the treasure aboard, then we fastened the rowboats against the side of the ship. I wiped my arm across my forehead and leaned against the mast.

"Is it over?" Bo questioned, already elbow deep in inspecting what treasure remained.

The crew's eyes settled on me, hoping for confirmation that our struggles were over. That our debt died with Admiral

Bones and we'd secured this treasure safely for ourselves. That the worst of our problems was behind us.

I knew the reality of what would come next, but I couldn't disappoint them now. I showed them my foot. "The oathbind is gone."

Cheers went up, and hats were tossed.

Emme threw her arms around me. "Thank you for not giving me up." Her hair tickled my chin as the weight of her head leaned into my chest.

"I thought about it. It was a close call, really," I teased, and got a pinch in the side for it. My voice dropped. "And thank you for what you did back there, Emme. I never wanted you to have to experience that part of a pirate's life."

She glanced down to her pistol and gnawed on her lip. "It's okay."

"I know how hard that was for you." I cupped her chin up to mine. Her hazel eyes studied mine from beneath dark lashes. I'd taken this innocent girl and brought her down a path where she'd seen more violent death than I'd ever thought she would with me. She made a brave decision in a moment of chaos. But I couldn't tell what she made of it.

Her brow crinkled, and she drew a deep breath. "It was an accident."

At her words, my heart twisted. She'd become a killer, and not by choice.

"I had to be fast," she said. "He had his hand on his pistol, and I reckoned he could draw in an instant. I was aiming for his hand to keep him from shooting you, but this disease, I'm so shaky, and I missed. I didn't mean to kill him." She closed her eyes, as if the sight of it still burned in her mind.

I tightened my arms around her and let her head rest against my shoulder. "At least that horrid man can't harm anyone else." She sniffed. "Things are not as simple as I once thought them to be. Nor am I as simple as I once believed."

I leaned back to see her. "You are anything but simple, my darling."

"At least it's over now," she breathed. At my tightened expression, she frowned. "What?"

"That's the thing. It might not be over. My oathbinding is gone, but I still owe the money. Those records are kept in his books. He has a son who will likely take over for him and might want that debt repaid, or at least revenge on the one who killed his father."

"Have you met this son?" she asked.

"No. I only know that he exists."

"I thought it was finished, Arn." Dismay filled her face.

"It might be. I don't know anything about his heir or what kind of man he is. Unless his son shares the same . . . feral tendencies as his father, I can't know what I'm up against. If nothing else, you've bought us time and made tracking me difficult for them. That's something worth celebrating."

Uncertainty lingered in her eyes, so I took a risk to comfort her. My head tilted forward, and my eyes asked the question for me. Her gaze softened and she raised her chin to meet her lips against mine. Worry became only a tiny wave breaking against the shore.

"Bring out the ale," Bo shouted, sitting atop jewels and placing a crown on his brow. "Tonight we celebrate. We are some of the richest men on the high seas!"

44

EMME

I stood on the deck. The sea spat water on my neck and the wind wiped across my face like a blade until my skin felt numb. I couldn't remember how I got here, or why I came in the middle of the night; all I knew was I stood at the helm and faced the main mast.

Thick ropes wound against the post, shifting as someone grunted from the other side. "Help me," they cried out in anguish.

I ran to free whoever was there, but when I reached the mast and saw the captive, I jerked to a halt. Admiral Bones sat against the post. His crisp hair was now mishappen, and his clean clothes were riddled with holes and smut. The ends of his pants were cut in uneven lines, and his shoes were no more than pieces of leather tied together with string.

His eyes looked so desperate. "Help me."

I wanted to help him. Everything in me said to bring out my dagger and cut the bonds loose. But instead my hand reached for my pistol, and I cocked it.

"No." He stared down the barrel of the gun. "Please."

Bang. Bang. Two shots, straight to his heart. Just as my mother had taught me. This time the bullet went right where my hands aimed.

But the wounds didn't bleed. Instead, the blood seeped across my hands, turning from a trickle into a flood of thick, red liquid oozing over my body, until his blood was covering me.

A voice in the wind spoke. "His death is on your hands. His blood is yours to answer for."

I couldn't move. I couldn't cry. All I could do was watch his blood overtake me until I was drowning in it.

I knew it was a nightmare. But it told me nothing that I wasn't responsible for. This was my punishment for not feeling more guilty. I was to relive the moment over and over until I regretted my decision.

Half a year ago, remorse would have engulfed my soul, but not now. I had saved Arn, and that's what I was supposed to do.

"Wake up! To your posts!"

The sound jolted me from my sleep, and I rolled from bed.

"We're under attack." Arn burst through my door a moment later.

"Who's attacking?" I quickly strapped on my weapon belt.

"The black ship."

My hands froze. This was the moment we'd been anticipating—and dreading—over the past few months as that mysterious vessel insisted on trailing us. And it was happening now. Arn grabbed my cutlass and put it in its sheath at my side while I twisted around to put the knife in my back pocket. I checked my pistol and glanced up.

I savored the look of him—the tight waves in his hair and the thick eyebrows drawn in a straight line. The gold tattoos of the ocean curled on his chest and across his arms.

"We're finally going to see who's captaining that blasted ship," Arn said. He gave me a final look over before pulling me after him toward the sounds of gunshots and shouting in the air.

We stopped at the bottom of the ladder as the ship rocked

violently. "Be careful." He kissed me, and it tasted like rum and fear. A tremor of nerves slithered down my spine as we climbed the ladder and looked out.

Either we'd grossly underestimated the size of this ship, or it grew overnight. It dwarfed us; we were a dolphin next to a whale. Twenty cannons rolled out from its side, each pointed at us with deathly stares. They were firing one by one, their ammunition landing in the water in front of us and sending the *Royal Rose* swaying from side to side. It was near enough to score direct hits, so it had to be toying with us, igniting our fear.

The crew ran about in a frenzied panic, shouting at one another but not really knowing what to do. Our own cannons were loaded, but six of us stood on deck so only two men were manning them.

"Fire!" Ontario leaned over the side, hollering. "Fire again!"

Cannonballs crashed into their ship, breaking through the wooden boards. A cheer rose, but one shot wouldn't take down a ship such as this.

Despite the chaos, we still saw no one aboard the other ship.

"Come and face us, you devil!" Emric waved his pistol in the air. "Come fight!"

I drew my gun, but kept it lowered until a target presented itself.

"Show yourself," Emric shouted. His face was soaked with water as waves pummeled the side of the ship and flooded across the deck. His feet positioned wide, his pistol now scanning the other ship, waiting to be told where to shoot. He was the only one who didn't look panicked.

The temperature in the air plunged, and a woman's voice as deep as the bottom of the sea laughed. "You should not be so eager for danger, young one."

Our hearts stilled in our throats.

"You wish to see me?" the voice mocked. "Here I am."

From the starboard side of the ship she appeared, climbing atop the railing, her long white jacket flapping in the wind and her hair like a wool blanket billowing around her. Her skin was the shade of dark rum, and white tattoos circled her arms, five simple bands across her forearms. In her hand she held a rope.

She pointed forward, and her ship lurched toward us.

We began to fire at her, but she moved too quickly to be caught. She threw herself upward, swinging from the rope across her whole deck and propelling through the air. As the rope reached its end, she let go and dropped to land on our deck to perch on the bow.

"Here I am, boy." Her voice came from her body now, instead of floating in the wind. "Kill me if you can." She drew two cutlasses from her sides and crossed them in front of her, staring us down with a taunting smile on her lips.

Emric charged at her, while the rest of us fired our weapons when we had a good angle. No matter how true I aimed or how confident I felt in my shot, nothing struck her. Our bullets had only passed around her as if she wore a shield of wind. Soon Emric was before her, and I wasn't confident in my ability to aim without striking him.

There was a harsh metallic clang as their swords clashed in the air.

I turned to Arn. "Do you know her?"

He shook his head. "Never seen her. She could be a ghost like Bernabe De was. See how our weapons aren't hurting her?" His expression changed, and he darted for the hatch on the deck. Without giving an explanation, he dropped below.

Ontario discarded his pistol first and drew his cutlass. With a mighty battle cry, he ran to Emric. The woman raised her other sword and fended them both off as if it were nothing. The strength she possessed wasn't natural. Bo joined them, but she swung at him with such force that it sent his cutlass clattering across the deck. Another twist, and Ontario's blade went into the ocean.

As the woman fought, she turned her head and looked directly at me. Those silver eyes froze my blood. Not once taking her eyes off me, she hooked the end of her cutlass around the hilt of Emric's and yanked it hard, pulling it away. It dropped on the ground behind her.

I cried in alarm and started to go to his aid, but my feet were stuck to the deck and wouldn't be moved, no matter how hard I tugged. I'd rip my legs from my body if I pulled any harder, and so remained planted on the deck in frustration. Just as I'd been one of the first times we encountered this black ship.

What devilish magic did she possess to hold a person so captive? Eyes still on me, she spoke. "You should not be here."

Collins attacked while Bo retrieved his sword. The two of them fought together, and Arn returned above deck. From below, Bishop and Timmons continued firing the cannons. The woman might be unbeatable, but her ship was beginning to sink. A small sliver of hope in this dire situation.

Arn was next to me. "The box from the mermaids. If I'm right about what she is, this will trap her." Arn tilted the box into my arms so he could hold his cutlass again. He kept his bandaged wrist tucked to his side.

I tucked it into my jacket just as the woman disarmed Bo for a second time. Now alone, Collins took a few shaky steps back.

Emric had realized as the rest of us did that his weapon would do nothing against her. He threw it aside and jumped at her.

They collided, and rolled to the floor together in a tangle of limbs. He attached his hands to her neck, but she pried his fingers away.

I grabbed Arn's arm. "She's not a ghost. We can touch her. She's powerful, but she's not a ghost."

"Then she can be killed." Arn sprinted to Emric's side. I tried to move, but my feet still wouldn't obey. Abandoning formal weapons, Emric threw a punch and connected with her stomach. She hunched over. A second swing grazed her cheek. He wound up again, but her hand caught his before the blow, and she raised her head with a devilish gleam. A trickle of blood ran down her face.

"Strong spirit. Much like your mother. My quarrel is not with you, boy." She twisted her grip and threw him across the deck. He collided with the main mast and sank to the ground where he lay motionless.

At the sheer power she displayed, we all paused. She'd thrown a grown man halfway across the ship with no more than a flick of her wrist.

Arn only hesitated a moment before taking Emric's place, but the woman ducked under his cutlass and placed both her hands on his arm, tearing the weapon from his grasp. He flailed his other wrist at her, but without his second hand he couldn't do much. Just like with Emric, her strength propelled him across the deck just at Bishop and Timmons opened the latch from below to see the commotion. Their eyes widened as Arn slammed into the ground in front of them.

Her silver eyes surveyed the ship. "No one else? Very well, I shall take what I came for."

To my horror, she reached for me. I ground my teeth as I strained to free my feet from whatever bonds held me. Her slender arm extended, and the air turned colder as she drew near, and I snapped my mouth at her hand.

She drew her hand back and grinned. Then she reached out again and grabbed my throat with an ice-cold grasp that tightened over my neck. I clawed at her thick skin. That did nothing. My mind cleared for a moment, and I managed to pull the ghost box from my pocket and threw it against her, but it rolled off her back and fell to the floor. She didn't even glance at it. My head grew heavy with its need for air, and I thrashed desperately. Perhaps if I were stronger, I could have stood a chance. But with the disease inside, my strength failed me.

Her grip on me was suffocating as she hauled me to the rails. In horror, I realized she was about to take me off the ship. If she got me away from my crew, I'd be helpless.

"Emme!" Arn pulled himself from the floor with a shout and retrieved his cutlass. He ran forward with it raised high, but she reached up with her own blade and blocked him.

He grunted and struck her with his wrist but to no effect. She brought the hilt of her blade crashing down against the side of his head. He fell to his knees and tried to yank at her legs. She kicked his temple, and he collapsed.

At the sight, the other men found their courage, but she stretched her arm toward them, and they all sank to their knees.

"I'm done playing games." She released me, throwing me to the ground. The freedom I felt was fleeting. In the next breath, with strength a woman of her size should not possess, she picked me up as easily as plucking a flower and threw me over her shoulders.

All around the ship, the crew stirred, but none fast enough. The woman carried me to the edge of the ship where she grabbed hold of the rope that had brought her to us. I tried to roll off her shoulders, but she kept a tight hand on me, pinning my body against hers.

"Who are you?" I struggled to rasp the words. My hair tumbled over my face, blinding me to her face, and she looked over her shoulder at me.

"Someone who sees who you might become," she replied. I couldn't know if her words came from her lips or my mind. "The Fates have spoken to me about you. You have a potential for great darkness, just like your mother. It's not safe to leave you in this world."

My jumbled mind registered one word. *Darkness.*

The last words sunk in.

It's not safe to leave you in this world.

The Fates had shown her some false future where I brought ruin, and now she meant to kill me to keep that from coming to pass.

All the visions, all the haunting nights, she'd been trying to drive me mad. Beckoning me to the water where I would have drowned. Scaring me off the seas. But I'd survived her nightmares, and I'd survived the Island of Iilak. She was done waiting for me to die by other means.

My nails dug into her side, but she hardly flinched. I bit into her shoulder until I tasted blood, but she didn't pull it away. "Never again will I let such destruction fall upon the world," she declared. "May your death be my payment for what I allowed with the Nightlock Thieves."

I remembered the tale, the one about the girls who brought horror to the world. This was her. And however she'd lived for this long, my death would be her redemption.

She'd been the one to frighten Mother off the seas. I'd been too ignorant to heed the same warning.

There was a roar, and Emric hurled himself into her. I fell to the deck at Emric's feet just in time to see the woman turn, draw out her cutlass, and plunge it through his belly.

I gave a voiceless scream.

My brother's blood dripped over me as he stumbled forward. The woman reached for me once more. I kicked at her while screaming out my brother's name. Hot tears rained, clouding my vision.

Emric was still moving. He wrapped his arms around the woman and heaved them both overboard.

Their bodies splashed into the water, and I tottered to lean over the side. "Emric," I cried his name into the void. "Emric!" No reply came. No sign of them was seen. Just dark water and a ripple from where their bodies had plunged below. Frantic, I was about to jump over when Arn grabbed my arms. "You're weak right now. Let me."

The crew who had regained their strength worked their way to the side to peer into the vast waters for a sign of their fallen captain. Arn was about to straddle the rail but he froze, his eyes straight ahead.

We all watched the black ship shimmer and disappear.

"What in the devil's name?" Arn swore.

"Emric!" I cried again and again. Arn dove into the water, and Ontario threw himself after him. The others furled the sails so the wind didn't move us too far.

We waited with tight hands on the railing and breaths clotting our throats. Arn and Ontario popped up for breath before diving below again. After the third time, Arn paused to meet my eyes, and tears slid down my cheeks. Emric needed air, or else he would drown.

I climbed onto the railing and dove into the water after them. The seas were difficult to see through, but I flailed my limbs, begging the Sea King Valian to let me find my brother and to let him be alive. I'd never hoped in the existence of the sea king more than I did now.

When I came up for breath, Arn grabbed my arm and pulled me into his chest. "He's not there, Emme. He's not there."

I spat water out of my mouth and flung my head around, eyes wildly searching beneath the water. "He has to be. Let me go." I pushed, but Arn held tight.

"It's been too long. He was severely wounded. It's too late for us to help him now." His words were like knives to my chest, and I didn't want to believe them.

"The ship is gone. He killed her. He survived," I protested

as I struggled to keep my head above the chilly waters. "He's alive."

The crew threw down a rope, and Arn took hold of it. Ontario slowly climbed back up the ship.

"No." I kicked away from Arn and went underwater again. I swam deep to peer through the darkness, seeing nothing but murky waters around. The strong salt burned my eyes and filled my tongue. I stretched out my hands over and over again, each time grabbing hold of nothing but more water that coursed through my fingers.

When I could hold my breath no longer, I drifted back to the surface feeling numb. "He has to be alive," I insisted again. "I have to find him." I filled my lungs with air and prepared to swim down again, but Arn grabbed me.

Water trailed down his temples where a bruise was forming. "You'll drown with him if you keep trying. He's gone, Emme. They are both gone."

I didn't believe him, but I let him pull me back to the boat where we were both dragged onboard. I lay in a puddle of water with my chest heaving and my heart ready to burst. All I could think of was the cutlass stabbed through my brother's stomach and his body going overboard.

"He's alive," I kept repeating, though none echoed the sentiment. "He has to be alive."

45

ARN

Emme was a ghost on the ship, wandering the deck and staring into the waves with an empty expression, as if she were one gust of wind away from teetering over the edge herself.

This was worse than the nightmares. At least with those she would wake up and know that it was all right. There was no waking up from this. Her brother was dead, and she'd lost a part of herself.

Emme didn't believe that he was gone, and I couldn't decide if that made it better. She couldn't mourn him this way—and neither could we. She'd allow no funeral for a man who wasn't dead.

We decided it'd be best to return her to Kaffer Port where she could have some of the treasure we had kept from Admiral Bones to buy her sheep farm inland. I asked her if she'd be okay living on the farm where she once lived with her father and brother, but she only shrugged. "I don't know what to do. I don't know anymore."

Emric's death weighed less on me than the others, and for that I was plagued by guilt. I was frankly more concerned with regaining control of my ship than for the one who had taken it from me. When Bo finally brought up the question of captain,

I perked up. It'd been three days since Emric went overboard, and the *Royal Rose* longed for a commander.

Emme went below deck. None of us knew what to say and let her pass without a word. My hand caught hers quickly, but she drifted out of my hold.

"I will happily take back over command," I said with a bow once she'd disappeared. When I raised my head, I caught Collins and Bishop exchanging glances.

"I don't know how comfortable I am with that," Timmons confessed as he sharpened his blade in the doorway of the cabin on deck. The sun beat down relentlessly today, creating a glare from his blade that swept over the cleaned deck. We'd shed our jackets, unbuttoned our shirts, and tied up our hair to keep cool as we sailed back toward warmer weather.

My arms swept to my sides. "Why? I've been giving orders most of the time."

"But captain?" Bo asked. "Ye almost got us all skinned alive by the admiral. I say Ontario deserves the role. He didn't lie to us."

Bishop nodded in agreement.

Ontario sat on the stairs and played with the round earring in his ear. At his name he rose to his feet. "Yes. You won't regret it."

I choked a laugh. "Do you care to tell them, or shall I?" Ontario frowned. His lips stayed tight as a trapdoor. "Fine." I faced the men. "You think Ontario didn't lie to you? He knew about Admiral Bones the entire time." I glared at Ontario.

"Aye, but I didn't sign the deal. There was no oathbind on my foot. All I did was follow the orders of my captain. After all, loyal was my mantra." If he could bring up what the old boot told him, then I should remind them how it told me I was captain, but Ontario wasn't done. He strode across the deck to the other men. "I am the reasonable choice. I am brave, intelligent, and honorable. And I promise to lead you well."

This was ridiculous. But they were all nodding their heads. "Men," I said. "I have let you down, but I swear it won't happen again. We will take our revenge on Landon for what he's done and prove ourselves unbreakable, despite our sorrows."

Collins drew his mouth in a straight line and looked to his feet. Bo frowned and put up his hand. "We need a captain we can trust. Right now, that's not you. All vote Ontario?" He looked to his mates, who said aye. "Then there you have it."

Ontario didn't move for a moment, but when he did, he lifted his chin. "Finally." He glanced to me. "I have been overlooked for far too long." He made a great show of ascending to the wheel, where he stroked the spokes. "How many of you want retribution for what Landon has done to us?"

They had to move from the cabin door to see him, but they all responded, "We do."

"Death to the scoundrel!" Bo shouted.

"Very well, then. Once we are sure that Emme is taken care of in Kaffer Port, we will plot our revenge on Landon and prove to King Valian that we are worthy pirates aboard his seas."

The sight of Ontario commanding my precious ship made my chest tighten. I scowled and turned away, vowing that I wouldn't let this last. Ontario didn't have the assertive nature needed to captain a pirate crew, and soon they would see that. My sins had stripped my ship from me, but I would win it back.

I swear by King Valian, I will take back what is mine.

46
EMME

Arn knocked at my door, but I wasn't inside. I held a bowl of beef broth against my stomach, savoring the sweet smell that drifted up as I walked down the passageway toward the deck. "I'm here," I called to him through the spoon between my teeth.

Arn turned. "You aren't in your room?" He wore his cream top with the strings almost all the way unlaced, gold tattoos showing on his chest. His sleeves were rolled carelessly around his elbows, and his hair was tied in a tight bun at the back of his head.

I shrugged, almost causing the soup to spill. "I think I've wallowed in sorrows enough."

Arn removed the spoon from my mouth. "Your brother died, Emme. It's acceptable."

I faltered. I'd grown weary of correcting people over Emric's death when my heart wasn't sure what to believe. I'd seen him go overboard. He never came back up. And yet, a part of me clung to the hope that somehow, he'd found a way to survive.

I changed the subject. "Has the crew made plans on where to sail next? I assume we'll be needing more crewmates?"

Arn raised his brows. "Have you forgotten that you need another healing nut? We sail there."

Right. I nodded. "Sorry, these past few days have been a haze." He started climbing the ladder to the deck above, but I hesitated. A few days ago, I didn't care what happened next. Losing my brother was as bad as if I'd been impaled, and all I could think of was surviving for the next few minutes. The pain of it hurt worse than the disease in my bones. The thought of Emric's body swelling with water, decaying at the bottom of the sea, fish eating his eyes . . . I had to stop thinking of it. This would drive me mad.

"What does the crew plan to do after that?" I asked, staring into my soup.

"Revenge on Landon."

I brought my eyes up to his as he reached down from above to take my soup so I could climb.

I went up the ladder a few steps. "Take me with you."

Clouds formed behind his head, making the blue in his eyes appear gray. "Are you certain? Once you're healed, we can take you back to Kaffer Port. Your sheep farm—"

"The farm can wait." I climbed atop and inhaled the fresh sea air, and Arn handed me my bowl. I stared over the endless waves. Wind kissed my cheeks, breathing life into me again. I'd missed the mist in the air and the beautiful sound of water breaking against the hull. "Aye, I'm certain," I told him. "I'm not ready to leave the waters yet, especially if Emric is still out here . . ." My voice drifted off.

"It'd be good to see Bart again, and I bet Kaffer Port could offer us some new crewmates. But then, if you'll have me, I'd like to join your crew." I looked up at him. "For real this time."

I felt him take a deep breath. "You mean it? You'll stay with me?"

For the first time in the past few days, my heart felt something other than crippling sorrow. I placed a hand against the tattoos on Arn's chest. "Who knows?" I echoed his words from months ago. "Perhaps we'll make a pirate out of me yet."

"Arn, help." I had rolled out of the bed. Ontario had allowed me to keep the captain's quarters for my room—for now, he said—and I crawled to kick at the door. "Arn!"

Footsteps pounded, then my door opened. Arn's voice was thick with sleep. "Emme?"

I clawed at my socks until they were ripped from my feet and held my foot out to him. Terrible, sharp pains shot from my toes all the way to my head, making my skin feel on fire. He crouched beside me.

"The oathbind, it hurts s-so bad." I clenched my teeth. "It's killing me."

"That's impossible, you haven't—" A bright glow from the tattoo cut his words short. For a moment, I thought it really was on fire. The design lit up in magnificent gold that illuminated the entire room. My tattoo came to life before our eyes; the waves danced off my foot, and the ink lifted to fill the room. Arn's brow furrowed as he leaned closer to my foot, running his hand through the glow.

My voice spoke, though I didn't move my lips. It filled the room with its soft whispers. "I, Emme Jaquez Salinda, bind myself to you in this oath, that when you call upon me for a favor, I will obey."

I braced myself with my hands behind my back and stared wildly at Arn. "It's time," I whispered. No one told me the oathbinding would hurt so bad when called upon.

"Your oath is ready to be fulfilled." The voice was Sereena's this time. Her face appeared before us, the piercing eyes, short blonde hair, and tattoos that covered her neck. "And here is the favor you will do for me. See, I have found a way to regain my place in the ocean court of King Valian. To do so, you must assist me." She smiled as if nothing could please her more.

I knew she desired to be reunited with her sea prince and be free of the lonely island. Without her help, Arn would be dead right now. If there was a chance for her to do that, then it'd be an honor to assist her.

Then I heard her demands.

"You must kill the king of Julinbor and bring me his head. But make haste. You are not the only one seeking to murder him."

I gasped. I knew she was raving mad. I never should have oathbound myself. Attempting to kill my king would bring me nothing but death.

But a grin crossed Arn's face as the glow of the oathbinding danced across his own skin. He gave Sereena a firm nod.

"Happily."

47

EMRIC

I almost didn't survive the fall to the water. My vision blackened, and I struggled to keep a hold on the woman.

I'd known she was the same one who sought after my mother. But it wasn't until she asked penance for what she'd done with the Nightlock Thieves that I connected her to the old tale as the one who wandered the sea to be sure none grew too powerful. She'd seen something in Emme's future that scared her and planned to kill Emme before that future came to pass.

Whatever shield protected her from our bullets on the ship didn't protect her from my grip. She thrashed, but my body weighed us both down. *If I'm to die, then she will drown with me.*

I could hardly see her face as her silver eyes darted around, and her head thrashed as she attempted to tear herself away from me. Blood trickled up from my wound. It wouldn't be long before the beasts in the sea smelled it and came looking for us.

Let me go, her voice demanded in my head. *You are not the one I'm after, son of Arabella.*

My strength was fading. The pain in my stomach was overwhelming, and my eyes struggled to stay open. My lungs begged for air. One of her arms slipped from my grasp, and her hand clawed into my other arm, digging her nails through my skin.

Something brushed against my back, and smooth arms wrapped around my sides. Their touch brought the warmth that the ocean lacked. The figure curled its body around mine and pressed its nose into my cheek. Vibrant blonde hair floated by her face, and green eyes stared into mine.

Coral.

"You will not die today, my love," she said into my ear. Her voice alone renewed my strength. She took a knife from her fins and placed it in my hand.

It tingled. Magic.

She nodded to me, and together we drove it into the woman's chest.

I twisted the knife deeper. Her grip on me released, and her blood mixed with mine until the water between us was ribboned with red. Somewhere I heard Emme's voice crying out, though I couldn't be sure. The woman's eyes rolled into her head, and her body went limp. A few seconds later she disappeared, leaving me in a tide of blood.

Coral placed her hand over the sword still in my stomach and pursed her lips. Pain erupted from my stomach as she pulled the cutlass out with a swift motion.

I must get air. I tried to swim upward, but my body didn't listen. Coral grabbed my shoulders and caressed my cheeks, but I had little strength left to look upon her beauty one last time.

Death would find me here.

"King Valian," Coral's sweet voice pierced the waters. "My lord, I beseech you. Let him live."

If King Valian answered, I could not hear it, for I was too far gone.

Waves lapped against my toes and washed the hair around my head. Trickles of water rolled into my eyes, even as I turned my head the other way. Warmth beat upon me, and light snuck through my eyelids, beckoning me from the darkness. Coarse sand settled over my skin, shifting with each wave against the shore. I searched for the feel of Coral, but her presence was not there.

It took a while for my eyes to find the strength to open, and it wasn't until a shadow passed over the light that I peeled my lids back. A figure with long brown hair hanging over her shoulder was staring down at me with the halo of the sun behind her head.

I tried to sit up, but my stomach cried out in pain.

"Rest, dear one, you are still weak," spoke a smooth tone. At its familiarity I blinked to focus on the face. The sharp nose, the rounded cheeks, the point in her ears. Her hand wiped hair back from my sweaty brow, the same hand that had cared for me as a child. The same hand that taught me how to shoot a pistol and swing a cutlass, and that pointed me toward the sea each day growing up.

"Hello, my son," my mother said. "Welcome to Alvalla."

48

ONTARIO

I was no longer just a first mate. I was *captain*. This would earn me many ladies at port, no doubt.

Arn didn't think I could handle this obligation—his expressions told me that much. How I looked forward to proving him wrong. To do that, we'd first need to acquire more men for our crew. It was decided that whatever portion wasn't given to Emme or used on provisions would go to buying slaves to work the deck. But we might get lucky in finding eager lads willing to join our ranks.

A ruffling from behind made me jump. A large bird with black eyes shifted on the railing behind the helm with paper tied to its foot. I glanced to the deck, but as the night had fallen the men had drifted below.

"What do ye got there?" I reached my hand out, and it lifted its foot for me to pull at the twine. As soon as the message was freed, the bird flew back off into the cloudy night.

I would have opened the letter regardless of who it belonged to, but to my surprise, it was my name scrawled across the rolled-up parchment. Eager fingers peeled open the paper to read.

Ontario,

I regret to inform you that your father has passed away. He left his business and all he owns in your name. Please come visit soon so we can speak of the details.

— Mother

Father must have had no trusted advisors to have left his inheritance to his estranged son. Once over the shock, I almost laughed at the irony. Little did we know that as we raced to provide Admiral Bones with what he was owed, he would end up giving it all to me.

First a ship, and now my father's business. King Valian had blessed me today. I wouldn't squander it like Arn might. I would bide my time. Surely overseeing the Bones legacy would give me riches beyond compare, and with that money I could do anything I liked.

Finally, I would get the respect I deserved.

ABOUT THE AUTHOR

Victoria McCombs is the author of The Storyteller's Series from Parliament House Press, and *Oathbound*. She writes young adult fantasy and adores stories about treacherous pirates and traitorous princes.

Her favorite things include peppermint hot chocolate, peanut butter ice cream, game nights with family, and Jesus. She has her mom to thank for allowing so many medieval weapons inside the house as she was growing up, which cultivated her love for that time period.

She is a mom of three little boys and a wife to the handsomest accountant there is. Together they live in Omaha, Nebraska.

ACKNOWLEDGMENTS

There are so many people to thank for making this book happen, but first I want to thank my oldest son for all the times he asked about my pirate book. I'm delighted to finally be bringing you a pirate story.

Second, I couldn't have done this without Jonathan. Literally. Thanks for being you. I love you a lottle.

Next, the team at Enclave who has made this all so easy for me. You are a delight to work with! Huge thanks to Emily for designing a cover that makes me want to buy a hundred copies and display them in every room. My editor, Lisa Laube, and copyeditor, Lindsay Franklin, who took my ramblings and honed them into a coherent story. Trissina Kear for putting up with my constant emails and teaching me the ways of marketing. Jamie Foley, the production and interior design genius. And Steve Laube for allowing me into the Enclave family.

All of my Instagram friends, you are priceless. Thank you to Stephen, Danielle, Caitlin, Brian, and Casey for putting up with a million questions in your inbox about writing. I appreciate you guys so much! Ruth, you are there for me whenever I need you, and I'm so grateful for you. And Kalliopi, who loves the story as much as I do. Your excitement has motivated me through the tough parts. Thank you to my amazing early readers who sent me excited emails about the story and encouraged me to keep going.

To my family for supporting me always, and for watching the kids so I can work. Thank you a million. And thank you to Eric, who was the inspiration behind Emric, even though I somehow didn't realize that until halfway through.

Biggest thank you to my readers. I couldn't do this without you.